Praise for _USA TODAY_ bestselling author

KASEY MICHAELS

"Kasey Michaels aims for the heart and never misses."
—_New York Times_ bestselling author Nora Roberts

"Mistress of her craft Michaels uses her signature wit
to introduce...[an] intricate story, engaging characters
and wonderful writing."
—_RT Book Reviews_ on _What an Earl Wants,_
4 1/2 stars, Top Pick

"The historical elements...imbue the novel with powerful
realism that will keep readers coming back."
—_Publishers Weekly_ on _A Midsummer Night's Sin_

"A poignant and highly satisfying read...
filled with simmering sensuality, subtle touches of repartee,
a hero out for revenge and a heroine ripe for adventure.
You'll enjoy the ride."
—_RT Book Reviews_ on _How to Tame a Lady_

"Michaels' new Regency miniseries is a joy.... You will laugh
and even shed a tear over this touching romance."
—_RT Book Reviews_ on _How to Tempt a Duke_

"Michaels has done it again....
Witty dialogue peppers a plot full of delectable details
exposing the foibles and follies of the age."
—_Publishers Weekly_ on _The Butler Did It_ (starred review)

"[A] hilarious spoof of society wedding rituals
wrapped around a sensual romance filled with
crackling dialogue reminiscent of _The Philadelphia Story._"
—_Publishers Weekly_ on _Everything's Coming Up Rosie_

What a Lady Needs

KASEY MICHAELS

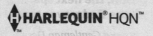

HARLEQUIN® HQN™

Recycling programs
for this product may
not exist in your area.

ISBN-13: 978-0-373-77764-8

WHAT A LADY NEEDS

Copyright © 2013 by Kathryn Seidick

Printed in U.S.A.

To my readers.
Thanks for all the hours of pleasure you've given *me!*

Dear Reader,

In the first book of this series, *What an Earl Wants,*
I introduced the Redgrave family—those scandalous
Redgraves—whose family history includes whispers of
hosting a salacious hellfire club known only as the Society.

Now the whispers are back, and it's up to the Redgraves
to find and destroy this new, treasonous incarnation of
the Society before it not only destroys the family, but
England as well.

The earl himself, Lord Gideon Redgrave, located the first
clues. Now, to keep his sister, Lady Katherine, safe, he's
advised her to search for evidence of the original Society
at Redgrave Manor. Evidence he's certain isn't there.

But never underestimate the determination of a beautiful,
headstrong young lady, or the mischief that can unfold
when an unsuspecting Simon Ravenbill, Marquis of
Singleton, is sent to ride herd on her.

I think you'll enjoy Kate and admire her courage, even
as we all shake our heads at her methods. When Simon
gives up on any notion of controlling her and realizes the
inevitability of loving her, they set off for the adventure,
and discovery, of a lifetime.

Enjoy! And please visit me online on Facebook or my
website, to catch up on all my news.

Kasey

www.KaseyMichaels.com

What a
Lady
Needs

Oh, what a tangled web we weave,
when first we practice to deceive.
—Sir Walter Scott

PROLOGUE

1810

THE HISTORY OF the Redgraves could be traced to the days before the beheading of the House of Stuart's Charles I in 1649. Meandering through the years, the family managed to stay on the good side of the Cromwell Roundheads. They then lightly danced through the return and second exit of the Stuarts, before managing to be favored with quite good seats for the Westminster Abbey coronation of the first monarch of the House of Hanover. All accomplished without ever forfeiting any of their lands or fortune and, more important, any of the family's heads to the chopping block in the Tower of London.

There was one hanging, but that was the twelfth earl, and really didn't count. He'd accomplished the deed himself in his study as the consequence of steep gambling debts and a genuine horror of his lady wife learning of them while he was still able to hear her screeching. After all, it was a matter of honor that before he kicked the chair out from beneath him, he had first settled said gambling debts by prying the major stones out of his wife's jewelry and replacing them with paste. Not that women, who had no real notion of honor, understood such things.

But the thirteenth earl backed faster horses and could

count trumps with the best of them, so that the Redgrave holdings once more increased. Their social status never wavered, and the paste gems were replaced thanks to the earl's brilliant marriage to a lovely young thing whose father's enormous fortune was a full generation away from the smell of the shop.

So much for the history of the Redgraves and the many earls of Saltwood.

The *scandal* of the Redgraves began in 1789, thanks to Barry Redgrave, the handsome, fashionable seventeenth Earl of Saltwood, who unexpectedly found himself quite dead one winter's morning, facedown in an icy puddle on a makeshift dueling ground. How he came to this ignominious end, when even as he'd aimed his pistol he'd been planning his order for breakfast once his wife's French lover was disposed of, has a simple answer. His lady wife, the fiery Spanish beauty, Lady Maribel, had shot Barry in the back. As noted earlier, women have no real notion of honor.

After all, not only did the countess coldly dispatch her own husband, but she and her lover had then fled to the Continent, leaving her four young and now fatherless children behind, motherless, as well.

Oh, the scandal! This was no nine-days wonder soon forgotten, especially when coupled with rumors Barry Redgrave had been the leader of some sort of debauched hellfire club, the group known only to its members, and then only as the *Society.*

Everyone knew such clubs were only excuses for otherwise respectable gentlemen to don cloaks and masks and behave badly with women from the lower orders, indulge in drunken orgies and dabble in other disgusting yet titillating experiments, such as opium eating. And, of course, it goes without saying there was also this business of sacrificing the odd billy goat here and there, just to keep their end up on the satanic-chanting, ritual-ridden hellfire side of things.

Except the rumors surrounding the late earl's hellfire club after his death went deeper than that, all the way to political conspiracy and admiration of the French citizens bent on taking down their king. One side of the Channel or the other, the chopping off of heads still registered the ultimate in displeasure by both the masses and monarchies. So, naturally, having managed to outwit the headsman thus far in their history, the Redgraves were quick to deny Barry's possible seditious leanings to George III—who had just come out of a year in a straight waistcoat, no longer foamed at the mouth and had been declared fit to rule once more—so it is anybody's guess whether or not he understood.

But a titillated society was mostly certain Barry's little hellfire club was all about the orgies; if nothing else, they were much more delicious to contemplate. Perhaps his wife's affair with the Froggie had been merely to register her dissatisfaction with her spouse's licentious activities outside the marital bed? Had she only known about them, or had the round-heeled beauty been a willing participant? You never knew about those foreign types. Hot-blooded and volatile, the lot of them. Oh, how delicious to speculate!

Nothing could be proved, of course, as the so-called Society was made up of people whose names were not known, and none of them thought it would be jolly fun to publish his memoirs recounting something like: *The Society: a Chronicle of Great Times and Lascivious Pleasures with Barry Redgrave, the Other Lads, a Cast of Willing Trollops and the Occasional Billy Goat*. No, definitely not.

There was also the dowager countess to add into the mix of conjecture; Lady Beatrix Redgrave, who was herself a scamp of the first water. She took lovers by the dozen, helping to keep alive all those rumors about *her* late husband, Charles, who'd had all the circumspection of a satyr, even decorating his Mayfair mansion in a way the majority of the world would term salacious. That Trixie hadn't had the decency to have fig leaves plastered to the larger-than-life marble statues lining the curving staircase after the man's death only proved the woman was no fit guardian for her grandchildren.

Still, the years passed, and the four Redgrave siblings somehow managed to reach adulthood without growing horns or bursting into flames when passing by a churchyard. The current eighteenth Earl of Saltwood, Gideon Redgrave, had entered society with his head held high and an unspoken challenge to anyone who might dare speak ill of his late parents or attempt to rake up that old scandal.

A few did try him on, to see how far they could go. That was their mistake, and the beginning of the belief the Redgraves were not only scandalous, they could be downright dangerous. Intelligent, yes, smoothly sophisticated, yes...but there was just something about them that warned the wise that to scratch a civilized Redgrave was to reveal the barbarian beneath.

Gideon's brother Maxmillien went off to sail with the British Royal Navy at a ridiculously young age, and he managed to be on the deck of the *Victory* to witness the heroic death of the illustrious Admiral Nelson at Trafalgar.

The youngest Redgrave son, Valentine, traveled about the Continent in the way of younger sons, cleverly avoiding areas of increasingly hostile action as that upstart Bonaparte randomly flexed his muscles.

And their sister, Lady Katherine, had made her curiously belated come-out a scant year ago, in 1809. A true beauty, it appeared she would take London by storm. She very well might have, except for That Unfortunate Business at Almacks.

After all, it wasn't every day London got to see a debutante fracture her dancing partner's nose with a brilliantly executed right cross. Lord Hilton, the fool, had dared to say something *amusing* to Kate about her family tree as they came together in one of the movements of the dance. The abused gentleman had bled copiously all over his waistcoat while pressing both hands to his abused proboscis, screaming, "My node! My node! She broke my node!"

With all eyes in the room wide with shock, all ears open for what would happen next, Kate had told him to stop being such a baby, then serenely strolled off the dance floor, declaring London society to be a sad waste of her time, just as she had predicted. It may not have helped that the dowager countess followed behind her, laughing so hard she had to walk nearly bent double.

No overt gossip resulted from this shocking event, no barely veiled references to the incident were reported in the daily newspapers, no limericks were composed by young wits. This was not amazing. Gideon, Earl of Saltwood, made the rounds of all the gentlemen clubs the next day, seemingly ignorant of the scandal his sister had caused, and everyone took their cue from him, then breathed a collective sigh of relief when he moved on to the next club. A message had been delivered, and they'd all heard it, loud and clear.

Not that the Redgraves weren't by nature an affable

bunch. The line was pure—if somewhat clouded by the Spanish wife-murderess—the pockets were deep, the progeny tall, strikingly good-looking, very nearly exotic thanks to that touch of foreign blood.

There was just something about each and every one of them, some nebulous something that whispered rather than shouted a warning: they're being affable only because it suits them, even the old lady.

The Redgraves were lions, one surprisingly insightful gentleman had whispered. Seemingly indolent, they could lie in the sun for hours, secure in themselves and seemingly indifferent to the world about them. But the more they relaxed—and nobody could relax with quite the magnificent sangfroid of a Redgrave—the more everyone else knew to stay on their toes and keep their wits about them.

Because if you did catch their notice they might look, blink and turn away, or they might pounce. Not that any of them had—with only a few notable exceptions no one ever spoke of—but the possibility was there, very clearly. After all, it was in the blood. Nobody knew what would happen if they took on a Redgrave because, thanks to those few notable exceptions in the past, nobody was foolish enough take on a Redgrave.

Except now, something indirectly has. The Society, the legacy of Barry Redgrave, and that of his father before him, has been resurrected by a new, even more deadly dangerous brand of hellfire members. Its unknown leader, building on the surviving members of the supposedly defunct Society, is employing every vice possible to lure both members and victims, the ultimate aim destroying England from the inside out and then handing the empire to a grateful Bonaparte.

With the help of the earl's new bride, Jessica, whose

recently deceased father had been a member, and the information all but bullied out of the dowager duchess, the Redgrave siblings set out to swiftly and quietly find and destroy this deadly reincarnation of the Society, from its members to its leader, relying on Trixie's memories, and in hopes of locating the journals detailing the sordid, even treasonous history of the hellfire club.

It's imperative this rejuvenated Society be identified and stopped, with the Redgrave name not connected to its actions in any way. Otherwise, this time, the resulting scandal could destroy them, and possibly the monarchy itself, forever.

CHAPTER ONE

"EXPLAIN TO ME again why you get to perch there chomping on an apple—and I do mean chomping—while I've been put to crawl around on my hands and knees, tapping at the woodwork while Tubby keeps insisting on licking my face. Not that I mind, do I, Tubby?" Valentine Redgrave put down the small hammer so he could tug on the spaniel's ears. "There's a good old dog. Fat, decrepit and with the fetid breath of a mongoose, but I love you, truly I do. You're a good old dog."

Lady Katherine Redgrave employed her tongue to push her most recent bite of apple against the inside of her cheek, looking much like a squirrel gathering up nuts for the winter. She was sitting on the back of one of the enormous leather couches in their brother Gideon's study at Redgrave Manor, her bare feet pressed onto the cool cushions, her long, lithe body still clad in her simple cotton night rail and dressing gown, although it had already gone noon.

"He knows when you're being facetious," Kate pointed out to the sibling closest to her in age of her three brothers, which had made him both the best friend and chief tormentor of their youth. "You could have said good dog, good dog all day last year, when you were so careless as to trip over dearest old Tubby and tumble down the stairs, taking Duke and Major along with you, poor animals. Tubby still knew you were angry. Everybody did. After all, you howled worse than the hounds."

Valentine sat back on his haunches, wiping at his damp face with his handkerchief as the spaniel watched, tail wagging in ecstasy and ready to launch himself, tongue first, at his master again. "I broke my damn leg and all three insanely concerned mutts kept leaping on it until you could pull them off, or has that part of the incident escaped your memory?" he grumbled, and then went back to crawling and tapping, tapping and crawling.

"It still aches, you know, when the weather's about to change, although I suppose you'd think that a good thing. So you can make sure you have your umbrella handy, except you like getting soaked to the skin, don't you? In any event, being a weather soothsayer was only amusing the first time I bet Jeremy it would rain by dusk before he figured it out, and then blabbed my secret to everyone. I still want to know who left the gate open at the bottom of the stairs so the dogs could get up them in the first place. Because I could swear I'd closed it."

Kate examined her half-eaten apple, as if looking for the next logical area to bite, which was safer than looking at Valentine, and much safer than having him look at her. "It's a petty man who holds a grudge. I'm certain the person is most exceedingly sorry."

"And you damn well should be, instead of talking me into crawling around Gideon's inner sanctum looking for secret passages."

Kate slid down the back of the couch, her night skirt billowing out around her as she plopped onto the cushions. "I never said it was me. I?" She waved the apple about in frustration. "I never could get the straight of that one, no matter how Miss Pettibone tried to drum it into my head. I know—I never said I forgot to latch the gate."

"You never said you didn't," Valentine responded reasonably. "You don't lie, Kate. You just don't tell the truth if you can find a way around it."

"Well, that's true enough. You've gone beyond the length of the couch now. You want me to help you push it back against the wall?"

"I told you nobody puts a secret passage behind a hulking great piece of furniture. Scrape marks would show on the floor every time it was moved, and be a dead giveaway. There's probably some sort of switch somewhere that operates a lever that opens some cleverly disguised door. Maybe hidden in all that carving around the fireplace—not that I'm saying there is a lever, or a door."

"No. I checked there. I checked all the obvious places before you arrived to bear me company. Now I'm working on the unobvious places, obviously. But if you're so certain I'm wrong, why did you volunteer to help me?"

"Again," Valentine corrected, unnecessarily dusting at his clean breeches, for Redgrave Manor was run by Dearborn, the butler, and Mrs. Justis, the housekeeper, who oversaw a multitude of well-trained servants. No bit of dust or dirt had dared to even think of being caught out lingering anywhere on the premises for at least thirty years, not even beneath the couches in the eighteenth Earl of Saltwood's study. "That's why I am helping you *again,* since you've been getting into scrapes all your life, left to your own devices. But the answer to that rephrased question is both obvious and simple. I'm not helping you. I'm keeping you out of trouble."

"How so? Why would I be getting into trouble? Gideon asked me to do this."

"Really? The way I was told the thing, our clever new sister-in-law asked you *not* to go hunting the journals, at the request of our big brother, which meant you immediately made plans to return here and do it. But that got you to leave London, which is what Gideon wanted Jessica to get you to do any way she could, since you were demanding to remain after the wedding and things could have turned dicey. It was only when he realized you might actually *find* something that big brother began to panic like an old woman."

Kate didn't know if she should be amused, surprised or angry. She quickly decided on amused, knowing Gideon's bride had truly tricked her. A person could admire that. "And that's why you're really here, instead of London? To make me stop?"

"Clearly not, or I wouldn't have spent these last miserable minutes crawling around on the floor. We're still to look, but you aren't going to be searching alone. Those were my marching orders from Gideon—don't let that idiot girl out of your sight. My God, Kate, what would you do if you found those infernal journals our father and his cohorts kept?"

She moved her shoulders a time or two, trying to act nonchalant, as if she hadn't yet contemplated that possibility. "I don't know. Read them? Write to Gideon at Yearlings and announce I've found them?"

"Exactly. You'd do both, and in that order."

Kate grinned. She never could fool Valentine. "Are they really that naughty?"

"They don't describe the Society's lawn parties, I'll tell you that much. I've read the single one we found, and one was enough, more than enough, even for me. Now, let's get this couch back into place."

Sticking the apple between her fine white teeth once more, Kate pushed with all her might, helping to slide the couch against the wall. It wasn't easy to do, which was why she hadn't yet searched the area, and in the end, Valentine had to do the majority of the pushing. "You're right. Nobody would hide a door or secret panel behind that monstrosity. That really cuts down on my list of possible hidey-holes, doesn't it? And in a house with seventy rooms, I can't tell you how that cheers me. Where shall we search next?"

Valentine glanced at the mantel clock. "No more today, Kate. I've got a friend arriving from London in less than two hours."

"Please say it's not Jeremy. He keeps looking at me with his mouth hanging open. I can nearly see his tonsils."

Valentine chuckled as they left the study, arm in arm. "He can't help it. He's mad for you. Except when he's afraid of you, which is most of the time."

"That's ridiculous. Why would he be afraid of me?"

"I don't know. Probably because I said you'd eat him for lunch." Valentine grabbed Kate's elbow and turned her toward the large pier glass in the hallway. "Look at you."

"I don't have to look at me—I know what I look like, Val, for pity's sake."

"Do you? Just because it amuses me, let me tell you what Jeremy sees. Jeremy, and any man with two eyes in his head and not dead below the waist—and don't try to be coy and tell me you don't know what that means, because Trixie gave you the same talking-to she gave all of us, God help us."

Kate was checking out her reflection in the glass, pushing a lock of hair back behind her ear. "Oh? So she told you if a man misbehaves you're to *kick him hard in the fork* and then run away while he's on his knees, whimpering and calling for his mama?"

"My God. It's even worse than we'd imagined she say." Valentine rubbed at the slight twitch that had started up beneath his left eye. "Thank you for not doing that last year, at Almacks. Really, I mean that sincerely. Now, shall we continue?"

"I'm not continuing anything," Kate said, trying not to grin at her brother's embarrassment. "You started this, remember?"

"Yes, for my sins, I do."

"We make quite the handsome couple, don't we, Val? Same dark hair, same amber eyes. Why, your eyelashes are nearly as long as mine. Does that bother you?"

"Not as much as it does Max. Why else do you think he's grown that mustache? Now pay attention, Kate. First, your hair. Black as the ace of spades in most lights, golden-black in the sun. Hair like yours is rare as hen's teeth in London, land of the insipid blond, blue-eyed miss. Then there's the sheer amount of it. And the curls when you let it hang loose, which is most of the time, because you're a lazy sot. Females live to be told they're old enough to put up their hair, and you let yours hang. I'll bet Trixie told you to do that."

Kate played with one of the fat, soft curls that reached halfway to her elbows. "So Jeremy's shocked into imbecility by my hair? Which, yes, Trixie told me to continue wearing down because the only reason to put it up would be so men can do nothing but concentrate on finding a way to take out the pins. Why not give them what they want beforehand, because that way maybe they'll retain enough brains to actually attempt coherent conversation."

"That woman's a menace. And dead wrong in this case, or hoping to keep you looking younger so she doesn't feel older. In any event, you let them start thinking lascivious thoughts having already arrived at step two of their plan for you—and with your help. Luckily for you, Jeremy hasn't the expertise to have ever gotten past step one to even begin thinking about step three. You confound him, poor fellow."

"Intriguing. What's *your* step three, Val?"

"None of your business, brat. All right, so much for the hair. We've discussed the eyes as to color. The problem with yours is, you don't lower them, not to anybody. You don't simper, you don't flirt, you don't flutter. You look at the world with beautiful eyes, granted, but beneath those lashes and those tip-tilted ends you've got going so nicely for you, you're a man, and they know it. You think like a man, you look boldly like a man, you appraise with your eyes. Also damnably unnerving."

Kate looked at herself looking at her eyes. "Good. I like that."

"Wonderful. I'm trying to explain something, and all I'm doing is handing you more ammunition to use against my own gender. Your mouth? That mouth is self-explanatory, and probably a sin to think about, not that your older, wiser brothers see it for more than it is, which is bold, and definitely opinionated. Leaving us with your body."

"We are not going to discuss my body." Kate tried to tug her arm free of her brother.

"No, no, let's finish this. First, it's noon, and you're not yet dressed for the day. Not because you're lazy. Lord knows half of London's debutantes are just now waking up to their morning chocolate. But they're hidden away in their chambers, not tramping about the house in their bare feet because of a sudden insuppressible desire to have me poking around behind a couch."

"I wanted to catch you before you went out riding, or something."

"We could argue that one point for hours, Kate, but we'll let it go with the easiest explanation—you want what you want when you want it. Just like Gideon."

"Thank you," Kate said cheekily, knowing she was making her brother crazy. "Now you're going to compare my body to Gideon's?"

"No, mostly I'd compare it to our mother's. I'd compare all of you, and most of the rest of us, to our mother. It's what you do with your body that is like Gideon, or Max, or me, or men everywhere, at least the ones who aren't wearing red-heeled shoes and mincing about like nincompoops."

"Speaking of nincompoops, do you know Adam sleeps until eleven, and then takes two full hours to bathe and dress, only to come out of his rooms looking the brainless fop, his scent arriving in any room a good ten seconds before he appears?"

"Jessica's brother is a good example of the men you don't resemble," Valentine said, grinning. "You haven't been tormenting him too much since you brought him back here from London, have you?"

"No," Kate said, peering at her reflection again, trying to understand what Val had meant about her body. She'd been tutored by Trixie, she was all of twenty years old—she should know what he'd meant. "He can fairly well make a cake of himself all by himself. And does, frequently. A spider crawled up his silly pink clocked stockings out in the garden the other day. He screamed, worse than any female and ran in circles until I could catch him and flick the thing away. I like him, though. He's almost my same age, I think. We've agreed to cry friends, as long as we're banished here together to keep us out of the way."

"You two weren't banished here to keep— Oh, all right. I'll grant you that one. On the other hand, you weren't Adam's age since you were five. That's still not what I'm trying to say, so if you'd please shut up I can be done with this. And not a moment too soon for my comfort." He looked toward the ceiling, as if hunting his next words, and then said carefully, "You didn't quite get the hang of London last year."

"Oh, nonsense. Don't tiptoe around the thing. I know exactly what London is. I just didn't like it."

"Yes, I've seen Lord Hilton's crooked nose. Actually, it helps one forgive his nonexistent chin. But what I'm saying is you have a woman's body, but you comport that body like a man. You slouch when you want to, you cross your legs at the knee, for God's sake. You walk with purpose, your strides too long to be dainty. You fold your arms across your chest when your hands should be neatly curled in your lap. You put your feet up on the table and let your ankles show. And look at you today. Traipsing about here in your nightclothes, as if you have no notion of what's proper. And when you finally get dressed, nine times out of ten it's in one of your riding habits and a pair of boots."

She truly didn't understand his concern. She was who she was, just as her brothers were who they were, and what was good for the goose should also be good for the gander. Who'd decided only men could be comfortable? Probably a man. "Oh, dear. Surely I should be locked up. Or is that shot?"

Valentine r̶ ... of dark hair. "You ...
of all people, and in ...
ers who probably set a ...

"Probably?"

"I'll ignore that. But you a...
Kate, no matter how much you ...
be. You're a female, and these thing... ...
in London for less than a week when y... ...Al-
macks and performed your little party tric... ...w I've
got a friend coming to stay with us for a few weeks. A
sophisticated gentleman. A marquis."

"Oh? And you're ashamed of me, is that it? Wait—
it's worse than that, isn't it? You're *matchmaking?* I
refused to go back to London for a second season, so
you're bringing London to me? With all that's going
on here, Val, with the search for the journals, the caves
where the Society met? Have you entirely lost your
senses?"

"As you just said, probably," Val muttered, turning
away from the glass, refusing to meet her gaze. "All I'm
saying, Kate, is…well, it's time to grow up, be a lady.
You can do it, I know you can, Gideon made sure you
had lessons. You *need* to do it."

But he turned back at the sound of a short, hurriedly
cut-off sob, and held out his arms to her. "Aw, Kate,
I'm sorry. Come here."

Kate walked into his arms, to lay her cheek against
his chest. Her brothers were all such sweethearts, they
really were. But even her love for Valentine wasn't
enough to contain her giggles for long, and he soon
put his hands on her shoulders and pushed her away
from him enough to see her grin.

"Why, you—"

just acted like a lady. You
I didn't fall into a ladylike swoon.
this marquis of yours begins courting me on
ers from you—"

"Now wait a moment, Kate. It isn't as if I deliberately invited the man for you to practice on. We were both bored hollow with the season, and Gideon had already asked me to come here to watch over you. I just opened my mouth and heard myself inviting Simon to join me," Valentine corrected quickly. "The rest was an afterthought."

"Well, that at least sounds like you. Always quick to lend assistance. And, as I always remind you, one day you're going to drop yourself into trouble, being so helpful."

"I just think it would be a good thing for you to get in a little…practice before you descend on London next spring. Because you are going back, Kate, and at twenty-one some will already say you're getting a bit too long in the tooth for a debutante. Gideon's already working on securing another voucher for Almacks, although I doubt even he can manage that miracle."

"Right up there with the loaves and fishes, I gather? Bunch of high-in-the-instep matrons who think they're more important than they are. But tough nuts to crack, hmm? Maybe Gideon ought to petition the heavens for help."

Val pointed a finger at her. "See? *That's* what you do. Young ladies don't say things like that. What you need is practice, and me for a mentor, God help me, because I'm the only one available except for Trixie, and we can all see how that turned out the first time. So practice on the marquis while he's here, and I'll guide you."

"That depends, Val. Can he join in our treasure hunt?

We can call it that, at least. Gideon said there may also be a treasure of sorts in the cave when we find it, remember? A golden rose with a diamond in it as big as a pigeon's egg, perhaps?"

Valentine's eyes went wide. "Who in bloody blazes told you about the rose?"

Really, men were so simple. "Nobody. I just happened to hear something about it somehow. You've only just confirmed it for me, thank you. And gentlemen don't say *bloody* in front of ladies, even sisters. I'm not the only one in need of a mentor, it seems."

"Never mind that. Eavesdropping, were you?"

She jammed her fists onto her hips. "How else am I supposed to learn anything? Of course I eavesdrop. The members of the Society all wore a golden rose in their cravats, to show they'd brought a virgin into bloom, correct? And, somewhere on the estate, there's possibly a very large golden rose, with a diamond in it as big as a pigeon's egg. Maybe. Perhaps. Or at least Gideon was thinking that way early on, when he suspected someone was poking about the grounds last winter. You know, lights moving through the trees, that cave-in in one of the greenhouses that exposed some bit of collapsed cave or tunnel?"

"Do…do you have any idea what you're saying? About the rose?"

Kate lowered her head, this time truly close to tears. "Yes, I think our father was an exceedingly bad man who did exceedingly bad things, much if not all of it done here, at Redgrave Manor. I can't ask Trixie, because that might hurt her. That her son was evil. Our father was evil. I've stared and stared at his portrait in the long gallery since I returned from London. He was very handsome, like some sort of blond god. I don't see evil, except perhaps in his eyes. They're cold, aren't they, and mocking. He's got one of the golden roses stuck in his cravat. That couldn't have made our mother happy, could it? No wonder she shot him."

Valentine pinched at the bridge of his nose. "God, I'm done. I came here to protect you, and you already know more than you should."

"I know you're all after a murderer, who probably killed Jessica's father and some of the other older members of the Society who possibly didn't agree with the new leader. Trixie said that right in front of me in London. She was half in her cups, poor thing, but she couldn't help it. After all, her lover had just—"

"I know what happened that night," her brother said, looking pained.

"I'm sorry. I'm simply trying to help, that's all. I should be allowed to help. Tell me about the murderer. Who all did he murder? What other bad things has the Society done?"

Valentine shook himself back to attention. "Now we're more than done. You learned about the journals, and Gideon decided you could search for them, certain you wouldn't find them, that Trixie had found them years ago and burned them all. And then he had second thoughts. Concentrate on the journals, Kate. Finding them would be an immense help."

"So you won't tell me about the murderer. Why? It's all of a piece, isn't it? The Society, the journals, the murderer?"

"We believe the *murderer,* as you call him, is the new leader of the Society. Murder is not their true purpose but only, as I said, a weeding out of the members from our father's time who might not agree with what's happening now. Tell you what, Kate. Find the journals, and I'll tell you the rest. All you have to do is promise me you won't open them, and that in the meantime you won't badger me incessantly to know what nobody wants to tell you. That's a fair bargain, isn't it?"

"Is there a lot I don't know?"

"God, I sincerely hope so."

Kate considered this for a moment. Either way, she'd learn the whole of it, eventually. But if it made Valentine happy? "All right. We'll shake on it."

"We bloody well will not. Women don't shake hands to seal a bargain. If they do anything, they offer their hand and allow us gentlemen to bow over it."

"So stuffy, Val. All right, pretend I just did that, assuming you agree to the rest. We'll let this marquis of yours join in the treasure hunt, unaware of what we're really looking for. If we don't, and you insist on being with me as I search in case I find something—which I'm determined to do—he'll have nothing to do all the day long otherwise but twiddle his thumbs. That and have his ears banged on by Adam, which isn't always as jolly as it sounds."

"And," Valentine said, apparently feeling he had the advantage now, "you'll behave like a lady in the man's presence. Seriously, Kate, much as we all adore you, you need the practice."

She could give in, but never completely. It wasn't in her nature. "I'll *try,* that's the best I can say. However, if he should be so impressed with my ladylike behavior that he attempts whatever step three is, be aware, Val, I'll kick him hard in the fork. I really will, and then I'll blame you."

"I need a drink. Go get dressed."

Kate held out one side of her dressing gown and sank into a deep curtsy. "La, sir, you're so very masterful.

I shall of course rush off now, begging your leave, to do your bidding."

"Two. Make that two drinks…"

CHAPTER TWO

SIMON RAVENBILL, LATE of his majesty's navy and now marquis of Singleton, both thanks to the unexpected death of his older brother the previous year, reined in his curricle at the crest of a hill overlooking Redgrave Manor.

This is where it all began, he thought, looking down at the enormous fieldstone country mansion that had probably stood there for well over a century, with each new earl adding his own touches by way of wings that seemed to jut out willy-nilly on three sides. Spread around the main grounds were at least a dozen more stone buildings of varying sizes, as if the main house had pupped and the hodgepodge of structures was the result of several strong litters.

There were sheep milling about, their purpose to keep the acres of grass neatly gnawed, but the animals were kept away from the buildings and gardens by means of a ha-ha, a gracefully meandering but rather formidable sunken fieldstone wall. Simon eyed the height of the wall from the distance, took in the several high stone pillars fitted with heavy iron gates that kept the ha-ha from completely circling the grounds. The road leading to the gates took the same deep dip and rise of the ha-ha trench, rather like a moat.

He decided sheep weren't the only unwanted visitors that could be kept at arm's length.

The ha-ha's wide top was encrusted with bits of colorful broken glass and sat level with the scythed lawns nearest the buildings. The wall must be a dozen feet high, seemingly grown up out of the twenty-foot-wide ditch that then gently sloped back up to the level of the rest of the property. A sheep could amble in and out of the grassy ditch easily enough, but only on the same side on which it had entered. The same could be said for any man hoping for entry anyplace other than one of the gates, unless he brought his own ladder with him, and a stout pair of leather gloves.

Green grass, white sheep, the sunlight dancing on the broken glass and setting off small rainbows of color. Bucolic. Picturesque. Deceptively deadly.

All that was needed was a drawbridge. Then Simon remembered where he was: southern Kent, not more than a mile from Hythe and the Channel. Beautiful, but with a sometimes violent history. Smugglers had been active here for centuries, and probably would see the coast for what it was, a spot seemingly fashioned perfectly to ply their trade.

Invading armies saw it likewise, most recently Bonaparte himself. Although Simon agreed with the current theory that the new self-proclaimed Emperor Napoleon was now too busy annexing every country in Europe to attempt an assault of England by sea.

All the strong brick Martello watchtowers hastily constructed along the southern coast in earlier years of the new century were left now to inferior troops who spent their days napping and their nights in the local dockside pubs as guests of the friendly local smugglers.

Hopefully, nobody noticed the building of the towers, mostly abandoned a few years ago, was quietly taking place once more, with the goal of having more than one hundred of the things fully manned before they were done, their cannons all aimed out over the water.

It took an army to win a battle, but only a few determined men could completely alter the tide of a war. That those men could be English, and their goal the collapse of their own country was why Simon now found himself the guest of a man he'd met only the once, and a reluctant actor in a romantic farce dreamed up by Prime Minister Spencer Perceval himself in order to appease Gideon Redgrave and gain his cooperation.

Or as the earl had affably stated as he relaxed in Perceval's office as if it were his own: "We Redgraves will see these traitors brought down, I assure you. However, if you wish for me to continue to share information, you'll do things my way. I keep you apprised, you keep me apprised, and nothing appears so much as vaguely suspicious at Redgrave Manor." He'd then stood up, shot his cuffs and smiled one of the most appealing yet threatening smiles Simon had ever seen. "We're agreed? Otherwise, good day, gentlemen, and good luck."

Only days earlier Simon had still thought Gideon Redgrave a possible traitor himself because of who he was, and suddenly his family was to be their savior. He didn't like it. In fact, he was all for bringing in troops and ripping Redgrave Manor apart, and the devil with this tiptoeing about as if the man were in charge.

But as the prime minister had pointed out, Simon hadn't made much progress on his own in the matter. With one of the two men he'd been investigating now dead, and the other claiming illness and retiring to his country estate, Simon had to agree. Now, thanks to the Redgraves, they had hopes of more information, and had already uncovered one nasty plot at the Ministry level to criminally divert the timely delivery of food and ammunition to their troops on the Peninsula.

Perceval was no more comfortable with the thought he'd been unknowingly harboring traitors in his own midst than Gideon Redgrave had been to realize his family's long-ago shame could end up trotted out for another airing, this time with high treason not an accompanying rumor but a proven fact.

"All of which has resulted in me arriving here, about to play houseguest to a man I don't know and possible suitor of his bound to be half-witted sister, if she'd be fool enough to believe any of it." Then, wondering when he'd begun to talk to himself out loud, he released the brake and the matched pair of bays in the traces responded to his light touch on the reins. "That's it, boys, let's get this over with."

Redgrave Manor got larger as Simon drew closer, even as, in parts, the sparkling top of the walls of the ha-ha disappeared here and there, following the rises and dips in the land. He kept to the well-tended road, which he was certain had run through the huge expanse of property during the last mile of his journey, noticing a grassy avenue lined with ancient trees off to his right. Could that have been the scene of the long-ago duel turned murder?

To his left he could see what had to be only a small part of the extensive gardens drifting away from the rear of the mansion, along with a moss-covered stone ruin. It was probably a true ruin, and not especially built to appear to be one, as there was at Singleton Place, thanks to Holbrook, who'd thought them the height of good taste.

Then again, his late brother had harbored many

strange tastes. And, as it had worked out, one of them had proved fatal.

As he approached the main gate a pair of what could have been farm laborers sidled out from small doors cut into each of the massive stone pillars. Now that he was nearly on top of them, Simon could see the pillars were actually a clever pair of gatehouses, complete with colorful potted flowers below the windows and stout iron bars behind the leaded glass panes. Again, it was discreet, but the place had all the beauty of a fairy tale while carefully disguising its many defensive strengths.

He gave a moment's thought to the existence of a dungeon in the cellars, one with a well-greased rack.

The servants stood at their ease just behind the gates. Nonchalant. Waiting. One of them raised a hand to poke a finger in his ear, wiggle it and then visually examine what he'd managed to dislodge. It would appear the Redgraves didn't stand much on ceremony. Either that, or they liked their visitors caught off guard and more than slightly confused. Was he facing two none-too-intelligent country dullards, or was he facing a fortress?

"Good afternoon, my fine fellows," Simon called out cheerfully if facetiously. "The Marquis of Singleton, to see Mr. Valentine Redgrave. Is that sufficient information for you, or is there also a password?"

The two young men exchanged puzzled glances before one of them tugged at his forelock and pulled a large iron key from his pocket. "You're expected, my lord. I'll just open these gates and Liam here will hop up behind you lickety-split so as he can take your horses around to the stables and see they're bedded down all nice and tight."

"That sounds reasonable. Tell me, are these gates always locked?"

Again, the servants looked to each other before the one called Liam answered. "I'll be bringing up that there trunk you have tied up behind the seat, my lord, once I've got those pretty horses tucked up. You want to open the gates now, Dickie, I suppose?"

Simon thanked him as the lad hopped up behind him. So much for any idea of cultivating the servants for gossip. Redgrave had trained them well, if not then dressed them accordingly. Suddenly eager to see more of Redgrave Manor, and its inhabitants, he released the brake again, only to set it a minute later as he reined in his team halfway around the wide circle that sported a gray, weathered sculpture at its center. He couldn't be certain, but he believed the marble had been chiseled to resemble Hades, Greek god of the underworld. Why else would the marble hound seated next to him have three heads?

"If you're so concerned about rumors and speculation, you don't invite it in by greeting visitors with *that,*" he murmured under his breath as he hopped down from the seat just as one of the massive front doors opened and the tall, darkly handsome Valentine Redgrave bounded down the stairs, his right arm extended in greeting.

"Simon!" he said, pumping the man's hand as if they were old school chums reunited. "I heard someone was loitering up on the hill, and hoped it was you. Gives a grand view of this pile, doesn't it?"

"And a grand view of anyone loitering up on the hill, obviously. You have sentries posted, sir?"

"No, no, not sir. And not my lord. Val and Simon, Simon and Val. We cried friends months ago, somewhere in Sussex, I believe we'll say."

"I met you for five minutes in Perceval's office, and

told you then I'm not happy about this ridiculous play-acting."

"So you did," Valentine said, draping a companion-able arm around Simon's shoulder and walking him away from the open front door. "I advised you to learn to like it, which you better have done, because Lady Katherine is about to do some playacting of her own, which might put you a little off your game unless you apply yourself."

Simon stepped away from the man. "Excuse me? She knows about the deception?"

"Not quite. She leaped to an erroneous conclusion this morning and I allowed her to leap, even pointed her more firmly in that direction one might say. Kate's a stickler for the *why* of things, so it seemed best to have her think she'd guessed correctly." Valentine hesitated a moment before continuing. "Oh, about that. She thinks I invited you here so she can 'practice' on you. Let me explain. Some would say she didn't fare well during her first foray into society. You may have heard of it?"

A truly splendidly delivered right cross, Singleton. You should have seen it. "I may have heard a few whispered words at one of my clubs. Should I consider wearing some sort of protection?"

Valentine immediately glanced down at Simon's crotch, which unnerved the marquis just a little bit. "No, of course not. Look, Simon, it's simple. I told her you're my friend, we're both bored with London, I invited you here for some respite and, hopefully, to let her practice her feminine wiles a tad before we haul her back to the city next season. It was too soon to take her back this year. You, however, have no idea you're here to act the role of interested *parti* in between searches for those damn journals and hopefully, a cave or tunnel that hasn't yet collapsed from age."

"Have you poked around that statue? It could be the portal to the *underworld*." Simon wasn't feeling particularly cooperative.

Valentine laughed. "Good point, we'll have to give it a look. Maybe one of the hound's heads swivels and opens a stairway or some such thing? We call him Henry, by the way. Hades, not the hound. String him with holly at Christmastime. Our grandmother told us, in the old days it served to keep the locals on their best behavior, but now Henry is mostly a family joke."

"Do you have many such *jokes* about the place?" Simon asked.

"Well, there's the ha-ha, but that's only funny if you're not sixteen and don't attempt to climb it after you've stayed out past the time the gates are locked, enjoying the company of the extremely accommodating barmaid at the Eagle." Valentine looked down at his palm. "I can still make out a few of the scars."

"From the broken glass embedded in the top of the wall, or the extremely accommodating barmaid?"

Valentine threw back his head and laughed. "No, she left her marks on my back, as I recall the thing."

Damn. Simon was beginning to like the fellow. Probably because that's what he was supposed to do. "All right," he said, deliberately turning back toward the open front door. "So I'm playacting as your friend, brought here by you to distract your sister, hiding the fact I'm really here to find the journals—which she doesn't know. In her turn, Lady Katherine is set on finding the journals, but now she's also playacting as a—what?"

Valentine sighed. "Much as it pains me to say it, she'll be playacting as a lady."

"I beg your pardon?"

"Don't concern yourself. I'll soon be saying those same words to you, if you aren't careful. The thing is, it's imperative she stops searching for those godawful journals on her own. Imperative. One of us has to be with her at all times. She *cannot* read them, not so much as a single page. Remember, Simon, I've read one of them."

"I haven't. Your brother didn't pass it along to us."

"As Gideon convinced Perceval, there was no need. That journal is only the first small piece of a very large puzzle. But since we can't stop her, I could be called away at any time, and nothing less than binding her hand and foot and shipping her off to one of Gideon's other estates will even begin to put a spoke in her wheel—like a pigeon, she'd somehow find her way back here again—we're doing three things. Distracting her with your handsome face—but carefully, my friend, or I'll be constrained to hurt you—keeping her on her toes as she attempts to impress me with her ladylike accomplishments and accompanying her on any searches. Those are our goals. She's really quite acute, Simon, and beyond tenacious. If those journals still exist, she'll find them better and faster than any dozen hounds we could put on the scent. Gideon will have both our heads on a platter if she finds them without us."

"I think I might be able to do with a glass of wine before you introduce me to your sister," Simon said as they neared the wide steps to the mansion. "Perhaps more than one."

"That's strange. My interlude with Kate this morning ended much the same way. She can have that effect on people."

"Well, if nothing else, *Val,* you've certainly piqued my interest."

Valentine grinned. "Yes, she has that effect on people, as well."

Simon was impressed with the house the moment he entered it. Massive. Everything about it was massive, from the size of the entrance hall to the height of the dark, polished oak paneling and woodwork in the fashion of another time. The heavy wooden staircase, again massive, began with three steps up to a landing, then turned toward a full flight, currently blocked by a sturdy yet ornate wooden dog gate that told him the Redgraves loved their animals, but they didn't love them everywhere.

He directed his eyes upward and saw the staircase had another landing, another turn, and then the railing seemed to wrap itself about three sides of the hallway before rising again to the next floor.

"Impressive, isn't it? All that magnificent oak is from our own lands, when they were cleared to build this pile. Horribly out of the current style, but we like it, although the maids tend to grumble while they're polishing that staircase."

"Beauty being in the eye of the beholder, as opposed to the labor of the worker."

"Oh, we've all polished that staircase at one time or another. Our grandmother considered it the perfect punishment. I was given the job for one day each week for six months after I had the happy notion to slide down the entire staircase on a large silver tray. If the dog gate hadn't been closed, I might have made it all the way to the tiles."

Simon gave another look to the sheer height and tricky landings. "How did the tray fare?"

Valentine grinned. "That was sent off to the blacksmith, to be hammered back into some semblance of its former self. Now, about that drink…"

But Simon was still looking at the staircase, which meant he was the first to see the exotic vision that had just appeared at the wooden railing to peer down at them, her long black curls hanging slightly over the railing. "My God," he breathed quietly.

Valentine looked up, as well. "Oh. It's only Kate." He waved his arm at her. "Come on down, Kate. Our guest has arrived."

Lady Katherine turned toward the stairs, keeping her right hand on the railing, using her left to hike up her hem a few inches as she took on the first few steps. Then she stopped, took a breath, let go of her skirt and continued her descent, this time with her head held high, and at a much more sedate pace.

Simon prayed she'd continue to take her time, stretching out the moments he could simply stand and stare at her. And hopefully figure out a way to get his tongue unstuck from the roof of his suddenly dry mouth. *Please let her open her mouth and squawk like a parrot. Otherwise, I'm doomed.*

"So?" Valentine asked.

"Hmm?"

"So, do you think you can do it?"

"Do what?" Simon asked, finding it difficult to believe the beautiful creature had just winked at him.

"You know, Singleton, I don't think I thought this new twist on our little game through as well as I could have, and should have just let Kate be Kate," Valentine said on a sigh. "Because this is beginning to show all the hallmarks of a bad, *bad* idea."

KATE HAD ALREADY lifted her right leg to cross over her left before she caught herself in time and carefully placed her foot back down on the carpet. Five minutes into the thing, and she had almost proved Valentine correct—she didn't know how to behave as a lady. It would have been thirty seconds into the thing, if her brother had seen her wink at the marquis, but he hadn't, so that didn't count.

But she hadn't been able to resist. The marquis had looked so adorably flustered as he watched her descend the staircase, yes, like a lady. It was just as Trixie had promised: men were lamentably easy, as they rarely thought with their brains. She probably should have asked her what they used instead, but Trixie had seemed to think she understood, and she hadn't wanted to appear blockheaded. Still, she believed she was beginning to get an idea.

Now here they were, all cozy in the enormous main drawing room, the introductions behind them, and she was wondering why she continued to find his lordship so appealing.

Perhaps it was his coloring. Her brothers were dark-haired, and none of them had such startlingly green eyes. Perhaps that was it—the marquis was a new experience for her. Not that she hadn't seen her share of light-eyed, blond-haired men. It's just that none of them had looked anything like Simon Ravenbill, or dressed half so well. In fact, although his clothing was more than two decades out of date, the man the marquis put her in mind of most was her father, and the portrait that hung in the long gallery.

Maybe it was fate, sending her a warning. Was there something hidden beneath the appealing surface of the marquis, as there had been evil lurking behind the smiling face depicted in that portrait? It still didn't seem sensible to her that Valentine would have invited a guest to Redgrave Manor now, of all times. Was her brother playing her for a fool? Why?

"Kate?"

She shook herself back to attention. It wasn't like her to allow her mind to drift. The marquis must think her rude, or shallow…or simple. "A thousand apologies, Val," she cooed sweetly; she'd learned at Trixie's feet how to deliver a cutting line with an accompanying smile. "Did you say something of interest, and I missed it?"

The marquis, just then in the midst of taking a sip of wine, gave a short cough and then swallowed, seemingly with some difficulty.

Kate could like this man. If she wasn't so suspicious of him.

"I was saying, Kate," Valentine pressed on, ignoring the jab, "I think Simon would enjoy joining us in our small treasure hunt. You know, the jewels supposedly hidden somewhere on the estate by that band of smugglers who then set out on another run, only to drown to the last man in a storm."

Oh, that was fairly good. Valentine must have put some thought into that fib; to mention the golden rose by name would have been a mistake. Still, it was a lengthy explanation of his lie, and he probably should have kept it shorter. And probably would have, if she'd been paying him the least attention when he first uttered it.

"Really?" she asked, turning to the marquis. "I doubt

there's any truth to the legend, but I will admit to being intrigued ever since I heard the tale a few weeks ago. My brother Gideon thinks it all a great hum, but Val here has promised to help. You don't think us incredibly silly?"

"Not at all. There isn't a little boy in all of England who hasn't dreamt of finding buried treasure. I don't see why it should be so different for the fairer sex."

She smiled at him, careful to bat her eyelids, just the once. "La, my lord, how forward-thinking of you. Many would suggest we of the fairer sex are too fragile for such undertakings."

"Not true. But I would be remiss if I didn't add joining you and Val here will also afford me an excuse to spend more time in your fair company."

Oh, now I know I'm being led by the nose! Such stuff and nonsense, and laid on with a trowel, it's so thick! "You put me to the blush, my lord."

She sensed Valentine looking from the marquis, to her, and then back again. He then got to his feet, rubbing his palms together. "Good! That's settled, then. Kate, isn't it soon time for some afternoon refreshment? I'm sure Simon is hungry for a little something before dinner."

"Yes, of course. A poor hostess I'd be, indeed, if I hadn't thought of that myself." *Don't ask me to be perfect and then continually test me, Val, or you'll be sorry you ever began this farce. Although I suspect you already are!*

As if he'd been hovering outside the door awaiting his cue to enter, Dearborn stepped into the room to announce the arrival of refreshments, "as requested by Lady Katherine" (she'd asked him to add that last part). In marched a trio of maids, all carrying silver trays laden with sandwiches, cakes and a large pitcher of lemonade. They could have fed a half-dozen ravenous men with this display of food, but then, the Redgraves did nothing in a small way…and the servants would enjoy the remnants that returned to the kitchens.

The marquis surprised Kate by taking on the role of mother, pouring them each a tall tumbler of lemonade. "So you don't have to strain to lift such a heavy pitcher," he told her, handing her one of the glasses.

"Oh, too kind, too kind," she purred, smiling around gritted teeth, mentally exchanging that trowel for a shovel. "We're quite informal here, my lord. Please feel free to help yourself to anything you'd like."

"Yes," the marquis said slowly, his back to Valentine, looking at her rather than the trays of sandwiches and decorative cakes. "I'll do that."

Kate felt herself being put to the blush, an occurrence so rare in her experience she couldn't remember the last time it had happened. "Val? Aren't you hungry?" she asked quickly.

Valentine was looking at his own glass with barely veiled horror. Kate believed she could read his mind: *Lemonade? Is the man mad? What in bloody hell am I supposed to do with lemonade?*

"Not anymore," he grumbled, eyeing the drinks table.

Kate had to bite the inside of her cheek to keep from laughing. She didn't know how long she could last with this ridiculousness, but she was certain she could hang on longer than her brother. Besides, it was rather fun being flirted with, even if the man was doing it on orders from his new friend—because that had to be the answer, it was the only answer that fit. Val had told *both* of them to flirt, his lordship in order to do his friend a favor, and Kate in order to play at being somebody other than herself. Or could her brother actually have brought them both together, spinning lies for both of them, all in order to matchmake? Clearly her brother had no head for intrigue. No matter what, Valentine was in trouble!

Kate reached for one of the plates holding a cake iced with some lovely pink confection. It was time to learn more about their guest. "Valentine tells me London is very flat this season, my lord. Is that true?"

"London is London, my lady, and in the end, I suppose what you make of it," he answered, having somehow already downed half his sandwich, rather like a person who has learned to feed his belly as quickly and efficiently as possible. Someone like a soldier, perhaps?

"Yes, and I made a shambles of it last year. It was really quite enjoyable."

"Kate," Valentine said warningly.

"There's no sense in pretending it didn't happen, Valentine. Now is there, my lord?"

"I'm certain you were quite justified in your actions, my lady."

"No, I wasn't. I could have done any number of things. Walked off the floor, for one, cutting the man dead. Claimed a sudden indisposition and asked him to return me to my grandmother. Feigned an overturned ankle. Any number of things. I simply preferred my chosen rebuttal to his statement."

"Again, may I say I'm certain you were quite justified."

"Thank you." She turned to Valentine. "Now, see how simple that was? Rough ground gotten over swiftly and smoothly. It had to be said, didn't it? Elsewise, it would hang over us all. My goodness, she's the barbarian who bloodied that man's nose last year at Almacks." She gave a slight toss of her head. "I feel much better now. Shall we cry friends, my lord, as you and Val have already done? We prefer to be informal here at Redgrave Manor."

"I would be honored," the marquis said with an inclination of his handsome head. "Kate."

"Simon," she answered, again feeling heat climbing into her cheeks. She was going to have to be extremely careful around this so pretty, so pleasing man. "I'm certain Dearborn is waiting outside, to show you to your rooms."

As Kate rose, he stood up, as well. "I would like to change out of my traveling clothes, thank you."

"We keep country hours, Simon," Valentine told him. "Dinner gong goes at six, tea at ten and then early to rise. We might think about a ride over the estate in the morning?"

Simon looked to Kate. "Do you ride?" His tone implied if she didn't, he wouldn't, either.

"I do," she said, "thank you for asking."

He inclined his head to her once more. "My mount will be arriving shortly, if it hasn't already, along with my coach and valet. I eagerly anticipate the dinner gong, so that we may become more acquainted."

She dropped him a small curtsy, then watched as he strode out of the room. Grabbing up one of the well-cut sandwiches, she plunked herself back down on the soft couch and clunked her heels, one after the other, on the low table before crossing her legs at the ankle. "All right, where did you meet him?"

"Is it impossible for you to employ correct posture for more than ten minutes?" Val asked, seating himself on the opposite couch and repeating her action with his own legs.

She spoke around a bite of ham shoved between a split roll spread with their own homemade mustard. "No, but that doesn't answer my question, does it?"

"Sussex. Somewhere in Sussex, I disremember where. We met again in London, at some insipid affair, and soon I was regaling him with the beauty of Kent. Did you have to bring up Almacks?"

"Of course I did. Everyone knows, even if Gideon made it clear no one was to talk about it. You can't stop gossip, Val, you can only make it whisper instead of shout. Why else did you all decide I shouldn't return for another year? Simon was sure to have heard, so why not admit it and be done?"

"I'm not certain I like you addressing him as Simon."

Kate rolled her eyes. "I'm not overjoyed with his blatant flirting. You might consider advising him to not lay it on so thick and rare."

"You don't use cant expressions like thick and rare," Valentine said, almost as if the correction was by habit, without having to think about it. "And I did *not* invite him here to flirt with you. You're to be practicing on *him,* remember?"

Poor Valentine, trying so hard to elude the ensnaring net of his lies. "Yes, certainly. Such deep intrigue confuses me. Poor Simon has simply taken one look at me and succumbed. Much like Jeremy, except he can still speak. Being older, he probably knows Step Three, as well, don't you think? Or should I say, shouldn't you have thought of that before starting this? I mean, as it would appear your hoyden of a sister is irresistible when playing the lady." Then she grinned at him.

Val sighed theatrically. "I never should have mentioned Jeremy. I think we need Trixie here, but she refuses to leave London, saying you've more than enough guardians here without dragging her away from her fun."

"Fun? Jessica told me she was off to the countryside to attend a funeral."

"Two funerals, actually. As I said, our grandmother didn't want to be dragged away from her fun. And, no, I'm not going to explain that. It's enough you were there to see—"

Kate held up one hand. "Ah-ah, I thought we weren't going to talk about that. Although it was all rather jolly, except, of course, for that poor old fellow. You should have seen Gideon's face, he was that appalled. I laughed so hard I ended up with a bout of the hiccups."

"Dead men in our grandmother's bed amuse you. Wonderful. May I now critique your first attempt at behaving like a lady?"

"No, I don't think so. Was Simon in the army?"

"Now why the devil would you ask that?"

Kate shrugged, and sank a little lower on her spine. "I don't know. Trixie trained us all to be observant. He eats like a man used to consuming his meals in a rush, and he walks with some command to his step. It seemed a logical conclusion."

"Logical, but not completely correct. He served in the Royal Navy. Had his own command as a matter of fact. But his brother…died last year, so now he's the marquis."

Kate sat up a bit straighter. Aha, now she'd stumbled onto something. "You hesitated before you said *died*. Why?"

"Once in a while, I wish you wouldn't be so awake on all suits. The man hanged himself. Nobody speaks of it, just as nobody speaks of that right cross of yours or the Redgrave family scandals, but everyone knows of it. Holbrook Ravenbill wasn't in debt, a victim of some new heartbreak—any of the usual reasons for putting a period to one's own existence, not as far as anyone knows. If he left behind any sort of explanation, Simon's the only one who knows it, and no, I didn't ask him. And neither will you."

"Your confidence in me is sadly lacking, brother mine. I would never be so rude as to ask a grieving brother such a thing." *But he'll tell me, eventually.* "Now I suppose you'll want me to change my clothes yet again before dinner, which is a sad waste of time."

"Nobody said being a lady is easy," Valentine quipped as she got to her feet.

"Nobody said it was logical, either. Just be grateful I have all those gowns upstairs that never got to see the light of day in London. But for now, I'm off to the west wing. Liam told me his grandfather told him old houses were sometimes built with hidden staircases that could lead all the way from the attics to secret rooms in the cellars, but with no other openings along the way. Odd, isn't it? Since *our* grandfather ordered the construction of the west wing, I've been thinking perhaps Liam's grandfather might know something about that construction, that it isn't just a tale he told to entertain Liam."

"You think our grandfather and father had everyone climb up to the attics just to descend four floors into the cellars? In a parade of masks and cloaks, I'd suppose, dragging a braying goat behind them?"

Kate pulled a face. "I didn't say I was positive. And I would think only the journals could be hidden in such a place. I doubt they performed their silly rites in a cellar. But now that I don't have to ask you and your friend

Simon to move every heavy bed and couch pressed up against a wall, I thought I'd give it try."

"There's dedicated, Kate, and then there's— Bloody hell, I don't know what to call it."

She put a finger to her chin. "You know, just because couches and beds and chests are where they are now doesn't mean they were there all those years ago. A secret panel could still be hidden behind one of them, somewhere. Seventy rooms. Quite a task. But perhaps we should—"

Valentine held up both his hands. "No. No, no, no. I think you and Liam's grandfather might have stumbled onto something here. Go. Crawl around the attics of the west wing, tapping your little hammer. Really. Enjoy yourself."

"And what are you going to do, that you can't join me?"

"I, um, I haven't yet looked at today's post. I may have letters to answer."

"What a hum. You couldn't come up with a better excuse?" Kate rolled her eyes. "You know, Val, it's just as Trixie says, a real conundrum that women don't rule the world. And, also according to Trixie, that's only because we don't have—"

But Val was already stalking out of the room, his ears looking faintly red.

"Power!" she called after him. "Only because women don't have power." And then she ended quietly, "Or some other word beginning with *P*..."

CHAPTER THREE

SIMON BELIEVED THE Earl of Saltwood could comfortably fit any three rooms at Singleton Place inside his dining room and still seat a dozen diners. Not that Ravenbill was small; it was a fine estate. But everything about Redgrave Manor was immense. Most families suffered setbacks over the years, the centuries. The Redgraves seemed to have never taken a backward step.

That meant either unbelievable good luck, or a long line of crafty, intelligent men and women who always chose the right side, the correct moment; when to act, and when to retreat. So how, if what he believed was true, did at least the last two earls reconcile all this bounty with plotting to overthrow the monarchy? It made no sense.

Unless...

"I hope you don't mind," he said conversationally as the servants passed around yet another course, "but I spent a bit of time earlier with your obliging butler, familiarizing myself with your beautiful home. Quite an interesting and certainly extensive lineup of portraits in your gallery. From the change in dress, I'd have to think the Redgrave line goes back a considerable distance."

"Ages, yes," Kate said from her seat across the wide table. The four of them were gathered at one end of the immense table, with Valentine at the foot and young Adam Collier sitting beside Kate, alternately stuffing his face and attempting discreet peeks at her bosom, fetchingly outlined by her lightly golden silk gown. The puppy. And did he actually believe that pale paste he'd rubbed onto his face really succeeded in covering his spots? Simon sent up silent thanks he was no longer eighteen.

Valentine took up his fork. "True, Kate. Ages. All the way back to the Stuarts, the first time they held the throne, even before the first earl wrangled himself the title. We carry a few drops of Stuart blood, actually, although you'd have to apply to Gideon for the particulars, as the study of our family tree became lost on me by the time our tutor had got to the fifth branch."

"Descended from kings. And you're not interested?"

"Good Lord, Simon, who's even to say what side of the blanket our supposed Stuart was born on in the first place?" Valentine looked to Kate. "And *you* did not hear me say that."

"Oh, no, definitely not. But there is that small portrait of the first King Charles in the long gallery, remember? The one who had his head lopped off?"

Valentine widened his eyes in what seemed to be real shock. "I really should have paid more attention, shouldn't I?"

"I would have. No choice, really," Adam said, speaking for the first time in long minutes, an interlude he'd clearly felt had been better spent in seeing how many peas he could line up on his knife and then slide into his mouth without dropping any. "My father had me study the monarchies of every last country in creation. Boring stuff mostly, but I haven't been able to boost it out of my head now it's there. Charles the first was followed by that Cromwell fellow, and then his son, before the Stuarts came roaring back for a second go at things with Charles the second, but when Queen Anne died, everything went to our first George of the House of Hanover, thanks to a few drops of Stuart blood in him somewhere. You know, Valentine, like you Redgraves."

"Yes, of course. My brother should be sitting on the throne right now. Idiot."

"I think the Redgraves are smarter than that, Adam," Lady Katherine said, patting the boy's arm. "As I said, kings can be beheaded. Kingship was a messy business back then."

"They do sillier things than that! Did you know when the Stuarts got back on the throne they dug up Cromwell the first and chopped off his head because the first Charles had his chopped off? I mean, Cromwell had already been dead for dog's years, but it was a show of power, m'father said. Very important in kingships, showing off your power. Chopping off heads, poisonings, perhaps even drowning royal dukes in barrels of Malmsey wine, whatever that is. Then there were those poor boys in the Tower. Nobody knows who did that, not for certain. You have to be careful most times in not letting what you did get followed back to you, you see, or at least not be the only one who might be blamed. Now, consider Julius Caesar, for one. He was Roman, you know, and—"

"Eat your peas, Adam," Valentine instructed wearily, and turned back to Simon. "You'd never think our new relative has been tossed out of every school his late father managed to get him into, would you?"

"Only five, my lord, not all of them. One burned down—but it wasn't me who did it, I swear. Mine was only a small fire, nothing quite so spectacular. I still got the boot, though. Picky things, deans," Adam grumbled, plucking an errant pea out of his lacy neck cloth.

"The only reason I'm not in school now, your lordship, is I'm in mourning. Both my dear parents died in a coach accident, you know. The oil from the outside lanterns caught fire when the coach overturned, and they were both burned up. I'm devastated."

"Yes," Simon said blandly as Kate hid her smile behind her serviette. "Yes, I can see that. Allow me to offer my condolences, Mr. Collier."

"Well, it was nearly two months ago, and Gideon tells me I'm rich as Croesus now, save for the fact he's my guardian for another three years, and now that he's married my sister, I'm family, as well. I'd rather be in London, but it's as his lordship says, one can't always have everything one wants, at least not while he's in charge of me, and he lives only for the day I reach my majority. But he likes me. I'm certain of it. Everybody likes me."

This was all said with such artlessness, such nonchalance—and probably a dearth of brainpower backing his words—Simon felt himself unable to reply.

Kate, however, wasn't so reticent.

"That's because you're such a lovable looby," she said, nudging Adam with her elbow.

The boy carefully patted at his hair, dark and stiff with pomade, so that it probably wouldn't have moved by a single strand in a gale. "Thank you, Kate."

Lady Katherine rolled her eyes. "You're welcome—looby."

"Yes, well, Kate, shall we have our dessert in the main drawing room?" Valentine broke in. "We'll join you and Adam there in an hour."

Kate agreed, and the men all rose as she departed the room, smiling over her shoulder at Simon, who nodded his acknowledgment of her favor. He fought the urge to follow her.

"You're going to have brandy and cigars now, aren't you? I'd rather stay here with you and the marquis. My father and his friends used to step outside after dinner and piss off the balcony into the garden. I think they held contests. Do you do that, too?"

"We most assuredly do not," Valentine said coldly. "Or, as my grandmother the dowager countess would say, were you raised by wolves? Now go harass Kate while the grown-ups among us talk."

Simon watched the boy mince off in his red-heeled evening shoes and sat down once more. "That's Turner Collier's son? Was the man sure? I'd worry my wife had played me false if I ended up with a popinjay like Adam."

"Jessica says he's his mother's child, down to his ridiculous shoe tops. Jess, um, she left home when he was only twelve, leaving behind, she vows, a sweet, bashful child who sang songs with her. Gideon ended up with the guardianship of him a few months ago, thanks to Collier's ridiculous will that named the Earl of Saltwood, but didn't happen to mention which one. You know Collier was involved with the Society in my father's time, correct? From what we've been learning, he was also his closest friend and associate. Wait. Don't answer yet."

The baize door opened and Dearborn himself carried in a tray holding a crystal decanter and two snifters. He then employed the small key he'd carried with him to unlock a drawer in the immense sideboard. He extracted a rosewood humidor, smartly snapping back the lid and offering the selection inside first to his lordship's guest, and then to Valentine, who took two, pocketing one for later, probably.

The butler then deftly managed the ceremony of assisting in the tip-cutting and lighting of the cigars for each man by way of a short candle also on the tray, bowed and retired from the dining room.

"He loves doing that," Valentine commented as he puffed on the cigar and then smiled in satisfaction. "Ah, wonderful. Count on Gideon to have nothing but the best. I'm more of a cheroot man myself, but cigars take longer, leaving us more time to talk before we'll be expected to rejoin the children."

"Children? Your sister made her come-out last season. She's hardly a child."

"True," Valentine said, putting a finger to his lips before quietly pushing back his chair. "Follow me. Quietly."

Simon did as he was told, casting only one regretful look at the decanter of brandy as they headed for one of the many sets of French doors leading onto some sort of balcony. If the Earl of Saltwood's good taste in cigars was matched by his selection of spirits, he knew he was missing a treat.

"What's all this about?" he asked as Valentine gently closed the door behind him.

"Notice we're on a balcony, Simon. It runs the length of the dining hall, with the only entrances leading from that room. If Adam's right, I finally realize why the balcony may have been constructed this way, but I chose it because we're a good twenty-five feet above the gardens and Kate won't be able to hear us."

"She'd eavesdrop? Why would she do that?"

Valentine leaned against the stone balustrade. "Because I'm an idiot, but she's not. Within a minute of your going off with Dearborn, she asked me if you'd been a soldier. Because, if you can believe this, you eat quickly and efficiently, and walk with command in your step, or some such nonsense. It has been less than a full day and I already have the headache, watching her pretend—badly, I might add—watching you pretend. If I didn't know you're acting on orders, I'd actually believe you saw her and were instantly struck. But it isn't going to work. Sooner or later, Kate is going to see through the thing from both sides. Hang Gideon and Perceval for sorry plotters and me for thinking I could boost Kate through some hoops of my own as long as we were putting on this charade. We have to call it off."

"I thought I was doing fairly well," Simon said, damned if he'd call it off, not if Valentine was going to use the failure to send him on his way. He was here to find those journals and anything else he could find. Besides, pretending an interest in Lady Katherine wasn't the hardship he'd imagined. Not by a long chalk.

"Simon, if you did any better I'd have to pop you in *your* nose. But that's probably because you haven't met Kate yet. Not really."

Simon smiled. "She's a bit of her own person, isn't she? She's beautiful, entrancing, really, and quite unexpected."

Valentine looked at the glowing tip of his cigar. "Go easy, my friend."

"I'm doing my best, but even a brother should be able to recognize her unique beauty. That said, don't think I was unaware that she was—how should I say this? Putting me on? Yes, that's it. Crude, but correct. And all while somehow already knowing I was doing the same thing. Hell, Val, I'd compliment her, and her eyes would fill with laughter, all through dinner. So how do we fix this?"

"I'd say by you taking yourself back to London, but I doubt you'd go without a fight."

Simon's jaw tightened, and he wondered if the reaction was all because of his hunt for the journals, and had nothing to do with learning to know the intriguing Kate better. "And you'd be correct."

"Which leaves us with telling her the truth, although Gideon won't ever see it that way. Against all common sense, he still harbors the hope we can keep Kate away from the worst of this. Are we agreed?"

"Agreed," Simon said, reluctantly pitching the cigar over the balustrade.

"Oh, too bad. Dearborn doles out Gideon's prize cigars very carefully to younger sons," Valentine said, peering down into the gardens. "I was going to ask Kate to join us in the dining room. She quite likes the smell of a good cigar." Then he laughed and reached into his pocket. "Here—take this one, and I'll go find her, bring her back here."

"Don't you think you should first tell me what she knows. I don't want to say anything to shock her."

"Redgraves don't shock easily. Besides, what she hasn't yet been told she's probably conveniently overheard."

"And Adam? What does he know?"

"I'd have to say he doesn't even know how to find his own backside with both hands, but the truth is he was a font of information for us, even though he has no idea what his father was preparing him for, which was membership in that damned Society. That business about learning all the monarchs? Mostly, what his father was attempting to teach him was about assassinations, governments being overthrown, the *how* of the thing. What worked in the past, what failed. That, and giving him an education that went well beyond the usual visit to the local tavern on your sixteenth birthday and the trip upstairs with one of the barmaids as the entire taproom cheered you on your way. Can you imagine? Lessons in debauchery."

"I noticed him ogling your sister overtop his peas," Simon said, suddenly not finding the boy's antics so amusing.

"Yes, we'd thought about having all the younger housemaids fitted with chastity belts. Either that, or arming them with pikes, so they could fend him off. But we've found he's more boasting and wishful thinking than anything else. Collier had him keep a yearly journal of his conquests. Gideon said it read mostly as very bad fiction, which isn't to say he hasn't had his successes, willing ladies who like the feel of heavy coins in their palms."

Simon rubbed a hand across his mouth. "And that's how you—"

"Adam mentioned the lessons, the journal, to Jessica, and we quickly learned the boy also had a copy of his father's journal for last year, given to him to use as a reference or some such thing. Dates, the participants, the, um, the *actions taken*. As I said, Adam's entries were mostly that of an overactive imagination, but Collier's journal was something else entirely."

"So I've heard. The members' names all listed somewhere in it, although in some sort of code. It's how you discovered Sir Charles and the late Mr. Urban, correct? Again, I'd like to see one." *One in particular...*

"And again, no, you wouldn't," Valentine said, shaking his head. "We especially dread finding anything our father wrote. And our grandfather, as well. Believe me, Simon, this isn't easy for any of us. According to our grandmother, the Society members kept yearly journals from the beginning, during my grandfather's, shall we say, tenure as leader of the group. And then the Keeper, as that privileged member is called, the latest one being Adam's father, gathers the journals every year, compares them and dutifully records everything into their unholy bible. All the names, the secrets, the intrigues, the debaucheries, the supposed crimes, going back all those years. God knows who some of their *guests* were. Prime ministers, royal princes, men of letters, leaders of our military. Seduced, corrupted, blackmailed. Sometimes eliminated. Nobody knows the true extent of the Society's activities. But we're certain of one thing, none of that information can ever see the light of day."

"I begin to see your point." Simon had to tamp down his excitement at this revelation. The answers were in the bible. He had to find the bible. "I hadn't heard of any bible. Just the journals."

"Really? Gideon always did play his hands close to his chest. The journals will give us more clues, we hope, although we'll be dealing with those blasted codes. Only the supposed bible will give us everything, all neatly spelled out for us. My brother has hung his hopes on it, at least. But now that you're here, you might as well know the rest. We're looking for one other thing."

"And what would that be?" Simon spoke quietly, aware Valentine was speaking with some reluctance.

"Not what, who. The seventeenth earl," Valentine said, forcing a smile. "A tree fell against the mausoleum last winter and broke a lovely stained-glass window— not that you need know all of that. We don't visit inside the family's final resting place unless we're walling up a Redgrave, so nobody had noticed our father's crypt had been broken into, or knows when, but we've decided it had to be shortly after he was interred. In any event, the old lech's remains have been taken, providing we don't believe he somehow got up and toddled off on his own with a whacking great hole in his back."

The Redgraves had a lot to hide. Their sordid history going back two generations—and now a missing earl. "The Society took him? Why?"

Simon shrugged. "We don't know. Gideon believes they propped him up somewhere and held their own ritual. Remember, the rumors include that of devil worship, and Barry was their exalted leader or some such rot."

"Yes, I'd heard about that aspect of the Society. Rites, rituals, rumors of virgin sacrifices."

Valentine looked at him curiously, and Simon realized he just may have said too much. The man bantered so easily, it was easy to forget he was a Redgrave, and probably much more intelligent than he let on. Gideon Redgrave got what he wanted through sophisticated intimidation; Valentine Redgrave probably did just as well with his outward charm.

"Is that so. Well, that's discouraging, isn't it? How would you know about that?"

"I've been investigating the two men you found for more than a year before you Redgraves joined the party, we could say. That included familiarizing myself with hellfire clubs in general. Scratch most anyone in one of the London clubs and they'll soon come up with stories their grandfather told them about Sir Francis Dashwood, and others like your father," Simon answered carefully, because he hadn't heard any of that, not officially. But he'd made it his business to learn anything and everything he could about the Society. In the past six months, he'd made the Redgraves themselves targets of his investigation, half hoping they were behind it all and he could get back to his own life.

Then again, who could say whether or not the Redgraves were acting out of loyalty to the Crown, or in some convoluted, self-serving way meant to take suspicion away from them? Give the Crown one small success to prove their loyalty, and then be able to operate with Prime Minister Perceval's full assistance. Simon wished he wasn't so inclined to like this odd family. Especially when it came to the quixotic Lady Katherine.

"In any event, we hope he's here, somewhere on the estate. We already know there were tunnels, because one caved in last year, as well as caves, although I've never seen one, so if they exist they've been cleverly disguised. It's a large estate."

"I'll agree with that."

"Our grandmother doesn't know. We just want to find him and put him back. Barry was a rotter to his toes, from all accounts, but he was her son."

"And your sister knows this, as well? That the body has gone missing?"

"She does now."

Both men turned to see Kate standing at the other end of the balcony, more than half-hidden in the shadows. She stepped forward, her face pale in the moonlight, her arms wrapped about her as if she'd taken a chill. Simon felt an insane urge to go to her, hold her in his arms, comfort her.

"When were you going to tell me, Valentine? When I tripped over him?"

"Kate, I—"

"Never mind. I probably know the rest. The journals,

the bible and the rest of it—the reborn Society and its plans to open England's door and let Napoleon stroll in. I'm a woman, yes, but I'm a Redgrave first. I'm a part of this. God help us, it's our heritage. So now that the farce is over, and not a moment too soon, we'll meet tomorrow morning at seven to take that ride, and then resume the search. Oh, and one thing more. Simon, I don't know how you're involved, or why Gideon allowed you here, but know this. You stay the bloody hell out of my way or I'll have your liver on a stick."

With that, she pulled open one of the other French doors and was gone.

Valentine took a long pull on his cigar and then rather violently tossed it down into the garden. "My apologies, Simon," he said tightly. "I didn't have a chance to introduce you before she took her exit. *That* was my sister Kate."

Simon was still looking at the empty spot where Lady Katherine had stood. He felt incredible helplessness, not unmixed with guilt. "Shouldn't you go after her? Clearly she's upset."

Valentine looked at him in some surprise. "That's what you got from that? She's upset? She's homicidal, man, not that I blame her. Hell of a way to find out about old Barry."

"I wouldn't care for the method, no. Does she even remember him?"

Valentine shook his head. "No, she was only an infant. I don't even remember him, or my mother for that matter. You can look at Barry in the Long Hall, but Maribel's portrait is up in the attics if you want to see her—or you could just look at Kate."

Simon thought for a few moments. "Sometimes it's

more comfortable to build castles in your mind than to actually live in one."

"How marvelously obscure. But I understand what you're saying. Kate probably built our parents into perfect beings in her mind, victims of circumstance and a cruel fate. They were far from that. Our grandmother told her everything she felt she had to know before her first season, but these past weeks have been a painful revelation to all of us. Kate probably most of all. You're right, I have to go to her. If I don't appear by the time our mounts are brought round tomorrow morning, check to see if my body has been stuffed behind a rosebush. Here, take your cigar."

Simon nodded his thanks, but then slid the cigar into his pocket for later in the evening, as he doubted he'd find sleep easily tonight, so a head-clearing walk in the gardens might be in order. For the moment, he was going to find his way back to the long gallery and take another look at Barry Redgrave, and then hunt up the portrait of his father, the sixteenth earl, as well. He'd thought he'd seen something in the background of Barry's portrait earlier, but he'd dismissed it. Now he wanted a closer look without Dearborn standing behind him, because he'd imagined he'd seen the faint outline of a draped tartan painted in one dim corner inside the frame.

Not the Hunting Stuart tartan, which could be worn by anyone, but the distinctive red and green of the Royal Stuart, reserved for members of the Stuart line, and worn only with the permission of the king.

But that would be insane....

CHAPTER FOUR

KATE WATCHED AS Simon mounted his horse, a fine shiny brown stallion with a white blaze on its handsome face. The horse was ready for a run, but the marquis controlled it beautifully. Not that she'd compliment him on either his fine judge of horseflesh or his horsemanship. Not now, and not if he cleared two five-bar fences while sitting backward in the saddle, playing the flute.

She wasn't feeling in charity with Simon Ravenbill this morning. She wasn't very happy about the world in general.

At least Valentine had now answered all her questions, promising he was holding nothing back and there would be no more unpleasant surprises.

The marquis of Singleton wasn't Valentine's new friend, but working for the government, and here with Gideon's blessing. She was only the silly young female who should be hoodwinked, tricked, cajoled if necessary, even romanced, just to keep her from knowing what any fool could see was happening beneath her own roof.

Gideon would get a scathing letter from her in the next few days. Valentine had already received notice of her displeasure with him, and Simon Ravenbill could just go hang, for all she cared.

"Where are we off to?" Valentine asked from atop

his bay gelding. "Kate, which fields are lying fallow this year?"

"The entire West Run, but first I want to see the mausoleum."

"Kate," Valentine warned, but his tone was resigned. "All right, as I'd rather you didn't go on your own. Do you mind, Simon?"

Kate looked at him, her chin raised defiantly.

"Not a bit," he said affably, and then raised one eyebrow at her as if to say *happy now, brat?*

Clearly the gloves were off, for both of them. She didn't like him, and he— Well, she didn't know what he thought of her. Nothing good, surely, not after her explosion last night on the balcony.

She really should attempt to be a better hostess. If only any of her brothers ever brought home somebody *normal.*

Valentine dismounted, tossing the reins to one of the grooms. "You two go on ahead," he said as he walked toward the door. "I'll hunt up Dearborn and get the key."

Kate felt her stomach do a small flip. She did not want to be alone with the marquis. "No, we'll wait for—"

"Excellent idea," Simon interrupted. "Is it far? Hector here is on the frisk. I'd like to give him a short run rather than have to fight him."

"Kate, take the long way," Valentine called back over his shoulder. "I'll meet you there."

Kate was considering hot coals heaped on Val's head, and didn't immediately respond.

"You're thinking up a way to lose me in the woods?" Simon asked, drawing his mount up alongside her Daisy, who wasn't shy about indicating her interest in the stallion.

"No," she answered honestly. "I was mulling punishments for Val. But you were next on the list. What are your feelings as to thumbscrews?"

"I'm not particularly enamored, thank you, anyway. You know, I'd wondered if there might be a dungeon somewhere in this great pile of stones."

Kate acknowledged the jab with a small smile as she urged Daisy ahead at a walk. "I suppose I should apologize for my behavior last night."

Simon returned her smile, still easily controlling the eager stallion. He didn't pull at the horse's mouth by trying to rein it in, or dominate the animal. It was his calm manner that had Hector obeying him. She could admire that sort of talent and understanding. And he really was quite handsome. He couldn't help that his hair was blond.

"The eavesdropping, or the designs on my liver?"

"Excuse me?" She'd really have to begin concentrating on what he was saying rather than how he looked. After all, he was only a man. She refused to be impressed.

"I was inquiring as to the possible subjects covered in your apology."

Now who wasn't listening? "I didn't apologize. I said I supposed I should."

"Ah, yes, you're right. I see the distinction. Would you mind if I apologized?"

She shook her head. "No, that would take too long, as I consider the list to be quite lengthy. I'll just graciously accept." They were clear of the circle now, and about to pass through the gates held open by Dickie and Liam. "To the top of the hill, my lord, and then bear to your right and follow the trail. It eventually leads us back around to the other side of the stone fence. You'll be able to see the mausoleum tucked into the trees at the crest of the far hill. Show off if you feel the need, as I'm certain your mount can best mine, but please don't frighten the sheep."

And with that warning, she was off, urging Daisy into a full gallop.

She needed this. The morning sun on her face, the breeze blowing away the cobwebs in her head and easing the heaviness in her heart. Kate's life had been one long fairy tale here at Redgrave Manor, and even Trixie's explanation of her parents' tragic end had been something out of a storybook, made romantic in her mind. A misunderstanding, an impetuous challenge. A warning shot gone mortally astray. A devastated mother forced to leave her beloved children to escape arrest, but vowing to return for them, only to perish in the French Terror. Nearly a Shakespearian tragedy.

Kate could have been content with that fairy tale for all of her life, knowing she was deceiving herself, still embracing the deception. Now her world had turned upside down, and she'd been forced to grow up and face the truth. Oh, how that hurt. It hurt so much.

And it seemed every day brought a new revelation, a fresh ugliness to light. Kate couldn't go back to her carefully constructed cocoon of wishful dreams, but she couldn't look away from the nightmare. That the world could end up knowing every Redgrave secret was to be averted at all costs. That Simon Ravenbill already knew those secrets was humiliating past all bearing.

But there was no getting rid of him, not if Gideon approved of his presence. She'd have to face him every day until the journals were found. If she hadn't had good reason to search for them before, she certainly had one now. Every time she looked at the marquis she would know he knew. And probably judged. Who wouldn't be suspicious, at the least, and disdainful at the most, of any offspring of two such immoral, deadly monsters who were their parents?

She heard the sound of hoofbeats behind her and moved to the side of the riding trail.

"I'll be mindful of the sheep!" Simon called out cheerfully as he and his mount blew by her as if Daisy were moving at a sedate trot.

"Show-off, indeed," Kate muttered, watching him go, the stallion's hooves kicking up great clouds of brown dust from the dirt trail, the breeze blowing it all straight back at her. She now had two choices: ride the rest of the way eating dust in Simon's wake, or reining in the mare and only following once he was off the trail and onto the grass. She chose the latter alternative. "Daisy," she said, brushing dust off the shoulders of her dark blue riding habit, "I do believe this means war. And as he threw down the gauntlet, it's left to me to choose the weapons—or something like that."

Wasn't it strange? She felt much more in charity with Simon when he treated her as her brothers did… as his equal. But this was still war, and he had to be taught a lesson!

By the time she'd reached the mausoleum, Kate had made her choice. Valentine wanted her to practice? She'd practice. But she'd do it her way, as herself and not as some simpering debutante, and Simon would either tumble madly in love with her or go running back to London in fear for his sanity. After all, she was a Redgrave, so it could go either way. And, either way, she'd have his solemn vow to never speak a word of what he knew before she, at least figuratively, kicked him out the door.

Yes, it was the perfect plan. Hadn't Trixie told her women always win any battle between the sexes, because they are born with more interesting weapons. Kate at last believed she truly understood what her grandmother had meant.

Simon, who had already dismounted and had been sitting on an iron bench placed outside the mausoleum, quickly rose and went to assist Kate from the saddle. But she was far ahead of him, intent on being Kate: she merely tossed him the reins, then lifted her leg to disengage from the pommel, kicked her other leg free of the stirrup and lightly leaped to the ground.

"Very neatly done," Simon complimented her coolly. "And here I had been so hoping to help you dismount. A man lives for such opportunities, you know. My hands spanning that narrow waist, drawing you closer as I slowly lower you to the ground. A chance for an accidental brushing together of bodies…"

"And an even greater chance of suddenly finding yourself rump down in the dirt." Kate, far from missish or easily flustered, responded without heat, already looking past him to the large stone mausoleum. She ignored completely the small tingle just then running up her spine. What a maddening man—up close like this, he even smelled good!

"A risk I'd eagerly accept."

"Then more fool you." He wasn't going to stop, was he? This called for a change of subject. She kept her eyes on the mausoleum, certain if she looked at him his green eyes would be laughing. How dare he find her amusing! "But thank you for your attempt at distracting me, although it hasn't worked. Imposing up close like this, isn't it? And even larger than I remember from the one time I thought it might be interesting to peek inside, although the stained-glass windows prevented that."

"All right, I'll stop teasing you now. Yes, quite imposing, like everything else at Redgrave Manor. The pillars make for a nice touch. Do you come up here often?"

"Never." Kate shook her head. If she visited her father's grave, it would only remind her of her mother's probably unmarked grave in France. But she wouldn't tell him that. "Trixie always says the dead can keep each other company well enough. It's not as if they're really *here,* you know." She shook her head again. "Well, Barry isn't, that's for certain, not unless he's haunting the place, looking for his body. Do you believe in ghosts, and talking to the dead?"

Simon had tied Daisy's reins to a tree branch on the opposite side of the mausoleum from his stallion, and now stood beside Kate once more as they both stared at the family tomb. "I don't think I've given the subject much thought. I would like to speak to my brother, though. A lot of questions could be answered if we had the chance of hearing a voice from beyond one last time."

Once again Kate thought about her mother. Had Maribel lingered long enough to kiss her infant daughter goodbye, or had she just run off with her French lover? She sighed and turned away. "But we might not like the answers."

Simon put his hands on her shoulders and turned her toward him. "Look, Kate…every family has its share of scandal of one sort or another. I'm not judging, and I wish to God I didn't need to know what I need to know. But I am here to help. Not to be overly dramatic, but lives depend on us finding those journals, that supposed bible. So, can we forget yesterday ever happened, and begin again? With you being you and me being me, and all three of us dedicated to the search."

"I don't know," Kate answered, avoiding his mesmerizing green eyes, his open and honest green eyes. She felt so...*drawn* to him. The idea that had seemed brilliant not ten minutes earlier was now hastily discarded as she remembered swords cut both ways. Trapping him, she could end up trapping herself. Trixie had never mentioned that possibility. Her grandmother could snap her fingers and walk away from anyone except her adored grandchildren, whom she'd kill for if necessary, and without a blink. Love was a game she played well, but Kate was surprised and dismayed to realize perhaps she didn't share Trixie's prowess.

She took a deep breath and turned to look at him, determined to face him down. "In other words, no more outrageous comments such as the one you made about helping me dismount?" And felt her knees melt as he smiled at her, his eyes twinkling with mischief once more.

"Ask me not to breathe. It would be simpler."

Oh, enough of this! Kate willed her knees to stiffen and then rolled her eyes at such blatant nonsense. She didn't know if she was impressing him, but her defensive actions hadn't done much for her still slightly wobbly knees. Compliments, sweet words, made her nervous, that's all it was; she never knew how to respond. "So, you being you means you're prone to spouting ridiculousness like that at the drop of a handkerchief—not that I'm dropping mine, let's be clear about that. If so, you could stop now, because I know you don't mean it."

"I don't? Are you certain of that?"

"I'm certain you're nothing like anyone I met in London." She rocked on the heels of her riding boots, every nerve in her body tingling with an awareness the two of them were quite alone at the top of this dratted hill and out of sight of the house. Next thing she knew, Simon would start waxing poetic about her fetching smile, or some such rot—and how would she respond to that? When one was complimented, did that make one beholden to send a compliment winging back? And where would that lead? At the rate Simon was moving, she'd soon find out what step four is! Oh, where was Valentine? What was taking him so long? It was only a stupid key.

"That's probably because I was never meant to be the marquis."

"What?" Kate realized her mind was wandering, perhaps even running in panicked circles.

"You said I wasn't like any men you met in London, and I offered that this might be because I wasn't raised to be the marquis. I happily chose a more rough and tumble life, as suited my embarrassingly plebeian nature. Or so my late father said as he happily agreed to buy me a commission and pack me off to sea. London truly does bore me. In the Royal Navy, the chain of command has a reason. In society, it's all a bunch of self-important people deciding who should bow lower to whom because of who their father was."

Exactly as she felt about the patronesses of Almacks. How strange. "People bow to my brother Gideon because they'd be fools not to," Kate pointed out, not without pride. "It certainly can't be because of who our father was. Gideon is his own man."

"And you are very much your own woman, if you'd let yourself realize that, and not allow Val or Gideon or your grandmother or anyone else to tell you to change. The last thing you aren't, however, is either of your parents. Or am I wrong, and the fact I've learned certain things about your family isn't what's standing between the two of us getting to know each other better?"

Kate tilted her head to one side, rhythmically tapping her small riding crop against her thigh. Too close, he was getting too close. "You know, Simon, just when I think I can begin to like you, you go and say something like that. What makes you think you can presume to peek inside my head?"

"I'm not sure. Perhaps it's because we're more alike, you and I, than you know. We feel…responsible."

"And what is *that* supposed to mean?"

Simon looked past her, down the hill. "It means you're not the only one who would like all of this to disappear, have never happened. Can I trust you?"

Kate could feel her heart pounding against her ribs. For the first time, she knew he was being deadly serious. "I don't know. Should I trust you?"

"I won't presume to answer that for you, Kate. Make up your own mind. I'll be waiting with Henry and his hound at midnight. Some things are easier said in the dark."

"Henry? Who told you about Hen—?"

But Simon was walking away from her, his right hand already extended to grab the bridle of Valentine's horse. "Did you get lost along the way?"

Valentine dismounted, looking somewhat harassed. "Nothing that simple. It seems Adam got himself locked in a linen cupboard."

Kate looked at Simon, who was a distinct distraction and puzzle, and then to the doors of the mausoleum, which were both beckoning her and repelling her, and decided, for the moment at least, she'd much rather hear about Adam.

"How did he get locked in a cupboard?" she asked, joining the men. "More important, whatever possessed you to let him out again?"

"It wasn't an easy decision, believe me. Then again, listening to him bleat about there possibly being spiders sharing the dark with him was equally embarrassing as the reason he was in there. When nobody seemed able to locate the key, I suggested a hatchet, but Adam screamed I was trying to kill him, so we gave that up as a bad idea. As to the why of the thing, it would seem our new relative woke early today, feeling amorous, and spied out a maid bending over the fireplace grate. Needless to say, Adam needed no further invitation."

"Oh, the poor thing," Kate said in dismay. "Who is she?"

"I didn't ask, but I'm told by Mrs. Justis the girl is fine. I sent her my compliments and gave her the rest of the day off. Now, let me get on with the story, which I'll relate quickly. The nameless but brilliant maid suggested they postpone their liaison until she quickly did something Mrs. Justis asked her to do. Adam was to await her in the large linen cupboard on the third floor, as Adam's valet was just in the other room, because, and I quote, 'I gets noisy sometimes, you know?' All of which he agreed to, of course, because he's a bumble-brained idiot. She waited in the shadows until he was inside, then snuck up and locked the door before disposing of the key. She threw it from the nearest window. It took six of us to locate it."

By now Kate was nearly bent in half, suffering a case of the giggles. She'd have to find out which of the maids was involved, and then invite her to her bedchamber so she could hear the story again, with many more of the details.

"Excuse me, Kate, for this indelicate question, but I have to know," Simon said, "as I'm already building a picture of this in my head. Val, were his breeches on or off?"

"On," Valentine responded, his smile lopsided, at last losing the glowering expression he'd arrived wearing. "But buttoned incorrectly. Otherwise I might have been tempted to choke him with them. That boy needs some straightening out, with no thanks to the claptrap his father fed him. I ordered him to present himself to me—properly buttoned—in Gideon's study in one hour. If you knew what he said to me—" Again, he looked at his sister. "Never mind."

"Don't look at me like that, Val. I don't need to know *everything*. Besides, I'm busy building my own unlikely pictures, although I'm having some trouble painting one of you being the stern voice of reason and maturity."

Valentine looked relieved she hadn't pressed him for more. "Don't pin all your hopes on that eventuality, Kate. I may bring home my points by repeatedly dunking him head and shoulders into a horse trough until he either drowns or promises me he understands."

They all laughed, but then Kate remembered the last piece of Valentine's tale. "If you're busy schooling Adam, does that mean we can't continue the search until this afternoon?"

"No," Valentine said, extracting a large black key from a pocket in his hacking jacket, "you two can manage well enough on your own this morning without me, I'm sure. It may be time to broaden the search from the house to the grounds, anyway. Now let's get this over with, not that there can be much of anything to see."

Kate looked to the heavy iron doors, suddenly not so anxious to go inside the family tomb as she had been the moment she'd heard about the theft of her father's body. She'd never been inside the mausoleum, not in all of her life. No Redgraves had died in her lifetime except her parents, and Trixie was adamant about leaving the dead in peace, even going so far as to say she'd probably haunt anyone who dared disturb her rest with weeping or the cloying smell of too many flowers.

Now Kate found herself wondering if her grandmother feared death, and deliberately avoided any reminders Redgraves weren't immortal. It certainly couldn't be just any mausoleum that bothered her; she'd just tripped merrily off to a pair of funerals. Or was it that she couldn't face evidence of her only son's death in particular?

"Kate, are you coming?" Valentine called to her. "This was your idea, remember?"

"I remember," she said, allowing Simon to take her hand as he stood on the marble steps, to assist her. "You can let go now," she reluctantly whispered as they followed Valentine into the high-ceilinged, dome-top crypt. It was both cold and dim inside, the only light provided by the leaded glass panes in the ceiling and two small stained-glass windows, one definitely a recent replacement, as its many-colored panes were grime-free. Clearly even Mrs. Justis and her small army of maids considered the mausoleum out of bounds between interments.

That explained why it had taken nearly twenty years and a fallen tree branch for anyone to discover her father's body had gone missing. It didn't explain Trixie's avoidance of the final resting places of both her son and husband.

Or was Kate now looking at everything she believed with new eyes?

"You won't see much if you don't open your eyes," Simon told her softly, leaning in close to her as if he knew she was all but shaking in her boots. "Stacked to the dome on three sides. Extremely impressive. There must be more than a hundred tombs in here."

Kate kept her chin lowered and peered upward through her lashes, not really wanting to see. Simon was right. Everything was excruciatingly neat, almost mathematically so; row upon row of long cubicles, each fronted with marble and inscribed with a name and two dates. They'd started at the top, and descended from there, row by row, as if the tombs were a linear depiction of the Redgrave family tree.

The family must have dug up any ancestors who had been planted elsewhere and brought them here when this enormous mausoleum was built. And wasn't that… disturbing.

On the right wall there were still four rows of empty shelves. Twenty more bodies and the mausoleum would be filled. They looked like dark, empty maws, awaiting their prey.

Kate looked away, feeling ashamed. She'd never considered herself fanciful, but she could swear all these generations of Redgraves were calling to her; pleading *fix this, don't allow us all to be shamed by the actions of a few.*

"Here it is, Kate," Valentine said, directing her attention to the last opening on the fifth shelf. "Gideon thinks they chiseled out the stone and then carefully put it back, but with inferior mortar. That's what happens when supposed gentlemen are forced to put their hands to real work. The stone was found on the floor, cracked in two, and Barry's coffin gone. You can see bits of mortar sticking to the iron shelving and the stone, as well. Now can we get the hell out of here?"

"In a moment," Simon said, still holding Kate's hand as he approached the violated tomb, but then passed by it to the next one. "'Charles Barry Redgrave, Sixteenth Earl of Saltwood.'" He rubbed his hand across the stone. "It looks as if something was affixed here, just below the dates, and then removed. See the holes, and the damage to the stone? As if someone went at it with a chisel, and rather angrily at that." He leaned in closer. "A coat of arms, perhaps?"

Valentine repeated Simon's action, and then began examining other stones, walking around the room, stopping here and there. "Well spotted, Simon. It looks as if each earl sports a replica of the Redgrave coat of arms, all done up out of silver and colored enamels. I suppose we need to replace my grandfather's, and Barry's, as well, if we can find it. You're certain it didn't just loosen and fall out?"

Now Kate took her turn in front of the stone, running her gloved fingers over it, still able to feel the small chinks in the otherwise flat surface. "But wouldn't both have been found on the floor when Gideon came to inspect it after the servants' report about the crypt being empty? Do you think they were stolen?"

"They're silver, Kate, so it's possible. But why steal only two when you can take them all? Besides, Dearborn actually keeps the only key inside a locked box, and that key with his ring of butler keys that never leaves him. Nobody comes in here unless they've got his permission. Any other suggestions? A ghostie wielding a hammer and chisel, perhaps?"

Kate pulled a face at her brother and turned to leave

the mausoleum. She didn't know what she'd hoped to
find, or feel, or learn here. She'd just known she'd had
to come. Now all she wanted was to be gone, flying
across the fields of the West Run with Daisy, the chill
of the stone tomb and the stench of stale air replaced
by the warmth of sunlight and a clean, fresh breeze.
She needed to take herself as far from death as she
could get.

"Here, I'll boost you up," Simon said from behind
her, even as his hands clamped about her waist and she
was lifted high, then settled into the sidesaddle with
such ease it was embarrassing.

"You didn't have to do that," she told him, adjusting the military shako hat that had slipped down over
her eyes. "I could have managed. My brothers never
believed in coddling me, and I actually much prefer it
that way. I often ride alone on the estate, and they felt
I should know how to remount if I fell off—which I
never have."

"That very nearly makes sense, except for the part
about you riding out without a groom in tow, which is
bloody stupid." He handed her the reins. "Very well,
remind me to do you no more favors."

Rough and tumble. That's what he'd said was how
his father had described his younger son. And for all
Simon's outward polish, clearly something about her
allowed him to speak and act as his real self. She believed she could be either flattered or insulted, and
immediately decided on flattered. Especially since it
allowed her to be herself.

"I have reminded you, repeatedly. I'm not helpless,
and don't care to be made to feel that way." She raised
her voice so Valentine, who was still locking the doors,

could hear her. "I'm heading for the West Run. You can follow or not."

"And the breeze will dry those tears you don't want anyone to see," Simon said quietly, shaking his head. "You're the prickliest woman I've ever met. Have you ever wondered what you're trying to prove?"

Kate opened her mouth to say something scathing, but then realized she had no answer for the man. He'd bested her. She tugged on the reins with more force than care, so that a confused Daisy actually turned her head as if to be sure who was atop her before setting off toward the fields of the West Run.

Maybe somewhere along the way, Kate thought, she might discover why she felt it so important to keep Simon Ravenbill at arm's length. She'd already thought up and discarded several reasons, from his hair color, to his and Valentine's attempted deception, to her family pride. But did she really want him gone? Even her foolish plan to keep him away had hinged on deliberately drawing him closer.

Was she afraid of Simon Ravenbill? Or was she afraid of how Simon Ravenbill made her feel? He made her feel like a woman, and she wasn't certain she was comfortable with that.

CHAPTER FIVE

Simon watched as Kate rode off, her spine ramrod straight, wondering if he looked long enough whether he'd see smoke emanating from her ears. She was the most interesting, maddening, not romantically inclined, exotically beautiful woman he'd ever encountered, and the more she pushed him away the more he longed to know her better.

He might consider her actions to be a ploy meant to draw him closer. But, no, not Kate. He was more than certain she said what she meant. Or what she thought she meant...

So. Did he now tag along after her like some love-sick swain hoping for crumbs—or possibly a rousing argument—or did he ride back to the Manor with Valentine to tell him what he was beginning to suspect?

If he told Valentine without including Kate in the telling, he would be at least figuratively putting his life in her hands.

Then again, chasing after her could pretty much guarantee the same result.

Simon laughed softly as he considered his dilemma.

But, if he was going to be hanged, it might as well be for a sheep rather than a lamb.

"She says you allow her to ride unaccompanied," he said, watching Valentine mount.

Valentine settled into the saddle. "Oh, she did, did

she? At least she almost got it right. It's more that we'd rather she do it openly than sneak behind our backs. Either way, she rides when she wants to ride. Did you see the bell nailed to the stable wall?"

"No, I haven't yet visited the stables. But doesn't the bell go on the cat?"

Valentine laughed, acknowledging the joke. "Whenever Kate rides out alone one of the grooms rings the bell, an action repeated across the estate by those who hear it. Rather a heads-up to be on the lookout for her, you understand. If she's off to the West Run, we know it by the bells. Toward the village, we know that, as well. Et cetera. She's not as alone as she thinks, everyone watches for her. When she returns, the groom rings the all-clear. It sounds convoluted, I know, but believe me, it's much simpler than trying to keep Kate to the rules."

"And she doesn't realize this?"

"Of course she does, unless she thinks some bloody angels are ringing mystical cowbells as they greet her along the way. She doesn't acknowledge it, which to my sister's mind is rather as if it isn't happening. I suppose you could say she's being accommodating. She may even think she's won. You never know with Kate."

"Yes, I'm beginning to see that. No cowbells needed today, I'll go after her. In a moment. What did that henwitted twit say to you?"

Valentine brushed at the sleeve of his riding jacket, as if attempting to remove a smut of something unpleasant that had got stuck there. "Nothing worth committing to memory, I assure you. He's as ready to go as any young lad of his age, but with twice the brass because he's been convinced he's *entitled*. He's a parrot for his father's teachings, you understand. What randy young pup doesn't want to hear women have been placed on this earth to please him? Men rule the world and are, again, *entitled* to anything they want. Oh, although we can thank our lucky stars Turner Collier hadn't gotten so far in Adam's lessons to actually *show* him how men gain strength and power by bedding as many women as possible, most notably during their supposed ceremonies. So everyone can observe and join in, perhaps applaud, you understand. The mind fairly boggles, doesn't it?"

"It's disgusting," Simon said, fighting back a mental image he could feel forming in the back of his brain.

"Despicable, I agree. But useful for keeping members in line and blackmailing their carefully selected guests—the journals, remember? Gideon remarked that it comes down to a simple strategy of play tonight my good fellow, to the top of your bent, unaware you'll pay tomorrow. You've had your every sexual whim provided for, and will so again—we just ask you to first do us this one small *favor*."

Simon nodded. "Such as the recent attempt to divert supplies meant for the troops massing on the Peninsula. Not traitors, not primarily, but weak-minded men who don't want their pleasures taken away."

"As far as it goes, yes. You're forgetting the implied or *else*. Lord only knows the forms the threats might take. We think the first *favor* is fairly innocuous, but then they've really got the man on their hook. After that, they own him pretty much body and soul, and the favors turn to outright crime, even treason, poor bastards. Didn't Gideon share all of this with you in Perceval's office?"

"He skirted the issue quite neatly, but I suspected as much." *I know as much. Your brother isn't the only one who says only what must be said.*

"My apologies. Since the strategy began with our father, perhaps even our grandfather, I doubt Gideon wished to elaborate more than he thought necessary. In any event, we believe that same system of control remains the current Society's reasoning behind whatever the hell they're plotting now as concerns our government, as the current Society seems to have ambitions that far outstrip those of my father."

Simon bit his tongue, not about to say: *If what I suspect now is true, I think these current traitors are aiming far low of your family's ambitions.*

Valentine seemed to wave away any further discussion of the Society. "Enough of that. Getting back to our resident randy young goat, what stuck deepest in Adam's mind and holds there is his enthusiastic belief a woman's place is on her knees. Literally. So to answer your earlier question truthfully, yes, the idiot's trousers were hopelessly tangled around his ankles while he crouched in the cabinet, the most visible sight when I opened the door his pasty white rump."

Simon knew he shouldn't laugh; this was a serious problem in desperate need of solving. But surely he could be allowed a small smile? "Tangled. Or you would have strangled him with them, you said?"

"Not really. My brother Gideon quoted something Robert Burton supposedly wrote a long time ago and said I was to repeat to myself whenever I was tempted to throttle the twit. 'Diogenes struck the father when the son swore.'"

"The blame goes to the father. Yes, I can see that. But the father's dead. I don't quite picture you in the role of the boy's new, much more stern father, though, Val."

"Neither will Adam," Valentine muttered, shaking his head.

Simon allowed the anxious Hector to dance in a small circle for a moment, eager to be off. "I know *how* you'd like to point that out to him, but it isn't true. You can't literally beat sense into a person's skull."

"No, but I can tell him some home truths about his father, about the Society. Jessica wanted to keep it from him as long as possible, but the only alternative I can see is to geld him, and Jessica might not approve. He's still young enough to save."

"I sincerely hope you're right. I wish you luck, then, and would appreciate a recounting of his reaction later, perhaps over brandy and cigars. As for me, I'm off now to bell the cat." Simon turned Hector toward the West Run even as Valentine shouted a laughing warning after him having to do with exactly who could end up gelded.

He'd soon catch up with Kate, who was doubtless holding back her mare, saving her for a good gallop, and did the same with his mount. He believed she needed some time to settle herself after the visit to the mausoleum. His family had actually enjoyed picnics on the grass just outside the Ravenbill mausoleum while their parents told their sons stories about their ancestors. The Redgrave family avoided their dead like the plague, mostly, it would seem, on Trixie's orders.

He'd have to find a way to speak with the Dowager Countess of Saltwood at some point, even if he doubted she'd be more than marginally cooperative.

As he rode, he thought about Holbrook, the *if onlys* ringing in his head, keeping pace with Hector's hooves. If only he'd been the older son, able to ride herd on Holbrook and his mad starts. If only his brother had confided in him. If only Holbrook hadn't so much money, so few restraints put on him, such a burning need to be accepted by those he wished to impress. If only he hadn't been such an easy sheep to lead, never realizing the promised pleasurable path could lead to the slaughter. If only, if only...

Simon caught sight of his quarry and her mount at the end of a tree-lined path looking out over fallow fields that seemed to stretch to the horizon. Redgrave Manor wasn't an estate, it was a damn kingdom.

He pulled up beside her, Hector still unhappy and not reluctant to show it. Simon's quick glance told him Kate was composed once more, and faintly belligerent, probably because he'd been stupid enough to comment on her tears. It couldn't be easy, being a woman. Not when no matter how resolute the resolve to have her sex be a secondary consideration, no matter her wish to be treated as well as to behave like her brothers, as every man's equal, she was still undeniably female.

Didn't she realize it was only womankind's softer hearts that kept men from total ruin?

Still, to politely inquire about how she was feeling now would be courting disaster, Simon was certain of that much. So he chose to talk about Redgrave Manor, which clearly held a good portion of her heart. At least then he could reassure himself he was working on his assignment, not selfishly pursuing the prickly young woman who had invaded his dreams last night.

"I didn't realize your family's holdings are so vast," he said, casually lifting his right leg and hooking it in front of him on the saddle, as if willing to settle in for a comfortable chat. He deliberately waved one hand across the view to include the entire estate in his next words. "Your ancestors must have pleased somebody very much, to be given all this."

Kate chuckled. "The trick, Trixie told me, lay in not *displeasing* anyone overmuch, and holding firmly to the policy of prudently shifting loyalties as required. They were a crafty, slippery bunch, my ancestors. What they couldn't manage to wrangle as gifts from the Crown, they bought out of hand, sometimes paying twice the land's worth, just to have it. An earldom isn't that high to reach for a man of ambition, but it was as far as they wished to rise. Earls are more easily overlooked than dukes, you understand, when someone is hunting up a titled neck to put on the block."

Simon looked at her profile. "You sound proud of them."

"I'm not ashamed of them, no. Our father and grandfather, between them, nearly doubled our already vast lands, and I don't doubt they would have been happy to double them again if they both hadn't died at relatively young ages. Gideon is a magnificent steward of the proud Saltwood legacy." She lowered her chin slightly as she turned to face him. "With a few notable recent exceptions, not quite so laudable."

"Yes, but let's not talk about them now. Hector here is still looking for a good long run. Possibly from here to that circle of trees and boulders off in the distance?" he suggested, pointing to an area in the midst of the vast, low hedgerow-lined fields someone must have decided not worth the effort needed to clear it.

"From one graveyard to another?" Kate asked, wrinkling her delicious nose. "Very well."

"The hedgerows barely present a barrier to either of us, I'm sure. Wait. One graveyard to another?"

"I'll tell you about it when we get there, if you'll first tell me why you named that magnificent stallion Hector. I named Daisy when she was a foal and I was much younger, but I can't see the same excuse for you. Did you name him for some Greek god?"

"Nothing so dramatic, no. My Scottish groom called him *Eachdonn,* which I could barely pronounce, as I'm sure you've already noticed. So he suggested the English form of the word, Hector. Put simply, in either language, it means brown horse."

"That's it? Brown horse? That's a description, Simon, not a name. And not a very good one. Clearly you have no imagination."

Simon smiled, possibly grinned, as he cocked one eyebrow. "Are you quite certain of that? I'd be willing to offer to change your mind, by way of a brief demonstration I believe would convince you otherwise."

Kate let out her breath in an exasperated huff. "You're the most *maddening* person I've ever met. And certainly not a gentleman."

"Then we're doubly well suited!" he called after her as she put Daisy to an immediate gallop, leaving Simon to hastily shove his right foot back into the stirrup as the impatient Hector took off after the mare, clearly a horse on a mission.

"Men," Simon grumbled, tamping down his curly-brimmed beaver that was in danger of blowing off his head. "We're all of us pitiful specimens, Hector, led about by the ladies."

Kate cleared the first hedgerow ahead of him with no difficulty, and Simon relaxed, belatedly realizing she would have taken his words as a challenge, even if she'd never jumped a hedgerow in her life.

From then on, it was every rider, and horse, for itself. Their finish line was farther away than he had first imagined, thanks to the rolling nature of the ground that had shortened his assessment. Kate knew the fields, and he didn't. She sat her horse as well as he did, and was clearly fearless, a neck-or-nothing rider. All of which didn't mean he held back to let her win, knowing she'd blister his ears if he did. She'd already admitted Hector was the faster mount.

Simon had dismounted and looped the stallion's reins around a low-hanging branch when Daisy plunged to a pouting halt, neighing at Hector who, being male, and stupidly proud, returned what many would construe a horsy laugh.

"Well run," Kate congratulated him, and then smiled as she added, "and you did tolerably well, too, Simon."

"Rather cheeky for the one bringing up the rear, aren't you?"

"Never mind that. Aren't you going to help me dismount?"

Something went sort of *ping* in Simon's chest. Progress. They were making progress. "I wouldn't so insult you."

"I wouldn't be insulted, since I asked. Don't be thick, Simon. That wasn't easy to say in the first place. Besides, you said a man lives for such opportunities, remember?"

"I was being facetious?" he suggested, tongue-in-cheek.

"You are now. Very well, pretend I didn't mention it."

She hadn't made a single move to dismount in the short (very short) second Simon took to realize only an idiot would not hold out his hand for a ripe plum poised to fall into it.

He put up his arms as she disengaged her leg from the pommel, and she allowed him to touch her. "My hands spanning that narrow waist," he said, from memory, even as he marveled at the smallness of that waist above wonderfully flaring hips. "Drawing you closer as I slowly lower you to the ground," he continued, and then following his words with action.

She had her hands on his shoulders now, presumably for balance. Her eyes shone with mischief even as her breasts rose and fell with each quick, shallow breath. "What was next? Oh, yes. A chance for an accidental brushing together of bodies. You mean like this?"

Their bodies were touching now, as he eased her feet toward the grass. She was looking up at him, her full wide mouth a whisper away.

She had no idea what she was doing to him. Or perhaps she did.

"Yes, precisely like this. And then, as naturally follows, I steal a kiss."

She was gone so quickly he barely had time to realize the way she bent her knees, pulling down and out of his light grasp on her waist. In a heartbeat, she was standing a good five feet away from him. She had her arms crossed tightly beneath her breasts, and she was still breathing rather hard.

"Very neatly done, Kate. You do this often?"

Her cheeks had gone faintly pink, but Simon didn't believe the flush was in anger. "No, I most certainly do not. You shouldn't ask questions like that."

"No? Well, then, how about this one? How many men have kissed you, Lady Katherine?"

There went the chin again, aiming for the sky. "That's absolutely none of your concern. But if you must know, several. A lot. *Dozens*."

He began advancing on her, slowly. "Then one more certainly shouldn't matter, should it?"

She was backing up now, still with her arms hugged tight round her body, as if she might fly apart if she let go. "Perhaps not dozens."

He took another step forward. She was backing straight toward a wide tree trunk that would halt her retreat, not that he was about to point that out to her. "Perhaps not even a lot? Shall we agree to settle on a *few?*"

Kate's mouth must have gone dry, because she was clearly working her tongue around the inside of her mouth, even employing the tip to moisten her lips. "Maybe…maybe not anyone."

All right, now she'd shocked him.

"And you're how old?"

Finally she dropped her arms to her sides. "What does my age have to do with anything?"

"I'm not sure, but it seems at least minimally important. No one? Ever?"

Kate rolled her eyes as if weary of discussing the subject with someone so incredibly *thick.* "I've never seen the need, is that so difficult to understand? My brothers bring home stultifyingly boring men, most of them married and the rest of them silly—those last would be Val's friends. There's no one within miles of Redgrave Manor who would dare, again, thanks to my brothers. And I wasn't in London last year long enough to meet anyone who possessed a brain larger than any of the peas Adam insists on playing with at the table. There, are you happy now?"

"I'm not certain. Never seen the need? Really?"

"Really." But as soon as she said the word she turned her head away from him, as if not willing to maintain eye contact.

And hope springs eternal in my shameful breast, Simon told himself as he followed her into the trees, the boulder-strewn ground also dappled with shafts of sunlight filtering through the leafy branches. He imagined the boulders had been those dug up when the land was first plowed, and had been dragged here, out of the way. But why was "here" created? The rocks could just as easily have been lined up along one of the hedgerows. Why was this area left intact?

"Very pretty spot," he commented, looking up at the dusty rays of sunlight as he walked, and then tripped over something solid and found himself sprawled on a thick carpet of damp, moldy leaves. He quickly turned himself about so that he was in a sitting position, hoping that looked better than shamefully leaping to his feet. "Well, wasn't that graceful of me? Care to join me?"

"I think not," Kate said dryly. "But, while you're down there, say hello to Torr Gribbon."

Simon had belatedly taken out his handkerchief, and was wiping at his palms. "I beg your pardon?"

"You should probably ask that of Mr. Gribbon. Considering you're sitting on the man."

All right, so she'd managed to get him leaping to his feet, popping up like some inane jack-in-the-box. He looked down at the ground and saw the small tombstone he'd stubbed with the toe of his boot. Sure enough, the name Torr Gribbon was chiseled into it, along with two dates he couldn't quite make out thanks to the long grass.

Then he noticed the other graves. Six of them.

"You did say we were going from one graveyard to another, didn't you?"

"Mr. Gribbon owned what we now call the West Run," she explained as she walked over to a nearby boulder and boosted herself up onto it. She pointed to her left. "His house and stables supposedly were somewhere close to this spot, but the house burned one night, and the family all perished. My grandfather bought up the land immediately from some distant cousin who didn't want it. Grandfather termed it a present to his wife for having presented him with a healthy son only a few days prior to the tragedy."

"He deeded it to her?"

"Hardly. There's nothing that isn't entailed with the estate. It was a symbolic gesture only. But as the destroyed buildings were being razed, Trixie begged my grandfather not to disturb the graves. She'd been bosom chums with Alice Gribbon. In fact, it was Mrs. Gribbon who delivered Trixie of my father when the local doctor didn't arrive in time. Those few days later, the woman was dead, and my grandmother couldn't even attend the burial because she was very ill. In fact, she would never bear another child, the doctor warned her, and if she did conceive she'd never survive another childbed. Just a terribly sad story, all the way around."

"Indeed. A compounded tragedy." *Especially for an ambitious man who undoubtedly felt the need for more than one son.* Simon was beginning to form another theory.

Kate nodded her agreement to his agreement. "Trixie told me all about what happened one day when I announced I was going to ride in the West Run. She asked me to check on the stones to make certain they were still in good repair, as she no longer rode herself. I need to send Liam out here with the scythe again, don't I? There are other, older graves, as well, hidden in the grass and leaves."

"The dowager countess concerns herself about the state of these graves, yet never visits the family mausoleum? Does that seem in the least strange to you, Kate?"

"No. Why should it?" But yet again she averted her eyes. "I'd like to go back now. Dearborn will be fretting over the platters, worrying about the food all growing cold on the sideboard. He always expects me back by nine when I take an early ride. Not that he'll say anything, but he does have this way of speaking with his eyes." She hopped down from the boulder. "Shall we? I mean, unless you want to continue your ride. It's not as if it's a rule even guests be in the morning room by ten."

She rolled her eyes and rather huffed out an exasperated sigh. "I'm babbling, aren't I? I didn't think I was the sort who babbled."

Simon approached her, taking her hands in his before she could turn away. She was too intelligent not to wonder, not to see the facts as they may have been. She was also vulnerable at the moment, and might not be again. He had to say what he was thinking. "The doctor, Kate. Did he suffer a fatal tragedy soon after, as well?"

"I—I never inquired." She attempted to pull her hands free of his. "I never should have told you anything."

"Yet you've thought about it, haven't you? Thought about it, supposed about it. Your grandfather must have been incredibly angry at the unexpected turn of events, don't you think? But you didn't want to upset your brothers with what you now suspect, so they don't know what Trixie told you that day. I'm a stranger, easier to confide in, aren't I? How long have you been worrying about this? Ever since your grandmother told you about these people, or did it all only begin to make some macabre sense in these past weeks, when everything changed, when your sainted grandfather and murdered father were exposed as past leaders of the Society?"

Her eyes went wide. "You're wrong. I've never sus— I don't know what you're talking about."

"And if I suggested we share your thoughts with Valentine?"

"Why? You're the one saying these horrible things, not me." Again she tugged at his hands, but Simon held fast. "Let me go."

"Horrible, yes, but logical, once we understand the man. They'd have to be punished, wouldn't they? For nearly losing his wife and son, for robbing him of the chance for more sons. And then there was the happy coincidence of being able to step in and purchase this lovely land we're standing on."

"You're a hateful person with an evil mind!"

Was he? Was he seeing conspiracies everywhere now? "I don't know, Kate. I don't think so. But I do wonder how long your very young and suddenly barren grandmother would have lived had it not been for your grandfather's death within a year of Barry's birth. How did he die, do you know?"

"Stop it, Simon. Just stop it!"

"You understand now, don't you? You've walked the long gallery. You've begun to see what everyone else has so far missed. Your grandfather was building himself a small kingdom, wasn't he? And your father, as well. No matter the cost."

"I said, *let me go.* You're here to help find the journals, even if Gideon doesn't want you here. You've no right to say anything about my family."

Simon held tight. "Then why tell me about Alice Gribbon and this land? Why not tell them? I think I know. You're afraid to ask your brothers, your grandmother, what you now suspect. Was it easier to say it to me, test my reaction?"

"I love my grandmother," she said quietly. "I love my brothers. Everything else is yesterday. It has to be."

"And we're all going to try our best to keep it that way, including me. But more and more I'm realizing that to understand today, we have to know about yesterday."

She shook her head. "No. Whoever is using the Society now is doing it for his own reasons. None of us is involved. It's only the journals they want, those and the supposed bible."

"In case their names were mentioned, at least those who were members before the new leader arrived to take over and called a halt to the journal keeping. More important, we're all fairly certain Turner Collier disobeyed the order to cease and desist in his position of the Keeper, and continued to update the bible every year. Perhaps he thought he could hold the information over everyone's heads, that it would keep him safe, instead of being the same as signing his own warrant of execution. Men have done stupider things. Locate the bible, and we could know all the names."

She stopped tugging against his grip. "Do you want to know what I think, Simon? Before they killed him, Adam's father told the Society that everything is here, at the Manor, but didn't divulge the correct location. I know if I had no chance of saving my life I certainly wouldn't tell such monsters the truth with my last breath, but just enough to be sure they believed me."

Simon cocked his head to one side, surprised by this statement. "You have put a lot of thought into this, haven't you?"

"I do realize how important the journals and bible are. They're also probably hot to find Barry's so-called plans, hoping to use them, to use some damning information about the members and their invited guests from his time, or their heirs if the members are dead, to use for leverage now, planning to make them dance to the new leader's tune."

"Really? All of that?"

And there went the chin, raised in defiance. "Am I right?"

"Anything's possible. I won't say you're wrong."

"Thank you. And we'll not mention the Gribbons again, because that was long, long ago, a half century ago. A whole different time, Simon. It has nothing to do with anything. Not anymore."

He said nothing.

"Simon?"

"Agreed. For the moment. But if I decide what happened is important, I *will* bring the earl and your brothers into it. And the dowager countess."

"And me?"

"You tell me, Kate. For someone as intelligent as you, as perceptive as you, you also seem to want to cling to the fairy tale. There's no fairy tale here."

"No. But there is an ogre," she declared as he let go of her hands. "At least you don't lie to me. I thank you for that."

She really was quite adept at mounting the sidesaddle on her own. What he hadn't expected was how swiftly she then bent and snatched up Hector's reins before turning both the horses, the stallion making no protest as he happily followed behind the mare.

It was going to be a long walk back to Redgrave Manor.

Or should he think of it as the *castle?* After all, there was almost a moat....

CHAPTER SIX

KATE PUT DOWN her fork. "Stop looking at me that way, Val. He won't perish from exhaustion or some such thing. I sent Dickie out with the pony cart as soon as I got back."

"The pony cart. Marvelous." Val sat in his tipped-back chair, dusting toast crumbs from his neck cloth. "So he'll only perish of embarrassment. Riding backward on the cart, his boots near to dragging on the ground. Really, Kate, you're too kind."

"I know," she said brightly, digging into her coddled egg yet again. "At times I amaze even myself. But I could hear him laughing as I rode off with Hector. Unless that's because he was already planning his revenge," she ended, smiling.

"I don't care for that smile. So you're definitely attracted to the man?"

Kate shifted the fork in her hand, so it suddenly more resembled a weapon than a simple silver utensil. Pointing it across the wide table at Valentine (unfortunately still with a bit of egg hanging from it), she said, as if they were still in the nursery, "Take that back this instant, Valentine."

"Take back what, Kate? I was merely putting forth a supposition. No, only a question. Perhaps with an idle jest tossed in there somewhere. Gauging by your reaction, however, I'd say there's no longer any question.

What first drew you to him? We men are usually at a loss to understand women and how they know they're attracted, indifferent, or instantly take a man in dislike in the blink of an eye. We poor gentlemen often don't know our own hearts until we're figuratively banged over the head with Cupid's shovel, so anything you could offer would be much appreciated."

"Sorry, Dearborn," Kate mumbled as she withdrew the fork so that the butler could make quick work of sliding a knife beneath the fallen bit of egg and neatly lifting it clear of the tablecloth. She often wondered what he thought of Redgrave family conversation, but as always, his expression did not change. Then again, he never absented himself from the dining table, even when the footmen handled the serving, so he couldn't be bored. *She* was never bored. She leaned forward once more. "Cupid's *shovel?*"

"When the arrows fail, yes. Desperate times call for desperate measures. Now answer my question, if you please."

"And how shall I answer it?" Kate propped her elbow on the table and cupped her chin in her palm. "Perhaps he reminds me of my dear brother Valentine? I have always so admired you. Your quick intelligence, your generous nature, your delicious way with witty repartee…your incredible gullibility."

"You forgot to mention easily amused," Val said, tossing down his serviette as he stood up. "I really should warn the man."

Dearborn helped her move back the heavy chair. Before she could follow Valentine the butler handed her a perfect apple he'd shined on his black coat sleeve, just as he'd done every morning since she'd first been allowed at the table. Some other young woman would think she was being needlessly coddled, or she simply deserved such personal treatment, but Kate never forgot the affection demonstrated by Dearborn's gesture. It humbled her, when little else did.

"Thank you, Dearborn," she said quickly before catching up to her brother in the hallway, matching him stride for long stride. "You mean you haven't already warned him about my unladylike behavior?"

"Numerous times, although you've already proved that on your own, haven't you? Any man of sense would be running the other way by now, which clearly he isn't, and you're being of absolutely no help if you're encouraging him, which is the last bloody damn thing I ever suspected you'd do. He touches you, Kate, and it won't be you having his liver on a stick, and perhaps mine, as well, all with Gideon's compliments. Now excuse me. As our brother and your guardian isn't here, I'm off to the stables to greet Simon, and ask his intentions."

The apple halfway to her mouth, Kate blurted, "His— Oh, my God!" She tossed the apple back over her shoulder (to be deftly caught by one of the under-footmen), as she raced forward to stand in front of Valentine, to block his way. "Don't you even *think* to do anything so silly."

"Silly, is it? Why is it silly, Kate? Because you've absolutely no interest in the man? Or are you worried he might have no interest in you?"

"*You're* the village idiot who told him to pretend to flirt with me, and for me to *practice* on him."

"I'll grant you half of that. I did suggest you might attempt to hone your very meager ladylike skills on the fellow, yes, and I apologize, although you haven't as yet whacked him in the nose, so perhaps the idea had some little merit."

Kate pulled a comical face. "One small punch in the middle of Almacks, and I'll never hear the end of it."

Valentine grinned at her. "Not while I still draw breath, no. I'm going to tell your children and grandchildren, so they'll have it to hang over your head when you admonish them to behave like ladies and gentlemen. Mostly, however, the plan was truly a ridiculous idea, meant to divert you from the real reason Simon's here. *Mea culpa* for that, et cetera. But the rest of it was Gideon's idea, and Perceval's, not mine, or even Simon's for that matter. Besides, I thought we were starting over."

"There are some things you can't start over, Val. Like…like peeling an apple. Once begun, you may as well continue, for there's no putting it back the way it was."

"Wonderful. Now my sister is a philosopher. A rather poor one, but I understand your point. The two of you are enjoying a flirt. Good for you. Now you understand my point."

"You don't want Gideon to murder you," Kate said, nodding. "I understand that, as well. But for the love of heaven, Val, asking the man his *intentions?* In these few short days? As if Simon would take you seriously in the first place, and if you're fearful of Gideon's wrath, perhaps you might stop to consider mine. I'm a lot closer than Gideon."

"I can always send you to him, trussed up and tossed in the coach if I have to. Because you're right about that apple. Or at least the point of the thing about it not being possible to put some things back the way they once were."

Kate tipped her head to peer up at her brother through

her lashes. "My goodness, Valentine, I do believe you're blushing."

"And I do believe Gideon should have married you off at eighteen, so you'd be too busy now with your own brat to make my life a living misery."

"Married me off to whom, Val? You all scowl down any man who comes near me."

Val grinned at her. "That's because we like most of them and didn't wish to lose them as friends once the fog of infatuation cleared and they realized they'd been bracketed to a whirlwind."

"Ha-ha," Kate grumbled. "But it's fine with you if I'm bracketed to a near stranger intent on poking his inquisitive nose into every area of our family history, on the lookout for scandal?"

Val stopped just as they'd reached the drive. "And precisely what do you mean by that, Katherine?"

Oh, now she'd put her boot in the muck! This was what happened when a person let a man into her mind. Disaster in the form of a weakened brain connected to a loose tongue. Which, of course, conveniently made her verbal slip all Simon's fault. She supposed she'd now have to protect him from his own folly by lying through her teeth to Valentine. Really, that man owed her *so* much.

"Nothing," she said quickly. "You know I never cared for Gideon's idea to have the man here. We're Redgraves. We solve our own problems."

Valentine continued to look at her, as if considering her answer. "Now you sound like Trixie's pet parrot, reciting her words."

"She doesn't have a parrot."

"I don't know about that. The person I'm looking at seems to have ruffled feathers at the moment. So you and Simon aren't…aren't getting to know each other better?"

"Just well enough to dislike each other. I mean, not *dislike*. I suppose he's a likeable enough fellow. But there certainly is no whiff of April and May in the air, for pity's sake. We have had a mission set before us, that's all, and you can't expect me to be happy having to include him in our search. I'm simply attempting to make do the best I can with the situation. Naturally, I'll have my small lapses—"

"Ha! Forgetting where you left your riding crop is a small lapse. Stealing a man's horse is more than a small lapse. One might even term it a whopping big lapse. I mean, if you're soliciting opinions."

"I'm not." Kate pulled a face at him. "To continue. I'll have my small lapses, such as this morning, but they mean nothing. You're so fanciful, Val. And to think such things of your sister?" *Always end accepting blame and then accusing him of a greater guilt of his own—that ploy has worked on Val since we shared the nursery.*

Valentine looked off into the distance, seeing what Kate did not know or care, and then sighed. "All right. I agree it's a mildly uncomfortable situation for all of us, Simon included. I won't embarrass you by asking his intentions."

Kate breathed a sigh of relief. "Embarrass me? Think of yourself, Val, if he said he has no intention to do anything but his job, and quickly at that, so he can be shed of us."

"Another good point. You know, Kate, I'm not quite so dull-witted with other women. But sisters are a whole other species. Part of me is dotty with pride about you being all grown up now and so surprisingly beautiful, so intelligent and independent, while another part remains staunchly committed to the innocent child I remember never coming to any sort of harm. Which makes it damned difficult to even consider that someday some man will look at you in a totally different light. See the woman, but not the child."

"I'm fine, Val, and more than capable of taking care of myself. Why, you've just admitted as much, and I thank you for that." Kate went up on tiptoe to kiss her brother's cheek. "I'm the woman I am because of my brothers. And before you say something such as, *yes, for our sins* to ruin the moment, I didn't mean that facetiously."

"Thank you, Kate. But you're also the woman you are because of Trixie, which is enough to keep your three brothers on their toes at all times."

Kate laughed softly. "You're right. She has taught me a few things that would probably keep you all up nights. Now, since you've changed your mind about confronting Simon, please allow me to go to the stables and wait for his return. I should apologize."

"Should, but won't," Valentine said, displaying how well he knew her. "I'll be off to see how Adam is doing with an assignment I gave him earlier. With any luck, he's finished covering all the schoolroom slates with *a true gentleman is born to responsibilities, not entitlements.* With more luck, he'll have spelled responsibilities incorrectly and I'll be forced to make him do it all over again."

Kate was still smiling as she approached the stable yard, only to see a tall male figure cresting the grassy hill nearly a half mile away, Dickie and the pony cart following behind. Simon must have ridden most of the way, to arrive so quickly, but he wasn't about to let her see him still in the cart. Now that she considered the thing, he'd probably shifted Liam to the cart while he took the reins. Vain man. All men were vain. But women continued to best them, time after time.

The smug smile faded, though, to be replaced by a scowl, followed hard by realization and resignation, knowing she had declared victory too soon. Because Simon put two fingers at the corners of his mouth, whistled, and Hector, who had been roaming free behind the paddock fence, picked up his head, made short work out of clearing the top rail and trotted immediately uphill to his master.

If Simon had whistled as she was leading the stallion away, she probably would have been ignominiously jerked out of the saddle before she could think to release the reins. At the least, she would have been embarrassed. At the most, she could have been badly hurt. So, instead of risking either, he'd decided to walk back to the Manor in his tall riding boots.

The man was a gentleman.

She watched as he grabbed on to Hector's mane and neatly hoisted himself up onto the stallion's bare back, holding on with his tightly clasped knees as horse and rider rode triumphantly (smugly?) into the stable yard.

The man was a show-off.

He doffed his hat to her as a groom rushed up to slip a bridle on Hector, and then Simon slid his right leg up and over the stallion's head and neatly leaped to the ground in front of her. He looked tall, somewhat warm, his thick blond hair damply mussed and falling onto his forehead. His green eyes were shining as he replaced the curly-brimmed beaver, seating it nearly at the back of his head.

The man was irresistible.

He looked down at her for long moments while Hector was led away, a smile slowly twitching at one corner of his mouth. "If we're keeping score, I think this was ultimately my trick," he said at last.

Kate said nothing. She did no more than blink her eyelids twice and continue looking up at him. She had nothing to say, nothing she could say. However, a part of her brain prodded, Valentine would have had *plenty* to say if he could see her now, see how Simon was looking at her now...how she was looking back at him.

"I've been thinking on my pleasant ride back here. What I've been thinking is, it's time we got this over with before we manage to kill each other. Come on," he said, grabbing on to her hand.

Protest was useless, especially since her heart wouldn't be in it, so she simply allowed him to lead her around the stables and into a deep shadow caused by the morning sun striking the tall, gabled stable.

Still holding her hand, he deftly maneuvered both their arms behind her back, which had the happy result of bringing her upper body forward until they were pressed together, chest to chest.

"Just one," she managed, wishing her voice didn't sound so curiously raspy.

"We'll begin with one."

"You're arrogant," she countered, her gaze riveted to his mouth. Could he feel her heart beating, racing? Did he have to sound so smug? Did she have to sound so incredibly stupid? Couldn't she be pithy, say something that would make him apprehensive about what he planned to do?

"I'd like to say *confident,* but that would be bragging, wouldn't it?"

Why was he still talking? "Oh, just shut up and kiss me."

"I do so adore a willing woman," he said, his mouth claiming hers just as she opened it to say something certain to be wonderfully pithy, or something incredibly stupid that could even talk him out of what he planned to do.

No one ever told me, she thought wildly as a toe-curling wave of what had to be desire swept over her. She'd never experienced such instant heat and this most curious *hunger.* Simon was doing things to her mouth that, if described to her, would have had her pulling a face and saying *no thank you!*

He let go of her hands and sudden panic struck her. *No! Don't stop!* She grabbed at his cheeks, pressing her mouth against his, returning exotic favor for exotic favor.

Simon's hands skimmed her waist, then rose to cup her breasts. Kate thought the top of her head might simply explode. She moaned against his mouth, and then gasped as he slid his thigh between hers.

And then he was gone, just as she had escaped him earlier, leaving her to stand there, rocking, wondering when Mother Nature had turned up all the colors of the world until they made her blink.

Simon held up his hands. "Enough," he said, although he seemed to have some trouble getting the word out without taking another quick, shallow breath.

"Yes…I think so." She took a deep, shuddering breath of her own. "Well…well, that was interesting, wasn't it? As in, that is…by way of experimentation."

Simon leaned his shoulder against the sturdy brick of the stable wall, crossing his legs at the ankle, his folded hands clasped together below his waist. "In case you're wondering, that doesn't always happen. In fact, I'd have to say it's damned rare. I think, Kate, we're dangerous for each other."

"It's not as if this was my idea," she bristled, wondering if he might be surreptitiously attempting to hide his— No, she wouldn't think of that! "However, I concur. My curiosity is satisfied, I assure you. Now, if you tremble in your boots at just the thought we'd have to be in each other's company as the search proceeds, please don't feel as if your continued presence is required here at Redgrave Manor."

"Ah, so polite yet firm. Now she's Lady Katherine, lady of the manor. Too late, Kate, I know who you really are. And I'm going nowhere." He ran his gaze lazily up and down the length of her body, and then smiled. "Unless we travel there together."

"You can't put the skin back on the apple, so you might as well peel it all," Kate mumbled beneath her breath, and then shook her head. "Go eat your breakfast, Simon. You can then join me at the greenhouses or not, as is your pleasure."

"Yes," he said, pushing himself away from the wall. "Pleasure. A lovely word, don't you think?"

"Oh, go hang yourself!" she exploded, and then stomped away, slowing only once she had turned the corner of the stables, to wonder if Simon's posture after their kiss had been rudely nonchalant, his teasing only in good fun—or if he'd had as much trouble regaining his equilibrium as she had done.

CHAPTER SEVEN

DEARBORN HANDED SIMON a well-polished apple as he made to leave the breakfast room after a satisfying meal of slab bacon and curried eggs.

"Why, thank you, Dearborn," he said as the butler curtly bowed and signaled for the footman to clear the table.

"My pleasure, my lord," the butler said. "But the apple is for Lady Katherine. She seems to have misplaced the one I presented her with earlier."

Simon snatched up another apple from the fruit bowl on the massive sideboard. "You assume I'll be seeing her?"

Dearborn pulled himself up stiffly. "I seldom assume, my lord. You'll be meeting her at the greenhouses. We watch over her, you understand. Closely."

"Well, that put me in my place," Simon muttered as he headed out of the house, munching on one apple while lazily tossing the second up and down in his hand, attempting to appear nonchalant, just in case he was being watched from some hidey-hole. From cowbells to watchful servants, Kate was about as unprotected as the crown jewels in the Tower. Could their kiss have gone undetected? He was beginning to believe it hadn't been quite the private moment he'd supposed. *Wonderful*.

He'd earlier noticed the morning sun as it was reflected off the hundreds of large panes of glass making up the roofs of the greenhouses, so he knew where he was going. Although, if he hadn't known, it may have been possible to call out *which path leads to the greenhouses,* and have a half-dozen heads poke up from the shrubberies to point him in the correct direction.

The enormous trio of structures—the buildings at the Manor all were constructed in various versions of enormous—lay some distance from the main house, long enough that he'd supposed servants employed the pony cart to haul flowers and fruits to the kitchens.

There was a glass-domed conservatory attached to the East Wing, but that was probably simply for the lady of the household, if digging in the dirt interested her. The real succession houses were now straight ahead of him.

"Hold there a moment, Simon, if you would."

Simon stopped in his progress across the scythed lawn, to see Valentine Redgrave approaching at a near trot, his overly long black hair flying, his fists clenched, his expression considerably less than pleasant.

Before one of those fists possibly ended up smashing his face into bits, Simon held up his hands to indicate surrender—if Kate was that good with her fists, Simon wasn't in a hurry to receive firsthand knowledge of the pugilistic prowess of her brothers.

"What in blazes are you doing?" Valentine asked as he approached, looking at Simon's raised arms. "My God, man, do you think I'm on the attack? Why would I do that?" Then his dark eyes narrowed. "Why would I want to do that, Simon?"

"I have no idea," he said, lowering his arms, knowing Valentine Redgrave wouldn't let it go at that. "Possibly because I kissed your sister behind the stables, not realizing Kate is never really alone?"

"She damn well was alone this morning. Her watchers keep their distance, for God's sake, else she'd have our ears. The servants watch over her, yes, but they don't dog her steps like puppies." Then he sighed. "All right, you kissed her. I suppose it was only a matter of time. I'm not so unawares I've missed the sparks I've seen flying between the two of you since the moment you met. So. How did that go?"

"How did it—?" Simon goggled at the man. "Very well, all things considered, thank you," he then answered, dumbfounded. "I'm quite prepared to offer for her hand at once, of course."

Valentine rolled his eyes as if this was the most absurd thing he'd ever heard. "And what makes you think any of us would dare to make that sort of decision for Kate? We'd have better luck ordering the rain to stop falling. I admit I'd earlier thought about asking you to tell me your expectations with Kate, until she pointed out I'd only be making a dashed fool of myself. Well. Let's see now, Simon, shall we? Where do we go from here?"

"I have no idea," he admitted honestly. "The only rules I'm conversant with in the matter appear not to apply to Kate."

Valentine nodded his agreement. "Although Gideon doesn't share Kate's belief, mind you. Do you think you could love her?"

Simon had already been half expecting that question. "I don't think I honestly could answer that either way, not at this point."

"I understand. It's early days yet. Sometimes it takes a shovel."

"I beg your pardon?" Was he to *dig* for the answer? Or was someone considering conking him on the head with one? Perhaps all the Redgraves were insane…or he was. Either way, Simon hadn't been put so far off his stride since the age of ten, when his father asked him just what he thought he was doing sneaking out of the man's study with a pipe tucked in his waistband and a handful of tobacco.

"Never mind. But have you given it any thought?"

"Some, yes. I think, in time, she might drive me straight around the bend," Simon confessed.

Valentine draped a companionable arm around Simon's shoulders. "Then there's our answer, isn't it? Kate calls the tune, just as she's done since the cradle. We can blame Trixie for that, by the way. We blame her for everything else," he ended, grinning.

"Yes, four innocent children, doomed by their heritage and then corrupted by the deliciously *outré* dowager countess. Those scandalous Redgraves, those unpredictable Redgraves. I can't say I wasn't warned. But my informants had it wrong. You're simply who you are, with no pretense, which may make you four of the most independent-thinking and therefore most civilized people in all of England. There aren't many of us who can say that. I envy you."

"That's all well and good, although I cannot but point out if you ruin her we variously accused Redgraves will not scruple at hanging pieces of you on every lamppost in London."

"A friendly warning, Val?"

His smile was wide, but it was his words that Simon took to heart. "Nothing friendly about it. A kiss is a kiss, and probably to be expected. But she can be quite inquisitive. Don't let the girl seduce you unless you intend to meet her at the altar, understood?"

"Understood." Feeling lucky to have survived the

past few minutes without having to play the gentleman and let Val knock him down, Simon then asked, "So why were you chasing after me?"

The scowl returned instantly. "You mean now that we have that other settled— It is settled, isn't it?"

"Most definitely. The only question left to me is, am I more afraid of Kate or her brothers?"

"Trixie. Fair warning, my friend. Be most afraid of Trixie. There are hidden depths to that woman even we reckless Redgraves would never dare to plumb. In fact, I stand rather in awe of you for having dared that kiss, knowing what my grandmother is capable of if displeased. In any case, now that we understand each other, perhaps I can feel more at ease with what I have to tell you. It would seem you and Kate will be on your own for a while."

Simon shot a glance toward a nearby shrubbery. "*Relatively* speaking, you mean, if you don't mind the pun?"

"True enough. Very good, Simon. Yes, but not really on your own. I'm leaving for London."

"Is that a fact," Simon commented without inflection, although the statement had surprised him. "May I inquire as to the reason?"

"I would venture to say not, no." This, again, was said with an accompanying smile. Such a handsome, well-set-up man. Smooth, eminently affable and easygoing. Simon was beginning to think an adversary should be more concerned with Valentine Redgrave's smiles than his scowls.

Then again, Simon wasn't easily put off. "Personal pleasure, or something to do with the Society?"

"There can be nothing more personal to us Redgraves at the moment than the *pleasure* of unmasking the Society. All right, since you're not going to stop, are you, I may as well tell you the rest. Our only other known avenue to answers at this moment is Lord Charles Mailer, now that his cohort, the late Archie Urban, the only other Society member whose name we know, is busily feeding the worms. Post and City. Meaningless code names found in Jessica's father's journal, until you somehow figured them out without our assistance. I don't believe it was ever mentioned—how you did that."

"Damn if you aren't correct. I don't believe I shared that information," Simon said, and then most deliberately smiled. More than one could play at this game.

"And we didn't impart our method to you, or Perceval, for that matter." Valentine looked at him for a long moment. "All right. No matter what avenue you took, we all somehow arrived at the same destination, didn't we?"

"Until Urban was run down by a cart—highly suspicious—and Mailer decided it was time he withdrew from London to rusticate in the countryside. There are some who believe he should have been arrested, you know, and thoroughly questioned about those misdirected supplies."

"You among them, I'm certain. But in this case, we Redgraves managed to convince Perceval a bird who believes he is free to fly is more useful to us than one locked in a cage, steadfastly denying his guilt. You've not the most subtle of approaches, my friend, dogging their steps everywhere they went during the Season. You half frightened Jessica to death that night at Almacks."

"I apologize. That was back when I was wondering if this generation of Redgraves was involved in the Society."

"No apology necessary. God knows I would have thought the same thing had I been on the outside, looking in. But to return to your question. Now that Mailer has calmed his fears of having been found out and ventured back to town, a finer hand might be called for. Mine, in point of fact. Although there's always the fear the man only remains aboveground because the Society is using him for bait, assuming someone is on to them and that's why Urban is dead. And they most certainly know by now these unknown someones somehow managed to thwart their scheme, implemented by Mailer, to misdirect the supplies meant for the Peninsula. Yes, the man would make perfect bait, meant to draw us in. Dear me, always so many possibilities. My mission is not devoid of its pitfalls."

"Agreed. You could be walking straight into a hornet's nest, cultivating Mailer. Urban was most certainly murdered. I'd thought—"

"We'd done it? Let's say this—we didn't stop it. But it was a better death than he deserved. I could be prodded into telling you the whole of it, once we've cleared this mess we're in currently. In any case, I leave for London in the morning."

"Kate may decide to go with you."

Valentine shook his head. "No, I doubt that. She's determined to locate those journals, and now, I fear, our father's body. Besides, you don't really believe I'm a slave to truth when explaining my numerous absences to her these past few years, do you? With luck, I'll return in a week, or some other of us will show up."

"You have my word as a gentleman. I'll watch over her," Simon told him, nearly childishly reaching up a hand to cross his heart. He couldn't believe his good fortune. Or was that his bad luck? Either way, the next days should prove interesting. Lord knew how much had already been packed into this first full day at Redgrave Manor. And it was far from over yet!

"And the servants will watch over you, with Consuela trading in her senior maid's duties to act as Kate's duenna. Consuela arrived on these shores from Spain with our mother, and is fiercely protective of her charge, not to mention the proud possessor of arms like ham hocks. Should be delightful having her about as chaperone, don't you think?"

Valentine turned to start back toward the Manor, before swinging about to add, "Oh, and don't attempt to make friends with Dearborn, or else he'll be convinced you're a rotter of the first water and you'll never see another of Gideon's cigars."

Simon waved his understanding, and then stood quite still, lost in thought for some time, attempting to understand the Redgraves. It wasn't possible. The only conclusion he could come up with was the notion he, Simon Ravenbill, had been accepted into this strange, fairly eccentric family. Trusted. Why this pleased him so much, he had no idea.

Then he realized this supposed trust also damn well put a heavy damper on any amorous plans he might have harbored about Kate…and he was fairly certain Valentine knew that. His sister's virtue couldn't be safer inside a nunnery than it would be with Simon on the premises.

Damn, they were a diabolically clever bunch!

By the time he reached the greenhouses, Simon was smiling at his predicament, mostly because he believed Kate might not see the humor in the thing once she

realized why he was keeping his distance. And defi
nitely wouldn't if she was truly attracted to him. "God,
I would be the pursued rather than the pursuer. Now
that could prove interesting."

One of the gardeners paused in his pruning of some
low shrubbery, to point Simon toward the last of the
trio of succession houses and then dutifully returned
to his task—which seemed to be clipping the air just
above the neatly trimmed greenery.

He knocked on one of the sparklingly clean panes at
the open doorway and called out Kate's name.

"Stop!" she shouted from somewhere behind the
carefully stunted pear trees blocking his sight of her.
"Don't move, for God's sakes—can't you see that gap-
ing hole?"

Since he'd been looking forward as he walked, no,
he hadn't seen a need to examine the center pathway.
The ground was the ground. But he looked now. He'd
been two steps away from a minor disaster.

"You never had the collapse filled in?"

She stepped from the trees, appearing on the other
side of the miniature abyss, pressed her fists against
her hips and peered down into the darkness. "Gideon is
still debating digging the whole thing wider, although
when he first was lowered inside, he saw the collapse
had hidden any hint of what we assume to be more of
the tunnel. It still could be nothing but a result of heavy
rains and the fact Gideon had ordered the direction of
the stream rerouted in order to make it more convenient
to carry water to the succession houses. The hole actually fills a bit whenever it rains, even beneath this roof.
It could collapse on itself anytime, Gideon says, and
any information lost to us, or collapse enough to point
us in the direction of the rest of the tunnel. My brother

is, of course, hoping for the latter possibility. Do you know if it rained last night?"

Since he'd been up half the night, attempting to sort out what he knew and didn't know, Simon was able to answer her. "Yes, it did. And if you know the ground isn't all that steady, why are you in here?"

"Because I agree with Gideon's suspicions, what we're looking down at right now is part of a man-made tunnel. I'd hoped to locate more of it somewhere else in here."

"Man-made? From your father's time?"

Kate shrugged. She looked delicious, dressed as she was in a midnight-blue riding habit, not to mention that tempting smudge of dirt on her left cheek. "Or my grandfather's. Or possibly even from the days our ancestors may have dabbled in a bit of smuggling."

"The upstanding earls of Saltwood—smuggling?"

"Don't pretend to be shocked. Smuggling is a time-honored profession the nearer you are to the coast, yes. Or did you believe the Redgraves totally depended on crops and forestry and the like to build their empire? There's many an exalted family could be traced back to horse thieves and smugglers. Trixie told me of one insufferably high-in-the-instep peer she had on good authority owes the majority of his fortune to his grandfather's clever hand with a marked deck."

"As opposed to those who made their way via assassination, poisoning and the occasional tragic midnight tumble down the stairs, for example. Yes, I see the distinction," Simon said, attempting not to smile.

"Don't be snide. Smuggling is barely criminal, nearly laudable, as it keeps the local residents from starving in bad years, and there isn't a landowner from Dover to the marshes of Sussex who would not look the other way or turn down a few bottles of French brandy or several ells of Flemish lace deposited on his doorstep once or twice a month. In thanks for allowing the owlers to cross their property, you see, or to store their cargo in a handy cave until a caravan of land carriers and their ponies move everything inland to its final destination."

"So then you approve?"

She shrugged once more. "Of smuggling? In general, no. It can be a bloody business. But we like to think *our* smugglers are more civilized. Not like some of the competing gangs who once operated in Kent."

By now Simon had managed to gingerly make his way around the collapse and join Kate on the other side. "You're saying the owlers, as you call them—and allow me to admit I'm amazed at your ladyship's wide vocabulary on the subject—still operate near the Manor?"

"With our heads conveniently turned away, yes. But Gideon more or less frowned on the practice during time of war, so any activity has been sporadic these last years, what with us seemingly at war with France one moment and forging a truce the next, skirting the edges of combat while Bonaparte seeks new conquests. But this time, with France capturing Spain, it will be all-out war until the Little Corporal is in a cage, won't it? That's what Max told me before he left for the Peninsula."

"You worry about him?"

"Max? No. He always lands on his feet. The same for Gideon." She sighed as she turned away from the collapse and headed down the main aisle. "It's Valentine who worries me enough for the three of them. He's got such a soft heart."

Simon smiled as he followed her. "And that's a flaw?"

"In a Redgrave, yes. And makes him easy prey to any sad story. He always seems to be riding off to help some supposedly unfortunate soul. I worry one of these days he's going to tumble into trouble by falling prey to a conniving female with a heartbreaking tale of woe."

Simon's bark of laughter startled a few small birds that had made their home in the rafters of the lofty structure.

Kate whirled to confront him. "It's not funny," she told him—warned him. "Women are natural-born connivers, at least once the skill is pointed out to them."

"And you should know, hmm?" he said, recovering from his unexpected bout of mirth. "Being your grandmother's student."

Kate's smile slowly crept all the way up to her dangerously exotic eyes. "Exactly. By rights, Simon Ravenbill, you should be quavering in your boots, terrified of what I might do next. I already managed to frustrate you into believing you wanted to—no, *needed* to kiss me."

"Oh, is that right," he said, advancing on her. The devil had taken hold of his mind, and he couldn't resist. "Rather sure of yourself, aren't you? May I suggest a wager?"

Her eyes widened, and she stepped behind a rather straggly bush clearly brought into the greenhouse to be revived. "What sort of wager?"

"I *wager,* for the space of seven days and nights, I can be completely indifferent to you."

"Really." God, she looked smug. "And am I to wager in return that I will be able to remain *indifferent* to you for that same time period?"

"That only seems fair, doesn't it? And, as I'm only a helpless man, and you are a self-admitted born con-niver, it shouldn't be much of a challenge on your end. Therefore, the forfeit has to be considerable. Agreed?"

"I don't know," she told him, revealing more than she knew by nervously stripping the leaves from one flopping branch. "What did you have in mind?"

That was a good question. He'd been so intent on the wager, he hadn't yet considered possible consequences. And then inspiration—or the devil—had him saying, "If we both resist, the wager becomes null and void in seven days. However, if your attractions should become too difficult for me to resist and I cannot help but kiss you, I will climb to the top of the highest church steeple in Hythe precisely at noon the very next day and sing every last chorus of 'God Save The King.'"

"All of them. Really." Simon could see the corners of Kate's mouth quivering, but she was holding out, asking, "And my forfeit?"

He continued to push, genuinely enjoying himself. "When you find you can no longer resist me and beg for my kiss, you mean?"

"If, Simon. Not when. And a highly improbable *if* at that."

"Why, then you will marry me." *Because the wager may be ended by a kiss, but what would inevitably follow that capitulation could only end at the altar.*

"That's ridiculous! I won't agree to any such thing."

Simon made her an elegant bow. He had her now. "You flatter me, madam, with your refusal. Clearly you're afraid you will find me irresistible."

"Stop that ridiculous bowing, you look like an ape. I'm not afraid of—I'm not afraid of anything." She stepped out from behind the shrubbery and her position that clearly proved otherwise, and stuck out her hand. "Agreed. And you will sing loudly enough to be heard over the bells in every church steeple in Hythe, because they all always strike at noon. You'll be both deaf and hoarse for weeks."

He shook her hand to accept the wager, and then pulled her close against his chest. "I believe my ears and voice to be safe. You'll make a lovely bride."

She peered up at him through her lashes. "Give over, Simon, I'm not going to kiss you. I've no need. You're already halfway to losing. I suggest you practice those lyrics. Beyond the first, they become rather tricky, as I remember."

He brought his mouth to within a whisper of hers, closer to capitulation than even she might think. "One kiss behind the stables and she believes herself the master of all men. How amusing, Kate, but I don't think so. By the way, you've got a smudge on your cheek," he said, and then let her go.

"You insufferable pig! I've got half a mind to—"

What Kate might do with half her mind Simon was never to know, because at that moment Adam Collier stepped into the mouth of the greenhouse and called out, "Yoo-hoo! There you are. Look at me—no, don't! I'm beyond mortified. My second-best rigout, and I'm *covered* in chalk dust. My valet will be brushing it away for *hours.* And my hand? It's all but in a cramp from writing and writing. Really, Kate, I'm going to have to complain to Jessica about—"

"Don't take another step, you idiot!" Simon commanded.

"Oh, seriously," Adam trilled, mincing toward them, "I may have exaggerated some little bit. I'm not quite *that* bad. See, although my lace cuffs are all but— *aaaaahhhh!*"

Simon and Kate rushed toward the collapse. "I suppose no one ever thought to cover the opening with stout boards?" he commented as they approached.

"The doors are kept closed and locked," Kate countered. "Most of the time. Is he all right?"

Simon was certain the pit caused by the collapse was a dozen feet deep, but at least the boy's landing was soft, thanks to the mud. "Adam. Adam! Can you give us a shout?"

"What—what happened? One moment I was…and then I was— My God, I'm in a hole! What am I doing in a hole? *Gaak!* It's *wet* down here, and my lovely shoes are mired in mud. They're *ruined!*"

"That's one piece of good news, at any rate," Kate muttered as she, too, looked down in to the darkness. "You'll have to climb out, Adam. Just stay there until I get someone to bring a rope."

"Where would he be going?" Simon asked facetiously, bent over with his hands on his knees. The sides of the collapse were more mud than solid earth, and he couldn't be sure thanks to the shade cast by the pear trees, but there was possibly a good two feet of water at the base. "And you might want to hurry a bit."

There was the sound of a splash, followed by a good deal of sputtering and a loud appeal from Adam that nobody leave him to drown.

"Then stand still, man, and stop jumping about," Simon advised, stripping out of his jacket. "The ground down there isn't all that stable. You don't want to knock anything loose."

"Knock *what* loose? You…you don't mean— *My God, you have to get me out of here!*"

Simon dropped flat on the ground, reaching one arm into the hole. "Adam! *Adam!* Stop bawling like a mired calf and listen to me. You either stand still until Kate comes back with a rope and some help, or you take your time, find footholds and handholds in the rocks I can see jutting out until you can take my hand and I can pull you the rest of the way. Can you do that? Good God, look who I'm asking to help himself! Adam, forget what I said. I suggest, highly, you wait for Kate."

"No! I'm going to do it. I can't survive down here another moment! I can see your shirtsleeve. I can reach it, I can. I'll just do as you say and dig my hands and feet into this horrible mud—"

"Not the mud! *Rocks,* you twit, you can't expect the mud to hold you!"

"But it is! And— See! See me, I'm climb—"

Three feet of the edge Simon lay prone on gave way all at once and he went sliding into the hole. He would have landed headfirst in the muck if it weren't for his quick thinking that had him twisting his body with all his might. The wall of sodden, packed earth trapped his body, but not his right arm, head or shoulders.

He struggled to clear his face of mud and attempted to look about in the darkness. "Adam! Collier, where the devil are you?"

"I'm up here!" the boy called out triumphantly from the new edge of the now much rearranged collapse.

"Thank you, Simon. When the side came tumbling in, it made a near walkway to the top. I was out of there lickety-split, although my rigout is now ruined beyond redemption. Why don't you come up now? You can't possibly like it down there."

Simon looked at the far side of the oddly shaped pit in time to watch a new section of mud slowly break away from the rest as if surrendering to the blade of a huge knife, and slowly slide into the disturbingly deepening mud. Adam had climbed out, up and over the mud that had taken Simon down…thus over Simon himself. But now the "walkway" the boy had employed was also gone. Adam Collier couldn't be more of a menace if he put his entire minuscule mind to the task!

"If I get out of here alive, I'm going to strangle that paper-skulled idiot," he muttered, attempting to pull himself free of the mud. More of the wall collapsed, as if the hole was attempting to fill itself in, further pinning his chest and legs. But he couldn't panic. Panic was his enemy. "Where the bloody hell is Kate?" he asked. But he asked quietly, trying to not even breathe heavily.

Kate's face appeared over the edge. "Simon? For the love of— What are you doing down there?"

Someone held a lantern out over the pit—it was surely a pit now—lighting the mud walls and the mostly buried Simon. And there were rotting beams here and there, sticking up from the mud. Gideon was correct to believe the cave-in was the result of a collapsing tunnel. Although surely there could have been a better way to learn that fact beyond tumbling headfirst into the hole.

"Don't let anyone tramp too hard up there, Kate. Every move seems to bring more of the walls down on me in slices."

"Oh, my God. Oh, my God, oh, my God, ohmyGod!"

"Less than helpful, Kate," Simon pointed out, attempting to stay calm himself. He was in a predicament, no ignoring that. If slices of the wall kept splashing into the mud and water, he'd soon be completely covered. Perhaps he should console himself with the idea there would always be flowers on his grave.…

"I know that. But I'm fine now, Simon. We need

more rope and shovels. And some stout boards. We need to shore up the sides. Somebody—get them! But first secure this rope. I'm going down there."

"First man up there who obeys that last idiocy is a dead man!" Simon shouted, and then prayed his voice wouldn't bring down another section of heavy mud. It was as if he was to be buried beneath brown, extremely heavy slices of cheese.

"You're hardly in any position to threaten anyone, my lord," Kate told him. "Toss the rope up and over that rafter, Liam, and then secure one end around the support beam beside you. *Do it!*"

Simon watched in amazement as Kate stripped off her jacket, revealing the lace-edged white silk chemise beneath, and tossed it down to him.

"Grab that, Simon, wad it up and try to place it behind your head."

Moments later a rope was hanging down into the middle of the pit.

Kate made a dangerous grab at the swinging rope, caught it then launched herself into the air, wrapping her legs around the rope, aided by the divided skirt of her riding habit. She lowered herself, hand over hand, until her boots sank into the mud.

Simon would never admit it, but he couldn't recall ever being so happy to see anyone in his life.

"They're getting more men, more shovels," she told him as she unceremoniously pulled the jacket from behind his head and tucked it in around his neck and shoulders. "There, that should help for a while." Then she dragged herself through the muck, wresting his head forward before letting it drop onto her thigh as she sat beside him. "We have to keep your head above the mud until we can dig the rest of you out. Honestly, Simon, how did you manage anything so stupid?"

"Practice," he muttered, relieved she hadn't broken his neck. Who knew she was so strong? Or was that just bloody determination? "It takes practice. I think the mud has slid as far as it's going to slide."

"You're an expert on sliding mud?" she asked him, pushing his sodden hair away from his face. "Isn't that fortunate. I know it eases my mind mightily, although it certainly doesn't explain how I could leave you safely standing up there and now you're down here."

He looked up at her, into her clearly worried eyes. "So you're an advocate of kicking at a man when he's down, are you? Good to know."

"And you joke when things are at their worst. Also good to know." She then yanked the jacket away again, wadded it up and stuck it behind his head as she withdrew her supporting thigh. "I can't do anything with your head on my leg, and I want to try to dig some of you out of the muck while we wait."

"Isn't that strange. I could imagine any number of things I could do with my head on your thigh, but this is probably neither the time or place to enumerate on them."

"I'm not certain what that means, Simon, but for a man who may have only a few precious breaths left to him, you might want to consider uttering something more profound."

"Marry me," he said instantly, wondering where the words had come from. He must have suffered a glancing blow from one of the rocks during the collapse. God, he barely knew her.

She was already digging with her hands, attempting to reach his left arm and then, apparently, wrench it out of its socket. "First I'd have to kiss you, and that would mean missing your performance from the church steeple. I'd never do that. Especially since I'm already thinking of something Valentine calls *side bets,* and winning a purse of gold coins."

Simon would have been hurt by this remark, but he was much too interested in the way her chemise gaped open as she continued her industrious two-handed dig. Strange. It would appear even males on the verge of swallowing a fatal dose of mud could still be diverted by glimpses of the soft, deliciously bouncy curves of the fairer sex.

"Now pull, Simon—*pull.* There! Now both your arms are out. I don't think we'll need risk more people down here, or shovels. We can just secure the rope beneath your arms and pull you out. Brilliant, yes?"

"Astonishingly so. But now I can manage putting the rope around myself, so they'll first pull you out."

"Don't be asinine. What if I'm on my way up and more mud comes down?"

"What if *I'm* on my way up and more mud comes down?" he countered.

"You're in no position to argue, you know. Besides, I can stand up and hold on to this rope if that happens. You're still half-submerged, like a pig in a sty. Ah, and they're back." She raised her head as another rope was lowered beside the first. "Pull it up again, Liam, and make one of those sliding knots in the end. You know… like a noose?"

"Only if you plan to fasten it around his neck." Valentine's head and shoulders appeared in the light from the lantern. "This is how you take care of my sister, Ravenbill?"

Kate shot Simon a quick, questioning look. "What is he talking about?"

An outright lie seemed to be the safest way to go at the moment, Simon realized. "I haven't the faintest idea. Oh, look, here comes the noose. I don't want to rush you, Lady Katherine, but we might want to make haste about leaving this charming place. There's far too many people standing about up there, close to the rim, to make me comfortable."

"I'll have an answer from you, once we're out of here." Kate somehow managed, with Simon's limited assistance, to secure the crudely constructed "noose" under his arms. She looked up toward the rim of the pit. "Pull!"

The rope went taut and Simon waved a silent good-bye to his new Hessians as he was slowly, and definitely not painlessly, unearthed, the mix of mud and water making a sickening sucking sound, as if reluctant to let him go. He believed he could now identify greatly with any poor soul who had been stretched on the rack.

At the same time, Kate struggled to her feet, her riding skirt sodden with mud and the rest of her streaked here and there with it, making her still the most beautiful woman in the world. Especially since her smile bordered on the triumphant.

Simon let go of the rope and grabbed her hard against him, his arms like steel bands around her waist. "Arms and legs wrapped around me, Kate. Now! And then hold on."

"Simon, no! You can't hold me. The rope could snap. Let me go!"

But Valentine was calmly issuing orders above them as he now held the lantern over the edge. "Hand over hand, men. On my command. Pull— Stop. Pull— Stop.

Again. Pull— Hold up, they're spinning like tops down there." He reached for the rope and somehow held it steady. "All right, we begin again. Pull— Stop. Once more and we'll have it, boys. Pull— Stop!"

Kate was snatched from Simon's grasp just as their heads appeared above the rim, leaving him to dangle and swing like a watch on a chain. But that was all right, because Kate was safe.

The next thing he knew, Valentine himself had grabbed hold of his buckskins at the center of his waist. In one quick, wrenching upward jerk on the cloth that could have rendered Simon's manhood a deathblow, Valentine one-handedly lifted him up and over the rim as the men pulled one more time, not stopping until Simon was a muddy lump lying facedown a full ten feet away from his possible burial spot, wondering if outright whimpering would be allowed.

"What in bloody blue blazes were you doing down there?" Valentine shouted, clearly still overcome with fear for his sister, or possibly anger. Probably a mix of both. Although he, like Kate, had been markedly cool-headed while affecting the rescue.

"The side of the hole caved in when Simon was standing there, keeping an eye on Adam until I could bring help," Kate explained as she sat on the ground, her knees raised, her arms balanced on her knees. It would seem the strength she had employed while in the pit had deserted her. Simon understood that feeling, as well. He felt weak as a kitten, probably thanks to the weight of all that mud on his legs and chest.

"Adam? What does he have to do with anything?"

"Perhaps if you ceased your shouting, we could tell you," his sister pointed out in some belligerence. Simon sighed, and attempted to rise. Pluck to the backbone, that was his Kate. Even when she should keep her mouth shut.

"Look, Val," Simon said, but then quickly put out a hand to steady himself against a support beam. Prudently, he held on as he gingerly lowered himself to a sitting position in the dirt. "Adam fell in, I slid in after him when the ground I was standing on caved in, and now we're out."

"All right," Valentine said, running a hand through his hair. "You're out. You don't have to tell me why Kate was down there. It's just like her to want to play the heroine. But where's Adam? My God, are you saying—?"

"Your pardon, sir," Liam broke in, "but it's after a bath the boy is, or so he told me when he was tiptoeing past as I was bringing more rope to haul up his lordship. I'm to dig out those queer red shoes he wears, he told me, and then I can have them mayhap I wants them. Now what, beg pardon, sir, does that queerboots think I'm to do with the likes of any such things? Sir."

"Off to take a bath while I'm half drowning in mud," Simon said, shaking his head. "Now there's a sailor I'd not want standing at my back in battle. I'd be taking a cutlass in the gullet while that blockhead was employing his knife to pare his nails."

And then the strangest thing happened. The sound began as a sort of weak chuckle, but within moments became real laughter—complete with a few unladylike snorts. Kate was laughing. She was laughing so hard, she had to lean her back against the leg of a nearby worktable.

"Katie? Katie-girl?" Valentine asked, kneeling in front of her. "Are you all right, sweetheart?"

"I—I'm fine. Really. It's all over now," she said, and then burst into tears.

Her brother scooped her up into his arms, and she buried her head against his shoulder, her muddy arms clinging tight around his neck. He turned to glare at Simon. "You and I will speak later."

As all the servants save Liam put their heads down and shuffled off, clearly embarrassed to be where they were, Simon pulled a clump of mud from his tangled hair and threw it in the direction of the pit. "Yes. I'll just wager we will."

Liam chuckled, clearly delighted.

"Go away, boy. I'll be fine on my own."

"But, m'lord, you're a sorry mess, sir. And you have no boots. Begging your pardon."

"No begging necessary. Wait. Is there a pump nearby?"

"No, my lord. But the stream is out there just a-ways. And trees lined up all along it, if I take your meaning."

"You do. Send my man, won't you, telling him to bring soap and enough clothes to dress me from the skin out."

"Mrs. Justis will like that, my lord. Mr. Adam and her ladyship are dragging enough mud home with them to put her into a rare taking."

"Yes, I am a considerate sort. Oh, and have my man bring me a bottle. Uncorked. I've no need of a glass. Make that two bottles."

"Yes, sir, your lordship!"

Once the servant was gone, Simon managed to push himself to his hands and knees, figuring his next move would be to use the post to get all the way to his feet.

That's when he saw it.

When they'd pulled him free of the pit, it would appear as if something in the mud clinging to him had been dragged along with him, and was now half-buried again in the dirt.

"It can't be," he told himself as he crawled toward what he was already certain was a not yet completely decomposed human hand.

CHAPTER EIGHT

ONLY AFTER HER second bath did Kate finally feel both clean and warm again as she curled up beneath the covers in her chemise, Consuela having ordered her to nap. Who would have thought mud could be so cold? Or perhaps the cold had grown inside her and had to work itself out.

When she'd peered over the edge of the collapse, to see Simon three-quarters buried in mud, the world began to spin and she thought she might faint. She'd read and heard about tunnel collapses, and how men had been swallowed up by the shifting earth and left there, as it would have been too dangerous to attempt to dig them out again for a proper burial.

She hoped Simon hadn't known that, but she was nearly positive he did. How brave of him, to attempt to divert her, worry for her—even peek down her bodice when he believed she wasn't looking—when he was only a few watery inches from a horrible death.

It had taken everything inside Kate to maintain her facade of calm and keep thinking, keep doing, keep scrabbling in the mud to keep it away from his face.

She may have made it a point to learn everything she could about caves and tunnels in the past weeks, to aid her in her search for the journals, but nothing she might have imagined could have adequately prepared her for the sight of layer after layer of nearly solid slabs of mud breaking away and splashing down on top of Simon Ravenbill.

For she already knew an extensive network of man-made tunnels from the coastline to nearly five miles inland, used as hidey-holes for contraband and ponies in order to evade the king's revenue men, was more fiction than fact. Not in this area of England. Much of the ground was unstable for tunnels; even caves near the shoreline often filled with water at high tide. Digging around rocks prone to shift, or burrowing beneath the water table, had the unhappy result of more cave-ins than engineering victories.

There were precious few long-term successes in the way of man-made tunnels or hand-dug caves. Unless one had firsthand knowledge of their location, or a map, the entrances to those successes were all cleverly disguised and nearly impossible to discover. Although a few years ago, one had been found beneath the altar of a village church.

Gideon had explained all of that to her when the ground first opened up inside the succession house. When he'd redirected the stream, the water must have found a way around and over unstable underground rock until it found a place to gather, weakening an area of the tunnel until one storm or another provided enough water for a section of the thing to collapse. Work had begun on returning the stream to the route nature had intended for it, but clearly water was still finding its way beneath the greenhouse.

Valentine, once he'd variously assured himself she was all right, and had harangued at her for being so stupidly brave, had already ordered—and the devil with Gideon's hopes and plans—the pit be filled with rock and gravel beginning tomorrow morning, or he'd know the reason why. Valentine was such a dear when he was being protective. No wonder everyone begged his assistance....

There was a light tap on the door and Consuela bustled into the bedchamber, having already discarded her maid's apron for an entire rusty-black, widely skirted rigout that included a heavy black lace mantilla perched atop a curious high comb, and lace-edged black gloves. Mantilla flying out behind her, she approached the bed looking very much like a prodigiously large raven fruitlessly attempting flight.

Kate attempted to hide her smile. If the sight of Consuela wasn't enough to frighten Simon into fleeing back to London, perhaps she should begin to think his flirting held more weight than simple nonsense meant to provoke her.

"We will rise now and go downstairs," the one-time nurse, now senior upstairs maid and temporary duenna declared even as she rather ruthlessly pulled the covers to the bottom of the bed. "We are to bear witness as Mr. Valentine murders the marquis."

Consuela had come to England over thirty years previously, as one of the young maids meant to serve the then-new bride, Maribel. She had been left behind to care for Maribel's abandoned children, the infant Lady Katherine in particular. Consuela was not a woman to take her responsibilities lightly, and in many ways had come to be as English as her beloved charges.

She spoke the language quite well, with her only noticeable lapse a continuing problem with pronouns (or else she was employing the kingly "we," which was an amusing thought). She wore English clothes—today being a remarkable exception—excelled at training the younger maids as she patiently waited for one of the

Redgraves to fill the nursery for her again, and she clearly greatly enjoyed English cooking. And Leonard, the head groom, although she steadfastly refused to marry him.

But when it came to protecting Maribel's children, even now they all were years beyond the nursery, the blood of a smattering of Moorish warrior ancestors ran hot in her veins.

Kate slid her legs over the edge of the bed. "Val's not going to murder Simon, Consuela. He might want to put a few dents in Mr. Adam, but the marquis wasn't at fault for what happened. You look very…nice in that gown. Um…queenly."

Consuela attempted to lift all three of her chins. "We do, yes. The trappings of a duenna. It was left behind by Doña Fermina in the rush to escape, and now it is ours. Here, put on this wrapper. We cannot waste time. We were given five minutes to arrive in the study."

"This?" Kate grimaced at the worn, deep green velvet banyan that once belonged to her father or grandfather; she'd used it earlier, after her baths, and now it lay at the bottom of the bed. She'd unearthed the robe years ago on a rainy-day search in the attics, pretending she was after buried treasure. Kate had found it wonderfully comforting after her bath on cold winter evenings, as it had a high quilted plaid shawl collar, the sleeves fell below her fingertips to end in quilted plaid cuffs, and the hem reached all the way to her toes. But, goodness, even she knew enough not to wear it outside her chambers. "Are you certain there are no shrouds about, Consuela? Where's Sally?"

Then she remembered. Her personal maid had gone off to hang Kate's riding habit near the kitchen fire until it was dry enough to, hopefully, brush the clinging mud from it. "And then most apt burn the thing, more's the pity, for it won't work, m'lady, much as you love it and hard as I'll try."

Consuela remained adamant. "Five minutes. There is time for nothing else. We remember Mr. Valentine in the nursery. Such tantrums! We will not risk them. Not today."

Kate smiled as she dove into the banyan before tying the sash tightly around her waist. She lifted her long, still faintly damp tresses out from beneath the collar and allowed her hair to hang freely, and somewhat wildly, below her shoulders. In her agitation, Consuela seemed to have forgotten the necessity for slippers, and since her feet were covered by the banyan, anyway, Kate decided it would be delicious to present herself to her brother barefooted. That would teach him to measure his words when summoning her…and perhaps take his mind off any lecture he'd prepared for her.

Five minutes, indeed! "If he throws his toy soldiers, I'll be certain to disappear behind one of the couches." Then she shrugged. If Valentine wished to play the master of the house, *ordering* her about, then let him explain to his lordship why his sister had appeared in the study most resembling a rag-and-bone lady, while bringing her very own black crow with her.

Before she had time to reconsider, Consuela sounded the small wooden castanets tied to her thumb and middle finger. Kate had believed them long banished to the nursery, although she could still recall her dread at hearing their sharp *click-click, click-click*. Somebody was in trouble when the castanets were heard, usually Valentine or herself. At the absurdly young age of ten, Gideon was already allowed downstairs with Trixie, and Max was too smart to ever be caught out doing any of the many things he shouldn't have been doing.

But Val and Kate? They neither one of them seemed to survive breaking the rules of the nursery unscathed, and being called to attention by the castanets probably hastened the development of what the siblings preferred to think of as their "independent thinking." Or, as Valentine once said, "The fine art of getting away with things."

"You aren't really going to use those while acting my duenna, are you?" she asked the maid, who simply held up her fingers and *click-clicked* again. "Oh, you are, aren't you?"

"Four minutes," Consuela pointed out, brushing past Kate on her way to the door, leaving a nearly chewable scent of camphor in the air. Her eyes stung and nearly began to water. Poor moths. No wonder the black gown had survived so long. A pity, really.

Her slim shoulders drooping only a little bit, Kate resigned herself to trailing along behind Consuela to the main staircase, following her down so that the maid wouldn't see her bare feet.

It was strange, though. She was being Kate, being herself, and the devil take the hindmost. But suddenly it wasn't so enjoyable to play the hoyden. Either she was, as her family would have said, "at last" growing up, or this strange feeling was Simon's fault. Probably the latter. It was always easiest to blame Simon...except she knew where the true blame belonged.

"Val can wait. I'm going back upstairs to get properly dressed," she told Consuela just as they reached the second landing, only to turn about to face Simon descending toward her. He looked wonderful, unruffled, none the worse for wear, making her feel stupid, frumpy and horribly gauche.

"Interesting plaid," Simon said as he came toward her. "It looks fairly ancient. Where did you get it?"

"That's it? That's all you can say?"

"For the moment, yes," he answered, fingering the shawl collar. "Although I do intend contemplating what lies beneath."

The sound came snapping up to them from the foyer. *Click-click, click-click!*

"What was that?"

"Not what, whom. Consuela. My duenna. Apparently she disapproves of you pawing me."

"Pawing—I'm bloody well not pawing—"
Click-click, click-click.

"Now you're yelling at me. And swearing. Consuela apparently disapproves of those, as well. Plus, you haven't let go yet."

Simon raised both hands and glared past Kate to the maid. "All right, all right, I get the point, *senora*."

"*Senorita*. Now you're in her black books for certain."

Simon made an elegant bow, which was quite a feat when performed on the stairs. *"Mil perdones, pierda. Estoy asombrado de que tal belleza ha no todavía se quebró por algún hombre con suerte."* Then he turned back to Kate to whisper, "Your brother has sicced a dragon on me. Wonderful."

"I was beginning to see the beauty in it, yes," Kate groused. "But now you've flattered her all hollow, telling her how amazed you are such beauty as hers has not been snapped up by some lucky man. And in Spanish, no less. A show-off. It may be your biggest fault, you know, among a plethora of annoying shortcomings. Now please let me pass."

"I don't think so, no. May I assume you've been likewise summoned to the study? If so, I'd like your brother to see this banyan. Or has he already seen it?"

Kate frowned in confusion. "No, I don't think so, I only wear it after my bath, in the wintertime. Today I was cold enough to use it. Consuela decided it was modest enough to cover me today because of Val's demand I be downstairs in five minutes— And why am I telling you all of this? Oh, I remember. She worries Val may otherwise throw one of his toy soldiers or the equivalent."

Simon rubbed at his forehead. "I'm going to ignore as much of that as I can. Come on, take my arm, and damn well smile so I don't get clicked at again."

Kate did as he said. "You swore again. I didn't drop you into the pit, you know. You should be growling at Adam, although you'll have to wait him out, as he's taken to his bed with what his valet assures Mrs. Justis is a fatal chill."

"We're not that lucky. The idiot *climbed* over me. I swear he even stepped on my head," Simon said, and this time in a definite grumble. "Listen, Kate, we're going to have to take our medicine on this one, I'm afraid. Val has every right to be angry with both of us. Accident or not, your life was in danger while you were in that pit with me."

"But not my virtue, which seems to be in danger any other time we're together."

"You believe so?"

Kate could see the humor in his eyes, and belatedly realized what she'd said, what she'd given away to the man. "Never mind. I was aiming for amusing, but clearly missed the target."

"I don't know. I would rather hope you'd hit the mark quite nicely. Your nose is shiny, by the way. I like it. And your hair smells like jasmine. I could become quite comfortable with your unconventional ways, if not to mention your myriad other attributes. God knows you never bore me."

"You don't ever stop, do you?" Kate halted just outside the study doors. "I really should go back upstairs to change. Val will tear a strip off my hide if I walk in there with you, dressed this way."

"You couldn't be more modestly covered in a shroud."

She looked up at him in shock. "That's what I thought— Oh, drat. Hello there, Val. I was just about to—"

Valentine pushed back the double doors, quickly recovering after goggling at his sister's outfit—or simply resigned to her sartorial mischief. "Kate. Simon. I thought I heard you two out here, indulging in your favorite sport—provoking each other. Come in, if you please, and even if you don't. Consuela, you look marvelously regal. *¿juntos nos mantendrá en jaque, sí?* But for now, our charges will be safe with me, you may retire."

"Simon speaks fluent Spanish, Val," Kate pointed out, trying not to laugh. "You and Consuela will keep us in check, will you? Surely we're not *that* bad."

"I'm still considering which of you is the worst, actually, although I think you just got a leg up with that monstrosity you're wearing," Valentine said, ushering them inside the study.

"Be on the lookout for flying toy soldiers. Consuela was only partially correct," Kate whispered out of the side of her mouth. "It's not just you—he's going to kill us both." She then hastened inside the study and curled up on the leather couch she'd just so recently—although it felt years ago—had Valentine move for her.

"We've got something to discuss," Simon said as Valentine walked behind Gideon's desk, taking up the role of stern headmaster, or so it seemed to Kate.

"True. But if you don't mind, Simon, I believe that's my line in this small farce we seem to be enacting. Although only one of us is in costume," he said, shooting another sharp look at his sister as he sat down. "Shall we begin with the pit?"

Kate knew that tone, that look, which was why she hadn't stuck her tongue out at him. Well, and because Simon was in the room, and for some reason she didn't want him to think she was little more than a nursery brat. Valentine was wound tightly as a clock spring. She hoped Simon had heeded her warning.

So much for hopes.

She watched, goggle-eyed, as Simon pulled a straight-back chair around and straddled it, so that he was sitting between Valentine and herself, able to see both of them. He seemed so confident. He'd probably appear confident in front of a firing squad. Did that make him brilliant…or brick stupid? "No, I'd rather we end there."

Valentine raised an eyebrow at this "down to business" pose, and she glanced up at the coffered ceiling, surprised to see it wasn't falling in on them. But then her brother surprised her. "You've discovered something, haven't you?"

Kate exhaled. They were going to behave like gentlemen. And here she was, barefoot and smothered in fairly ratty emerald green velvet, her damp hair hanging down her back, looking as out of place as a court jester at a king's war council. She had to listen carefully, and come up with at least one brilliant question, or else neither of them would take her seriously again. Or maybe just order her to leave the room and let the grown-ups talk.

Simon spoke again. "A theory, yes. And, possibly, some evidence to support that theory. I was going to tell you both later this evening, but now more pieces have fallen into place."

"Since the cave-in," Valentine prodded, nodding.

"Since the cave-in, yes. But my theory had its beginnings in the long gallery."

"I'd be an idiot if I said I wasn't intrigued by that statement. Since I was only going to read you both a stern lecture on the dangers of making mud pies twelve feet below the ground, I suppose it can wait. It can wait forever, as a matter of fact, because nobody more clearly knows how lucky you both are to even be here, or can give me back the year of my life I lost when I first looked over the pit and saw you. Very well, begin with the long gallery."

And Simon did. Kate sat stock-still, her knees tucked up beneath her chin, amazed at what she was hearing. He had taken bits and pieces, things he'd learned on his own somehow, things she'd told him and things he'd observed, and woven them together into a riveting story, even as he admitted much was born in supposition.

The Redgraves had chosen their ascent wisely, always careful to play the game of politics on the side of the winner. Doing so, they had changed their loyalties, even their religion, so many times their true ancestry became lost. Which was fine with them; they were happy at having achieved their goal, being the outlandishly wealthy earls of Saltwood.

But not all of them were quite so content to stop there, and decided it was time once more to move the target. When it began, Simon couldn't say for certain, but he was sure Charles Redgrave had nurtured more than a fondness for that old tale of the family hanging somewhere on the Royal House of Stuart family tree. Of course, at various times over the years, being a Stuart could literally end with them hanging *from* an entirely different sort of tree.

"I repeat, this is nearly all speculation on my part, backed with only the most pitiful evidence, but please allow me to begin by indulging in a short history lesson."

Valentine groaned. "Very short, if you please. Even mercifully brief, if at all possible."

"I'll do my best." Simon then told them about the time and travails of Louis XV, reminded them of France's Seven Years War with England that had commenced in 1755 and was not going well for them, mostly adding to the enormous debt hanging over the country. He then colored in the lines of a portrait of the aging Louis's reputation of lifelong libertine, eventually keeping dangerously young mistresses locked in a small mansion at the Parc-aux-Cerfs, commonly known as Stags' Park, double entendre probably intended.

Kate hid her face against her knees.

"The king had not been discreet in his love affairs, from having three sisters in succession as lovers, to Madame de Pompadour serving not just as mistress but, rumor had it, both political adviser and, in her later years, procuress. Add to that Louis's love for his deceased mentor, Cardinal Fleury, and his belief in a Catholic monarchy, the king's varied success and failure in war, his decreasing popularity with both the nobility and the masses, and here was a man who might be interested in a two-pronged coup that would make him the most beloved monarch in France's long history."

"Two-pronged, is that all? Sounds like an entire set of cutlery to me," Valentine commented wryly, handing Simon a wineglass. "Go on, I've always enjoyed a good fiction."

"Which it might well be," Simon reminded him. "Kate, am I boring you?"

"No, I don't think so," she said, nervously arranging the hem of the banyan over her bare toes. Here was her chance to be brilliant. "Two-pronged, you said. I suppose it would be a mighty triumph if Louis were to somehow restore a Catholic monarchy to the English throne, along with making free with the English treasury while he was about it?"

Simon looked impressed, and Kate tried not to preen. She adored puzzles almost as much as she loved solving them. Besides, now Valentine couldn't toss her out of the room. She was being helpful.

"Your grandfather died in 1759, only a year after your father was born. No one can say if he was actively dealing with the French, if he had gathered a secret Society of like-minded individuals rather than, shall we say, a group of fun-loving naughty chums who simply liked to prance about in devils' heads and tip over any female they could find to play with them."

"Here now, Simon. My sister's in the room."

Kate bristled. "Your sister grew up listening to Trixie's stories and isn't easily shocked, Val, or she would have daintily swooned at the mention of Stags' Park. Go on, Simon, please."

"Forgive me, but there are comparisons to be made. It's not outside the realm of believability your grandfather, and perhaps some who came before him, had been up to something involving the monarchy. Although I have reason to doubt that, which we'll get to in a moment. I believe this all began with your grandfather, if it happened at all. But, if he did harbor his own ambitions to replace the Hanovers and their limited Stuart blood with a bloodline he believed more potently Stuart, and he was amenable to yet another change in official religion, France was clearly the place to look for assistance. And what better way to get close to the king than through their mutual…interests."

"That's preposterous," Valentine said. "I mean, anything's possible, but I've never heard a thing about kingly ambitions, for God's sake."

Simon shrugged. "I'll get to the evidence later, such as it is. I am fairly, no, more than fairly certain he was, at the least, busily building his own small kingdom right here, so if he wasn't to become monarch, he would certainly have the lush background fit for a prince of the realm."

"Torr Gribbon," Kate said quietly, so only Simon heard. "One thread, Simon, and you think you can weave an entire tapestry."

"Conversely, pull one thread on a tapestry, and everything else begins to unravel. I'm sorry, Kate," Simon said, his eyes gentle for a moment before he turned to face Valentine once more. "Now, your grandfather is gone, your father grows to adulthood and, along the way, somehow discovers what his father had been up to. The journals from those times, the bible, everything. He's intrigued, to say the least. It's the 1780s. Louis XV has been replaced by the even more unpopular Louis XVI, and France appears ripe for revolution. Barry, along with many Englishmen fearing a revolution in our own country if the masses succeed in bringing down Louis, looks to France with an eye to convincing, even blackmailing England to intercede on behalf of the French monarchy. After all, the wealthy and titled have toiled hard and long to be where they are now, and a revolution could see them stripped of home, lands, title, wealth—and possibly their very lives."

"Making it time to dust off the devil masks and get back to corrupting the powerful, the gullible, the foolish, and perhaps even a return to the dream of somehow ascending the throne. Until Mama shot him dead, of course. That was inconvenient for him, wasn't it?"

Valentine sighed audibly. "Remind me again why you're in here, Kate, listening to all of this."

She smiled. "Because I'm completely without scruples and will find out everything one way or another, anyway. Oh, and I'm brilliant. There is that."

Simon laughed as Valentine tossed the letter opener he'd been fingering into the air and caught it again, saying, "That's the end of it, and not a moment too soon. I officially resign as your stand-in guardian. Gideon can have you back with my blessings. Simon? Before my sister so rudely interrupted, you were going to enlighten us, I believe, tell us our father's motives, his plans?"

Kate raised her hand. "But I wasn't done. Please let me finish and see if I'm right. Barry was following in the steps of our grandfather's plans, with the thought of being generously rewarded by a triumphant Louis for his assistance, in the form of an, at least nominal, seat on the English throne thanks to this nebulous Stuart blood. I imagine his court would have been made up of hand-picked members of the Society. I picture a coup, don't you? Instead of bewaring the Ides of March, King George would have had to beware the French-supported

Society he would have been led to believe had his back. Or something like that. It seems far-fetched, but Trixie has told me more than once about Barry's love of opiates. Anything may seem possible when one's head is swirling in the smoke of an opium pipe."

"Lovely," Valentine grumbled, reaching for a quill and dipping a pen into the ink pot. "Keep going, although we might now have crossed the bridge of fiction and are now in the land of fantasy."

Kate got to her feet, no longer able to sit still, and perched herself on the edge of Gideon's desk, forgetting the banyan and her bare feet. "But then Barry was dead, just weeks after the Bastille fell. The revolution had begun, Louis eventually lost his head, and now we have Bonaparte. We can only speculate as to what would have happened or not happened if one or both of them had lived to carry out their plans."

"Her Royal Highness, Princess Katherine. See her now in her lavish court trappings," Valentine joked, earning himself a scathing look from Kate, who already felt ridiculous enough in the ancient banyan. But it seemed to be something else that wiped the grin from his face. "Wait." He stood and reached across the desk, grabbing at the plaid lapel. "Where the devil did you get this?"

"I…I found it in a chest in the attics. It's either our grandfather's or Barry's, I suppose, as there were other things of theirs in the same area. Why?"

"Why?" Valentine repeated. "Simon, is this what I think it is?"

"I wondered when you might notice. The Royal Stuart plaid, yes, and as Kate and I have been just recently debating, perhaps another thread unraveled from the tapestry. I was as surprised as you when I first saw it.

I know you didn't mean to be so helpful, Kate, but well done in any case."

"But it's just an old robe." Kate touched her left cuff. "I don't understand."

Simon enlightened her. "Since the battle of Culloden, the Royal Stuart is worn only by the royal family or with permission of the king, although I hear that's soon to change. They may not have dared to wear kilts, but both your grandfather's and your father's portraits in the long gallery show a shadow of a draped plaid in the top right corner. The same Royal Stuart."

"Along with the small portrait of the first Charles I never noticed. The ladies use the long gallery for walking on rainy days, but for the most part it's ignored. I avoided it like the plague in my youth, preferring fencing lessons with Gideon and Max. That's no good excuse for never noticing the details of the portraits, but I'll offer it, anyway. I think we're seeing more fact than speculation now, even as I believe a pit is opening somewhere in my stomach," Valentine said quietly. "Is there more?"

"Perhaps there is," Simon told them. "Would anyone care to guess the coat of arms used to mark each of their tombs? If someone hadn't chipped them off, that is. I managed to convince Dearborn to accompany me back to the mausoleum an hour ago, and no other markers are missing, all of them displaying your own coat of arms. Which, still keeping to speculation, granted, leads me to believe this all began with your grandfather."

"But—but that's insane."

Simon nodded. "So is believing the Society continued on, if only in its more salacious form, striking deceased members from the rolls, bringing in new members to keep the number at the devil's dozen of thirteen. Until one of those new members tripped over the Society's true beginnings and purpose and decided perhaps it wasn't. Insane, that is."

Valentine refilled their wineglasses and returned to his chair. "And now, the wheel of France's always volatile history having taken yet another turn, rather than an unpopular monarch looking for a prime prize, we have Bonaparte and his seeming quest to conquer the world. I can think of no other man more eager to barter most anything if it gains him the British Empire." He set down his wineglass and clapped his hands. "My congratulations, Simon, I wasn't in the least bored. I find it all damned difficult to swallow, but the theories are intriguing."

"Not to mention we Redgraves are not at all involved, save for fostering the *idea* in someone's head," Kate said, stroking the offending plaid collar, eager to be rid of the thing. "Thank you for that at least, Simon."

"You're welcome. But there's more."

Kate's mind was flying in a dozen different directions. "Yes. There's the journals, and that so-called bible. We've been looking for names, and believing the journals to be diaries of their unnatural behavior. But if Barry and our grandfather had the keepers write *everything* down, as it would seem they did, those writings must also contain a treasure trove of tactics detailing *how* they thought their plans would be carried out."

She stood up and began to pace. "I know I'd want to see how it was done—was planned to be done—the product of delusion or not. Simon, you believe the estate itself played into those plans, don't you?"

"It seems logical, yes, that everything would have begun here. Especially when considering this area's long history of smuggling and its proximity to France.

Bonaparte long ago saw the use of English owlers. He's even established comfortable hotels for the men, to sleep, to replenish themselves before attempting the return crossing."

"Remarkable. Carrying English wool on the way over, French silks and brandy on the return trip," Kate considered aloud, "and a lovely rest and even ship repairs in the middle, I suppose, all courtesy of the emperor."

Simon nodded his agreement. "English wool to be made into French uniforms, yes, at times. But the smugglers are also a two-way conduit for information, the transport of agents and perhaps even escaped French prisoners. They transport London newspapers carrying the latest news of our battles and government arguments, even gold from English sympathizers, of which there are more than a few, I'm afraid. I've seen crude broadsides and pamphlets in London and elsewhere, extolling Bonaparte and urging our own revolution. But to continue. Some of the larger smuggling craft reach eighty tons now, and could hold a disturbing number of troops. One hundred disguised French land at midnight, to be safely hidden by sympathizers miles away by dawn, while the smugglers enjoy Bonaparte's hospitality for another night, never realizing how they've been duped."

"The action repeated all along the southern coast. Not an invasion. An infiltration. Bonaparte has actually provided hotels for the smugglers?"

"I understand he's ordered them constructed in both Gravelines and Dunkirk. Gravelines is supposedly the worst, a compound large enough to house several hundred English smugglers at one time. We've recently begun building more Martello towers, having stopped because we believed the threat of French invasion over. I wonder who ordered more to be constructed, and why, don't you? Fully equipped defensive towers, their guns pointed out to sea? Cannonballs can be launched at English ships as well as French."

"Now you're frightening me, Simon," Kate said honestly.

"Ah, Kate, but there's more. My head's been whirling all afternoon. The few ships allocated to patrolling the coast are slow and in disrepair, and the men themselves definitely not in the top tier of soldiers. Again, it's all something to think about, far-fetched as it might be."

"So was the Trojan horse," Valentine mumbled, having taken up his pen again. "Turner Collier was filling Adam's head with history, assassinations, all sorts of rot. Remember his contribution to the conversation last night at dinner? Conspiracies, ambitions, have been with us for centuries, probably since the beginning of time. Harebrained, brilliant, some succeeding, some spectacular failures. So, insane or not, improbable or not, can we really afford to dismiss *any* theory?"

Kate's heart was pounding now. "Well, then, that's it. We now have even more reason to locate the journals and the bible, quickly, praying no one else has already found them. We have to find the smugglers, their hidey-holes. If they're moving across Manor land, hiding French spies and such on our property, they must be stopped before anyone else finds them. No one would ever believe the Redgraves weren't involved."

"You're supposing anyone else will find a similar thread to pull?"

"It's possible. Look how easy it was for you to figure it all out."

"I'll attempt to see that as a compliment," Simon said, bowing.

"Oh, stop! You know what I mean."

"Adding the plaid and the missing coats of arms and the few facts we have about the Society in with what evidence we already possess? Yes, I know what you mean. There has to be more, but for a kingdom at war, that might be enough to encourage some very probing questions of you Redgraves. As I see it, and hope you agree, *we* have to be the ones asking those probing questions."

"Trixie," Kate said, wincing. "She has to know more. She was *there,* for goodness' sake. That isn't going to be easy, confronting her with what we know. But I see no other choice, Simon, do you?"

"No, but not until we know more. If everything I've heard is true, the dowager countess has survived on her wits for a long time. If she does know anything else, she's certainly kept it hidden from her grandchildren. After all, the men we're speaking of—possible traitors, seditionists—are her late husband and only son. She'll logically want to protect them, and her grandchildren, at all costs."

"Are you two enjoying yourselves?" Valentine asked from his seat behind his brother's desk, pen in hand and scribbling away industriously on what looked to be a third sheet of paper.

"My apologies, Val," Simon said. "We did seem to get carried away, didn't we?"

"Thinking about confronting Trixie? Yes, I'd term that to be in the realm of fanciful flights." He laid down his pen. "Although I can't help but remember how she always made sure to keep us from the mausoleum. Why wouldn't she have simply ordered our coat of arms put on the tombs?" Then he held up his hand. "Never mind. You two have already come up with too many answers. Is there anything else, Simon, before I get back to this letter to Gideon? I already foresee adding another sheet."

"No, that's it." Simon shot a look at Kate. "No, that's not it. I have enough trouble keeping the truth straight to attempt any more comforting lies. Kate, Val, I brought something up with me, from the pit. I don't know quite how. Perhaps it became caught on my clothing."

"Go on," Valentine said, casting a worried look at his sister, who immediately stopped biting at her bottom lip. Whatever Simon was about to say, she had to listen without blinking, without betraying how ill-prepared she felt for any more shocks today

"It was a hand. A human hand."

Kate grabbed at his arm, shaking him. "Barry? You found him? Oh, my God. That's it. The Society buried him in a tunnel after they were—after they were done with him. How could they do that?"

"I'm sorry, Kate, but no. I should have been clearer. The hand is from a much more recent burial." He turned to Valentine. "So you might want to tell Gideon it would seem he was right, what happened in the greenhouse was a tunnel collapse."

"A tunnel in use," Valentine said, rubbing at his forehead. "I was going to have the pit filled with rocks and gravel. Do you think it's safe enough for more digging?"

Kate took a steadying breath and rejoined the conversation. For a moment, just a moment, she had thought— but no, her father's body was still missing. "There's a lovely old book in the library, several actually, all about caves and such. Mostly mines. There were even drawings. Some of them showed how to dig an entirely new entrance, to rescue miners trapped below the ground. You don't dig where everything collapsed, Val. You dig down at an angle, and from a good distance away."

"Several books? Your family has an interest in mining?" Simon asked Valentine.

"Not that I was aware, no. There are more than three thousand books in the library. Perhaps our ancestors bought them by the yard, not caring what was in them as long as they filled the shelves."

"My late brother did that when he purchased a house in Bath," Simon said with a small, rather sad smile. "Not only by the yard, but by color, as well. He'd always felt the library at Singleton was too haphazard to be appealing. It's arranged by subject, you understand. Clearly aesthetically unacceptable to Holbrook."

"The library here is like yours at Singleton, and well-read, by the looks of many of the volumes. If the Redgraves really did once involve themselves with smuggling and cave digging and such, the books I found would make perfect sense. Wait, I'll go get them."

"In a minute, Kate." Val walked around the desk to take hold of her hands. "I can't think of a worse time for me to tell you this, but I'm leaving for London in the morning."

"No! You can't do that, Val. Not *now*. We're getting closer every minute, can't you feel it?" *Can't you feel the excitement? Or am I terrible to feel my blood running hotter after what we've just learned? Simon feels it, too, I can tell. He can barely wait to get back to the chase. Didn't you hear how splendidly our minds work together? Why, together, he and I can—* Oh. *Oh, dear. Yes, Valentine. Perhaps you should go to London....*

"All the more reason for me to go. We may not be

the only ones who are *getting closer*. If nothing else, I believe an audience with Perceval is in order, concerning the Martello towers, and why more are being constructed. There's a good chance the man didn't tell Gideon everything he knows. Either that, or somebody convinced him to recommence building, and that would be a name we'd want to know. But to be fair, I was already planning to leave tomorrow. There's a lady there who requires my assistance."

Kate pulled her hands free; at least now it wasn't difficult to make him believe she was angry with him. "There's always someone who *requires* your assistance, and most all of them are female. You'll have your heart broken one day, you know, not to mention your head."

"Yes, so you keep reminding me. My letter informs Gideon of my travels, and I've asked him to address any ideas or suggestions to Portman Square. With him and Jessica carefully out of sight and Max somewhere on the Peninsula, it's not practical to have all of who is left congregated in the same place, doing the same thing. I should be back in a week." Valentine looked to Simon. "In the meantime, Kate, you're in good hands. Isn't she, Simon?"

"Safe as houses, as my valet would say. Kate, why don't you take yourself upstairs to be rid of that fairly incriminating monstrosity. Then tell your woman to burn it and stir the ashes."

"You can't simply order me to—"

"Yes, he can, Katie, my love. It has already been discussed. For his sins, Simon is in charge the moment I leave. Or, as he seems to think, beginning *now*."

Already been discussed? Her chin went so high she could nearly see her own cheekbones. "The hell you say. We'll just see about that, won't we!" she exploded, and then left the room at a barefoot run.

Unfortunately not fast enough to miss seeing Simon and Valentine shake hands, as if some bargain had been struck. Of course! She remembered what Valentine had said while she and Simon were in the pit: *This is how you take care of my sister, Ravenbill?*

Oh, they'd pay for that, the both of them!

CHAPTER NINE

SIMON HAD WAITED near the statue of Henry and his three-headed dog until one, an hour after their agreed meeting time of midnight, never really believing Kate would appear. She'd probably been in bed for hours; Lord knew he'd felt all but asleep on his feet after what had seemed the longest day of his life.

Then again, her duenna may have locked her in her chamber, although something as paltry as a locked door didn't seem enough to contain Kate if she wished to be on the other side of it. He did admire her. He felt all sorts of emotions about Lady Katherine Redgrave. Most of them, if acted upon, would have ended with Valentine or one of his brothers feeding his entrails to the hogs.

Did he love her? That's what Valentine had asked him, even if he'd known it was much too soon for any such inquiry. Simon did already know he loved what she *represented,* however: freedom, intelligence, wit, fearlessness, a thirst for adventure, but all of it tempered by what he instinctively knew was a good and generous heart (at times well hidden behind a fairly fierce temper).

She was nobody else, and that was the main thing. She was simply Kate, and didn't seem to worry a tinker's dam about anyone's opinion of her but her own. Valentine hadn't just been optimistic in attempting to convince her to change her ways, he'd attempted the impossible; one should never attempt to tamper with perfection. And then there was the rest of her…those eyes, that mouth, those so-enticing curves.

He'd warned himself to stop thinking about Kate. It was too dangerous, especially with Valentine leaving in the morning, promise or no promise, wager or no wager.

Instead, he'd decided on a little investigating of his own. Thanks to the light from the lanterns flanking the wide doors to Redgrave Manor, Simon did at least manage to assure himself of one thing. None of the dog heads lifted or swiveled. There were no conveniently loose slabs in the base; the spear in Henry's fist didn't elicit a betraying click when he pushed on it, sending anything to shifting, exposing a staircase leading down to a man-made underworld.

In all, by the time he was done with his inspection, which included getting down on his hands and knees as well as balancing on the dog's back in order to push around Henry's marble face and eyes, tug on his ears, he was left feeling fairly ridiculous, as well as grateful Kate hadn't seen him making a grand fool of himself.

As he'd already begun feeling the physical effects of his time in the pit, and climbing old Henry hadn't helped matters, he'd then decided it was time to give in, give up and go to bed. Perhaps to sleep, most assuredly to dream…

The shaft of early morning sunlight that stabbed at his closed eyes came without warning. So did the jolt of somebody's body hitting the bed.

"Get up, you slug-a-bed. How can you sleep?"

Kate.

He pulled a pillow out from behind his head, then clamped it across his eyes. And mouth—for he knew he was about to say something best uttered only in the company of men. He said it.

"I didn't quite catch that, Simon. Naughty, wasn't it? Good for you. Now get up, rise, greet the day. Do you say morning prayers? I don't. I should, but I don't. Valentine's gone. That's one reason for thanking somebody, isn't it? *Get up.*"

"Bounce again and I may have to toss you out a window," he warned as, slowly, he lowered the pillow, to see her kneeling on the mattress, already clad in an emerald-green riding habit, a silly, matching shako and curled feather tipped ever-so-slightly on her head. He saw the smile on her mouth, the devil in her eyes. The minx! She was getting some of her own back for Val having put her under his care; she was giving him a lesson of just who really was in charge.

Clearly it wasn't him. But he'd play her game. For now.

"Are you bloody well out of your mind? Where's your duenna? Is she going to come *click-clicking* her way in here at any moment, swinging a battle-ax?"

He heard a *click-click* from somewhere else in the room, and groaned, "She's in here, isn't she? Of course she is, why am I asking? You two nodcocks believe this means you're adequately chaperoned? In my *bedchamber?*"

"Don't be an old lady, Simon. Besides, we didn't have any other choice. Your valet refused to wake you. Did you plan to sleep the entire morning away? I've decided we need to expand our search for caves. We only found the one, remember, and only a small part of it at that. Simon—*get up!*"

She reached for the top of the coverlet and Simon grabbed two great wads of the burgundy satin in his fists before Kate (and probably Consuela) had her first real anatomy lesson. "You probably need to know I'm not wearing a nightshirt," he said, biting back a smile.

"No?" Kate frowned. "Then what are you— *Oh!*" She hopped down from the bed with some alacrity and quickly hustled Consuela toward the hall. "I'll see that our mounts are brought round in the next half hour. Don't bother to break your fast. I've asked Cook to prepare a basket for us."

"Yes, your highness, at once, your highness," Simon grumbled as the door slammed behind the women, and then fell back against the pillows once more. He ached all over thanks to his time spent in the collapsed tunnel yesterday, with one particularly angry-looking bruise on his right hip, where he had landed on something fairly sharp that, in retrospect, could well have been the ribcage of the body now missing a hand. He'd been all but buried atop a decomposing corpse. Something like that could give a man pause, that's what it could do. By rights, he should be waking from nightmares for a month, screaming.

Not that anything seemed to upset Kate for more than ten minutes. Or slow her down, come to think of it.

Now she wanted him on horseback? Well, if nothing else, she wouldn't have to worry about him becoming overtly amorous anytime soon, the Manor swarming with Redgraves or just the two of them in residence (plus the black crow), wager or no wager.

A half hour later, having succeeded in convincing his valet he was not about to allow him to rub foul-smelling horse liniment on his buttocks, Simon was dressed and outside, eying Hector and visibly wincing when it became obvious to him the stallion expected a gallop.

Kate was already aboard Daisy, just as if she'd fully

expected Simon to obey her—that would take some thinking about at some point— a wicker basket tied at the rear of her sidesaddle.

"I think we should begin at the West Run and ride south to the coast, and start back from there, don't you? It's only nearly a spit of Redgrave land that reaches to the water, at least by Redgrave standards. There's several cottages nearer the coast, where it's not suitable for farming, but they're only leased. The land belongs to us. Do you think there may be a tunnel inside one of them? I don't know how we'd get inside, though. I believe it would take Gideon to manage that."

"I don't know. I think if we just politely knocked on doors and inquired if the occupants would mind us tramping through their cellars, tapping on walls, stamping on floorboards, no one would protest. Overmuch."

"You're a bit of a bear in the morning, aren't you?" she asked him as they headed their mounts onto the drive, and toward the West Run. "So's Max. He once threw a candlestick at me when I asked him to get dressed and romp in the snow with me before it melted."

"Imagine that. Tell me, had it been dawn yet?"

"Very nearly," Kate said, dipping her chin. "Still, I couldn't have been more than seven at the time. A person should make exceptions when there's an unexpected snow and the other person is only seven."

"And now that you're all of twenty?"

She allowed Daisy to dance a bit as they neared the split in the roadway; clearly both mounts were eager for a run. "Are you suggesting I apologize?"

"I wouldn't think of it. Just, next time, lock Consuela in her chamber. If you dare."

"I won't dignify that with an answer, Simon Raven-bill. Really, if I had known you'd—that you don't—that is… Oh, stop grinning! Besides, we have a wager to consider, if you'll recall. Since I fully intend to win, I would say you can consider yourself safe."

"And as I fully intend to win, I'll leave the invitation open." Simon looked out over the massive carpet of fields making up the West Run. "You lead, Kate. I'll follow."

"You don't wish to race? You know you'd win."

Simon stood slightly in the stirrups, then gingerly lowered himself once more. Win? He was still lamenting having forgone snatching up a pillow from his bed and tying it to the saddle. Why he didn't simply tell Kate he felt less inclined to indulge in a refreshing gallop than he did the prospect of climbing the steps to the gallows, he couldn't say.

It must be true, what one of his friends had told him: *Never allow your heart to become involved, it causes your brains to leak out from your ears.* Of course, that friend, Lieutenant Davey Filbert, had been bracketed to his Lucinda these past five years, and already had three infants in the nursery—one for every time their ship had docked in London.

Simon realized Kate had her head cocked to one side, and was looking at him curiously. "You're hungry, aren't you? Val's worth less than nothing before he's eaten. I should have waited until you'd time to break your fast. I'm sorry. I get an idea into my head, and just naturally believe everyone else will see the brilliance of it and—should we ride back to the Manor and get you fed a proper breakfast?"

The nearly silent *drip-drip* Simon imagined he could hear was undoubtedly a bit of his brains leaking from his ears. "No, don't be ridiculous. I'm fine, Kate. Hector's anxious for a run in any event. You lead the way and I'll follow." *He probably shouldn't have added that last little bit; not only would it give her ideas, but it was probably superfluous in any event.*

Her route involved hedgerows that needed to be cleared, three fences that must be jumped and some increasingly rough terrain as they neared the coast and the waters of the Straits of Dover could be seen in front of them, the spires of Hythe vaguely visible in the distance to their left. By the time she held up her hand and pointed to a stand of trees, Simon, if he'd been a lesser man, would have been whimpering.

But he'd proved his point, whatever his point had been—even if he wasn't quite sure there was one. Kate would have gone without him and attempted only God knew what at the cottages. That was one reason. Two, he would never let her believe a simple tumble into a pit was enough to have him take to his bed and...well, hell, Kate would have gone without him. That had to be reason enough; anything else would only serve to make him sound ridiculous.

He helped her dismount, ignoring the way she seemed to be purposely allowing her body to slide against his as he lowered her to the ground. The little devil; she was trying to make him lose their wager. And she'd picked a reasonable tactic for her first assault on him; the two of them, alone together, a picnic beneath a spreading tree...his never-strong resolve to keep his hands off her.

He untied the basket from Daisy's saddle, and assisted in spreading the blue-and-white-checkered cloth beneath one of the trees. He dropped to his knees, depositing the basket...and then he simply gave up and stretched out on the cloth, resting his head against his propped-up arm. It would take pistol fire to get him up again, at least for the next hour.

"Feed me, woman," he said, attempting an arch smile.

Which got him nowhere.

"Oh, no, you can't relax yet," she told him, opening the basket and removing a dusty bottle of wine. "See? I think it's a good one because I took it from Gideon's special side of the wine cellar, the side reserved for his most important guests and birthdays and such. But I don't want to uncork it incorrectly, because people can do that, can't they?"

All right, so she'd piqued his interest, especially if Gideon's choice in wines was even half as astute as it was in cigars. He managed to push himself into a sitting position. Other than to pour the bottle's contents onto his backside, having some of the wine inside him could go a long way toward easing his many aches and pains. "While you were pilfering, did you manage to remember to secure a corkscrew?"

Grinning, she reached into the pocket of her riding skirt and pulled out a familiar-looking silver corkscrew. "It's Dearborn's own. He wasn't using it."

"Since it's probably not even gone nine yet, no, I suppose he wasn't. You're very much a proponent of the 'may as well be a sheep as a lamb' school of thievery, aren't you?"

Kate shrugged. "I thought you deserved the best, considering the fact your valet told me you're a mass of bumps and bruises. Not that you'd ever admit it. Max once hid a broken elbow from Trixie for more than a week, just so she'd leave for London as promised, and we could be on our own at the Manor—we'd planned a sort of jousting tournament, you understand,

and Trixie wouldn't have approved of my participation. Max didn't so much as wear a sling until she left. Did it ever occur to you, Simon, that you males can be idiots? No, don't answer that. But you could tell me why you allowed me to coax you onto a horse, yet alone a gallop across country."

"I'm in charge of you now Val's gone, and Lord knows you can't be trusted searching out supposed smugglers' caves without being held on a stout leash as you go about it?" he offered, using his chosen answer, and then pretended to wince as she all but shoved the wine bottle at him.

"Meaning I would have gone, anyway, by myself." She handed him the corkscrew. "All right, I'll give you that one. But why didn't you attempt to talk me out of it?"

"Because although I may have hit the rest of my body against every rock and board—and bone— in that pit, I managed not to bang my head. The only thing that could possibly make you more determined to go would be for me to attempt to make you stay. Hmm," he said, looking at the markings on the bottle, "does your brother maintain a strict inventory of his bottles? Because if he does, I've never seen this one before in my life, and will swear to that on my mother's grave."

"It's that good?" Kate asked eagerly, leaning toward him.

The cork slipped from the bottle, and Simon took an appreciative sniff of its contents. "Let's just say, here's to sheep. You brought glasses, of course."

Kate's eyes shifted to the basket. "Uh, I brought bread and cheese. And ham. And apples."

"But no glasses, correct? In that case, kindly close your eyes, Kate. I'm about to commit an unforgivable sacrilege." With that, he raised the bottle clearly marked with the year 1720 to his lips and took three healthy swallows of double-aged Madeira.

"Your smile looks positively evil. Here, let me taste it." Kate grabbed the bottle from him, and before he could warn her, she'd taken more than a sip.

"Now that's just a bleeding pity," Simon lamented as Kate almost immediately spit out the Madeira in a spray of what some would call liquid gold. The expression on her beautiful face was priceless, and he wondered what she'd do if he were to offer to lick her mouth clear of any remaining wine. She'd probably clunk him on the head with the bottle and, worse, spill the contents; no, he should probably resist. "Then again, it leaves more for me. I believe I can already feel my aches and pains flying to the four winds."

"I'm delighted for you," Kate answered meanly, pulling out her handkerchief and blotting at the droplets of Madeira glistening like raindrops on the fall of lace she had pinned around her throat. "How can you drink anything so vile?"

"Madeira can be an acquired taste. Happily for me, during my travels with the Royal Navy, I acquired it. Have an apple. Clearly something that's only recently left the tree is more suited to your uneducated palate."

"I'd need a palate accustomed to pig swill, so I'm happy to leave it uneducated, thank you." But she did as he suggested, probably only because she really needed something to take the taste of Madeira from her tongue, and spoke next around a healthy bite of apple as she pointed toward Hythe. "Which of those churches are you going to pick, Simon?"

She was at it again, like a filly with the bit firmly in her teeth. "For our wedding? I've thought more about the chapel at the Manor, frankly. It will, after all, most likely be a case of marry in haste."

The half-eaten apple winged past his head and he neatly snagged it out of the air.

"I meant for your rendition of 'God Save The King,' you numbskull. There's never been a wager whose outcome is so assured. Or haven't you yet realized how unremittingly *annoying* you are?"

He was feeling better and better. So thinking, he committed a second sacrilege, and took another long drink of the Madeira. "Actually, I'm rather counting on that. Do you dream about me, Kate? I know you *annoy* my dreams."

She closed the basket with a slam of the lid and got to her feet. "We're done here," she announced, and then began tugging at one corner of the checkered cloth, as if she could roll him off it. "Don't think I don't know what's going on, Simon. You'd already promised Valentine you'd be my chaperone, or keeper, or whatever you two conspirators decided before you came to the greenhouse yesterday. That's why you made the wager, so I'd stay clear of you and you could keep your promise to Val. Admit it, Simon. I could all but throw myself at you, begging you to ravish me, and you wouldn't do it."

He got to his feet. "I don't know if I'd go quite that far with that sort of reasoning were I you," he said, grinning at her before lifting the bottle to his mouth once more.

Up went her chin. He loved when she did that. "Ah, a warning. Then perhaps that's just what I'll do. Because I won't marry you, Simon, for more reasons than I can count, although one of them has to be that you don't want to marry me, you only wish to…um…to *annoy* me. Besides, I already wagered five pounds with Mrs.

Justis that his lordship the Marquis will be singing from a church steeple within a week. So you have to lose."

He helped her fold the cloth. It was amazing how well they worked together, how splendidly they got along—as long as they were sparring with each other, that is. "Much as I hesitate to point this out, our wager included a limit. If neither of us loses within a week, the wager in null and void and you lose five pounds to your housekeeper, anyway. Only five pounds? That's almost insulting, now that I think of it. And all, I hesitate to remind you, supposing you can hold out that long, which I don't think you can."

"Oh, but you can, is that right? You're wrong, Simon, you did hit your head in that pit, if you believe you're so irresistible. I wouldn't have you served up on a silver platter!"

"Not even with an apple in my mouth?" he asked her, and then promptly produced the apple she'd tossed at him and clamped it between his teeth.

"You're impossible. You're the most impossible man I've ever—" She very nearly smiled. "Oh, give me that, you fool, you look ridiculous. And don't drink any more of that horrid wine. You're already too silly by half."

"Too late," he told her, holding up the empty bottle. He wouldn't admit she was right, but he probably should have broken his fast with some bread and cheese; at least the bread may have sopped up some of the surprisingly potent wine. He was feeling decidedly happy with himself at the moment, not at all marquislike, if that was an expression. He felt much more like the man he'd been before Holbrook died; young, even carefree. Not bosky; it would take more than one bottle of vintage Madeira to drop him entirely into his cups, but he would have to say he felt fairly well-to-go, especially with his aches and pains at least temporarily a memory.

And then there was Kate. He always felt better, more relaxed and natural, when he was around her. Even when she was tossing verbal darts at him. They simply couldn't seem to hide their real selves from each other, and he knew that ease and freedom amazed him, and just might amaze her, as well. "Do you think we should dispose of the evidence in the Channel?"

Kate had led Daisy to a nearby tree stump and was already up in the saddle. "I can think of something else I might want to dispose of in the Channel, if you'd be so kind as to load your pockets with rocks," she said. She then turned Daisy in the direction of the staggered line of cottages below them, leaving Simon where he stood, but not before he heard her mutter, "And they say we Redgraves are unromantic. Ha!"

So he'd been correct. This supposed early morning picnic was the opening salvo in her war to entice him to kiss her, and thus lose their wager. God only knew what she'd think up next.

Six more days and the wager would be null and void. Only six more days, or even less, and at least one of the Redgraves would have shown up at the Manor to save him. All he had to do was keep Kate busy and resist her charms—not to mention her plans and her wiles—for six more days.

How did that third verse go? Because he'd never make it.

CHAPTER TEN

ONCE THEY'D REACHED the half-moon-shaped shoreline, rather as if they'd arrived at the smaller end of a large, downhill funnel, Kate allowed Simon to help her from the saddle once more. This time she didn't bother with any pretense at innocently rubbing their bodies together. She'd been clumsy, amateurish; Trixie would have rolled her eyes at such a lamentably blatant effort at seduction.

That it hadn't worked was rather a letdown, though. Was she really that resistible? He hadn't seemed to think so the other day.

Not that she wished to seduce Simon. Far from it! Just a kiss. That's all she needed, and he'd be warbling from Saint Leonard's bell tower come Sunday. Which would serve to pay him back very nicely for all the trouble he was causing her; she could barely boost thoughts of him out of her head for more than a few minutes at a time. But clearly she needed a change in tactics, especially now she'd allowed him to see through her to the point where he knew what she was doing.

Brothers were easier to hoodwink, they really were. Of course, she'd never practiced her seduction techniques on them. For one thing, she guessed she really didn't possess any; she could shoot a pistol with much more finesse than she could flutter a fan beneath come-hither eyes (or would want to!). And for another— Well, who'd ever want to seduce one of her brothers? Jessica seemed happy enough with Gideon, but Kate figured she'd have to wait a long time before Valentine did more than flirt with any available woman under the age of forty who still possessed all her teeth. And Max? He didn't seem to much care for the species at all.

She did feel with Simon rather as she did with her brothers, though. She felt she could say anything to him. He seemed to laugh at the same things she laughed at…even if he occasionally laughed at her. She didn't have to sit ramrod straight, or always be in some frilly gown, pretending she was fragile. He loved adventure as much as she did, and didn't cavil at letting her come along with him as he went seeking it.

Yes, he could be one of her brothers. Except that he wasn't, and she was much too aware of that. Because Gideon and Val and Max were, well, they were Gideon and Val and Max. Simon? Simon was a whole new world to her. Dare she say a world of sensation? No, she shouldn't! But he was. Like when she was tempted to push his thick blond hair back from his forehead, and stare into his clear eyes, see herself reflected there….

Kate shook away her thoughts, knowing they were dangerous, and concentrated on her surroundings. They'd been wasting valuable time. It was more than time to get back to work!

The breeze coming in off the water, combined with the glitter of sunlight bouncing back at them from the many-paned windows of the cottages, made it difficult for Kate to believe anything nefarious ever went on along this wide stretch of peaceful, fairly isolated shingle-and-sand beach. Of course, Gideon had warned her never to ride down here, but Simon didn't have to know that, now did he?

There were boats pulled up onto the shingle, but they were loaded with fishing nets; clearly nothing out of the ordinary. The tenant cottages, she'd counted seven in all, were spaced widely apart, with small vegetable gardens surrounding them, some of those gardens in better condition than the others. There was a woman standing in the middle of one of the low-fenced plots, nearly bent in half as she weeded, or thinned, or pinched beetles, or whatever it was old women did in gardens.

"Tell me something isn't odd here," Simon said quietly, probably because who could know where the breeze could take his words.

She looked at him, puzzled by his remark, and then surveyed the scene in front of her once more. "I don't see anything odd. What do you see?"

"Let's walk," he said, turning in the general direction of Hythe. "I see seven cottages. I see four with nicely tended gardens and three nearly going to seed. This makes me believe there are women in four of the cottages."

"Because women tend gardens," Kate said, nodding. "Go on."

"Women also plant posies. They can't seem to help themselves. Those same four cottages have flowers growing in between the cabbages."

Kate sneaked a look back at the cottages. "All right. So you're wondering who, if anyone, lives in the other three cottages?"

"Not yet, no. I'm wondering where the other women are, although I know the one in the second cottage from the left dared push back the curtains to peek at us. I'm also wondering why the one woman who was already out in her garden has not so much as glanced in our direction. Think about it for a moment, Kate. How often could something like this possibly happen here? Two strangers, showing up on their doorsteps as if out of the blue. Riding fine mounts, dressed in finer clothes, the young woman beautiful—"

Kate dropped an insouciant curtsy. "Thank you, kind sir."

"You're welcome. The gentleman devilishly handsome, stylishly groomed and obviously of impeccable breeding—"

"You can never leave well enough alone, can you?" Kate said, giving him a quick jab in the side. "But you've made your point, Simon. We're being watched, but ignored at the same time. Well, I can certainly fix that."

"Kate, wait— Oh, hell."

With Simon quickly catching up to her, Kate headed directly for the woman just now straightening up, one hand pressed to the small of her back to ease the strain caused by her work…which was interesting, for there was not sprig nor turnip in the basket hanging from her arm.

"Good morning, madam," Kate called out cheerfully, stopping just outside the low, weathered fence. "I'm Lady Katherine Redgrave, sister of the earl, and this—as he has just assured me—impeccably bred gentleman with me is the Marquis of Singleton. And who might you be?"

The woman nervously shifted her eyes from side to side, as if attempting to locate that information. "Um, I be Maude, my lady," she offered even as she bobbed a curtsy, turned to Simon and bobbed another.

"Well, then, Maude," Kate persisted cheerily, "now that we all know each other, do you think you could find it in your heart to offer his lordship and me something to drink and a bit of shade inside your cottage on such a warm day?"

"Yer wants to go inside?" Maude asked this in approximately the same terrified tone she might have employed if Kate had asked her to kindly deposit her graying head in the basket hanging from her arm. "Ah, yer ladyship, yer lordship, it's an embarrassment ta tell yer this, but m'man's that poorly, and layin' straight in the middle of the place on a cot, seeking warmth from the fire, yer understands."

Kate glanced up to the stone chimney; there was no smoke. "Oh, the poor man. Perhaps I should send someone from the Manor to fetch a doctor for him? My brother is adamant that we Redgraves take care of our tenants."

The woman looked about to cry.

The front door of the cottage opened at that point, and the hulking body of a very large man filled the entry. "Ben's asking for you, Sissy. You haul yourself inside now."

Maude, or Sissy, bobbed another duet of curtsies and all but ran up the few flat stones to the cottage door, disappearing inside as the man stepped out, moving halfway down the path in a sort of rolling gait before coming to a halt. He was dressed plainly but well, his brown jacket reaching to his knees, bone buttons the size of small dinner plates marching down the front of the garment in two straight lines.

"Good day to you, my fine lady and gentleman," he said, his grin wide in his large head, his smiling eyes as open and guileless as a child's. "Or should I say, my lady, my lord. I was doing a bit of overhearing, I admit, seeing as how Sissy's dumb as a stump, sister or not. Never learned her way around a proper fib, though Lord knows she keeps trying. There's no fire in the grate, and no man anywhere but in her dreams. It's a poor house-keeper she is, but she wouldn't admit that to you, now would she? My name's Jacko. How might I help you?"

The man sounded polite enough, but he didn't bow, didn't touch his forelock like some of the tenants still did. His words and actions seemed to say *I'm not your equal, perhaps, but you're standing in my territory, and I'll behave as I behave.* He was a living wall. If he didn't want them inside the cottage, Kate decided, then they would not cross the threshold without a battalion of troops and a battering ram.

"Her ladyship was hoping for the courtesy of some refreshment," Simon said as Kate fought the urge to take a few precautionary steps backward…and then position herself behind him. She really needed to consider the possible consequences of her actions *before* she acted.

"Well, now," Jacko said, his jovial face belying the sorrow in his voice, "that's a sad thing, my lord, seeing as how Sissy isn't much one for tea and dainty cakes, her having fallen off the water wagon again, and with a mighty thump. But if it's a nip of spirits you're after…?"

"No!" Kate said, quickly amending that to, "no, thank you, anyway. Perhaps we can knock on another door."

"Perhaps that wouldn't be a good idea, little girl, see-ing as how you're neither of you none too bright being here at all, if you take my meaning," Jacko said, hitch-ing up his trousers, although there was little fat to shift; he appeared to be hard from large bearded head to top boots, except for that too-friendly smile. "Ah, now that was rude, wasn't it? It's only I'm that ashamed, you un-derstand, and wish myself home so that I didn't have to apologize for Sissy. She's a good woman, but not without her vices. Why, she wouldn't hardly eat at all, if it weren't for me bringing her food. Demon gin," he ended, shaking his head. "Good-day to you now, begging your indulgence yet again."

"Never quite lose the walk, Jacko, do we? You're a seaman. And one without much use for landlubbers."

Kate looked at Simon, wishing he could read her mind. For if he could, he would hear her screaming: *Let's go! He's only being nice because it's less trouble to him than finding a place to hide our bodies!*

"I was," Jacko responded, looking Simon up and down. "You've got the look of a man who's felt a quarterdeck rolling beneath his boots yourself. There's that squint we all sport, spending our days and nights searching the horizon. Here now, does that make us mates?"

"I don't know, Jacko, but I'm certain I'll find out, one way or another. Where's home to you, if it's not here with your *sister?*"

The large man walked straight up to the fence, his voice dropped to a rough whisper that was no less menacing than his joviality. "And what's that to you, my lord?"

Simon spread his long legs just a bit more, and locked his hands together behind his back. "Why, sailor, I imagine it's whatever I want it to be," he responded coolly, and equally as quietly. "At the moment, it's a friendly question, with Lady Katherine here. But it doesn't have to remain that. Would you care to meet again later, once I've escorted her home?"

"No need. I see where you're heading." The man smiled again, shrugging his immense shoulders. "You'd whisper in the earl's ear and have my sister tossed from the cottage. Just like the rich, striking at those who can't help themselves."

"Said like a man who'd look to someone like Bonaparte with admiration."

Jacko stepped over the low fence, and Kate nearly yelped. "Said like a man looking to wear his nose on the back of his head. But very well, your lordship, sir, now that we understand each other. I'm from down Romney Marsh way, and more than that you need not know. I earn my keep working for a loyal Englishman who'd eat your namby-pamby sort for breakfast, a man happy to be left in peace, but not blind to what goes on around him, if you take my meaning again. Don't ask me anything else, *mate,* because I won't answer."

"I think you've answered sufficiently. But do remember the name, if you please. Simon Ravenbill, marquis of Singleton, formerly commander in his majesty's Royal Navy. Currently I'm the guest of the Earl of Saltwood, all of us loyal, peace-loving Englishmen set on protecting these shores, all of us also not blind to what goes on around us. Can you retain all of that long enough to repeat it to your employer, Jacko, hmm? You know, the man who put Sissy here, the man who sends you to *visit?* Because we will meet again, you and I. I can feel it in my bones. Am I right to be hopeful about which side of the fence you'll be standing on when the moon dies?"

Show-off, show-off, show-off! You're worse than me! And I don't even know what the devil you're talking about! Kate tugged at Simon's sleeve. "If you two gentlemen are done crowing and scratching like cocks in the barnyard, I'd like to go home now, please."

"Of course," Simon said, holding out his arm to Kate. Raising his voice, probably for the benefit of anyone in the cottages who wouldn't otherwise hear him, he said, "Good-day to you, Jacko, and your lovely sister. Thank you so much for the directions. We were quite lost." Together, he and Kate walked back to where they'd tied their mounts' reins to a bramble bush.

But Jacko had followed after them.

"You beat the Dutch for brass, don't you, Commander? But I'm no fool, I see where you're sailing to, and at just the wrong time. I'll tell him," Jacko told him grudgingly. "Watch the moon, Simon Ravenbill, if you must, but then stay out of our way. We wouldn't want to hurt a hair on that clever head of yours by mistake, now would we?"

Only then did he finally bow—just a slight inclination of his head—and walk away.

Kate's hands were shaking as Simon lifted her up onto the saddle in one efficient move, and then lightly seated himself on Hector's back.

"Slowly, Kate. We'll leave the beach slowly. We were very lucky, it could have gone either way back there. The man could have broken me in two without any real effort, not that I could let him know I knew that, although I'm guessing he favors the sticker he has tucked in the sash beneath his coat."

"He had a knife? I didn't see a knife."

"You weren't supposed to, Kate. I was. The walk, the sash, the sticker, they told me all I needed to know. That said, the next time I'm so dimwitted as to ride out without a pistol in my possession, you may feel free to kick my shins purple."

"It doesn't matter. It would take a cannon to put a large enough hole in that man," she told him, doing her best not to look back toward the shoreline. Not that she feared being transformed into a pillar of salt, but because she didn't want to see Jacko's smile again. "What on earth were you thinking, Simon? You all but accused him of being a Bonaparte sympathizer and, as naturally follows, a smuggler working with France. Thank God he wasn't— I mean, he wasn't, was he? Either way, I'm not quite certain what a water wagon is, but I think you might want to climb onto one."

"Nonsense, Kate. You should be congratulating yourself on a brilliant stroke of inspiration, coming here today. We just made a friend, hopefully an ally."

Kate tried to speak, but was too flustered to say more than, "A friend? You swore you didn't hit your head yesterday!"

"Jacko and I understand each other. Now, tell me what you saw."

There were ways to kill this man, there had to be. Because he was driving her insane!

"I saw seven cottages. I've seen them before because they've been there for as long as I can remember. Gideon leases them to fishermen, I'm fairly certain of that, or at least to people who want to live there for whatever reason they— Stop smiling! I know I'm saying smugglers could be living in those cottages. They certainly have before. Nearly everyone along the coast either smuggles or in some way assists the smugglers. Everyone knows that."

"So everyone knows everything, but nobody speaks of any of it. That's almost poetic. Anything else?"

"Anything else," Kate mused as they walked their horses along a path leading back up to the very bottom of the West Run. She rather liked being tested this way; it was as if he valued her insights. "Yes. We were being ignored by the residents, which was clear enough. Even as we were being watched. Maude, the poor woman, was the only one out-of-doors and caught unawares when we arrived, or we wouldn't have seen her, or Jacko, for that matter. Which, by the way, would have suited me to a cow's thumb. The man makes my skin crawl."

"He's no smuggler, Kate. There's a lot of things he is and was, I'm sure of that, and we're probably safer not knowing, but he was here today for the same reason we were. If I had to hazard a guess, I'd say the Society has been careless. As you said, everyone knows everything, and tells nothing. But word will travel irregardless, in certain circles. I'd like to meet his employer, he could be of help to us."

"You must be joking. He's bound to be even worse than Jacko, and that man would slit your throat as much as smile at you. Wouldn't he?"

"I don't think it would trouble him much, no. But only because a namby-pamby like me might get in his way as he goes about his business. Are you worried about me, Kate?"

"Naturally I'm worried—but not about you. It's just that I'd have to explain to Valentine and Gideon why you ended up stuffed headfirst down a well when we were supposed to be hunting the journals, not smugglers."

"I'll leave them a note absolving you," Simon said maddeningly. "Now, you observed nothing else? Really, Kate, you disappoint me."

She sighed in exasperation. "I wasn't finished. The beach is a mix of sand and shingle, except where the shingle appears to be more concentrated and somehow extended all the way up to the rear of the last cottage, I mean on the side that seems to end at the rocks, not the hill that borders the other side. It seems natural enough,

I suppose, unless you're really looking. I imagine it would be easier to unload boats onto the shingle rather than to have the landsmen—they're called landsmen—have to slip and slide on wet sand and loose rocks."

"And?" he prompted, making her long to choke him.

"And there's precious little place for a tunnel, which could only go so far in any event because it eventually would have had to be dug uphill, and nobody digs a tunnel uphill because it would be too difficult to move the goods uphill. Plus, to dig so deep as to keep the floor flat? Not around here, because the ground is too soft to have so much of it overhead, or at least that's what I've been told— And we saw what happened in the greenhouse," she said, hating to admit that part of the thing. Discovering a tunnel would have been quite a feather in her cap.

"Very good. Keep going. *And?*"

She cudgeled her brain for something else to say. "And the cottages, all of them, sit too near the shore to consider them having cellars where contraband or people or whatever could be hidden until the landsmen could move everything inland. They may sometimes land a few boats here, but the sort of landing, the scope of it we've been thinking of, would have to be somewhere else. The area simply isn't right." She looked over at him, wincing as she repeated the word: "Right?"

"And?"

Now she was really angry. "There is no more *and.* There can't be. Dare to send over a hundred men and pack animals up this hill and across the West Run, and it wouldn't be long before you were discovered and taken to Dover to be measured for your hanging chains. Head toward Hythe, tunneling beneath the hill, and there's too much civilization about. More and more cottages, and then the straggling beginnings of the town. Head the other way, and there's all that rock. Rocks. Because they're all just loose rocks and boulders piled on top of each other, everywhere. It's as if every rock and stone and pebble found on the West Run, thousands and thousands of them, was lugged or dragged to the top of the funnel, and then allowed to roll down to the shore. For all we know, the Romans did it, or the gods."

"You see the layout of this land as a funnel? The *gods?* And you say you aren't romantical."

Kate shot him a look that would have felled a lesser man.

"We'll continue," he said jovially, clearly pleased with himself and his grand idea, whatever that was. "You forgot to mention the considerable number of cleared trees, or at least their stumps, although they're long rotted and gone. I think we could call that seeming outcropping nothing more than a large, some would say immense, sort of stone midden. A dumping ground. To the unobservant eye, that is."

"Meaning mine? You're right, I don't see the point of all of this," she admitted reluctantly.

"Then aren't you lucky I'm here, to show off my brilliance," he answered with a wink, again proving he was impervious to her most threatening stares.

"You'll pay for that, Simon Ravenbill. I don't know when, I don't know how, but then again, neither do you. Think about that."

They'd made it back to the tree on the hill, and without further comment Simon suggested they stop for a while before continuing on to the Manor.

"We've nothing to drink," she reminded him as he helped her dismount and lifted the lid of the basket.

"That's all right." He foraged inside for two apples. "Want one?"

"I suppose so," she said wearily, and then had to quickly catch the thing when he tossed it to her. "No end the gentleman, aren't you, *Commander?*" she asked, rubbing the apple on her sleeve.

"So I've been accused, yes. Now, tell me what you see when you look back down toward the coastline. On shore, Kate."

"Will you ever be done being cryptic? I'm weary of answering your questions. Clearly there's nothing to see except the roofs and chimneys of the cottages, the hill running down to our left, your so-called *middens* on the right."

"Correct. And, standing down on the beach, looking up here, all that could really be seen, as far as I could calculate when I was very slyly and surreptitiously checking—and making certain Jacko could see me slyly and surreptitiously checking—would be the very tops of these trees. Which means it's safe to leave the horses here and go see the full extent of the midden from the top down, as I don't think Jacko is the climbing sort."

"You're being annoying—again. Are you going to tell me why, or merely quiz me on what we find? Because, obviously, what's on the other side of the midden, as you call it, *is* the other side of the midden."

Simon tied up the horses and took her hand. "You'll forgive me if I still want to see for myself. You saw the way the shingle seems to be more prevalent there, correct? But what if, rather than leading to the last cottage and some cellar or small cave, it led to the rocks?"

"Sideways along the coastline?" Kate held on to Simon's coattails as they carefully made their way parallel to the shore for some minutes. The scenery never changed. There were loose rocks here and there, entirely too many prickly windblown bushes and a few stunted trees with most of their growth on one side. Ahead of and behind them; all around them. The area was less than hospitable, and no one would ever think to go strolling here unless some wandering sheep got itself stuck in the brambles or they were Simon Ravenbill, whose brilliance she was seriously beginning to reconsider.

Below them was a river of boulders; small ones, larger ones, many of them piled on top of each other, everywhere she looked. "Why would anyone dig a cave or tunnel sideways along the shore?"

And then Simon stopped, pulling her down with him behind a rotting tree trunk. He pointed to something in the distance, nearly at the shoreline. "Jacko," she whispered, her heart pounding as she watched the man climb onto the seat of a small cart.

Simon nodded. "It would seem our sailor, like many others long committed to the sea, isn't fond of riding. Rather than risk losing a wheel driving the rig around the outcropping of rocks, he very logically leaves it on this side, and reaches the cottage via the narrow beach. It certainly gives him a good explanation for why he's so free to move about the area, although I'm sure he's already raised some suspicion. Clever. Damn, I wish I had my glass. Now carefully watch where he's going, and how."

Wasn't it strange, Kate thought, looking down this side of the hill, to the seeming unending field of rocks. She was looking down on a giant's playground, her romantical side told her. They certainly made a mess with their toys, her more pragmatic side whispered in her ear.

Was this still Redgrave property? She imagined so. Yet it wasn't at all welcoming. It had no beach at all, no safe landing place for boats. It was rocks to the shoreline; rocks, rocks, rocks. Where did Jacko think he was going? There was no way a cart and horse could thread through the jumble of rocks.

"Wait a moment, this is interesting," she whispered. She was surprised to suddenly realize a narrow track threaded through the maze of boulders, the twisting, turning route Jacko was now traveling. "All right," she said after Jacko and his cart had disappeared beyond another out-of-place small mountain of rocks and stone. At some point the track undoubtedly joined with another one, and then another, as he headed toward Dymchurch and Romney Marsh. "It's your turn. What do you see?"

"If I wasn't searching out anything in particular? I see, as I'm convinced you do, as well, a stretch of shoreline not suitable for landing boats. We saw the track leading toward Hythe, thanks to a more forgiving coastline beyond the hill in that direction. But I would imagine most would think the few cottages in the cove were the end of the line for a while. At least as far as constructing cottages in the area, or smuggling, when it seems much more logical to unload closer to Hythe, or sail on to Romney Marsh and land the boats there. Yet it's all right here, under our noses, as Jacko has just so politely pointed out to us. The strange thing, Kate, is I never would have looked, never felt the least suspicion, if it weren't for Jacko being here today. I wonder how he and his employer found it."

"Found what? Are you saying someone dug a tunnel through all those rocks?"

"Not precisely. I'm saying some someones, obviously more than a few stout someones, *built* it. Hundreds of the boulders were probably already there, but they've had help in being piled that high. I'd hazard the barrier conceals thirty to forty feet of tunnel, or even some sort of crude lodging for patrols and the like. This area didn't have its start as a midden, Kate. It was a sort of seaside fort, a crude, early version of a battlement. Brilliant in its day, too, but long abandoned. The tunnel, barracks, whatever, would also open onto the maze constructed out of all those rocks and boulders. Defensive, for the Romans. Since then, perfectly set up for smugglers. The largest haul could be stored there until the following night, then transported inland. If the water guard is in pursuit, sow the crop, sacrifice the boats and the tunnel is their escape hatch to the maze."

"Sow the crop, as in tie the kegs together and lower them into the water and retrieve them later? And here I was, politely explaining smuggling terms to you. You could have told me."

"I enjoyed the lessons. But I somehow doubt this area is known for what it was to many people at all. In fact, it may be known only to the Society, used only by the Society."

Kate had to agree. "Because it's only from up here, ruining our clothing with burrs and in danger of sliding down this near cliff, looking down at the beach, that we can see a pattern to it all."

"Again, thanks to our new friend. Very, very clever, and if I'm right, more than a thousand years old. A lot can happen in a thousand years, Kate. The entire shoreline may have changed shape. What we're seeing today may have been another half mile inland back then, for all we know. What was once a raw structure was worn by time and wind and storms until it became seamless with the landscape, and to the casual eye, useless. I'm going down there. But first I'm taking you home."

She was still looking down at the so-called maze, mentally retracing Jacko's path through the boulders. Had Roman soldiers, with their gleaming breastplates and metal helmets, once marched along the same route? Had there been campfires down there, possibly a few stone buildings long since destroyed? The man-made tunnel perhaps employed as a stable for their horses in inclement weather, or used to store grain and firewood? Yes. Yes, she could see it. Well, mostly.

Belatedly, her mind translated Simon's last words to her. "Home? You are not!"

"Kate, don't fight me on this, because you won't win."

She tore her gaze away from the maze, hoping she'd committed it to memory, and looked at Simon. Oh, dear. She knew that look, had seen it on Gideon's face more than a time or two. He was right, she wasn't going to win. Not this round at least.

"You know this is killing me inside, don't you?"

His smile was actually sympathetic. "I do, thank you."

"You'll bring pistols back with you? And Liam."

"I can trust him? You trust him?"

She nodded. "His family has been at the Manor forever and ever. I'd only get in your way because you'd feel some silly responsibility toward me and perhaps not be as careful with yourself because of that."

"You've heard that lecture before?" Simon asked.

"Obviously." She looked at him for a long moment,

her hands going into fists at her sides so she wouldn't be tempted to reach out, touch him, before turning away. "You'll be in a hurry to be shed of me and go exploring. I imagine the horses are ready for another gallop."

CHAPTER ELEVEN

"Ahhhh." Simon lay back in the warm tub, resting his head on the rolled towel his valet had provided for him, and then waved the man out of the room, telling him he could take it from here. He didn't mind someone else lugging water buckets and preparing his bath, laying out fresh clothing, but he'd be damned if someone else was going to wash him.

His aches still ached, his pains still pained him, but the day's discoveries went a long way toward easing both:

1720 double-aged Madeira should be sipped, not gulped.

He rather liked his brains dripping out from his ears; Davey had never mentioned that part.

More than a year now separating him from his time in the Royal Navy, he was still alert on all suits, still at ease in a position of command…and still loon enough to deliberately agitate an armed man twice his size and believe his sense of presence adequate protection.

And he'd discovered the Society's ingenious smuggling route. That should be the topper, and it nearly was, although narrowly beaten out by the dripping brains thing. Possibly more than narrowly.

Definitely more than narrowly.

He'd decided against going anywhere near the cottages, to hunt for the opening to the tunnel from that side, and didn't waste time looking for its exit on the other side of the man-made boulder land-jetty, as he'd begun calling it in his head. Instead, he'd concentrated on the maze itself.

Some of the boulders were too large for anyone but the gods or an army of unfortunate captives to move from where they'd landed; some were haphazardly, it seemed, stacked atop each other, with flatter rocks employed to keep them from tumbling down again.

If he stood at the water's edge, all he saw were boulders; with no pattern, no reason to believe they were anything more than they were. After all, even if the land-jetty did possess a tunnel, all it did was go from one side of it to the other, so what was the point of it?

Liam had been reluctant to climb down with him. Ghosts, his grandfather had told him. Ghosts of long-ago soldiers who died in a fierce battle "right on this very spot, m'lord. Nobody comes here. Yer can hear the screams in the night, the swords banging. Makes your skin creep, that's what it does."

A story like that would help keep the curious away, Simon had decided, and left a grateful Liam up on the hill.

Although he'd felt he'd fairly well memorized the layout of the maze, once he was on the beach he found navigating his way through wouldn't be that easy, and if it weren't for Jacko's wheel tracks, he'd have just wandered aimlessly until he came to a spot where the boulders, most of them reaching a good three or four feet above his head, made further progress impossible.

He could see places where the "walls" had been patched or rebuilt. There were boulders so high they nearly blocked the sun, and a few open spaces along the way to make wrong turns possible, just enough to hide any hint in daylight that there was really a twisted but navigable maze here, visible in the day, unfathomable on a moonless night, if anyone was even clever enough to look.

And, from the look of it, only accessible by land in low tide. He could clearly see the marks on the stones, showing how far the water would reach at high tide. That alone proved his theory that the shoreline had greatly changed since the Romans landed. The beach on the other side hadn't been similarly affected; even at high tide the water wouldn't reach any closer than fifty yards below the cottages. This side? This side would be a death trap if you couldn't make it to the end of the maze in time, or climb up the cliff he'd just climbed down.

How old was this cove? How long had the stones been here? Soldiers could hide here, loose arrows at galleys rowing close to the shoreline, and then disappear among the boulders. Enemies could be lured into the tunnel, and then dispatched easily as they stumbled about to be slaughtered on the maze side of the beach when they emerged. Conversely, soldiers could use the maze and tunnel to spring surprise attacks on the beach side, where the cottages now stood. After all, England in those years was a very large and wild place, overgrown with trees, and settlements were mostly along the shores. What had it served to protect? Lympne Castle, perhaps, in any of its many incarnations, from the time of the Danes, the Normans, the Romans?

Other than satisfying his own curiosity, and fascinating as any history of the place would be, more important, he was certain the maze also concealed a route to—where? His investigation had answered half that question, again, thanks to Jacko. He'd enjoy telling Kate of his discovery.

"Do you always smile in the tub?"

"Kate! For the love of God..."

"Oh, I don't think He has anything to do with this. And don't worry. I learned my lesson this morning. I already knew you were... That you're not— Now you're grinning. That's really rather insufferable of you, you know."

Simon kept quite still, not knowing where she might be standing, and actually not all that eager to find out.

"You don't know where I am, do you?"

"I know where you should be, and that's not here. Where's Senorita Click-Click?"

"There wasn't room enough for her back here, not that she'd approve. Besides, Consuela's taking a nap. She naps every afternoon at this time. Your hair looks darker, wet like that against your forehead. It very nearly curls, doesn't it? That's so adorable. I'm almost tempted to come in there and kiss you."

"Kate, I'm going to kill you," Simon growled. Her voice was coming from somewhere behind him, yet somehow she was seeing his face. Ah, the mirror; she was looking at his reflection. But from where? He sank lower into the tub.

"Which I won't, of course—kiss you, that is. Because of the wager, you understand. So, what did you learn while crawling about on the rocks? Liam didn't seem to know anything."

Simon kept looking up into the mirror hanging above the dressing table. It had been tipped to a rather strange angle. Then again, he'd taken his last tub in his bedchamber, not the dressing room. Why had the tub been moved in here?

What did he see in the mirror? Not what Kate saw, he was certain of that. It all depended on the angle from which the person viewed the mirror. At least he could see the wall behind him reflected in the thing. Aha!

"Don't tell me those are your eyes looking at me from that portrait behind me," he said, trying not to laugh.

"You found me out. Very good, Simon. All the dressing rooms in this wing, reserved for guests, you understand, are similarly *available* for monitoring. Trixie showed me the false corridors, years ago. She never showed the boys, only me. She said someone had to know about them, and decide what to do with them once she's gone. I wonder if she thought Gideon would immediately close them up, and ruin all her fun. And only heaven knows what Valentine or Max would have done."

"Naughty little buggers, your ancestors, pecking at the ladies in their tubs."

"Yes, I suppose so. Trixie used the peepholes a time or two herself, she told me, to peek at the gentlemen. And once, to see two guests sharing a tub, and both were the same sex. She wouldn't tell me which sex or what that meant, but, then, I was only seventeen."

"She shouldn't have told you if you were ninety-two. For an innocent, you're pretty damn corrupt, do you know that?"

"Probably."

He could almost see her shrugging those magnificent creamy shoulders of hers. Yes, Lady Katherine Redgrave was one of a kind. Which was probably a good thing—the world might not be able to survive two of her.

"But I made sure to angle the mirror and tub so that I

can only see your face. *And* I waited until your valet left the room to sneak downstairs and pest Lily, one of our housemaids, so that I was certain you were in the tub. I do have scruples, you see. Just not many of them. So, what did you discover? Surely you found something."

Simon knew he could continue his protest, but there really was no point in it. "I found my way through the maze of rocks, nearly to the end, hesitating only briefly when I chanced to see a freshly bent branch on a bush, courtesy of our friend Jacko. I'm certain it marks a concealed tunnel entrance. Very clever. You'd expect the tunnel, if there were one, to be fifty yards farther along, at the end of the maze."

"Simon, that's wonderful! Where does the tunnel lead?"

He noticed the water beginning to cool. "I wondered how long it would take you to ask that. The answer is, I have no idea. I kept walking to the end of the maze, stood and scratched my head as if cudgeling my brains, shrugged my shoulders, angrily kicked at a small stone and then turned around and headed back. For anyone who might be watching, I believe I was the living picture of confusion and frustration."

"Or an exceedingly bad actor, there is that."

"Oh, really? Let's see, how did it go? Oh, yes. You'll pay for that, Kate Redgrave. I don't know when, I don't know how, but then again, neither do you."

"Aren't you amusing," she grumbled back at him. But, because she was Kate, she then went back to the point that interested her most. "This tunnel you think you found. It could lead anywhere, couldn't it? But it most probably runs beneath the West Run somehow, remaining on Redgrave property."

"Agreed." He smiled again, waiting for her to come

up with any number of wild ideas, all of which she'd insist he assist her in pursuing. He counted inside his head: *Four, three, two—*

"Simon!" The sound of his name was followed by a dull *clunk*. "Ouch! I hit my head on something. That will teach me to get too excited. It's entirely too close inside here, and dusty into the bargain. Still—Simon!"

"Yes, Kate?" he asked, the words rather rolling off his tongue.

"This tunnel could run all the way to join with the tunnel beneath the greenhouse. Or perhaps it's a natural cave, and not a tunnel at all. Oh, my goodness! Think about it. There could be a whole *warren* of caves beneath us. If they've lasted since the Romans were here, they're still useful, yes?"

"Unlike the man-made tunnel I was nearly buried in, yes. Interesting to contemplate, isn't it? Why don't you just go do that, Kate? Have yourself a jolly time, wondering and pondering. As for me, I'm done with my bath now and will be standing up in three seconds. Three, two—" He laughed as he heard the snap of a small shutter being closed, and looked to the portrait. The eyes of the long dead person depicted there once again looked as dead as the brace of pheasants pictured at his feet.

THERE WERE ONLY the two of them at dinner since Adam was still keeping to his deathbed, or three if one counted Consuela, and Kate knew she must. Therefore, as hostess, she was forced to keep the conversation quite general and boring, while Simon, drat the man, replied in nods, grunts and one-word answers. Mostly, he ate.

She could only think, hope to believe, he was in a hurry to get the meal behind them so that they could take a walk in the gardens—which they couldn't, because it was raining—or in some other way outmaneuver Consuela so they could be private.

So she ate. Although she had absolutely no appetite.

That lack was made up for by Consuela, clad in her black crow and camphor best, who seemed to enjoy sitting at the other end of the long table while in her role of duenna, being waited on rather than serving.

"There was a letter from Gideon today," Kate finally said, inventing an imaginary post. "He reminded me to ask you about something or other you were supposed to tell me."

"Did he, now. Did he happen to give you any indication of what that something is?"

Men were so thick—thick as planks! "I believe it had something to do with Henry."

Simon frowned (and if he frowned that obviously while investigating the stone maze, there wouldn't be a person in the world who'd seen that clearly contrived frown and swallowed it whole). "I don't believe I know any Henrys. Could you be a tad more explicit?"

"Henry Midnight. It would appear you and he were to meet someone just the other night," she pronounced through gritted teeth.

Consuela called one of the footmen over to her, signaling she'd like another slice of beef. Honestly, she probably wouldn't be satisfied until she'd downed the entire cow. And all in one sitting.

"No." This time Simon shook his miserable empty head. "Still can't say I recall a Henry Midnight. I'm so sorry."

If the table wasn't so wide as to make it impossible, she'd kick him, then he wouldn't have to feign being *sorry.* "That's strange. Because just the other night you patted his dog and poked your finger in his ear."

His lips twitched. "Oh, *that* Henry Midnight. I remember him now. Never much cared for the man. Now his sister? I always found Miss Libraria Midnight pleasant enough."

Libraria? There was no such name as— Oh! The *library* at midnight. So he wanted to meet her in the library. Wasn't that cute—the rotter! "That should be sufficient."

"I cannot tell you how gratified I am," Simon drawled, and deposited another forkful of beef between his smiling lips.

He'd pay for that, too. She was keeping a tally in her head. Perhaps he'd smile out of the other side of his mouth when she presented the final bill!

Consuela motioned over the footman and had him ladle more vegetables onto her plate.

Simon lowered his voice as he leaned toward Kate. "You might suggest Dearborn remove the candles. Before she eats them."

Click-click, click-click!

"Hearing's fine, isn't it?" he said from behind the serviette he'd raised to his mouth.

"Not the hearing so much as the eyesight. You were leering at me across the table."

"I was not," he said, sounding like a spoiled child. "Believe me, when I *leer* you'll know it."

"Could we talk some more about the you-know-what?"

"In code? I don't think so. My brain is taxed enough with all the balls we've already got in the air. One more, and they'll all probably fall on my head."

"Hopefully knocking some sense into it," Kate said.

"Because we really don't have any time to waste, Simon. We have to take advantage of every second we have."

Still with the serviette to his mouth, he said, "Although, in future, I believe we can safely sacrifice the minutes I'm in my bath."

So that was it. He was paying her back for his interrupted bath time. It seemed fair enough. "That probably wasn't my most overwhelmingly brilliant idea," Kate conceded, unconsciously touching her fingers to the slight lump on the back of her head. They both looked down the length of the table, just in time to see a platter of what had to be half a turbot being deposited in front of Consuela.

"Consuela favors fish?" Simon asked quietly.

Kate sighed. "Consuela favors food, in most any form. But yes, sadly, yes, fish is her favorite. She won't get up from the table until that platter's clean, which means neither can we, since I'm to go nowhere in this house without her." Then she turned to Simon. "Are you thinking what I'm thinking? Because it would present her with quite the conundrum if you and I were to adjourn, wouldn't it?"

"You're evil, and I applaud you," Simon said, putting down the serviette. *"Senorita,"* he called out even as he was rising from his chair, "Lady Katherine and I have important matters to discuss in the main drawing room. If you'll accompany us? Now, please."

Consuela had paused with a fork loaded with buttery turbot halfway to her mouth. She shifted her eyes to Kate. Her confused, pleading eyes.

"Oh, the poor thing," Kate lamented quietly.

"Now is not the time for one of your admittedly few scruples to rear its head," Simon whispered as he waved away a footman and pulled back Kate's chair for her. "Get. Up."

"It's all right, Consuela," Kate assured the woman as she got to her feet. "You simply take your time and enjoy your meal. I'll be safe as houses. After all, I am in my own house." She shot a quick look at Simon before adding facetiously, "and you're only a scream away."

She then slipped her arm through Simon's and allowed him to lead her to the drawing room, wondering how long it would take before he could no longer hold in whatever he was dying to say.

How long was answered the moment he shut the double doors of the drawing room behind them. "A scream away? Thank you *so* much, Kate."

"You're welcome," she said with a wink. "I wanted you to rest assured you're safe with me."

He threw back his head and laughed. "I could adore you, if you didn't scare me down to my boots."

"Thank you." Feeling smug, and for a reason he didn't yet know, she then suggested they speak while also passing the time with a few hands at cards, since eventually Consuela would be joining them and the last thing they wished to do is appear suspicious. It wasn't enough that she had allowed Sally to pile her hair up in curls, or that she'd chosen an ivory gown with delicate pink ribbons running around its fairly daring *décolletage*—that Simon hadn't yet dared to comment on. She wouldn't be content until she'd driven him completely insane. After all, other priorities or not, there was still a wager to be won.

And a kiss she really, really, longed to experience, if only the idiot would be a gentleman and lose the wager. Since he wasn't, she felt it only fair she give him some help.

They sat down at the card table and Kate unearthed a deck of cards from the small drawer beneath it. She politely pushed them toward him for the shuffle. "Two-handed whist?"

"German or Norwegian?"

"German, of course," she answered, just so he'd know she was no novice. "Stakes?"

But Simon was looking at the card backs. Intently looking at the card backs.

"I said—stakes?"

"Uh…um…a penny a point?"

"That seems reasonable. I'll just keep a tally for now. You can pay me later. Have you given any more thought to the idea there may be caves on the property?"

"No, and I won't, not until I've had a chance to see what's behind the hidden opening on the beach. I'd rather we got back to our main problem, locating the journals."

Kate tapped one of her cards against her chin for some moments, before playing it. "You're right. I can be so distracted sometimes, especially with the thought of an adventure. You know, exploring, as it could be said, virgin territory. Loathe as I am to admit it, you and I have made precious little progress so far."

He looked at her, she blinked in innocence (she'd had much more practice in appearing innocent than he did in attempting to be devious), and after a moment he shook his head as if shaking away an idea, and played a card.

In five more quick plays, she got to tally a win on her side of the line.

Simon eased a finger inside his collar, as if it had suddenly grown too tight. He gathered up the cards for another shuffle.

They were lovely cards. French, she believed. The backs of the cards were decorated in pastoral scenes, rife with twining vines and small flowers, and each with hand-painted cherubs and young couples in their French finery. Works of art, really; every single card was different. Subtle. Extremely subtle.

The sort of pretty deception an innocent young woman might easily fail to notice.

But while not overly explicit, still fairly instructive. Trixie had actually employed them when she'd sat Kate down to explain what she wasn't to let anyone allow with her until she was wed. She'd unearthed the deck in her grandmother's rooms earlier and slipped it into the card table drawer.

Simon swallowed with some effort, and dealt the cards. Wasn't that sweet? He would ignore the card backs so as to not embarrass her. What a gentleman! What a slowtop—he should be kissing her by now, and singing by Sunday.

She really had to give him a nudge.

This time she made rather a fan of her cards, slowly waving them in front of her as she frowned, biting her bottom lip as if contemplating her discard, lifting one halfway out of the fan, replacing it, lifting and considering another.

"For the love of God, Kate, pick one and play it."

"There's no need to shout, Simon." He was wiping at his brow with his handkerchief. The deck was only educational, for pity's sakes. And who said he had to look if he was embarrassed by what he saw?

Instead of obeying him, with one of the cards still held up clear of the rest of her hand, rather using it for emphasis, she told him her latest idea. He'd undoubtedly agree; the man looked as if he'd agree to anything, if she'd just play her card.

"Since it would be dangerous to go back to the area—don't you think?—I thought, at least for tomorrow morning—and only if you think it might prove successful—we could walk the area around the greenhouse, using long poles to penetrate the ground, just to see if the pole suddenly breaks through, into another part of the tunnel. Then we could repeat the action until we reach the end of the tunnel. Thanks to the rain again tonight, the ground should be soft and moist enough. What do you think? Simon? Simon, where are you going?"

He'd thrown down the cards and pushed back his chair, and was already heading toward the French doors leading to the stone terrace. "I need some air."

"But you didn't tell me what you think of my plan. Besides, it's raining," she reminded him. "You'll get all wet and your clothes will be ruined."

"Good point," he said, returning to the table to grab the cards from Kate's hand, gather up the remainder of the deck. "So will these. I'll see you at midnight."

As the door banged shut behind him—and it certainly hadn't closed quietly—Consuela walked into the drawing room, still patting at her lips with her serviette.

"He's leaving? Are we so frightening to him?"

Kate's smile was wide as she propped her chin in her hand. She hadn't thought the mere sight of her touching the cards would work so quickly. But that was men for you, she supposed. He probably hadn't even heard her question. "It would appear so, Consuela, it certainly would appear so. Isn't that wonderful?"

CHAPTER TWELVE

SIMON HAD EXCHANGED his sodden evening wear for breeches and a flowing white shirt, and arrived in the library a half hour before midnight. The room was huge, with many dark corners it would take a gross of candles to fully illuminate, but that didn't matter. What mattered was attempting to keep himself in check after Kate had so thoroughly scrambled his brains.

Pole. Penetrate. Break through. Tunnel. Soft and moist. He'd give her *virgin territory.* She'd flung that one at him on purpose.

But the rest? Bloody hell! She had no idea how she was killing him. All she'd wanted was to keep flashing those damn cards in his face. His imagination had taken care of the rest all by itself.

There was no possible way he was going to win their wager. He didn't want to win their wager. Wait out the days until the wager was null and void? Pray for one of the other Redgraves to show up to *save* him from something he didn't want to be saved from in the first place? It would be less painful to poke sticks in his eyes.

He was going to marry Kate. He knew he was going to marry her. She knew he was going to marry her. They might kill each other within six months of the marriage, but the marriage itself was as inevitable as the sun rising in the east. The bedding of her even more inevitable…and twice as urgent.

He'd made promises to Valentine. He'd given his word as a gentleman. Val was probably dancing around London, pleased as punch at the hell he'd plunged his new friend into, knowing how irresistible Kate could be whether she put her mind to it or not.

She was twenty. By next spring, she might even have reached her majority. That was fairly ancient for a debutante. Not to mention her first infamous Season, which would be raked up by the gossips the moment she arrived in town. She'd be invited everywhere, just in case she provided the *ton* with another delicious scandal when she got there, although there'd be no voucher for Almacks, as those stickler patronesses had probably blackballed her for life.

She was free and easy, which was another way of saying she was damn near uncontrollable thanks to her outrageous grandmother, a mixture of innocence and knowledge that was going to get her into deep trouble some day, if she ever met a man who wasn't a gentleman like him (a reluctant gentleman in this case).

Yes, the Redgraves needed Kate safely married, and if he were a betting man, he'd say the affable, smiling, quite clever Valentine had looked around at their dilemma and their prospects and settled on Simon Ravenbill as the answer to their prayers. He had the title, he had the money, he knew the family history and yet had not gone running for the hills of Scotland, and perhaps most important of all, he'd clearly shown the interest… and so had Kate, if repeatedly protesting she didn't want him was a sure sign she really did. And who would know that best but her brothers?

He'd walked into a trap, that's what he'd done. Val had said he'd made a mistake, a spur-of-the-moment idea of a contrived courtship that had almost immediately proved unworkable. The next time Val told him anything, it might be wise to have a ceiling-high stack of Bibles handy, for him to swear on...and even then Simon would have to make certain the man didn't have his free hand behind his back, his fingers crossed.

So, if he'd played the dupe, and he knew it, why wasn't he already halfway back to London?

Because he wasn't a total idiot, that's why.

"Now I'm patting myself on the back for only being a half-wit rather than completely witless, as if that's better?" Simon asked himself as he paced the carpet.

"Ah. Whatever I've been enjoying watching you debate these past few minutes clearly concerns a woman. Complex, aren't they, these feelings we need to sort out before we run eagerly for the cliff we always knew we'd choose. Thank you for being early, Commander, and yes, she'll be late. They don't care to appear too eager, bless them."

Simon whirled about in the direction of the voice, knowing he was defenseless against whomever was in the dark. So he bowed in acknowledgment, and said, "And clearly I am now addressing a gentleman of some wisdom and experience. May I ask the courtesy of your name?"

"The name Jacko will suffice as my introduction for the moment. I compliment you both on noticing the bent branch, Commander, and tamping down your natural curiosity, then as now."

Ah. Jacko's employer. "I'm a patient man in most things. You'll tell me what you want me to know, or else why would you be here? How did you get into the Manor by the way, as I do admit to some natural curiosity. At last count, there were five dogs in the house."

"True enough. One too fat and old to care, and four

out hunting rabbits in the rain. They found them." Simon could hear the slight rustle of expensive silk and imagined his nocturnal guest to be shrugging his shoulders.

"It would take more than diverting the dogs. Someone must have overheard Kate and me making plans to meet here at midnight. Someone must have summoned you, then directed you here and let you in through the French doors. One someone, probably more than one."

"A man must have friends."

"Meaning at least two of the Redgrave servants are also in your employ. Why?"

"For a patient man, you ask a lot of questions. But I will indulge this one. At the beginning of all this odd nocturnal activity on Manor land, I felt it necessary to assure myself of the Redgraves' place in it. As did you."

That last shocked Simon, but he managed to suppress a reaction, other than to say, "I've also been under your looking glass."

"For some time, yes. My condolences on the loss of your brother, which I'm convinced has much to do with both your connection to Perceval and your presence here at Redgrave Manor, although I've chosen not to satisfy my curiosity. However, clearly there's some serious game afoot, one that could bring renewed Preventive Service attention to the entire southern coast, and that very much concerns me. As I quite enjoy my private and peaceful existence these past years, I much prefer whatever is to happen to play itself out elsewhere, and have already been taking steps to be sure that it does. In plain language, Commander, you're very much in my way."

Simon was both surprised and angered. "How much do you know?"

"I know only what I hear, Commander, and my own conclusions. Much as you try to be otherwise, and laudably brave and daring, you—and I admit, a few of my sons—lack a certain finesse, probably as a result of your youth and natural belief in your own prowess. You would have been fierce in battle, and I'm sorry to not have been privileged to observe your tactics at sea. However, I once paid a heavy price, as did those dear to me, thinking myself invulnerable. A bit of advice, Commander. If you believe yourself invulnerable, it serves only to make you and those around you vulnerable. Your shipmates, your family…Lady Katherine. Because, you see, when attacked, your mind denies what's happening, and you don't react quickly enough to prevent disaster."

Simon, at the moment lacking anything to say, kept his response to a slight bow of acknowledgment. *Lack a certain finesse.* First Valentine, and now this mystery man. It must be true. Perhaps he was more like Kate than he thought.

"We live and learn, Commander, if we're lucky. Bonaparte, for all his brilliance and easy successes, refuses to correct that fatal failing of perceived invulnerability, and it will cost him dearly one day, as well as those around him. I personally predict the beginning of his fall will occur if he ever turns his ambitious eyes toward Moscow. As our chalk cliffs protect us, Russia's winters protect them, two forces of nature Bonaparte does not believe apply to him. But we'll leave intellectual discourse for another time. Tonight we'll discuss what happens, to quote you, *when the moon dies.* You have no idea how close you came to disaster the moment you uttered those words in front of another force of nature."

"I believe I do," Simon said, smiling toward the dark corner. He was beginning to be able to make out a shape, sitting in one of the chairs. But it was only a black outline, a shadow within the shadows, nothing more. "Luckily for me, I can also be charming."

Now his visitor laughed, a disarming chuckle that rose with him as he stood, advancing toward Simon, and the candlelight. "Jacko is immune to charm. He didn't wish to alarm Lady Katherine. More important, we don't need the earl and his brothers here, causing us no end of trouble as we monitor the coast from Dungeness to Hythe, which we consider our domain. Otherwise, Commander, you would have been tossed over his shoulder and dunked headfirst in the Channel. Repeatedly. Jacko has no love of the English Royal Navy."

"Pirates seldom do," Simon hazarded wildly, knowing he was once again taking a chance he didn't need to take.

"Clever. Also long ago and quite far away."

"Then I'm right. Pirates then, smugglers now."

"A protector of desperate people who depend upon me now. There's a difference." The man was now visible, but not much of him. He wore black from head to foot, including a black silk cape, skin-hugging leather gloves, highly polished black boots and a mask that covered the top half of his face. A few raindrops still glistened on his shoulders and black-as-night hair, proving that he had ridden here from somewhere, and arrived not long ago. He wasn't a young man, but he was tall, and extraordinarily fit. "Pardon the theatrics, but I've learned to never be sure of my reception."

"Valentine Redgrave would probably have already offered you a bag of gold guineas to know the name of your tailor." He motioned for the man to sit down in a nearby chair, which was declined with a slight shake of his head.

Simon could hear the clock in the hallway begin chiming out the hour of midnight.

"Ah, the witching hour. Although an enjoyable interlude, as I rarely communicate with outsiders, I must be going now, leaving you to your romantic conundrum. The moon will die the day after tomorrow. Our joint quarry is quite arrogant and predictable, always landing on the first night of the new moon. This will be their last run, although they don't know that yet. As we've managed to infiltrate the smugglers, I would ask you to observe from a distance if you must, but not take part. You won't recognize friend from foe, and that could be dangerous, both for us and for you."

Simon's answer was flat and immediate. "No."

There was that knowing chuckle again. "My apologies. That concludes your final test, Commander, you don't bother with lies. My man Billy will meet you at eleven in two-night's time, on the hill just above the cottages. You will, of course, not inform the lady of your plans for the evening."

"Oh, you can safely count on that, Mr....?"

"Lovely map of the Caribbean displayed on the wall over there, Commander. I can personally vouch for its accuracy."

Simon instinctively turned to look at the indicated map, not realizing his error until he turned back to see...nothing. No one. Just one of the French doors open to the rain. "Damn it. Taken in like a raw halfling."

Or was he? He picked up a nearby brace of candles and approached the large map, lowering the tapers to the bottom of the thing. *Commissioned by His Royal*

Majesty in the Year of Our Lord, 1803, researched and drawn by Mister Ainsley Becket, Gentleman.

What had he said when Simon tested him with the label of pirate? *Long ago and far away...*

"Well, hello, Mr. Ainsley Becket, sir. It was a distinct if not unmixed pleasure," he said quietly, stepping away from the framed map when he sensed Kate had entered the room.

He closed the French door and turned to look at her, smiling appreciatively when he saw she had let down her hair.

Then she moved into the center of the room.

"Woman, what in bloody hell are you wearing?"

"This?" she asked innocently, looking down at the overly large white linen shirt and breeches...and the shapely bare calves and feet below. "Consuela wouldn't leave my chambers until I was properly dressed for bed. I didn't have time to attempt buttoning myself back into a gown, and didn't think you'd approve of my night rail and dressing gown, because Valentine certainly doesn't. Oh, stop frowning, Simon. I'm decently covered."

"In your opinion," he said tightly. "I suppose your brothers have seen you like this?"

She crossed to one of the leather couches and sat down, pulling her legs up beside her and leaning her head on her palm. It remained true; nobody could relax quite like a Redgrave; how wonderful to know she feared him as much as she feared the couch she was all but bonelessly sprawled on. "Of course they have. I've always considered myself the fourth Redgrave brother, which seemed fine enough to them until a few years ago, when Gideon began getting starchy."

"Shame on the man, what could he have been thinking," Simon said, sighing. Kate was Kate, and nobody was going to change her. He was, in fact, surprised any-one ever had seen the need…which probably said more about him than it did them. Because he found her to be perfect, just the way she was.

Then he looked more closely at her feet. Her toenails were red! "Is that *paint?*"

She curled her toes. "Oh, I forgot about that. Con-suela did it. She said she remembered my mother al-ways had it done. It's supposed to make a woman feel feminine, even if nobody ever sees— Oh, that's right. You're seeing it. Pretend you haven't."

"I'll give that my best efforts," Simon said as he rubbed at his forehead, almost literally dragging his gaze away from her small, perfect toes. Mentally, he amended his earlier thoughts: *If we aren't married within six months, I'll probably have to kill myself.*

"Good. Because we're here to discuss what you wanted to discuss the other night, remember?"

"My brother, Holbrook. Yes, I remember."

Kate sat up, her wonderfully embellished toes now touching the floor. "Your brother? You suggested know-ing about my family's…history, keeps a wedge of sorts between us, on my end of things. Keeps us from getting to know each other better. Am I right?"

"You've a good memory. And then I suggested we're more alike, you and I, than you know. That we feel re-sponsible, would like it all to simply go away, have never happened."

She nodded, her expression serious. "Yes. And when I asked what that meant, there was something about trusting each other. I don't know that I did, then, which is why I didn't meet you the other night, even though I was there for a while, at least to watch."

"Watch me make a total ass of myself. Sticking my finger in Henry's ear."

"Well, yes, there is that," she said earnestly, not a single twitch of her lips giving away her certain enjoyment. "But I do trust you now, Simon. So I suppose it's only fair to ask if you trust me."

He sat down beside her—the spider who sat down beside her, hoping not to frighten Miss Muffet away—unable to resist wrapping one of her loose ebony curls around his fingertip. "With my life, yes. In several other ways, probably too numerous to mention, no, not at all."

She nodded thoughtfully as he tried not to smile. "Well, that's sensible of you. Sometimes I don't trust myself. You know about my family. Now tell me about your brother."

Wasn't it strange? He wanted her physically, with everything that was in him, but he also wanted her like this. Close, companionable, completely at ease and in harmony with each other. *Understanding* each other. *In tune* with each other. He could have known her all his life, and she known him all of hers. This was probably because she had three brothers, and had been comfortable with men since the cradle. As long as she didn't think of him as a brother, that was all right.

"Where to begin? Holbrook was four years my senior, which meant little at some times in our lives, and saw us miles apart in others."

"Let me guess. You were still plotting strategies with your toy soldiers—or planning your next sea battle, wading with your little ships in the estate pond—while he had begun educating himself via willing girls in the nearby villages?"

He'd given up being shocked at most anything Kate said, or pointing out she shouldn't have said it, and simply answered. "Something very much like that, yes. In any case, we grew apart, and I look back on those years and wonder if anything could have been different. If I could have changed anything."

Kate put her hand on his knee. "I think Trixie wonders the same thing. She hides it well, but I know she carries many regrets with her."

This wasn't easy. Simon stood up again, began to pace, as he'd often paced the decks aboard ship.

"Holbrook was naturally raised as the heir, while my father pointed out I didn't quite have the temperament of a feckless younger son who did nothing but spend his quarterly allowance on fancy clothes, gaming and women. He encouraged me to follow my dream of entering the Royal Navy, a suitable destination for a second son. He died shortly after I received my commission, with me at sea and not knowing for months, and Holbrook suddenly the marquis. He wasn't ready. He may never have been ready. My brother was a wealthy, titled man, answerable to no one, and quite devoted to indulging his own pleasures."

Kate shifted on the couch, once more with her feet tucked up beneath her, as if engrossed in Simon's words. "He wasn't your responsibility, Simon."

"Nor is your parents' history yours. Does knowing that change anything?"

Her chin dipped slightly. "I see your point. No, it doesn't. I still feel a responsibility to protect the family, as do Trixie and my brothers. Go on."

"I won't go into too much detail, because it would change nothing, but at some point, Holbrook drew the attention of the Society. You'll understand why in a moment. He sent me a lengthy yet also maddeningly rambling and hysterical letter, one I didn't receive until shortly before his death, begging me to come home, to save him from his folly."

Simon paused, remembering his immediate request for leave, and then told Kate of his mad dash to Singleton via the first ship to set sail, and what he found when he reached home. Holbrook had already been in the family mausoleum for two weeks. He'd committed suicide, hanged himself in his study.

"I'm so sorry, Simon."

"Thank you." He perched himself on a corner of one of the heavy library tables. "He didn't wait for me. The short note the butler handed me contained only his apologies. Perhaps he *couldn't* wait. Perhaps he was too ashamed, or too frightened to go on living."

"Frightened of the Society? Why?"

"His first letter explained all of that. The Society had given him anything he wanted, indulged his every desire, first as an honored guest, and eventually as a member. I would hazard Holbrook had begun to believe his only real happiness was within the Society. His valet told me he had been extremely lighthearted while yet secretive for several months, disappearing for days at a time. But then suddenly everything changed, and he refused to leave the estate. Near the end, he wouldn't leave his study, spent his days and nights mostly drinking heavily and smoking opium. He ate there, when he could be cajoled into a meal, he slept there. He died there. He was interred with a small golden rose tucked into his cravat because his valet believed it to be one of his favorite things, and by now we all know what that meant."

He looked up abruptly. "Christ, do you know? I'm never sure what you were told and what you may simply have overheard."

"I know. He'd brought a virgin bud into bloom during one of their horrible ceremonies. It's disgusting."

"And some sort of privilege of membership, according to Holbrook's letter. I found a pair of black leather breeches and matching boots, a hooded velvet robe embroidered with demonic or satanic symbols and a mask he must have worn. He'd written that he'd left them all safely tucked into a cupboard in my chambers."

"A devil mask?" Kate asked. "I would suppose a devil mask."

Simon shook his head. "I don't know what it was meant to represent. I'm certain its intent was to frighten. If anything, it resembles a particularly ugly gargoyle. Knowing Holbrook, he had to have been rapturous, at least for a time. But then the suggestion came. He should bring in a new guest, a particular one, to join in their fun. One of Parliament's leading supporters of recommencing the war with France. A man who was also Holbrook's best chum while classmates at school. When his friend evinced no interest in indulging his pleasures, Holbrook was told to try again, and if he couldn't convince the man, to summarily assassinate him. After all, Holbrook was the last man who would be expected to plunge a knife in the man's heart."

"Join, become one of us, do as we ask, or die." Kate shook her head. "They are monsters, aren't they, in every way."

"Monsters and dupes, the Society is made up of both. It was all in his letter, garbled and difficult to decipher, I grant you, and Holbrook thought the Society leader was joking. At first. But when he was immediately cut off, told never to return until he'd earned his way back—no women, no indulgences, no opium—my brother knew he was left with few choices. If he'd been ordered to murder his friend, whom he'd told only the slightest things about the Society, then what would the Society do with him, as he knew so much more? That's when he wrote to me for help. He couldn't murder his friend, but he couldn't exist without the Society. His letter made it clear he was terrified.

"The worst of it, if there could be a worst beyond Holbrook's suicide, is he didn't even know his fellow members, other than by some sort of code name. I know from his letter that he greatly feared the leader, who 'stole my soul,' and is 'dangerous beyond belief,' and the names of the two men who initially approached him. Lord Charles Mailer and the recently deceased Archie Urban, known to the Society as Post and City. Holbrook was Bird, of course, for Ravenbill, as it's a wretchedly simple code, almost too simple to see. I took the letter, the names, went straight to London and Lord Perceval's offices, and have been working with him ever since. It wasn't difficult for Perceval to believe me, as the man Holbrook was sent to recruit had just days earlier drowned in his own tub. Poor Holbrook. Taking his own life didn't save his friend. Val asked me how I knew the names, but I didn't enlighten him. And I won't."

Kate unfolded herself from the couch and walked over to him, putting her hands on his shoulders and her head against his chest. "Yet you've just told me. Thank you, Simon."

He slipped his arms around her waist, pressed a kiss to her head. "We can't go back and correct the past, Kate. But we can do our best to defend it from exposure, and to thwart an otherwise destined future."

She tipped her head back, looking up into his eyes, her expression determined. "We'll find them, Simon.

Find them and destroy them. The journals that represent the past, and the terrible men who want to dictate our futures. If we have a responsibility, that's it. And damn them all to hell."

"You're a fierce little thing, aren't you?" he asked, pushing the last minutes behind him and smiling down at her. "So are we going to take our poles and poke into the soft, moist earth, hoping to break through to the tunnel?"

"What?" Her frown was genuine. "Oh, *that*. I was just talking, saying anything I could think of to keep you looking at me, and the way I was terrorizing you with those cards. I should apologize for that."

She didn't move out of his arms, and he wasn't looby enough to let her go. "Yes. I'm keeping a list. I should warn you, it's growing rather lengthy."

"Trust me in this, Simon, it will get longer. But was it a good idea? The poles, I mean? Surely safer than trying to unearth more of the tunnel by climbing back down into that pit."

"If that's what you want to do, then that's what we'll do. Tomorrow morning. In the afternoon, we'll search anywhere you haven't yet searched. Agreed?"

"Agreed. That would be any shed or barn on the cstate. I haven't been at it all that long, you know. Oh, and the dower house."

At this, Simon raised his eyebrows in surprise. "You haven't searched the dower house? Why?"

Now she did move away from him, curse him for asking too many questions. "Because it's not ours, it's Trixie's. I mean, it belongs to the estate, but as she's the dowager countess, it's also hers, not that she goes there. It's been done up in Holland covers for decades, with only the maids going in to clean now and then."

"She never goes there? For *decades?* And this doesn't pique your interest?"

"No. Why should it?" Kate now looked just a tad mulish. "And I would have gotten to it, eventually."

Simon took hold of her hands, and brought them up to his chest. "Kate, who knows more about the Society than any of us, perhaps even more than many of the current members?"

"Trixie," Kate said quietly. "But—"

"Who would most want to avoid unhappy memories?"

"Again, Trixie, but—"

"And who would most want to protect the people who could be hurt by the truth coming out more than anyone else?"

She pulled one hand away and held up an index finger to his face. "Don't you dare interrupt me again, Simon Ravenbill. Trixie. The answer is the same. My grandmother. But she already told Gideon everything she knows, and has been marvelously helpful. She forgot about the journals, granted, until Gideon showed her the one Adam gave us, but then she explained why it existed and what its contents described. Trixie has already been endlessly helpful. You may speak again now, if you've anything of merit to say."

So, Kate had already been questioning what her grandmother knew and didn't know, what she'd shared and what she might still be hiding. Not that she'd come right out and say so. Her hint was more than enough. The woman had *forgotten* about the journals until Gideon had placed one in her hands? That was doubtful. Highly doubtful. Kate didn't believe that, and neither did he.

Especially if the journals, the bible, detailed the Society's insane ceremonies all the way back to its origins, when Trixie's husband the earl could have written his wife's name in them. Thanks to Turner Collier's journal, they already knew wives were sometimes included in the ceremonies, as willing or unwilling participants. No wonder the woman *forgot* about the journals!

"Thank you," he said gently, knowing, for a man planning to capture her heart, he was treading on shaky ground by pursuing his point. "But no, Kate, she didn't tell the earl everything. She couldn't have, or we'd know more than we know. She lived through the Society. Twice. With both her husband and her son. If anyone could help us in our search, it's the dowager countess. I've never personally met the woman, but I'm positive she's hiding something. With only the best intentions," he added quickly.

Kate retreated to the couch and plunked herself down inelegantly, her breeches-clad legs spread and her hands to her mouth. "I know," she mumbled, so that it was difficult but not impossible to hear her. She sat forward, her head in her hands, the picture of dejection. "But I don't want to know. That's why I have to find the journals, Simon. So nobody has to ask her. She must be terrified right now, knowing her own grandchildren are investigating, knowing what we might find. She may not look or act it, but she's not a young woman, and she's been through so much. The Society, my father's murder..."

Suddenly she was on her feet again, and belligerent. "You're *not* going to approach her. You're *not* going to ask her anything. You and I. *We'll* find what has to be found, or I'll do it on my own."

There were tears standing in her eyes, something

he didn't believe he'd ever see there. "You love her very much."

Somehow, Kate managed a weak smile. "She always encouraged me to make my own rules, my own decisions, just as she does. I always said I didn't ever want to really grow up, just like her. Until this happened, I never knew anything about…about the rest…"

"Come here." Simon drew her into his arms, again kissing her hair, rubbing lightly at her back, attempting to comfort her.

"Simon," she said, her head against his chest. "You've just kissed me. I think you kissed me before, but I wasn't certain, so I didn't mention it."

"The wager didn't include any language as to whether the kiss be mouth to mouth, not mouth to crown of head?"

"I don't think so, no. It also didn't include anything about a mutual calling-off of the wager if both parties agree, and it should have. That was rather remiss of us."

"Very nearly criminal," he said, feeling her relaxing in his arms.

"And did we spit on our palms before we shook hands? I'm not sure we did. Well, that's it, Simon. Clearly the wager wasn't official."

He rubbed his chin against her hair. "Your conclusion seems reasonable."

She sighed. "I think so."

"And fair-minded."

She ran her hands over his chest. "Quite adult of us, really."

"Oh, yes, quite," he said, his own hands going to the waist of her breeches, to begin pulling her shirttail from its confinement. "Eminently adult."

She took in a deep, rather shuddering breath as his

hand slipped beneath her shirttail. "And inevitable, I suppose."

"Again, eminently." He brought his hands around her rib cage and cupped her breasts. She wore no undergarment. "Christ..."

"I doubt He's anywhere close by. More likely his opposite. That...that feels rather wonderful."

He bent his head to place soft kisses on the side of her neck before whispering into her ear. "And wrong, and dangerous, and leaving no question as to our marriage."

"Even though I drive you mad?"

"In many ways, yes, you do. Before you ask, I enjoy this way best."

Her hands found their way to his shoulders, and she melded her lower body against his. She began nuzzling at the side of his neck. He'd wondered how long she would allow him to take all the initiative. She hadn't disappointed him.

He caught her mouth with his own, gloried in her open reception of him, felt his loins tightening in pleasure that could soon become pain if he couldn't get her somewhere much more private than this room.

So thinking, he broke off the kiss, slid his hands down to her waist. He considered the moves to fall into the manly category called temporary self-preservation. "Where's Consuela?"

"She wanted to sleep on a pallet outside my bedchamber door, but I convinced her to at least just take up the bed in the dressing room. Why? You certainly didn't think we could go up—?"

"No, no, I didn't. And Dearborn himself patrols the hallways at night, especially outside my chamber. Very obviously, so that I should know what he's doing. Any other suggestions, or do you want us to stop now? This library has too many doors. Because I'd understand if you—"

"The dower house." She took his hand. "I know where the key is kept."

"Are you sure? You weren't at all anxious to go there before we spoke of it just now."

"I know. But if I'm going to go there, I'd prefer it be with you. Come on."

They rather *slunk* their way to the corridor just outside the kitchens, where Kate took a key out from beneath a chair cushion.

"Dearborn hides his key to the key cabinet behind us under a cushion? I can't believe that."

"You shouldn't," she said, grabbing his hand once more. "He carries the key to the key cabinet with him at all times. This key is purposely obvious, too obvious, as many an industriously dusting housemaid has found out moments before being dismissed from service. It's Dearborn's idea of a test of honesty and trustworthiness. If the key is found, it should immediately be reported. If it isn't, the new maid assigned to clean this hallway is turned off, either for not reporting it, or for shabby work in not finding it."

"So it's a two-edged sword, that key. I understand. No, I don't. So what does this key fit?"

"Ah, that's Dearborn's real genius." She faced the slim wooden cabinet attached to the facing wall, bent her knees and inserted the key up into the bottom of the thing. The wooden bottom folded down with the aid of a hinge, and out dropped a much larger key.

"The key to the key cabinet," Simon said dully, shaking his head as Kate pulled open the door and extracted what he assumed to be the key to the dower house. "I still don't understand."

"Neither has anyone else, not in all the years I can remember. But if someone ever does, Dearborn said he'd immediately have that person put in chains and turned over to the constable in Hythe, for surely he or she was a master thief. There's curiosity in trying the key in the cabinet lock, you see, which is enough to have you turned off, but a real criminal must be placed in gaol."

"Which, although I probably would be safer not saying this, puts you in the category of *real criminal*."

She pocketed all three keys and turned to him with a grin. An unholy grin. "Not really. Because I'm only borrowing it and will put it back, and then politely ask him for it tomorrow. Only Valentine and I know about the secret compartment. We were left to our own devices a lot as children, you understand, and short enough to see beneath the cabinet. Now be quiet. Sometimes Cook falls asleep in her rocker and never goes to bed."

Doing as ordered, Simon followed Kate on tiptoe, so that his boot heels wouldn't strike against the stone floor of the immense kitchens, thinking Kate must be floating over that same stone—until he remembered she was barefoot.

Once outside, Simon lifted Kate into his arms.

"What are you doing? You can't seriously think you can carry me all the way to the dower house. Put me down."

"You're barefoot, if you haven't noticed," he answered, stating the obvious.

"Yes, and it's raining, if *you* haven't noticed. Soft, warm, lovely rain. Put me down, Simon."

She was right. She was going to get wet, no matter

what he did. He could only hope the rain wouldn't wash away the paint on her toes. He had plans concerning those toes....

He took her hand and they made their way slowly across the wet slates, notoriously slippery when they were wet, and then he lifted her down the few steps to the gravel path.

"You never walk barefoot, Simon? Gravel is not your friend when you do. Come on, we'll cut across the grass, which will be quicker in any event."

And they did. Hand in hand, they made their way the hundred or more yards, guided only by patches of light coming from the windows behind them and Simon's astute sense of direction...which he had to employ when Kate attempted to lure him beneath a tree for another kiss.

Not that they didn't kiss as they walked. Not that they didn't look at each other and smile. Laugh. They were having an adventure, that's what it really came down to, strange as that seemed. Life with Kate would be one grand adventure after another.

Her hair was sodden, clinging to her skull, and he could feel rainwater dripping off his nose. There is a point when you are wet, and cannot get any wetter; they met and passed that point in the first fifty yards, after which there seemed to be no hurry to get where they were going.

So they held hands as they made their way through the dark. And stopped now and then to kiss. And they talked.

Simon was certain he'd never remember a word they'd shared; he was too busy falling in love with Lady Katherine Redgrave. Completely, totally, eternally in love with his beautiful, unaffected, daring, unusual

Kate. He didn't have a choice, really. It had always been, as they'd both said, *inevitable*.

The dower house was Redgrave Manor in miniature, although that still made it larger than most dower houses, and oddly close to the Manor house, as well, as if the earls held their mothers in affection and wanted them gone, yes, but not banished.

"I can't see a thing," Kate lamented as they climbed the stone steps to the covered portico. "My hair keeps dripping in my eyes."

So Simon took the key from her and inserted it in the lock. Then turned to Kate.

"Last chance."

"Are you warning me, or reminding yourself?" she asked, pushing her wet hair out of her eyes.

"A little of both, probably. God, I want you."

She raised her hand to his cheek. "I want you, too. I'm not a child, Simon. And I know what I know, which is admittedly secondhand information. To be truthful, much as Trixie told me otherwise, I thought most of what she said to be either silly or embarrassing. Yet I've wondered what it would be like since I first saw you, which wasn't all that long ago, was it? Why do I feel as if I've known you forever? Because I find I can't remember much of my life before you stormed into it. What I'm saying, Simon, is that I look at you, and I think about everything Trixie has told me, and I want you to be the one who…who does that to me."

Only a fool wouldn't take that as her final answer. He didn't believe himself to be a fool. The key turned. The door opened soundlessly. Dry, dusty air welcomed them into the marble-lined entry hall.

"I'll do my best not to be silly or embarrassing," Simon told her even as he blinked several times, attempting to accustom his eyes to the pitch-black around him. He still held tightly to her hand; the last thing he wanted right now would be to lose her in the dark. "Dare we a candle?"

"Not on this side of the house, with the heavier draperies removed for the summer. Come on."

She stepped out with no hesitation, as if she could see where she was going, and led him forward for several yards, up a curved flight of stairs, and then unerringly to the right, and then to the left after passing down a long hallway. Simon figured they were now facing the rear of the house. He also suspected they were standing in the dowager countess's private bedchamber.

May as well be hanged for a sheep as a lamb...it might be their private motto.

"Stay here," she said, and then left his side, disappearing in the darkness, to soon be broken as she employed a tinderbox to light a large candelabra.

From what he could see, the chamber was inhabited by the ghosts of ancient furniture, all covered in dust sheets...including what had to be an enormous four-poster bed.

Bless Kate. She wanted what she wanted, and saw no need to play shy or coy about the thing. In fact, she was already stripping away the dust sheets and turning down the bedspread. *The hussy,* he thought happily.

He picked up the silver candelabra and deposited it on the table beside the bed. "I thought you respected your grandmother's privacy."

"I do. But she doesn't live here, does she? She never has. Val and even Max and I played here as children on rainy days. Playing at ghosts with the dustcovers, you understand, running about, making awful sounds and jumping out from cupboards to surprise each other. But

I don't go into her rooms at Redgrave Manor. Often," she amended, as if not wishing to be caught in a lie. "I'm beginning to feel chilled, Simon."

With the help of the candlelight, Simon looked down at her, seeing the way her taut nipples prodded at the wet linen of her shirt.

It was now or never. If he did, his life would never be his alone ever again; he would have given his life, his happiness, over to her. If he didn't, Kate would never trust him again, and he'd spend the remainder of his days stumbling through a life not worth living.

"Simon?"

He smiled at her, surprised to realize he was suddenly nervous. "Kate?"

She looked at him with those huge, tip-tilted brown eyes. "I don't know how I can be any clearer. I don't want to be a virgin anymore, and I've chosen you to rid me of my problem. But that doesn't mean I'm simply… curious. I really want it to be you, Simon. Please. I really do care for you. Very much so. I thought we'd agreed this was inevitable."

"Oh, bloody hell," he muttered, knowing what it had taken for Kate to say what she'd just said, reveal what she was willing to offer…although not conceding all the way. She hadn't said she loved him.

Then again, he hadn't told her his recent revelation: he loved her. Wanted her, needed her. But, mostly, he loved her.

She wasn't there yet, the brave, daring Kate unable to say the words first.

If she believed them. If she'd believe them if he said them.

For now, for his sins, he'd take what she did offer.

He bent his head, touched the tip of his nose to hers.

"You want me to take you where you've never been. I want that, too. But this first time…"

Up went the chin. That adorable, arrogant, brave chin.

"I know. Trixie told me. I'm still here, Simon."

"So you are. Let's get you out of those wet clothes."

Her eyes went slightly wider. "Yes, let's do that."

Her fingers went to her buttons, but he lightly brushed them away.

The release of each button merited a kiss against the damp, sweet-smelling skin revealed. The buttons on her breeches demanded the same tribute for each new success, her navel attracted the attention of his tongue, as well.

The breeches slid from her softly flaring hips to puddle at her feet, leaving her completely bare save for the open shirt.

He knelt in front of her as she leaned against the bed.

No undergarments. She'd said she'd dressed in haste. Or had it been more than that? Had she made up her mind that tonight would be the night?

He really didn't care, yet allowed himself to be flattered to think her hunger matched his own. There was no time for questions.

Not now, as he kissed her, touched her, learned her.

Not now as he gently spread her legs and introduced her to the delights he could give her with his fingers, his mouth, his stroking tongue.

Kate writhed against him, moaning softly, at times almost laughing, at times his name a near sob. She showed no signs of being frightened by this intimacy. She didn't try to shy away from him, but only allowed him to do what he would do.

And then her body took over, knowing what to do, pulsing with life and first-felt physical ecstasy.

She collapsed backward onto the bed, saying his name over and over again. He'd taken her without taking her. Given her pleasure without hurting her.

Now it was time for the rest.

He all but ripped off his own sodden clothing, then tugged Kate's breeches free and tossed them to the floor. He kissed the arches of her feet, the curve behind her knees, the soft warm insides of her thighs and then stepped between her legs. He took hold of her hands and pulled her upward, her head lolling back, her long black hair trailing damply, nearly touching the sheets.

He kissed away her right sleeve, and then the left, and wrapped her arms about his neck. He licked at her breasts, sucked lightly on the side of her long throat. He whispered to her in French, the language of lovers, and she sighed, her breath warm against his ear.

And then she did something totally unexpected. She reached between his legs and caught him, stroked him, guided him.

"If we get this over with, we have the rest of the night ahead of us," she told him, wrapping her legs around him as he took over, directing himself, finding, gently probing.

The pole, probing. The ground, soft and moist. Breaking through to the tunnel beyond...

Kate cried out, just a single time, and then bit into his shoulder even as she clamped her arms and legs around him as if she'd never let go.

CHAPTER THIRTEEN

"You could have managed to wipe that unholy grin from your face by now," Simon told Kate as he pushed back his chair and got to his feet when she entered the breakfast room.

"Now you're bragging," she scolded quietly as she brushed past behind him, managing to surreptitiously run her finger down his spine as a footman hastened to assist her at the buffet set up on the large sideboard. "Sit down, Simon, before your food grows cold. I'm ravenous, aren't you?"

He swiveled toward her, his smile twinkling with mischief, just as it had as the two of them sneaked back into the Manor, replaced the keys and then stealthily climbed the servant stairs...or as stealthily as possible, considering Simon was behind her, tickling and teasing so that she nearly giggled and gave them away. "And probably will be for some time. Whole decades, I'd imagine."

Kate laughed, longing to sit herself in his lap and partake of a few morning kisses. Once they were wed, they'd take their breakfast in bed. That way she could feed him bits of jam-topped toast and he could share his fruit compote with her. Among other things. Why, it might be months before they left their bedchamber at all. She still tingled all over, and had been terrified Consuela would notice something different about her

as she watched her being dressed. Some outward sign
of change in her. Ah, poor Consuela, she didn't know
what she was missing, or else she would be more understanding. To think, she was more experienced than
her duenna. Delightful!

And how strange. The intimacies they'd shared last
night seemed like something out of another world, their
world. Just theirs. She felt no shame, no guilt, no regrets. She supposed another woman might be somewhat shy this morning, avoiding her lover's eyes, at
least slightly embarrassed to be sitting across the table
so politely and impersonally from the man who had
wakened her to such ecstasy only a few hours earlier.

A devil at night, an angel in the morning.

Kate knew she didn't fit that category. She was Kate,
night or day, and she didn't wish to be anyone else.
Should she warn Simon? Tell him to beware of dark
corners, be prepared to fend her off as she made un-
toward advances each time they chanced to find themselves alone together for above a minute?

Then again, from the way he'd just looked at her,
perhaps he should be warning her.

The odd thing was, Trixie had warned her against
ever allowing a man to believe he might hold her happiness in his hand. At the time, they'd laughed about that,
about always maintaining the upper hand. To Trixie,
love was a game, and she was master of that game, and
had been for decades. It was difficult to ever think of
her grandmother being wrong; she had been correct
about so many things.

But Kate didn't want love to be a game. A contest
with a winner and a loser; one in control, the other
the supplicant. That was cruel. Moreover, that wasn't
Kate. She did nothing halfway, so if she was going to

fall in love, it would be with all of her heart, and with no reservations, no barriers thrown up in some sort of self-protection.

Did that mean she could be hurt…or that Trixie was once hurt, very badly, so much so she'd refused to ever care all that deeply again? The thought brought a moment of sadness to Kate, and she quickly shooed it away.

She sent a cheery *good morning* toward Dearborn, who had belatedly entered the room to take up his usual spot just in front of one of the windows (looking slightly breathless, as he'd probably warned someone to alert him when his charge entered any room where the marquis was already in residence).

Poor Dearborn, she thought, *destined to failure yet again at the hands of those naughty, unrepentant Redgrave brats.*

Poor Dearborn. Poor Consuela. Poor world. So sad for anyone who isn't me this morning.

As the footman held her plate, Kate loaded it with enough food to keep any of her brothers happy for a morning, and then swiped another bun from a silver platter while the servant was carrying her plate to her chair across the table from Simon.

"I trust you passed a pleasant night, my lord?" she asked innocently as she allowed her satin slipper to fall from her foot and reached out her silk-encased toes to locate Simon's knee. *Begin as you plan to go on,* that was always good advice. And since she couldn't seem to resist the urge to touch him, she may as well *begin* now.

"For the most part, yes, thank you," Simon replied, his green eyes still twinkling, which was just the way she liked them best. He'd reached his left hand below the table and was now running his finger lightly up and down her arch. *Delicious!* "Although there were moments when I was awakened by some rather high-pitched sounds."

She remembered the moments. Happily remembered them. But she hadn't been all that loud, for pity's sakes! Oh, he'd pay for that. "Really?" Kate asked, shooting him a warning look. Dearborn was old, and slowing up, but he hadn't turned brick stupid. "I can't imagine what that could have been."

"Caterwauling, if I may hazard a guess. Probably some bitch in heat, yowling to attract a mate. My papa kept plenty, and when they want it they want it, that's what he always said. Morning all, please congratulate me on my sterling recovery from the very edge of death. Lord, I'm famished."

Kate and Simon had turned as one to the doorway, to see Adam Collier standing there in all his town finery and natural woeful blockheadedness, striking a pose for them in yet another ridiculous rigout, this one sporting a sky-blue waistcoat and clocked stockings striped in red, blue and tan. Pitiful.

Simon was the first to recover, find his voice.

"You look like Paddy's pet pig, done up for the fair, and greatly offend the eye while you're at it, I might add. All that's missing is an enormous blue bow around your neck or you'd take the grand prize. Of course, that would probably mean you'd be hung from a hook by nightfall, being sliced up for bacon. You really need to give these things more thought, Adam, if only for your own sake," he said, returning his attention to his plate even as Kate used her toes to search the floor for her slipper. Clearly the teasing moment was over, and it was back to business.

"You look very nice, Adam," she said, still thanking

her lucky stars her mouth had been empty when he'd spoken, or else Dearborn would still be banging her on the back, to dislodge a bite of ham or some such thing. *Probably some bitch in heat?* Honestly, the idiot boy should have his mouth plastered shut until he learned to curb his tongue. "We're delighted to see you've made a complete recovery."

"I should say so. Elsewise you would have had a devil of a time explaining to Jessica why you dropped her beloved brother in a hole, now wouldn't you?"

"Dropped you in a— Adam, you're a bird-witted twit, do you know that?"

"Yes, Kate, I do. I'm told the ladies find that charming."

"The ones demanding recompense by the hour for their services," Simon muttered, and then stuck a forkful of coddled egg into his mouth. For her part, Kate decided it might be safer if she didn't eat another thing.

Adam oversaw the footman as he pointed to various dishes and then explained just how many spoonfuls he wished, precisely where it was to be placed on his plate. "No, no, man. Eggs most certainly do not come within so much as an *inch* of kippers. Runny things, getting in everywhere. Place them on a separate plate. No, don't try to hand that ladle to me while you get another plate—what do you suppose *I'm* to do with it?"

Kate grinned at Simon. "You aren't going to suggest something Adam could do with it? My, you must be in good humor this morning. Why is that, I wonder."

"Fishing for compliments, are you? Will they be returned?"

Kate felt her cheeks going hot, recalling a particularly intimate and daring portion of the evening. "I thought they already had been...reciprocated in kind."

Goodness! Now Simon's face appeared flushed. He must be remembering the same thing as she. How she'd taken his initial tutoring and turned it on him, not quite certain how to go about it, but clearly possessing some natural talent as she'd daringly kissed her way down his chest and belly, and beyond. At least gauging from Simon's reaction she did. Oh, my, yes. She believed the word he used to describe how he'd felt was *spent*. He'd been entirely *spent*. Or at least he had been until she'd begun to tease him again and he miraculously recovered. Poor man. Perhaps they shouldn't spend months in bed. Perhaps only a few weeks....

"What in blazes are you grinning at, woman?" Simon asked, tearing her away from her thoughts; odd thoughts for the breakfast table, even she'd agree.

"Nothing important," she answered and then quickly turned to Adam, who was just sitting down beside her and unfolding his serviette, which he then promptly tucked beneath his chin so as not to drip coddled eggs on his overdone, pouter-pigeon neck cloth. "Adam, we're going looking for the rest of the tunnel today. Would you care to accompany us?"

He looked at her in horror. "Would I care to— Are you mad? I won't go within ten yards of that horrible hole!"

Kate explained the plan, and that he'd do nothing more than use one of the poles to poke in the ground as he walked along, taking the air. "You do look dangerously pale, you know. There's fashionable, Adam, and then there's consumptive. I've had it on the best authority, my grandmother's. Only women ever wish to look consumptive, although I don't understand why they do. Come along with us, you've been moldering in your bedchamber long enough."

Adam immediately dropped his fork on the china plate and groped in his waistcoat pocket for a small, hinged case he flipped open to expose the mirror inside. He peered into the miniature glass, turning his head this way and that, touching his cheek, frowning, touching again.

The lid snapped shut. "I'll go with you."

"Oh, happy day. We would have been devastated without your company," Simon drawled, getting to his feet. "Kate, I'll see if Liam can round up some long poles somewhere and meet you at the greenhouse in thirty minutes. Enjoy your breakfast." He glanced toward Adam and smiled. "As I'm sure you will, with Adam here to keep you entertained."

Wretch, she thought, but then smiled. Whatever list he was keeping of grievances against her, he could now cross off at least one of them, for breakfast alone with Adam should pay it in full.

"So, Adam," she began sweetly as Collier picked up his fork once more. "Other than being locked barerumped in a cabinet, suffering a stern lecture from Valentine, being rebuffed by every house servant and milkmaid, and falling into a muddy pit, how are you enjoying your stay here at Redgrave Manor?"

Even Dearborn had to cover a bark of laughter with a cough on that one.

Adam actually looked, for a moment, as if he was considering how he could best answer her question, but finally grinned at her. "Not *all* of the milkmaids."

"Liar," Kate countered cheerfully. "You wouldn't dare risk Val's wrath. Or Gideon's. You're silly, but you're not anxious to be dunked head and shoulders in one of the horse troughs, now are you?"

"And you're no fun at all," the boy complained.

"Although Val's much worse, you know. Your brother threatened to have a bonfire of every stitch of my fine clothes and send me to Jessica dressed only in a sack. You're all rather evil, you know."

"Not just rather, Adam," Kate reminded him, but again, sweetly. "Val told you about what that journal of your father's really means, didn't he?"

Suddenly Adam looked as young as his years, and more than faintly bilious. "You mean he wasn't just trying to frighten me?"

Kate put her hand on his arm. "No, Adam. It's true. It's all true. It's why your parents are dead, among so many other things."

"I thought so, but didn't wish to believe it. What must he have had planned for me? That's really why I took to my bed, you know. I thought it was all about the willing women, not—" he lowered his voice to a whisper "—treason. A person can be shot for that! How do you stand it? Knowing, I mean."

"I don't *stand* it. What has been done isn't something to be endured. We have to fight, Adam. We've all set ourselves to stopping these horrible people. If, in our hearts and minds, that makes up for some of the sins of the past, that's all well and good. But what we really need to do is put an end to the Society, once and for all time."

"And that's why we're poking holes in the ground? It seems sort of silly." He gave a limp wave of his hand. "I suppose it was your idea."

"That's one of the things we're doing," Kate said evenly, wondering how she had suddenly become so mature she wasn't now boxing the idiot's ears for him. "Your father's journal is one of dozens, perhaps dozens of dozens. We need to find them all, and they might be in that tunnel, if we can trace it to its source. Do you understand now?"

"I'm not a simpleton, of course I understand. His lordship and I are about to humor you, and then get down to business in earnest." Adam pulled the serviette from his collar. "The journals must be found, at which point we will have saved the day. Let's get started— these eggs are too runny in any event."

"There are boots in the kitchens. You wouldn't wish to ruin those lovely shoes." Kate hurried to her feet before the footman could react. Goodness! Had she finally gotten through to Jessica's brother, when everyone else had failed? She longed to pat herself on the back, but would satisfy herself by telling Simon how brilliant she was.

"My lady," Dearborn called after her as she hurried toward the door. "Your apple, my lady."

Kate turned around and Dearborn tossed a shiny apple in her direction, unfortunately just as Adam stepped in front of her. Instead of catching it, he recoiled, squealing like a piglet stuck in a grate as the apple connected with his right eye.

"My eye! My eye!" he screeched, clapping his hands to his face as Kate, always quick to react, rescued the apple before it fell to the floor.

"You'll be all right, Adam," she encouraged him. "It was only an apple, and Dearborn didn't throw it hard. Did you, Dearborn?"

"No, my lady. But, regrettably, the apple itself is hard. My deepest apologies, Mr. Collier."

Still with one hand to his face, Adam sniffed, and told Kate he might meet with she and the marquis later, but he needed a lie-down. Then he toddled off in his red heels (had he an endless supply of the things?), already calling for his valet.

"Again, my lady, my apologies," Dearborn said, sadly shaking his head. "Not really one of us, is he?"

"He's one of something, though, Dearborn," Kate told him, smiling. "We can only hope there are no more of him."

Then she took a bite of the apple and headed for the kitchens for her half boots and then the greenhouse, thinking perhaps she wouldn't brag to Simon about her brilliance with Adam just yet.

He was just walking toward her, followed by Liam toting four long metal poles last used to prop up a canopy meant to shade the ladies while they watched some impromptu horseracing event Gideon had put on the previous summer. Or so Liam reminded her when she asked.

"If you'll hold on to Mr. Collier's pole for him, please, Liam? He won't be joining us quite yet, as he's temporarily indisposed," she told him as they headed back toward the area of the greenhouses. "And don't you say anything, Simon, because he really is indisposed," she added quietly. "Dearborn conked him in the eye with an apple."

"Good on Dearborn," Simon responded. "I won't even ask why, as there are too many possible reasons to count."

"One of them being Adam can't catch apples any better than he can locate willing females. But he is beginning to realize what a monster his father was, and his mother, as well, I suppose. And their plans for him. I'm thinking of sending him to Jessica. He needs family about him now, don't you think? We didn't do that at first, in case the Society somehow figured out

Gideon was their nemesis in London, but as nobody's come chasing after them, it should be safe for Adam to be there."

"And as welcome to the newlywed couple as the spring rain, I'm sure," Simon pointed out wryly, handing over one of the poles. "We've already tried in a few areas, Liam and I, with no success, but if you look toward those trees, I believe you'll see the ground leading up to it seems more like a faint trough than an even expanse of grass. Do you see it?"

Kate squinted into the distance. "No, I don't think I see any— Oh, wait a moment. The ground is still wet there, isn't it? As if last night's rain collected in it. Do you suppose—?"

"I can't be certain, no. But between the partial collapse, and the diverted stream—and then adding in the rain? It's possible. Shall we try? But be careful."

They began following on each side of the faint depression, Kate looking ahead, to see exactly where they were going. "It ends at a tree, Simon."

"A young tree, and an old tunnel. My hope is that it continues on the other side of the plantings."

Kate bit her lip. "You do realize, if it is the tunnel, and it does continue, it's heading straight for the dower house?"

Simon took her hand and squeezed it. "I noticed. If we think it does, we'll break off before we go that far, and tell Liam we were wrong, and the exercise was nothing more than a waste of time. Agreed?"

"You don't trust Liam?"

"I don't trust anyone, not right now. Except you, of course. Start probing with your pole, Kate, and then we'll stop at the tree, look perplexed and I'll send Liam and the poles on their way. We'll continue our search from inside the dower house. For one, no one will see us, and secondly, it will be safer. One encounter with a cave-in is more than enough for me."

The sun was warm, but Kate felt herself shivering. They were getting close, she and Simon. She could sense it. "Part of me wants to race to the house and get the key from Dearborn…and another part of me simply wants to run. Do you think we should send off messages to Gideon and Val? I doubt either would be happy if they weren't in on the discovery…and even less happy knowing I may have seen things they wouldn't want me to see."

"*I* don't want you to see whatever hell we might find. The difference is, I know you'll discover a way to do it, anyway, and I'd rather be with you. Ah, we're nearing the tree. Time to do some playacting."

To fool Liam. But she trusted Liam. She trusted everyone on the estate. Except now, thanks to a few words from Simon, she didn't. Her entire life was turning upside down.

"All right, Simon Knows-Everything Ravenbill, now what?" she asked loudly as she thrust her pole at him and jammed her fists on her hips. "I *told* you this was wrong. A tunnel would have to lead toward the shore. Any fool would know that. I knew we were chasing mare's nests the moment you came up with this ridiculous plan."

"Very nice, putting all the blame on me. I adore you," he whispered, then went back at her: "Then if you're so *brilliant,* why don't you tell me your ideas? Oh, I remember now—you don't have any, do you? Liam—take the poles, please, before I'm tempted to put them to use another way. As for you, *my lady,* I'll see you at luncheon. Right now I'm going to take a ride, clear my head. And no, I do not desire your company!"

"Nor I yours! You're as useless as Adam!" she called after him as he stomped off. He really was getting much better at this playacting business. "I'm sorry, Liam, you know how my temper can get the best of me. But, honestly, I have to do all the thinking for the three of us. Which reminds me. Did you ask your grandfather about the construction of the west wing? Are there any hidden passageways or anything of the sort?"

"I'm that sorry. Just the hidey-holes to peek at folks, my lady, and you said you already knew about those. He laughs about those all the time, that he does, but not when Da is about, as he thinks that's none of our business. Da just says the earl isn't a patch on your da and granda, begging your pardon."

Kate was taken aback. "Now what do you suppose he means by that?"

Liam bowed his head, as if only realizing he'd spoken out of turn. "He don't say, my lady, and I don't ask. Powerful temper he has."

"Then certainly don't ask," Kate assured him. "Your family has been on the estate for a long time, hasn't it?"

Liam nodded fiercely. "Back and back, my lady, all the way since your granda and mine were lads together right here at the Manor, Granda says. I'll be goin' now, if that's all right?"

Kate waved him on his way before turning back toward the house. She really would have enjoyed a ride, and some time alone with Simon, but they'd have to keep to their playacting now more than ever.

She stopped on the way to pick a beautiful white rosebud and one already fully bloomed, and smiled at them as she drew in their scent. Both were beautiful, but she believed she liked the fully bloomed one best.

And then her smile faded as she thought about the golden roses of the Society, and immediately dropped both blooms into the dirt. She knew what was right, and what was wrong, and that the blooms were innocent. In time, with Simon's help, perhaps she could look at them again and see only the beauty.

She turned to look back to where she and Liam had been standing, with a silent appeal to her brain for a change of subject. She'd think about Liam, and what he'd told her. His family had lived at the Manor for at least three generations. And although she knew them as the Cooper family, Liam itself was a Scottish name. Just like his father, Hugh. Just like his grandfather, Angus, who'd grown up as her grandfather's friend and companion.

Scottish names all.

Just like the Royal House of Stuart.

Perhaps Trixie wasn't the only one who knew more than she was telling....

CHAPTER FOURTEEN

IT WASN'T THAT difficult to locate the spot Ainsley Becket had left his mount the previous evening, thanks to the rain. He'd come alone, from wherever he'd ridden from, wherever he'd disappeared back to as the rain kept pouring down. It was equally simple to follow the tracks, the clumps of sodden earth his mount's hooves had displaced, until they reached the tradesman's gate.

The question was, who had opened the gate to him, although Simon felt fairly certain no one would ever know that particular piece of information until and unless Becket volunteered it. That gate was open now as a tarp-covered wagon made its way through after fairly effectively destroying the trail Simon had been following while pretending not to be doing more than enjoying a solitary ride.

Once through the gates, he guided Hector to the side of the gravel lane, but followed its direction, sure Becket wouldn't have kept his mount on the gravel, either. The last things he would have needed last night were a sprained foreleg or a thrown shoe, and he had to have been traveling fast the moment he was free of the Manor grounds.

And there it was; the telltale clumps of thrown earth, evidence left behind like a trail of breadcrumbs for Simon to follow. It was almost too easy.

He'd studied a map he'd found in the library, and

knew what lay ahead of him. He doubted Ainsley Becket lived cheek-by-jowl with what could be curious neighbors in any of the towns or villages along the coast. Especially since he'd admitted he rarely spoke with what could be termed outsiders. No, the man enjoyed his privacy, clearly. And the sea. Once a man loves the sea, he never strays far from it.

That left Romney Marsh. Smugglers' Heaven. Where else would the man who termed himself a protector of others reside? How else could he have discovered the smuggling taking place on Redgrave land?

Really, it was just a matter of putting all the pieces together.

Turning Hector in the direction of the coast, he zigged and zagged his way to the shoreline, figuring it the safer if slower route, staying away from the lanes, roadways and the recently completed Royal Military Canal. Martello towers seemed to have been unevenly spaced along the shoreline as if placed at random. But, mostly, he saw waving marsh grass and multitudes of sheep, all laid out in front of him in this nearly flat, harshly beautiful world.

Church spires dotted the landscape in the distance, but Simon knew if he attempted to make his way guided inland only by them he could soon find himself hopelessly lost. He needed to keep the shoreline in view. That presented other problems. Would the beaches welcome a man on horseback, or would they stretch ahead in fits and starts, causing him constant detours as he had to pick his way?

And one thing more. In this flat, unfamiliar land, he and Hector would be visible long before he knew what, or whom, he was riding toward.

He pulled out his timepiece. How much time did he

have before Kate would be champing at the bit to inspect the dower house? He smiled as he replaced the pocket watch. *Five minutes, at the most.*

Simon looked wistfully into the distance. For now at least, the Marsh and Ainsley Becket could keep their secrets. "Come on, Hector, I have a feeling our mistress is looking for us."

They made it back to surroundings now familiar to him before a lone rider walked his horse out of a small copse of trees twenty yards ahead and halted, blocking the hard-packed dirt trail. "Good morning, Commander," the man said, lifting his bent leg and resting it across the pommel, as if to show he meant no harm and expected none in return. "He said you were the inquisitive sort."

Simon accepted the hint and reined in the stallion no more than five feet away. The man was young, in his late twenties perhaps, but somehow the possessor of what Simon's grandmother would have termed an *old soul*. It was all there, in his eyes. "I thought it was easy, and that I was brilliant. Now I see I've been led around by my own arrogance, following a trail perfectly laid out for me. My congratulations." He chanced a look over his shoulder. "I've been watched the entire time?"

"Going and coming, yes. If you've been fretting about aligning yourself with an amateur, consider us wondering the same thing in return. But you did the wise thing, Commander. You satisfied your curiosity, somewhat, and then decided to give us the courtesy of not having to tie you up somewhere until we're finished here."

Simon laughed softly. "You overestimate me, sir. Curiosity almost won. It was fear of a lady's wrath that sees me returning here, rather than risking the dangers of the Marsh. My compliments to Mr. Becket. Please tell him I much enjoyed our conversation last night and look forward to continuing it at some other time. And that I value his trust in me and have from this moment forgotten his name."

"Courtland Becket," the man said with a slight inclination of his head, clearly returning gift for gift. "Now you can forget that, as well, as after tomorrow night we will not meet again."

"Have we met? I don't recall." Simon tried another smile, and this time Courtland Becket returned the gesture.

"He said you were solid. It's comforting to know he hasn't lost his keen eye. Jacko, however, frets like an old woman, you understand." Courtland swung his leg over and down, neatly finding the stirrup. "Good luck with the lady."

"Thank you. I'll need it."

Simon watched as Becket rode off. By the time he was halfway down the hill he was joined by another rider, and by the time they plunged into the trees bordering the West Run, there were four horsemen riding in single file, slipping into the trees via a narrow path he hadn't seen.

"Sonofabitch…"

He'd been watched from the moment he left the Manor stables to the time he'd stopped, rethought what he was doing. And all the way back again. First the Redgrave servants popping up from behind the shrubbery, and now Becket's men. And all without him noticing. It was rather lowering.

Simon decided he much preferred the sea. At least you could make out approaching sails a good mile away.

By the time he'd left Hector at the stables and made

his way across the wide lawn, Kate was waiting for him, tossing a ball for four of the dogs to chase, while the one called Tubby sat beside her, tongue lolling, his short, fat tail thumping up and down on the lawn. *Probably reliving old chases; at some point we all have to retire to the sidelines with our memories—a good reason to make sure those memories are pleasant, and entertain you, rather than haunt you each night under the covers.*

"Enjoy your ride?" she asked as she wrestled the wet ball from one of the hound's mouths and gave it a last toss before they dropped into step with each other, heading in the opposite direction. Only Tubby followed. "You rat."

He brushed the back of his hand against hers. "I'll say this for you, Kate, at least you don't keep a man hanging, waiting for the ax to fall. Do you feel better now?"

"I was wearing this same riding habit when I walked into the breakfast room, remember?"

"True. But after our public argument, I could hardly ask if you wished to go riding, now could I?"

"I know. I playacted my way into a box I couldn't get out of, didn't I? At least it gave me time to read the post, and took the liberty of opening one addressed to Valentine. It had already been sitting for days, and I was curious, in case the contents had something to do with...you know. However, it would seem Trixie is on her way here."

Simon looked quizzically at Kate. She didn't seem overjoyed to tell him the news. "Is she now."

"Yes, and I'm worried. Richard Borders—he's a friend of Jessica's and now Trixie's—wrote that she's not well, although she won't admit it. Two funerals,

Simon. She dragged herself to a pair of funerals. No wonder she's not feeling her usual self. But—"

"Yes? But?"

"But there was more. Richard passed along Trixie's request I be *removed* to stay with Gideon and Jessica. She learned I'm looking for the journals, and she *demands* my absence, and that Valentine wait until she arrives before continuing any search." Kate turned hurt eyes on Simon. "She's treating me as if I'm a child. She's *never* treated me as if I'm a child, even when I was."

"I see. And from this you're deducing—?"

"I don't know. It has to be the journals. What could be worse than the journals?"

Simon had his own thoughts on that, but wisely kept them to himself. He slid his arm around Kate's shoulders. "So, are you giving up the search?"

"I can't. Remember, Trixie doesn't know Barry's body has gone missing. I certainly haven't forgotten *that.* What if she has decided we'll succeed with or without her, and agrees to show us the entrance to some cave or tunnel, and we stumble over his body? Richard writes she's ill. God, Simon, that could kill her. She could arrive today, tomorrow, I don't know how long ago Richard's letter was sent. We have to move faster now than ever. Thank God we're close."

"We think we're close. Do you have the key?"

She touched the pocket of her riding skirt. "I do."

"And Consuela? You seem to be missing your shadow, both at breakfast and now."

"Ah, you noticed. She won't admit it, but she ate too much last night. She's tucked into the cot in my dressing room, vowing she'll never eat turbot again, moaning over and over, *Mi estómago está al revés*. She's truly miserable."

"If my stomach was upside down, I'd be none too happy myself. I imagine she begged you to remain indoors and you assured her you'd do just that."

Kate shrugged. "It would have been cruel to tell her we're going to the dower house. I was only being considerate."

"If I could lift the top of your head and peer in at your brains, they'd be twisted in a corkscrew, wouldn't they? But never mind." Simon took her hand and squeezed it, not giving a damn about how many Redgrave servants might be watching from behind every bush and tree. "Kate? Are you quite sure you're ready for this? What we might find?"

"No. I don't want to see any of it, even while I'm praying the journals are somewhere in there. I suppose you'd say I'm being corkscrewed again. But to show you I can be cautious if I must be, I'd even thought of summoning Gideon before we begin our search, let the two of you conduct it without me. Except that we're running out of time now, with Trixie on her way."

They'd reached the door to the dower house. "Tubby, you stay out here," she ordered, turning the key in the lock. "Simon, you only saw everything in the dark. Please don't be too shocked."

"Now that sounds ominous." Simon let go of Kate's hand and slowly walked into the foyer he'd first been through in absolute, dustcover darkness, nearly unable to take in the sight in front of him in one encompassing glance. His plans up until that moment consisted of nothing more than closing the door and taking Kate in his arms to kiss her senseless.

But he couldn't tear his amazed gaze away from what unfolded now in front of him.

The three-story, dome-topped area was resplendent with ivory marble and gold leaf. The large, round center table mimicked the ivory and gold. The golden sculpture atop it that of a nearly life-size nude woman with her arms stretched up toward the enormous crystal chandelier.

Kate was looking at her toes, as if embarrassed, which he could certainly understand; he was fairly embarrassed himself. "I sneaked in earlier and removed the dustcovers both here and in the drawing room for you. I doubt you need to see anything else. This is probably where the Society, um…held their parties?"

Parties?

"I didn't want to show this to you, and neither did Valentine, or else he would have while he was here, wouldn't he? It wasn't something you had to know, or at least we didn't think so. But if the tunnel truly leads here? Don't look at me like that, Simon."

Kate still didn't understand. She spoke as if she did, used all the right words, pretended to be worldly and knowing, but her mind couldn't possibly grasp all the evil that went on here at Redgrave Manor during her grandfather's and father's time. Possibly directly below their feet, or in some tunnel or cave that had its beginnings here.

Because this dower house, this place, in all its subtly erotic beauty, could, in fact, be only the antechamber to a hell beyond Kate's comprehension.

He peeked into what had to be a ground-floor drawing room, to see the theme repeated. It was beautiful. It was understated. There was art and statues everywhere, men and women both in various innocuous poses, all of them with nary a marble drape or fig leaf in sight. It could have been the setting for a refined Roman orgy.

Kate came up behind him. "You want to know something strange, Simon? When I used to sneak in here behind the maids, all I could do was giggle as I watched them with their eyes closed and heads averted as they used their feather dusters on…you know. But now, after last night…I see all of this, and it's not at all silly or amusing. Today I find it all quite…disturbing. How strange, that one night could make such a difference. Tubby! I said to stay outside." She retreated to the door and opened it a crack. "Go on, shoo."

Simon was looking toward the staircase now. "Do I want to know what the bedchamber we were in last night looks like beyond the bed?"

"Probably not, no. Nor would you wish to see Trixie's bedchamber in town, or the statues lining the curved staircase to the main floor. My grandfather had the decorating of both residences done years and years before he and Trixie married. She never changed anything, as she finds it amusing to live up to the reputation of being one of those scandalous Redgraves."

Simon glanced around once more. "Something like this should certainly accomplish that for her."

"Please stop looking. Although, as I said, she's never shown any interest in moving to the dower house. I wonder what she'll do now that Jessica will be taking over the role of hostess. Tubby!" She shut the door and they followed the dog back into the drawing room. "Honestly, he's usually better behaved. He knows no dogs are allowed in here."

"But you *sneaked* in here with the maids, that's what you just said. You aren't allowed in here any more than the dogs are," Simon said with sudden insight. "How did you manage to get the key from Dearborn? Because *that* you didn't say."

"I never gave it back last night, silly. I only pretended to, and you believed me. Even if I begged, Dearborn would no more give me the key than he would serve dinner in his nightcap. You have a lot to learn about being devious, Simon."

"I'm convinced you'll teach me," he responded dryly. "What's that dog up to now?"

Kate took one look, called out the dog's name and went racing across the drawing room. "If you dare to lift your leg against that wall, I promise you I'll—"

She jumped back, squealing, as Tubby began to bark, digging at a hole that clearly had been chewed through the ornate baseboard. "Blast it! Mouse!"

Simon laughed. "She's frightened of a mouse? Oh, how will I ever move beyond this disappointment. She isn't perfect."

She shot him a darkling look even as she hastily lowered her divided riding skirt, as if now confident the mouse wouldn't run up it to give her a bite on the nose, or some such thing. "I'm not afraid of mice. It simply startled me, that's all. I wasn't expecting it to poke its head out at me. Now, where did it go?"

"If Tubby's interest is any indication, friend rodent is now safely back inside the wall."

"Well. Good. That's where it belongs." She leaned down to grab hold of the dog's collar. "Come on, Tubby, time for you to leave."

"How big were its teeth?" Simon asked, approaching the wall.

"What? It was a mouse, Simon, not a fire-breathing dragon. Besides, I didn't notice. I mostly saw two eyes and a pink, wiggling nose."

As Kate began pulling a reluctant-to-leave Tubby away, Simon got down on his haunches in front of the hole. He knocked on the wall several times, and then stuck his fingers into the mouse hole. "A-ha."

"A-ha? What do you mean, *a-ha?*" Now Kate was hunkered down beside him, with Tubby still being held back. "Don't put your fingers in there!"

He took hold of her arm. "Stand up, Kate, and step back."

She rolled her eyes at him. "Do you have any idea how I loathe taking orders? If you've found something, *tell* me."

Simon got to his feet, brushing his hands together to rid the right one of any dust. "All right, since you asked so nicely. One, mice have sharp teeth, but it would probably take a dozen of them years to chew through a heavy baseboard such as the one in front of us."

"Well, they did have the time," Kate said consideringly. "Nobody's lived here in—in *ever,* I suppose. Our grandfather had it built after the original one burned down. I told you that, didn't I?"

"Another fire."

Kate narrowed her eyes. "Meaning?"

"I have no idea. It only seems coincidental, I suppose. If someone needs something gone, a fire is as good as anything else."

"Do you want to know more, or not? That one, the first dower house, had been a good distance away from the Manor itself, I understand. Our grandfather had the remains razed and there's a foaling stable there now, built right on top of the original foundation. Oh, I'm sorry. You were educating me on rodent teeth?"

He put the thought of coincidental fires—hellfires—from his mind, to return to the problems of the present.

"And baseboards, yes. This one is no more than two inches thick at its base. Considering its ornate design, all the layers of wood it takes to create such an intricate pattern?"

"Allow me to hazard a guess. It should be thicker."

"Yes. Layers. But this area is carved out of a single thickness of wood, just meant to appear to be layers. An entire section here is probably thinner, lighter, easy to slide behind the rest of the wall, or move in some way. Clever."

Kate was practically dancing in place. "So you're saying we've found it. A secret panel. You know, I always hoped it would be a secret panel. And that I'd find it, not Tubby. Because that's why you're knocking on the wall again, yes? The journals are directly behind this panel? Could it be this easy?"

"Or this logical. This isn't a dower house, Kate. It's a…" He struggled to find the right words. *Brothel? House of Pleasure? The Devil's Playing Ground?* "I can't believe this wasn't the first place everyone looked."

Kate jammed her fists against her hips. "That's because no one was looking, except for me, and *they* asked me to before one of them must have realized I might somehow manage to trick Dearborn out of the key and come in here, so Valentine was sent to distract me. *And,* for your information, *your lordship,* Valentine did look in here. He searched it top to bottom the very first day he arrived at the Manor. Thoroughly. Right after he told me if I dared to attempt to go inside, he'd make my life a living horror."

She left her arms drop to her sides. "And then he left, and here we are. He probably forgot he and I had long ago found the key. Satisfied now?"

"Valentine searched the building?"

"Isn't that what I just said? He did, and with his two paper-skulled dogs along with him." She finally smiled. "Clearly not mousers, are they, Tubby," she said, bending down to scratch behind Tubby's ears. "Good dog. Good, good dog."

While Kate was speaking, Simon was running his hands over the thick wooden panels decorating the wall. It wouldn't be anything too obvious, the mechanism that opened the wall, and nothing that could be easily activated by mistake, such as a maid cleaning a wall sconce with too much enthusiasm.

"In fact," he said to himself, turning to look at the rest of the room, "it might not be here at all."

That remark seemed to serve to clear Kate's mind of anything but the project at hand. "You mean you're wrong? For goodness' sakes, Simon, and here I was, all hot to tell Valentine he missed something so *obvious*."

"Move," Simon ordered shortly.

She did as he asked, this time without hesitation or argument. "You think there's some sort of mechanism beneath the carpet? But the footmen take the carpets outside once a year, to beat them. Surely they would have noticed a *mechanism*."

"You're right." Simon rubbed at his chin, once again inspecting their surroundings. There had to be something, or else his conclusion about the baseboard was incorrect. But it couldn't be. He'd felt cooler air against his fingers as he'd stuck them inside the hole. Why would there be cool air, when the drawing room should be backed by another room. At least the architecture dictated that, and the line of building and windows that stretched much farther than this room. No, it was all a matter of locating the damn trigger.

Fireplace? Too obvious. Chandeliers? A ladder would be necessary to reach any of them. Mirrors? Paintings? Again, a conscientious maid might discover the mechanism simply by cleaning either framed piece. Moving a certain book in a bookshelf? Except there were no books or bookcases in this room.

What else was there that wouldn't be dusted or lifted or in some way moved?

Think, Ravenbill! She's searching on her own now. If she finds the damn trigger before you do, you'll never hear the end of it! But this wasn't a contest, not at the heart of it. They should be working together, as a team.

"It doesn't move," Kate said, tugging on one of the pair of ornate sconces flanking the nearby fireplace. "I suppose that would have been too easy, in any event. Do you know what I think, Simon? I think we need simply to tear it down. I mean, who cares how it works? We just need to bash it to pieces and get inside."

A pair of sconces. Two. A team...

"Stay where you are, Kate," he said as she was clearly eager to go searching for sledgehammers. He walked to the other end of the large fireplace and put his hands on the matching sconce. He gave it a pull. Nothing happened. "Now we do it again, but this time we do it together. On the count of three. One...two...*three*."

Both sconces tipped forward. There was a clicking sound, and a four-foot-wide panel moved backward at least six inches, then slid to the left, disappearing behind the rest of the wall.

Kate let go of the sconce. "Oh, my God! Simon, we found it. We found it!"

And they had. Unfortunately, the moment Kate let go, the wall slid shut once more.

"It has to be both of us, at the same time," Simon

concluded. "The baseboard is thinner so that the panel can easily slide behind the wall. Clever. The real trick, however, is in getting the panel to remain open."

"No one person could do it, could he?" Kate asked. "If the sconces must be depressed in unison. Do you suppose then a third person somehow then props open the panel?"

"Too crude, after all this intricacy." Simon shook his head as he paced up and down in front of the fireplace. "Two is a shared secret, the highest honor to be bestowed by the Master. Three, as in most associations, would be unmanageable. Then again, if it takes two, it would be impossible to act without each other, unless a third was brought in, which clearly wasn't the plan. I imagine the two would be the Master and the Keeper, or in other words, your father and Adam's, and before them, your grandfather and whoever was the Keeper when he was alive. There would be absolute trust between them, as well as a subtle reminder that he who attempted to act alone would fail in any case. The devil's honor, I suppose."

He stopped and looked at the figurines on the mantelpiece. "Wait a moment. Let's try something, Kate. These brass figurines lining the mantelpiece. They have to play into all of this in some way. Ah, Eros and Aphrodite. The god of…desire," he improvised quickly, "along with the goddess of pleasure and eternal youth, among other things." *Such as the patron of prostitutes….*

"How do you know that?"

"I'm a man of many talents, Kate, including the ability to read. All the names are engraved on each base."

She peered at the dozen statutes, one by one. "Chaos, the Void. Nemesis, Retribution. Tartarus, the Abyss. Gaia, the Earth. Erebus, Darkness. Nyx, the Night.

Thanatos, Death, Apate, Deceit, Hypnos, Sleep, Moros, Doom. Eros, *Carnal* Desire—more than you said, Simon. And Aphrodite." She turned to look at him. "Why did you first say Eros and Aphrodite?"

"As I recall the thing, many believe them to be mother and son. Some of the rest of them could go together in various ways, but these two seem most obvious for your grandfather's purpose. Pick one up, Kate."

They each picked up one of the statuettes, Kate still puzzled, Simon praying he'd see what he hoped to see. And there it was: an opening in the back of the surprisingly heavy piece. He lifted the statute of Chaos, just to make certain he was correct. There was an opening in the back, but it had been cut in an entirely different shape. Hypnos also had a hole cut into its back, and that was cut in yet a third shape. Each also was a different weight. Unless he was right, they could be here all afternoon until they discovered the correct combination of gods.

"Simon? There's an opening in—"

He was truly excited now. "Yes, now let's hope I've chosen the correct pair. Go back to face your sconce. All right. Now look closely—feel behind the candleholders. We should be hunting something to hang them on. Ah, I've got it. Do you feel the hook, Kate? Behind the middle holder."

Her smile was part triumph, part terror.

"I do. We hang the gods at the same time, don't we?"

"On the count of three, yes."

She bit her bottom lip between her teeth, and nodded.

This time, when they let go, the panel remained open.

"A combination of weights and pulleys attached to the panel, I'd say," Simon told her as, together, they peered into the darkness. "Looks to be a set of stairs. I'd like you to remain here, Kate, while I investigate."

"I'm sure you would. I'd like any number of things, but we can't always have what we— Tubby! Come back here!"

But the dog, who had seen too many years and too many good dinners, was clearly feeling young and spry and hot to catch himself a mouse, kept going, disappearing down the dark staircase.

"Stupid dog. He'll go tumbling and break his stupid head. Tubby! Simon! Candles, we need candles," Kate said, even as Simon was employing a tinderbox on a small candelabra. "Hurry! This is all my fault. I should have put him outside immediately." She was already on the dark landing.

So much for keeping Kate upstairs; if I leave her here, she'll only follow, and I can't close the panel on my own.

"Just let me go first with the candles," he said, and stepped onto the short landing ahead of the marble steps. He took his time, Kate's hands on his shoulders, their major accompaniment the sizzle of generations of cobwebs succumbing to candle flame.

What would they find? The journals, lined up row by row, decade by decade? Clearly that's what Kate assumed they'd see, believing the Society met for its other functions upstairs, in the drawing room and other rooms in the dower house.

But Simon knew the contents of his brother's letter, his confession of the terrible things he'd done. If the beginnings of the Society were here, then what lay behind this door had to be at least somewhat a mirror of the chamber Holbrook had described.

Tubby was at the bottom of the staircase now, trapped

in a small foyer, facing a closed door and barking a demand for entrance. The stairwell itself, the door in front of them, had been crafted as well as anything else Simon had seen since entering the dower house. A small chandelier hung over their heads, festooned in cobwebs.

"We're about to see the journals, Simon. How can you simply stand there? Try the latch," Kate suggested rather obviously as she patted at her head, as if worried about more cobwebs.

"Yes, I never would have thought of that. Should I also pray it doesn't require a key?"

"Oh, for pity's sake, Simon, how can you stand there and joke when—" She took the candles from him and pushed past him to open the door, take several steps inside. "No, no. This isn't real. It can't be real."

It took only the faint light from the candelabra to tell them they'd just discovered the true meeting place of the Society. If the rooms above them were the antechamber, this was hell itself, and they were being welcomed into it by a statue depicting a woman and three men, all intermingled and unlike anything seen on the backs of Trixie's playing cards or in the rooms above their head.

"I thought we'd find the… Is this where they—?" Kate asked, taking a step back and handing over the candelabra. Her voice was none too steady, and he doubted his would be, either.

"Go upstairs, Kate, you've seen enough. Please, sweetheart—go."

She didn't fight him. She simply turned, her complexion white as chalk, and left him there, dragging Tubby along with her, the light coming from beyond the opened panel to guide her return upstairs.

Simon held up the candelabra, the shadows cast by

the candles even further distorting the look of horror and pain depicted on the female's face. He longed for that sledgehammer Kate had considered earlier, so he could smash this monstrous tableau into bits.

He walked about the room, hunting and lighting banks of fat white candles, strangely shaped red-and-black candles, until he could see into every corner. His heart pounded, his palms had gone moist. His brain silently screamed in protest as he believed he could hear the ghosts of raucous laughter, the tearing sobs.

The chamber was enormous, probably as wide and half as deep as the dower house above it. Even the dust and cobwebs and the scurrying of small feet as mice ran for cover couldn't mute the horror.

The statues and paintings here were anything but artful. They didn't hint at what went on here, they screamed it out in every way. Everywhere were depictions of coupling. Men, women…costumed beasts. Every perversion played out in stone, or on canvas, and even in large tapestries hung on the ivory marble walls.

There were fainting couches, everywhere, large red velvet cushions strewn on the carpets. Silver manacles hung from the walls. A variety of whips and paddles were propped on racks beside a spanking horse, a whipping stool and even a velvet-lined set of stocks.

An ornately carved wooden machine hanging with restraints and turning cranks could be nothing less barbaric than a crude stretching rack to be found in a medieval dungeon.

Dusty and flyspecked and discolored with age, mirrors hung everywhere; above couches, on the walls, set in swivel stands.

There was a small stage off to his right, two rows of chairs placed in front of it for the audience who had sat there to watch whatever bizarre performance could be enacted in front of them.

Every vice, every perversion, every curiosity, all satisfied here.

He nearly tripped over a low stone trough, and lowered the candelabra he held, only to quickly raise it again when he realized the trough was half-filled with a thin ribbon of lamp oil. The trough was only one of several that ran snakelike around the room. When the oil was lit, the low rivers of flames would twist and turn, curling about, casting weird shadows on the walls, mirrors and participants, turning everything around him into a macabre reflection of hell.

But what drew Simon, what he could no longer avoid after inspecting cabinets filled with rotting costumes and implements he didn't wish to put names to, was what held pride of place on a raised platform at the far end of the room, all but surrounded by thirteen pink marble phalluses, the centermost statue of the bizarre circle taller, and gold tipped. The flat-topped centerpiece they encircled had been fashioned in the form of a person; one with arms and legs spread, and complete with silver manacles. Its base was carved with skulls and devil's heads. Tatters of what once had been red tapestry draperies hung from the ornate, mirrored ceiling.

This was it, there could be no question. He was looking at the sacrificial altar.

Thank God Kate had only been able to see a few feet into this chamber of horrors.

Behind the altar was a door, again unlocked, that led to a large sitting room lined floor to high ceiling with wooden bookcases filled with leather-bound books.

They'd found the journals.

There were chairs and ottomans and couches, tables and smoking stands; several wine racks and dusty glasses and decanters. This was a library, one fashioned for the members who might enjoy stepping inside to do a bit of pleasurable journal-reading. A library for sophisticated ghouls.

But there was no larger tome anywhere, nothing that could be considered the Society bible. They'd made progress, but what Gideon Redgrave had declared the real prize still eluded them.

Holding up the brace of candles, Simon walked the bookcases, noted the journals were organized by year, and stopped only once, to remove two volumes bearing his brother's code name, Bird. He would respect the Redgrave privacy by not attempting to search out Barry's journals, those of Kate's grandfather and even those belonging to Jessica and Adam's father, Turner Collier; the Keeper. That would be up to the Redgraves themselves, God help them.

Dead men's names did him no good. It was the living members who concerned him, and the names to put with the codes were in the bible.

But he would protect Holbrook as much as possible. It had been a promise he'd made in front of his brother's tomb inside the family mausoleum. Eventually, if they ever located the supposed bible, his brother's name would be revealed there, yes, but never his private thoughts, his questionable deeds.

Tucking the journals inside his jacket, Simon turned his attention to the obvious once more: Was there a tunnel leading from this place? If so, where did it go? What lay at the end of it? The bible? Barry Redgrave's body?

Because he would not allow Kate in here, not if she had to pass through that damnable hell to see the journals. No. There had to be another way. He took up a single candle and once again walked along the bookcases, this time watching the candle flame intently.

CHAPTER FIFTEEN

BY THE TIME Simon had climbed the stairs and reentered the drawing room, Kate had replaced the dustcovers, and was sitting curled up defensively on one of the couches, Tubby beside her as she leaned her head against his.

"Kate?"

She didn't answer. She had nothing to say to him, to anyone.

"Kate. We probably have to lift the statuettes together."

Sighing, she gave Tubby a kiss on his ear and unfolded her legs, reluctantly standing up and heading for the fireplace. She was fine, she was in control, she would manage…she had to manage.

"On the count of—"

"I know! Let's just do it!" she exploded, surprised at the nearly hysterical vehemence in her voice. "Sorry," she mumbled, lowering her head. She was a cauldron, ready to boil over, Vesuvius about to erupt. Couldn't he see that? Didn't he understand? Oh, God, she couldn't allow her emotions to surface again. She had to hang on, just until she could be alone.

But Simon only calmly counted out the numbers and, together, they watched the panel slide back into place.

All gone. Hidden once more. But never to be expunged from her mind.

Simon merely stood there. Waiting. What did he want her to say?

"I...I expected a library of sorts. The journals," she said at last, feeling herself close to the tears she'd been suppressing while Simon had been...whatever it was he'd been doing. God! How could he have stayed down there so long!

"They're there," he told her, taking the statuette from her hand and replacing it on the mantelpiece. "Not the bible, unfortunately, but the journals are there, dating all the way back to the beginning."

Kate swallowed down hard, her dry throat paining her. "They are? And...and an entrance to the tunnel?"

"Also there, behind one of the doors. There was no need for secrecy once inside the...once inside. It's the other end of the tunnel we need to find. From this side, Kate, it will stop at the pit beneath the greenhouse. I found several other openings, smaller, brick passages leading straight up. For ventilation, you understand. We would probably find the openings in the shrubberies outside. But you're not listening to me, are you?"

She thought she understood what he was saying, save for the constant buzzing in her ears. "Trixie... my mother..."

"Don't, Kate. We don't know that," Simon told her sternly.

She felt her bottom lip begin to tremble. "Don't we? No...no wonder she shot him. I'd always blamed her, for leaving me. I always believed him to be perfect— perfect, Simon. What a fool I was." She looked up at Simon. "It...um...it would appear that either way, at the bottom of it, I'm descended from a...from a long line of monsters."

He tried to pull her into his arms, but she pushed him away. Pity would destroy her.

"No, Simon. Trixie made everything all seem deliciously outrageous and funny. The statues along the stairway in Cavendish Square? Naughty, yes, but only to discommode high-nosed people she believed feigned their outrage while their minds were filled to the brim with naughty thoughts. She laughed, Simon. We all laughed. But *this?* Why didn't she order it all taken away years ago, broken up, burned? *Why?*"

"That's something you'll have to ask her, isn't it?"

Kate's head snapped up. "How can I do that? I *can't,* Simon. I don't want to know. She must have her reasons."

"Or her fears. She couldn't dismantle everything without help, Kate, without someone telling someone else, until the secret was no longer a secret. So she turned it all, even this house, into a tremendous folly of her husband's, certain no one would ever find that panel."

"She should have removed the statuettes," Kate said dully. "She would have done that, yes? Unless she sometimes went down there to—what could she possibly *do* down there?"

"The cobwebs weren't disturbed," Simon pointed out, finally taking Kate's arm and guiding her toward the door. "For all we know, especially if she didn't trust anyone else to come with her, she never learned what we stumbled on today—how to open the panel. Let's just get out of here for now, all right? You can write to Gideon and Valentine, tell them we've located the journals. Gideon can take it from there. You're done, sweetheart. You did what you set out to do."

She shook her head. "Not completely done. There's

still the bible…and my father." She gave a short, choked laugh. "Maybe the Society didn't take his body. Maybe the devil came for it personally."

Once again, Simon attempted to take her in his arms. Again, she pushed him away. "Please don't touch me. How can you bear to touch me? I'm one of *them.* Don't you understand? I lured you, I tricked you, and now you think you must marry me. I'm no better than any of them. Trading favors for what I want."

She was trembling. She might even be sick, right here on the floor of the dower house, which would be rather fitting, she supposed wildly. Not that this place could be any more foul that it was.

The place she'd brought him. The place where she'd so freely given him her virginity…and more.

This horrible place!

I didn't know. I didn't know! I thought myself so sophisticated, so prepared for any challenge. What a fool I am!

"I left you alone up here too long, didn't I?" he said at last. "Gave you much too much time to twist everything about so that what we shared here together last night is now the nightmare, no longer the dream. And do you know something, Kate? Do you?"

"What am I supposed to *know,* Simon?" She lifted her chin; that way her tears might not escape her eyes to roll down her cheeks. "There's nothing you can say that will change my mind."

"Exactly. You've decided to feel sorry for yourself, and you're going about it as you do everything, with all that's in you. But do it knowing this, Kate. I won't try to convince you I love you, I won't say the words, not in this place, because love has never been here, has it? I'll wait you out, I'll give you time to cast out your demons or whatever the hell it is you think you need to do. I've got time. I'm not going anywhere."

He was so kind. So wonderful. It would be so easy to walk into his arms, forget everything but him. But she couldn't. She simply couldn't. Not now.

"Thank you, Simon," she said quietly, and then pulled open the door and left the house, waiting for him and Tubby to join her before locking the door. "I'd like to be alone now. If you don't mind."

"You're going riding, aren't you?"

She nodded, brushing at some dust and cobwebs on his sleeve. "There's cobwebs and cobwebs, Simon. Maybe I can find a way to get one kind out of my head."

He didn't fight her; he clearly meant to stand by his words.

"What did you do when you found out about your brother's involvement with the Society?"

His smile nearly broke her heart. "I crawled into a bottle for two days. I don't recommend it. Take your ride, but be careful."

She couldn't stand another moment near him, not without falling apart. So she only nodded, and turned in the direction of the stables, nearly breaking into a run once she turned the corner at the far end of the dower house. When she got there, it was to see the showy team of white horses being led out of the traces of her grandmother's coach.

Trixie had arrived, in all her usual glory. The woman Kate had always believed in, loved with all her heart; the outrageous, silly, daring-all-things, deliciously scandalous Lady Beatrix Redgrave, dowager countess of Saltwood. The woman the *ton* courted and petted, never daring to do anything less. The woman who never lied, but simply avoided the truth. The beautiful, petite, sweet-smelling angel who had overseen the raising of her four grandchildren without ever growing up herself.

The woman Kate had always striven to emulate, believing her the best of all people.

The woman who had known the worst of horrors about her husband, her son, had clearly been living a lie all these many years, keeping the worst of secrets in order to protect those she loved.

She looked toward the Manor house, imagining Trixie reclining on her favorite couch in the main drawing room, a glass of wine nearby, regaling a doting Dearborn with naughty stories, feeding sugarplums to her ridiculous little yellow pug dogs, looking so much younger than her years. The world as her oyster, Trixie the perfect pearl.

And all that time knowing, remembering. Protecting.

Kate roughly wiped at her tears, and called for Daisy to be saddled.

SIMON CLIMBED THE terrace steps two at a time, intent on entering the drawing room through the French doors and then aiming himself directly at the drinks table.

He wouldn't crawl into a bottle. As he'd warned Kate, that was never a good idea. But he'd visited hell in the past hour, and he needed at least one drink to clear some of the brimstone and ashes from his mouth.

His brother had…cavorted in a similar place. Earned his damnable golden rose at a similar profane *altar,* clad in his obscene, terrifying costume, not a man at all, but a beast, mindless, soulless, damned. Holbrook was dead, paying the ultimate price for his sins. But did that mean Simon couldn't be furious with him, wish he were alive so he could shake some sense into him? What kind of man resorted to such unnatural behavior? What sort of mind even thought up anything so heinous?

Haters of women. Even the willing ones.

Simon stopped just in front of the French doors as his mind whispered those unexpected words.

Debasing. Deflowering. Punishing. Controlling.

"Is that it?" he asked himself out loud, brushing at his sleeves, his waistcoat, trying to rid himself of any remaining dust or webs before stepping inside. "Am I to head back to London and scout about Mayfair to find all the unhappy marriages, all the frustrated sons? Aphrodite and Eros, remember—mother and son? Good God, that's half of London, perhaps half of England itself."

One ambitious man, believing himself to be royal, uses any means, any weakness, to further that treasonous ambition. Preying on the weak, gathering the greedy, tying them to him via their vices, their failings, their hungers; forcing them, if necessary, to do his bidding. Even going so far as to involve their own wives in the hellfire fantasy, proving their willingness to make *sacrifices* for the good of the whole. Promising much, demanding more.

Simon knew he shouldn't be surprised. Kingdoms had risen and fallen on sex for centuries. Wars had been fought, thousands, millions, had died. Women blamed for the lust of men. Men destroyed by clever women.

Sex, greed. The ultimate weapons.

First the father, and then, somehow, the son. Madmen, the pair of them. But clever enough to prove dangerous.

And now a third rebirth of the Society; employing the same methods, seeking its own end.

Could it all still be about the Stuart blood? Could he really be certain no Redgraves were involved? No, he wouldn't think that way; that way there be dragons, now that Kate was in his life. In time, she'd see the past for what it was, unchangeable, no matter how fervently she wished to somehow alter it. She'd come to terms with it, and he'd be there for her future, their future. But if he destroyed her family, past or present, she would never forgive him.

He lifted one last remnant of cobweb from his sleeve, thinking *Oh, what a tangled web we weave....*

Still shaking his head, he depressed the latch and stepped into the drawing room, now considering snatching up the wine decanter and taking it upstairs with him as he ordered a tub.

"Ah, and here's the clever lothario Dearborn has been telling me so much about. It has been impressed on me, mightily, that a betrothal is in order, perhaps even in some haste. Stealing kisses behind the stables? Naughty boy, you've shocked Dearborn all hollow, you know. Come, come. Closer, you handsome creature. I don't bite." There was the slightest pause. "Often."

A stolen kiss? Oh, madam, if you only knew...yet so much better you don't.

Simon forced himself to relax, smile, as he approached one of the couches situated just beneath the largest chandelier and the tiny woman who reclined on it, her painted toes visible, along with a slim silver chain around her right ankle. Her ladyship looked less a dowager than Adam Collier's outlandish rigouts resembled Beau Brummell's sober ensembles.

Her black gown was artfully cut, concealing her shoulders, a stiff, raised collar elongating her throat and somehow helping to accentuate the creamy skin of her chest. Poofed cap sleeves topped sheer black netting that enclosed her arms to her wrists, ending in lace-edged ruffles. A thin black ribbon was tied just beneath her small, uplifted bosoms, its ends trailing onto the couch.

She even had a black lace something-or-other tucked into her short, silvery-gold cap of curls, diamonds twinkling at its center, as did the diamonds in her ears, and ringing several of her fingers.

Her eyes were large and a startlingly clear blue beneath kohl-darkened lashes, her cheeks and mouth subtly rouged, and her scent reached up to tease at him rather than overwhelm him.

If this was the lady's idea of mourning dress, her evening gowns must be a sight to behold.

"My lady," he said, bending over the hand she so languidly offered. "Dearborn, it would seem, has preempted me. Yes, I do have every intention of wedding your granddaughter."

"Intention? Not every sincere wish, every humble hope? How direct you are, young man. And very unlike your late brother, both in looks and temperament. My belated sympathies on your loss last year, as long as I'm dressed for it." Trixie's self-deprecating laugh was the tinkling of silver bells, impossible to resist no matter how outrageous her words. "He was such an unhappy man ever since what cynics like myself might term his rude awakening."

After Simon excused himself to pour a glass of wine, and better marshal his thoughts, Trixie waved him to the facing couch on the other side of a low oval table.

"His rude awakening, ma'am?"

"Yes, and at the hands of a woman, just as in all the most cloying, overwrought tragedies. Leading him on a leash like a slavishly adoring puppy, but only to inflame her true target until he was consumed with jealousy and at last rescued her from the marriage mart. Your brother was crushed, and then embarrassingly incensed, I fear, very publicly declaring he was *finished* with all women, as they were nothing more than—I believe you can employ your imagination to picture the colorful list he spouted at White's. It was, at the least, extensive. You didn't know?"

The dowager countess propped herself more upright, so that she could reach her wineglass. "Oh, dear. I'm always speaking out of turn, aren't I? But that was all so long ago, and easily forgotten when the next *scandale* wiped it from the *ton's* minds, simple fools that they are. Shall we return to the matter at hand? My granddaughter. Where is she, by the way? Not that she would ever be the sort to tag along behind any man all the day long. No simpering, clinging miss, not my Kate."

Simon's earlier thoughts came slamming back to him. *A hater of women.* His brother? "She's gone out riding," he said absently. "About my brother—"

"Oh, you are the determined one, aren't you? I assure you, I know no more than that, and I refuse to repeat idle gossip, as I much prefer choosing to begin it. The subject is closed. I imagine you and Kate will be butting heads on a regular basis. Good for you, and good for her. A marriage of equals is much to be preferred, most especially where Kate is involved, or else the poor husband would find himself dismayed within a fortnight, wondering where on earth his balls had gone scurrying off to without so much as a farewell."

Simon nearly sprayed a mouthful of wine all over his waistcoat, except that a part of him didn't really believe what he'd just heard; that sweet voice, that sweeter smile, those totally unacceptable words. "I...I beg your pardon?"

Trixie gave a languid wave of her hand. "Oh, don't start doing that, or you'll never have time for anything else. Kate has undoubtedly informed you by now. I'm a perfect disgrace, although I consider my free speech a considerable portion of my unique, not yet faded charms. Lord knows everyone listens when I speak, for fear they'll miss a choice nugget they can whisper behind their hands at someone's dinner table the following evening."

Simon smiled. "She did indicate you rather enjoyed yourself."

"As I enjoy society's foibles so much, it seems only fair to give them an occasional bit of scandal or two as a return for my pleasure. Out riding, you said. And yet you're here. Were you naughty?"

"Do you consider it another part of your charm, this ability of yours to make someone's head spin? I can barely keep up."

"Yes, you can," Trixie said, and suddenly those wide, blue eyes weren't quite so innocent. "I know all about you, my lord Singleton. I have, over the years, cultivated and maintained some quite valuable resources, although I won't put you to the blush by disclosing my methods. My eldest grandson believes me beyond redemption, not that he turned his back on recently asking my help, since learning about the Society. Imagine my shock, dearest boy, to hear those words again after all these years. *The Society.* Now picture me figuratively on my knees before you, begging your help. For Kate, if not for me."

Simon put down his wineglass. Obviously he needed to listen to every word this woman said, measure every inflection. "I'm flattered, my lady. Go on."

"I have every intention of doing so. You wouldn't be

here if I didn't approve, or within a thousand leagues of anything to do with my family, most especially my granddaughter. Your brother was Bird, wasn't he? No, no, don't bother to agree or disagree. I saw the name in Turner Collier's journal when it was brought to me, and knew it couldn't be anyone but Holbrook, poor lovesick bastard. Not that I told anyone, dear me, no. He had to have been convinced they would come for him—the reason doesn't concern me—and chose to rob them of their fun. Good choice. Look at Collier and his whore wife. They didn't get too far, did they, and their end was less than pleasant."

She shrugged her elegant shoulders. "Cleopatra chose the asp, chose her own end. When the unthinkable becomes the inevitable, one should be allowed to select one's own poison. Your brother was very brave, having seen the inevitable, just as he had been selfishly greedy to succumb to the base allure of the Society. And yet, if we could see our fate before we act, imagine how dull the world would be."

The dowager countess took another sip of wine. Simon was surprised to see how steady her hand was, how cool and unruffled she appeared. They could as easily have been discussing the weather.

"You're looking less shocked now. Good. Again, I'm certain my dear grandchildren have told you all about me. All they believe they know about me, all I choose to let them know. You want my granddaughter, and I want you to have her. But as it's said, one hand washes the other. I did something for you, and now you're going to do something for me. The Society taught me that, at least."

"So you say, ma'am," Simon bit out, feeling suddenly angry.

"Oh, so rigid, so formal. *Ma'am.* Since we're to be family, I'll call you Simon, and you, of course, will please me by falling into the family habit of addressing me, of thinking of me, as the delightfully *outré* Trixie, and not the woman you see before you now. That's how it must be. I'm nobody's victim, Simon, and haven't been in a very long time."

"Ma'am… Trixie? Are you about to blackmail me? Kate, for some favor I perform for you?"

"Ah, wonderful. I knew you were quick. Spencer quite dotes on you."

She's spoken to Perceval? The prime minister was one of her carefully cultivated sources? The woman was correct; he didn't want to think about that.

"Yes, I've spoken with Spencer, among others. But do pay attention, for now I'm speaking with you. The journals, Simon. You were sent to find them, and dearest Valentine was conveniently called away so that you could, as Kate would have been similarly summoned, if she had taken an instant dislike to you. Yes, all my doing, all my spies, all my schemes. I'm a clever woman, Simon Ravenbill. And you are a clever boy. Have you located them? And the bible, as well?"

Simon hesitated. She had the power to have Val summoned to London, just to clear the path for him?

She put down her wineglass. This time her hand shook slightly. "Silence is as good as an admission. You have. I had put my faith in you, having no other choice, frankly. And now you will destroy them for me. Oh, don't frown. Not all of them. I've already told my family I'd burned all I'd found after my husband's death—a whopping-great crammer I was forced to invent in an instant. But they had no reason to doubt me, and I had no thought they'd still go searching, send Kate hunting for what they believed no longer existed, just to keep her occupied and out of trouble. I should have said I'd found Barry's journals, as well, but some lies aren't as brilliant as others. But no matter what, they cannot be found now, those of my husband, and those written by my son. Do we understand each other?"

Simon felt sure he did. "I think so, yes. If I refuse?"

"You won't. You've a lovely line to your jacket, Simon, my compliments to your tailor. Although I believe it could only improve with the removal of the journals marring its fit. Yes, I noticed when you so politely bent over my hand, but needed your confirmation to be truly certain. You understand my anxiety, as you feel the same protectiveness for your brother. That's only human nature, isn't it—to protect those we love. To be entirely clear, we're speaking of the journals from the beginning, up to the time of my son's death. They all must be destroyed, and the bible along with them. Are we agreed?"

God. She's terrified. And having seen what I've just seen, how can I possibly refuse her? But I'll be damned if I'll trust anyone here at the Manor, not even Dearborn. "We're agreed. However, I've failed to locate the bible."

Trixie's head snapped back, as if she'd been slapped. "No, no, that won't do. The bible must be found and destroyed. If my grandsons can't locate the Society through the journals alone, they're not the men I raised. The bible goes back to the beginning. To the *beginning,* Simon. Do you know when it began? With my husband, the most vile, perverted man to ever walk this earth. Now do you understand?"

"Yes, ma'am, I do. I truly do. I'll need your Mr. Borders, whom I understand traveled here with you. I assume you trust him?"

"There comes a time, even in a life such as mine, when it becomes necessary to trust somebody. Richard is the first man in a long time I've allowed myself to believe in. You're the second. Gentlemen in deed as well as word. Tell me, where are they? I searched for years without success."

Simon told her, leaving out the facts about how the panel was accessed, and that Kate had been with him.

"The so-called dower house? A secret panel? But I searched for them there, in that hellish place my husband considered his private retreat. For years I searched with no success. I wonder how Barry discovered them, unless one of my husband's nasty little coven of ghouls directed him to them. There are several I could point to, but luckily for them, they're all dead."

"It's all there, ma'am—" He could not bring himself to address her as Trixie, not at the moment. "The journals. The, um…the altar and the rest."

Trixie had picked up her wineglass once more, only to have it fall from her hand, to shatter on the floor. Suddenly she looked every day of her age, and probably more, her complexion white beneath her rouged cheeks. "No. No, that can't be. Don't lie to me, Simon. We have an agreement. I'll have the truth or nothing."

"But that is the truth, ma'am. Most sincerely begging your pardon, I'm certain you've been there, although you haven't directly told me you have. How couldn't you know?"

Trixie pressed her palm to her forehead, and when she spoke, she seemed to be speaking to herself. "That old bastard. That damnable old bastard! To the very end, he wouldn't tell me. His *legacy.* His cursed delusions. *Royal?* Royal *bastard."*

Simon leaned forward. "Descended from the royal Stuart," he said softly, hoping she'd tell him more.

Trixie snorted; she actually snorted. "The royal Stuart and some roundheeled chambermaid. Charles could have poured all his royal blood into a thimble, and even that would have been polluted." Her shoulders stiffened, and she turned those penetrating blue eyes on Simon. "How did you know?"

"The Royal tartan painted into the portraits, the missing coats of arms in the mausoleum."

"I never did get around to replacing those crests, did I? How uncharacteristically sloppy of me. It took me *hours* to dig them out of the granite. Spencer didn't exaggerate when he said you were up to the mark on all suits. Do my grandchildren know? Did you boast of your genius to them?"

"I'm afraid so, yes. Remember, ma'am, we may have to dig through many uncomfortable truths, but we're doing it to uncover and destroy a treasonous plot."

"Yes, yes, of course. All for the Crown and England, and all that rubbish. You'll have to pardon me for selfishly considering my family first, but pardon me or not, that's how it's going to be, understood? Might I trouble you for another glass of wine? I need to think about this for a moment. All of it."

Simon did as she asked, and then sat down once more, struggling to keep his silence, as he had a dozen or more questions in his mind, burning to be asked.

"I find the table has turned, Simon, and now I am at your mercy, and needs must trust your discretion. Are we again agreed?"

"We are. What we need, if we're to be denied the

bible, lies far from here, more probably somewhere in London. What happened here is the past, and has little bearing on what's occurring now, other than to begin to understand how the Society thinks and acts. We're convinced Turner Collier, in his role of Keeper during your son's time with the Society, somehow kept the bible current even after your son's death. It's probably why he was murdered, but we don't know how much, if anything, he told his murderers before he died. Which is why we're here."

Again, it was as if Trixie were speaking to herself.

"If Collier remained the Keeper, I doubt he told them the truth, or at least not all of it. If he knew he couldn't keep the bible safe, he would have destroyed it. I can only hope he had the time."

She seemed to snap herself back to her surroundings. "Collier was always a bugger for the rules. Born with a conscientious stick up his back, for all his devil-dabbling and fornication with anything that would lie still long enough, and I do mean anything, or anyone. Barry boasted about it to me when he explained he *owned* Collier, body and soul. After all, the Spartans believed it gave them strength, didn't they? My son was a master of self-serving expediency. A waste of effort on my part, ridding him of his father's influence, wasn't it? Then again, I'm still here, aren't I, even flourishing, in my way. There is that to consider. There always has to be a winner, and for that, there must be losers."

Simon said nothing. The entire conversation thus far had been otherworldly, as if he was listening to a bizarre, rambling soliloquy at Covent Garden. Will Shakespeare didn't have a patch on Beatrix Redgrave when it came to convoluted family tragedies.

"You really don't shock easily, do you?" Trixie took

a long drink of wine. "I suppose you're the one person I can tell this, if only in exchange for the destruction of the bible. We were always brought in via the tunnel. Opium administered by force, blindfolds, closed coaches, and then being led through the tunnel to the hell beyond. Charles was always waiting for us, robed and masked, standing there like some demonic Colossus of Rhodes, ordering us to our places."

He had to say something. The dowager countess appeared near collapse. "Ma'am, I don't need to know all of this, truly."

"Yes, son, you do. If you're to agree to thwart my grandson in order to help me, you need to understand the urgency of my plea. Now, about the cave. I would have thought, we all thought, we'd traveled whole miles. Clever, clever old bastard. Eventually, most of us learned it was easier to cooperate. Even when they brought in the whores, and made us watch. Even when they brought in the virgins. God…the stories I could tell you, and the stories those fools told me, never thinking to fear this cooperative, so congenial and flattering *vessel*. The men who then feared *me* these many years, feared what I knew. I kept them on their toes until the day they died, still believing I held the bible, had it safely hidden with a solicitor, to be turned over to the king should anything happen to me. None of those foul men died happily, by the way, I take pleasure in that. Although I suppose I should make an exception for old Guy, who cocked up his toes, among other things, in my—"

Now Simon believed it was he who didn't want to hear more. "Please don't think about that now. You're an exceptional woman. Not only did you survive, you shepherded a fine family who loves you unconditionally. I want to help you. Do you know where the entrance of the tunnel is, ma'am? It would assist me, immensely."

"I told you. We were blindfolded, led like blind lambs to the slaughter. Month after month, on the first night of the full moon. Sobbing, praying, pleading, all to no avail."

"That does help, ma'am. If they retain some of the old ways, we should pay special attention to the first night of the full moon."

She lifted her chin, reminding him of Kate, although the two women looked nothing alike.

"Good. Now I want you to know the rest. I refused to so demean myself, to either cry or rave. I won't attempt to justify what I did, how I learned to survive, even conquer, but I need to at least offer an explanation. I had been all but sold to Charles to settle my father's gambling debts. Which was their sin, not mine. I was fifteen when Barry was born. A difficult birth, and there were to be no more children, no more *royal heirs*. There was no longer any reason not to, as Charles drawled so poetically, toss me into the pot with the others. And he did."

Simon closed his eyes. "I'm so sorry, ma'am."

But Trixie was in charge once again. "Don't interrupt. When I saw his interest straying to someone else, no matter how *pleasing* I learned to be, I knew I would be replaced. She had the look of a fine brood mare, you see—large teats and broad hips. Not a looker, a breeder. After all, he had many other…outlets available to him for his pleasures, didn't he? His bastards fairly littered the countryside. But he needed the safety of more legitimate male heirs. That's when it became apparent what I had to do. For the sake of my child, who had to be protected at all costs. Until then, I reasoned I'd simply outlive him, be able to raise Barry without his father's influence."

Suddenly Simon recognized where this was all leading. He tried to ignore the shiver that went down his spine. "Please, you don't have to…"

Her smile was nearly beatific. "But, again, I find I want to, after all these years. Isn't that strange? Confession being beneficial, and all that nonsense. Perhaps I am growing old, and wish to cleanse my soul? Allow me to tell you something, Simon. There's no such thing as a convenient death, coming just when it's needed. That's the stuff of pennypress novels. Such fortuitous demises such as my husband's have to be… helped along."

She sighed, as if a weight had been lifted, but not completely. "Now I'm done. I suppose I'll feel better at some point, although I don't discern any change as yet. Please ring for Dearborn, and he'll locate Richard for you. You'll of course need the key. Dearborn believes he has the only one, but Dearborn has been wrong before, although he'd never admit such a thing, which is better for us in the long run. I'll have Richard get mine for you. How will you go about it? Destroying those journals?"

"A secret is best kept by two, Trixie, as I've recently learned," he said, at last taking up her invitation. "Mr. Borders and I are sufficient for this one."

Trixie nodded. "And you and I for mine. Kate must never know, none of them can ever know. Forgive my maidenly dramatics, but I truly couldn't bring myself to live on another minute, if they knew."

"They won't," Simon assured her. He already knew what he was going to do. After all, it had worked before. He bowed in her direction, turned to leave—and then turned back. "I have one more question, probably one you can't answer. As I dodged cobwebs in that hellhole, it occurred to me that somebody had to have done the cleaning of the place during the time the Society was active. Would you have any idea who that might have been?"

Trixie tapped a be-ringed finger against her lips. "In my husband's time, no. I wish I had. But with Barry? His man, Burke, and his wife and grown daughter ran off almost immediately after the interment. Very loyal, Burke. Perhaps it was them?"

CHAPTER SIXTEEN

KATE SAT WITH her eyes shut, unwilling to look at her reflection in the dressing table mirror as Sally stood behind her and brushed her hair, still damp from her bath.

How did one live a lie for more than half a lifetime? Not only live it, but thrive. Laugh. Joke. Dance. Hide all the horror, the memories, behind a facade that convinced the world, even her own grandchildren, that life was a beautiful, joyful thing.

Not once, but twice. First her husband, and then her son, repeating his father's sins. Monsters. Guilty of the worst crimes and abuses.

"I would have killed them both."

"Your pardon, m'lady?" Sally asked, pausing in the act of easing a tangle with the pair of brushes.

"Nothing. I was merely contemplating the idea of having you snip away at least two-thirds of this unruly mop."

"Oh, no, m'lady, you daren't do any such thing. It would be a crime for me to do such a thing, that would."

Kate smiled, and opened her eyes. "There are crimes and then there are crimes. I doubt anyone burned in hell for cutting someone's hair."

The maid took up her chore once more. "There was that lady with the veils and such. She cut someone's hair and then they cut off his *head*. That's surely worth a good burning in...in her nether regions."

"Netherworld might be a better choice of description," Kate said, her eyes looking somewhat alive again at last. "You're mixing Salome and her veils and John the Baptist with Delilah and Samson, I'm afraid, and I won't even bother with your misconception of where the nether regions are located in relationship to hell. Who told you these stories?"

Sally still looked confused. "The dowager countess, m'lady. We all so dote on her stories."

Kate's smile disappeared. "Yes, so did I. Are we through, Sally? Consuela looks more than ready for her bed—aren't you, Consuela?"

The duenna shook herself out of her near-slumber, to protest she was not in the least tired, and ready to guard her charge with every ounce of her blood and last breath of her body.

"Dear me, really? You're expecting an imminent attack from Delilah's Philistines, Consuela?"

"Only the one," she answered, pushing herself up and out of her chair. "We have spoken this afternoon with Mr. Dearborn, and we are aware the fox is attempting to breach the henhouse. Her ladyship thinks it all a delightful mischief, but we are not so easily amused. Until your brother the earl is approached, and gives his blessing, we will remain vigilant. We know what is proper."

"Yes, we certainly do, if only by listening to rumors and reading about it in books. But I highly doubt the marquis will be attacking my bedchamber door with an ax, demanding entry. Go to bed, Consuela. And you, as well, Sally. For the moment—or forever, if you have anything to say about it, Consuela—I sleep alone. Please, I'm nearly exhausted after an afternoon and evening of my grandmother's delightful but fatiguing chatter."

Kate continued to smile as maid and duenna curtsied and at last left her chamber, Sally for the servants' quarters, Consuela for the cot in the dressing room.

"The door, Consuela!" she called after the woman.

Apparently reluctantly, as it took some time, the dressing room door closed. That had been their agreement: close the door or sleep elsewhere. One night of burying her head beneath a half dozen pillows to attempt (and fail) to drown out the woman's snores had been more than sufficient for Kate to not feel terrible about making her demand.

And now she was alone. The mantel clock had struck eleven only a few short minutes ago, and she was alone; just her and her bed. That great, yawning abyss she alternately wished to throw herself onto to sob out her pain and longed to avoid because Simon would not be there to share it with her.

She untied her dressing gown, laid it out on the bed and climbed in beneath the covers, positive she'd never sleep.

How could she still want him, having seen the other side of what she had believed to be beautiful, wonderful, even magical? How could she touch him, feel his touch, without remembering there could be a dark and ugly side to what went on between a man and a woman? How could she look for pleasure where her grandmother and mother had probably known only pain, degradation, fear?

And hatred. They had to have felt hatred. Loathing. *Rage*.

Trixie had outlived her nemesis; Maribel had taken matters into her own hands, ridding herself of her tormentor. And good for her! There was no longer any question in Kate's mind as to why her mother had left her children in Trixie's care as she and her French lover made good her escape. For all anyone could ever know, the two women had made a pact.

Kate had worked all of that out in her head as she put Daisy through her paces along the West Run, as she'd industriously, perhaps with an edge of frantic, ruthless energy, pulled the weeds half obscuring the graves of Torr Gribbon and his family.

She'd felt Simon's eyes on her all through dinner, but they both had allowed Trixie to dominate the conversation with tidbits about the pair of funerals she'd attended, Richard Borders tossing her a name or subject when she seemed to lag, spurring her on to another hilarious, absurd tale as only Trixie could tell it.

Kate still had some trouble meeting Simon's eyes, yet at the same time longed to be in his arms. What did that make her? How could anyone see what she'd seen today, realize everything she'd realized today, and still long to feel a man's arms around her?

Trixie loathed men. Kate had convinced herself of that, too, during her long, introspective afternoon. She hated them, she used them…and, unbelievably, she enjoyed them. Had she ever known love? Kate doubted that highly. She would ask her grandmother the difference between wanting someone and loving someone, if she believed the woman would have an answer for her. But she didn't believe that.

Wasn't that sad…so sad….

Her eyes popped open wide when the hand came down over her mouth, followed by a low whisper. "We need to talk."

"Howd'youpropo wedo yat wit y'and over m'—"

"With my hand over your mouth, yes," Simon said, grinning down at her. "Good point. Will you come with me?"

Kate made note of the fact he still hadn't removed his hand. How trusting of him. As if she'd call for Consuela! She nodded, furiously. Mostly because she was furious. What sort of dolt did he believe her to be?

He kissed her forehead. "I wasn't certain you'd want to be…with me."

Her entire body relaxed. He was the best sort of dolt—the sweetest dolt in the entire world.

She nodded again as he stepped away from the bed, and pushed back the coverlet, Simon already holding up her dressing gown for her.

"Where are we going?" she whispered as they tiptoed to the door.

Once in the hallway and heading in the direction of the west wing, he answered her. "I'd like to say far, far away from here. But there is that inconvenient business of the gates. And the moat."

"We haven't got a… All right, we'll call it a moat. Where's Dearborn?"

"Taken care of," he said as they passed by the staircase. "It would seem he enjoys nothing more than a rousing game of dominos. He and Richard are in the dining room, betting fairly tame stakes while enjoying both your brother's cellar and his cigars. Every man has his weakness, I'm to understand, and Richard found Dearborn's."

He stopped in front of the king's chambers, never slept in by any of the realm's rulers, but when her grandfather had built the wing he'd foreseen all circumstances. To her amazement, he then pulled the heavy key from his pocket.

"How…?"

"Let's just say, thank you for having the foresight to return the cabinet key to its hidey-hole. Just, please, remind me to return it yet tonight. This is an impressive, but very large key. Dearborn would notice its absence from its hook in a heartbeat. Now, come on, let's see how kings supposedly live."

And suddenly, Kate froze where she stood. What had seemed so natural, even glorious, last night, now seemed sordid…even evil.

"Kate?" He cupped her cheek in his hand. "We're going to talk, remember?"

She looked at the floor, which held no answers for her, and then peered up at Simon. "Talk," she repeated. "This is…no, *I'm* being ridiculous. Why am I being ridiculous?"

"Because you're not made out of wood, I suppose. You've a mind and a heart and precious little experience, no matter if you don't think you're still more the girl you were yesterday morning instead of the woman you suppose yourself tonight."

"I have *no* idea what you're talking about, but we probably should continue this on the other side of the door?"

He smiled so sweetly at her, she wanted to cry. He had become her rock, without her realizing it; her anchor, her sanity in the midst of all the madness. "That was going to be my next suggestion."

Once the door was closed and locked behind her, Kate, led by the light from candles Simon must have lit earlier, made her way through the draped antechamber and into the cavernous apartment.

"It's just as I remember it when I'd trail in here after the maids," she said, looking about at the heavy tapestry draperies, the overly ornate furniture. "Possibly worse. Do you…do you know there are fresh sheets on that hideous bed? Trixie says it's mandatory. One must always have all in order, just in the off chance some mooching royal decides to drop in unannounced for tea. Or, as Trixie explained the thing, if you have the crushing stupidity and overweening audacity to *have* a royal chamber, you'd damn well better be prepared to see the occasional king."

She sat herself down on what had to be the most rigid, uncomfortable settee ever constructed. Again, as Trixie had told her, one has to make the king welcome, but not necessarily comfortable, or else he might decide to stay for days on end, his entourage and horses both eating their heads off at your expense. Trixie made everything and everyone a joke, and her descriptions of the foibles of society probably accounted for some of Kate's lack of fear and even respect of these silly people as she made her come-out. In retrospect, that may have been a mistake.…

She'd let her mind wander long enough.

"What did you do all afternoon while I was alternately feeling sorry for myself and strenuously biting my lip so I didn't mistakenly say anything revealing when I visited Trixie in her chambers?"

Simon sat down beside her. "Nothing too strenuous. At your grandmother's request, I accompanied Richard on a tour of the estate buildings."

She sat up straighter. "The dower house?"

He shook his head. "I didn't have the key at that point, remember? You took it with you when you went for your ride."

Sighing, Kate attempted to relax once more, but the settee made that impossible. The furniture in the king's chambers was constructed for the ramrod spines of royalty, not the all-but-collapsible ones of the Redgraves. "I can't sit here," she said, getting to her feet, intent on repositioning herself on the floor at his feet.

"Not there," he said, taking her hand. "I need to hold you. That's all, Kate. Hold you."

"I need that, too. Nothing else in this world seems solid to me anymore but you." She attempted a smile. "And this furniture, of course."

He led her to the bed, suggesting he approach it on one side and she the other, as it would most likely take the two of them to successfully turn back the heavy tapestry cover. "Otherwise, we'd probably smother," he joked as they then took turns tossing many of the heavy tapestry pillows to the floor.

"You'd best remove your shoes," she told him. "We needn't worry about wrinkles, however. None of the maids would ever be so foolhardy as to tell Mrs. Justis the sheets had somehow been put on the bed without first being pressed."

And then she ignored the wooden steps and boosted herself up on the mattress and arranged a few of the pillows behind her as she lay down, to peer up at the tapestry canopy.

"See anything of importance?" Simon asked her as he joined her on the bed, folding one arm beneath his head as he lay on his side, facing her, half the width of the immense bed between them. They'd been in much closer proximity on the settee; now she could barely see him, thanks to the velvet bed draperies that blocked most of the candlelight.

Kate was feeling stupid again. Panicked by his closeness, even as she wanted him closer. She wanted *him*. But what if she didn't? What would happen then?

What if she had asked him to stop last night? What if he'd asked her to do something she couldn't bring herself to do? Men were stronger, physically. Trixie may have been smarter, but even she hadn't found a way to stop whatever had gone on in that chamber of horrors beneath the dower house. Women were born physically vulnerable; it was the way they'd been fashioned. Weaker, softer. Vessels, not weapons.

And cursed with a desire to please.

She felt a touch on her shoulder and nearly jumped out of her skin.

"Damn. I should have followed you this afternoon, had this out between us before you had a chance to get everything tangled up in your mind."

Kate sat up on the mattress and turned to face him. "My mind is *not* tangled. We did what we did, I am who I am, and that's the end of it. You're the one who felt some great need to tack marriage on to what we did. I didn't. Can't you see what that says about me?"

Simon sat up, as well. "And what is that supposed to mean?"

"I don't know." She barely recognized her own voice. She pushed her hands through her hair and knew it was wild; she should have allowed Sally to braid it before shooing her away. "I'm...I'm probably unnatural. Aren't I?"

"Oh, sweet Jesus," Simon all but moaned. "Come here."

"No! I should be able to stand on my own. It's...it's wrong, so wrong to be...to be a slave to one's passions."

And Simon laughed.

He *laughed!*

Kate went on the attack. Without giving a thought to her earlier rejection of his touch, she turned on him, knocking the two of them back onto the pillows, trying to get at him, pummel him as he continued to laugh, and laugh. "Stop it! Stop that laughing right now. There's nothing funny about—"

"One night…one man who is soon to be your husband… and suddenly you're a…you're a slave to your passions?" Simon grabbed on to her wrists and rolled her onto her back. "God, I love you."

Kate stopped struggling. She tilted her head slightly to one side, allowing his words to play inside her head a second time. He'd said that before. Well, not exactly said it. He'd said he wouldn't say it, not while they were in the dower house, not while what she'd seen was still so fresh in her mind. Yes, that's what he'd said. She remembered now. At the time, she'd just wanted to be alone…but she remembered it now.

"You don't have to say that," she told him, knowing she didn't mean what she said.

He let go of her wrists, as if belatedly realizing she could believe he was holding her down, perhaps against her will. "That would be your opinion. Which, as it happens, doesn't concur with mine. I love you, Kate. I've probably loved you since the first day, when you winked at me on the stairs. You're beautiful, incorrigible, unexpected, passionate, brave, outspoken, beautiful—that bears repeating, probably headstrong does, as well— gentle, loving and caring, loyal, more than passably brilliant, and if you don't love me I'll probably wither and die without you, but I'll go. Do I go, Kate? Because I love you enough to do that, if that's what you want."

She looked up into his face for a long time. Searched his eyes for any shadow in them, any hint of loathing linked to the sins of her father, her grandfather…and perhaps Trixie and Maribel, as well. What she saw in those beautiful eyes had nothing to do with anything but caring, loving, acceptance. No shadows, no barely leashed lust. Just…yes, just love. Only love.

"Don't go," she managed to whisper through her sudden tears. "Please don't go. Never go…"

He kissed away her tears. Smoothed her hair back from her face, looked deeply into her eyes.

"I love you, Simon. I love you. More…I trust you. You'd never hurt me. You'd never lie to me. It's just as you said. The past is the past, but it's not our past. For us, there's only the future. I see that now, finally."

"Kate…sweetheart…we probably should talk about that a bit before—"

She put her hand over his mouth, just as he'd done to her earlier. "I think we've talked enough, don't you?"

He sighed against her hand. Nodded. Pressed a kiss against her palm.

And then they made love. Created it, between them. Nourished with kisses, stroked with gentle hands, coaxed into bloom with their joined heartbeats, brought to fierce, healing flame with the melding of their bodies.

Each touch a benediction, every sigh an affirmation. Together, they were invincible, untouchable. As long as they had each other, nothing and no one they might face in the future would have the power to change what they built between them this wonderful night.

Like the Phoenix, they went into the fire and then rose out of it again, soaring high and free, reborn.

ELSEWHERE IN THE Manor, a woman cried, and was held, and at last found what she never dreamed existed in the arms of a most unlikely lover; a short, portly, gray-bearded man long past his first youth. A man whose name might or might not be Richard Borders.

CHAPTER SEVENTEEN

"MORNING ALL!"

As "all" in the breakfast room consisted of Simon and Richard, both turned to see Adam Collier striking a pose in the doorway, clearly proud of his outlandish rigout.

"What in blazes are you dressed for, young man?" Richard asked around a bite of toast. "And where did you ever find those boots? You could fit another two feet into them."

"True, true," Adam said, advancing on what Simon secretly believed the brainless young twit considered his quarry. "There are only so many pair of my beloved shoes I am willing to risk, even in such an exemplary cause. These are Dearborn's, worn he tells me, when a portion of the cellars flood during heavy rains, not that it matters. These horrendous trousers belong to my valet, who begged my pardon for having them in his otherwise dull but acceptable wardrobe. Brown? What *could* he have been thinking? We're not tunnel hunting today?"

Simon and Richard exchanged glances. "No," Simon said, "sadly, we're not. But I'm certain Kate would be happy to join you." *Unless she kills me first for foisting you on her.* He got to his feet, and Richard quickly rose, as well. "Mr. Borders and I have other plans. And we're already wasting valuable time, aren't we, Richard?"

"My fault, entirely. I overslept. Mr. Collier?" he said, bowing in Adam's general direction. "The best of luck to you today."

"Well, I should hope so! It would be quite bad form to wish me ill luck, wouldn't it? I truly wish to help, you know. After a time of reflection I realized I don't speak French, so Boney has to lose. I mean, the clothes are one thing—fine, very fine—but I don't need the whole bloody bunch of them coming here, do I? Just the tailors."

Simon shook his head and motioned for Richard to precede him from the room. "You get used to it," he commiserated once they were some way down the hall. "The nearly overwhelming urge to bang his head against something solid until the action shakes awake some small bit of mostly slumbering brain."

"He was made Gideon's ward after his parents were murdered. Do you know, when presented with his sister after a few years lived apart, he didn't even recognize her? He first attempted to romance her, and then denied her, called her a fortune hunter. Jessica, who'd been worried sick about the boy she remembered as sweet and shy—and much younger, of course—promptly told Gideon he could keep him and stomped out of the Portman Square mansion. I think that's why Gideon married her—she'd bested him, you see. I understand not many can do that."

"I know I'm not in any great hurry to try. I'm told you and Jessica ran a gaming house in London."

The affable Richard suddenly looked anything but friendly. "And how would that be any business of yours, my lord?"

Simon immediately realized his mistake. "It wouldn't, and I sincerely apologize."

"Accepted. Now, here's the key Trixie told me to give you. What's the plan?"

"After finding a way to avoid Kate all morning, you mean?"

"Trixie's taking care of finding something for them to do, although I doubt she'll want to go searching for the other end of the tunnel, or cave, or whatever it is."

"I don't know about that, my friend. She's quite the brave woman. And the farther from the Manor she can boost Kate, well, the better it will be for us." Simon paused in the large entrance hall and looked up the staircase, just in case Kate was on her way down. He'd kept her awake until after four, and hoped she was still soundly asleep, perhaps even dreaming of him. But with Kate one could never be too careful.

He'd lied to her, a lie of omission, even as she'd praised him, saying she knew he'd never lie to her. He had that yet to deal with, and knew the discussion would probably take place uncomfortably soon.

And not one lie, but two, another lie of omission. Perhaps if there were only the one…?

"Richard, to save your own skin, would you allow a headstrong, admittedly capable woman to accompany you on what could possibly be a somewhat dangerous mission?"

"Should you take Kate along tonight when you meet with the smugglers? That is what you're asking, isn't it?"

Simon stopped dead on the flagstone walkway leading toward the dower house. "How—?"

"I think you know," Richard said with a smile splitting his beard, showing off strong white teeth.

"Trixie. She bribes the servants."

"No, she pays them. Quite well. Some to be obvious

in their watching, their observation, and some to be devious as the devil, even going so far as to tidy up behind someone like Kate, should she be less than careful, in order to help her keep her secrets. Any day, I expect at least three of them to announce they've pooled their earnings and plan to purchase themselves a tavern, or perhaps a small island."

"Are we being watched now?"

"No, not now. She gave strict orders. I might tell you this was not the easiest order she's ever given, as her curiosity nearly overwhelmed her need to feel safe at last. This has not been an easy time for her, ever since Gideon approached her about the Society."

Simon cocked a look over his shoulder at Richard as he inserted the key in the lock. "She confided in you?"

"Inside," Richard ordered shortly. Once the door was closed behind them, he looked at Simon, and sighed. "I found her last night, weeping as if her heart would break. Yes, she told me. She told me many things. Now, where do we go from here?"

Simon explained the mechanism for the secret panel, and they took up candles before heading down into Charles Redgrave's private hell.

Richard looked, sighed, but said nothing.

"The journals are in a room behind the altar."

"Never give such an abomination that name, if you please," Richard said at last.

Over the course of the next hour, all the journals covering the time since Barry Redgrave's death were carried upstairs and neatly stacked atop two Holland covers spread on the floor in the entrance hall.

Next, the remaining journals were pulled from the shelves and tossed into a pile in the center of the reading room.

Sweat pouring from both men, even though the chambers were underground, and naturally cool, they rolled small barrels of lamp oil Simon had found in two of the cabinets into place. They then poured some over the piled journals, added to the troughs that snaked through the main chamber, filling each to the brim, allowing more to run over those rims and soak into the carpets and velvet cushions.

The last of the lamp oil became a fuse of sorts, running from the room, to the staircase, to the main floor carpets of the dower house.

Richard put down the small barrel he'd just emptied. "Do you really believe the fire will be hot enough to collapse this pile onto itself, tumbling it all into that hellhole down there?"

"With any luck, yes. And melt the rest, even the metal of the..."

"Restraints, yes, I saw them. Some of them too large for a woman's wrists. Which of Dante's nine circles of hell do you think that place is?"

"All of them," Simon said, tying up the corners of the Holland covers, turning the dust sheets into sacks. "Limbo, lust, gluttony, greed, heresy, violence, fraud, treachery...even anger. All that's missing is madness. Complete and utter madness." He straightened once more, putting a hand to the small of his back. "Who would have thought arson could be such backbreaking work? Unfortunately, we're not done. I need to be sure the pipes leading up to the surface aren't blocked after all these years, as we need air to feed the fire once it's set. But first we'll get these journals to a safe place."

Richard picked up one of the sacks. "I've been wondering about that. Did you have one in mind, by any chance? I can't see us traipsing across the lawns and up the stairs of the Manor lugging them on our backs, do you? Although many others would," he ended with a soft chuckle. "Still, Trixie assures me you're brilliant."

"I appreciate her confidence in me, but I'm actually taking a page from the Redgrave books, sparing an unfortunately unquenchable nugget of apprehension Kate somehow was able to refuse Trixie's invitation and is still in the house somewhere. Still, I'm putting my faith in Redgravian audacity. It has worked for them, I believe, since the beginning. So yes, we are strolling across the lawn and up the Manor's main staircase with these sacks flung over our backs. With heads high, talking and joking, looking anything but furtive, as if we all lug sacks about with us in Londontown as a daily occurrence. Can you manage that?"

"I earned my daily bread with a deck of cards for many a decade, my boy. I can bluff with the best of them. Shall we?"

KATE HAD GIVEN in to her delicious laziness and agreed to take breakfast in her bedchamber. In her bed, actually, which she could barely remember returning to last night; early this morning, actually. Simon had carried her down the hallway, tucked her under the covers, kissed her lingeringly and then left her. She had probably fallen asleep before he was back in the hallway, softly closing the door behind him.

So only now, hours after she usually rose, bathed, dressed and made her way to the breakfast room, was she heading toward the stairs, eager to see Simon again, nearly as eager to load her plate with a hearty meal, for she was unnaturally famished.

The day would come when they'd spend each night together, wake to morning kisses and perhaps a pair of breakfast trays. Sally probably had best prepare herself to brushing crumbs from the bedsheets every morning. The thought brought a smile to Kate's face, and she nearly called out to Simon when she saw him in the upstairs hallway, walking toward the west wing with Richard Borders beside him, the pair of them carrying— What the devil?

She stepped into a recessed doorway, just in case either of them happened to turn to look over their shoulders and see her, and then slowly peeked out her head to watch as they disappeared around a corner in the west wing.

The journals. They had to be carrying the journals. Moving them from the dower house in order to inspect them without having to spend any more time in that horrible chamber.

The members of the Society couldn't have been prolific journalists, if all of their writings back to her father's time filled only two sacks—no, Holland covers; they'd used the Holland covers. Brilliant!

And moving them to Simon's own rooms certainly made sense. But couldn't he have told her what he was doing? Didn't he yet understand? Nothing remained a secret for long, not from her, at least. Although he was probably only attempting to protect her, keep *her* from having to return to the dower house ever again.

Which was very sweet of him. He was a sweet man. And he loved her.

She'd only make him suffer a little bit for thinking he could hide the journals from her.

Kate remained in the alcove, counting in her head, nearly reaching three hundred before Simon and Richard appeared once more, this time heading for the main staircase. Her body pressed against the door, she waited until the click of their heels on the wood stairs faded away before stepping into the hallway once more.

Figuratively, she rubbed her hands together, intent on heading straight for Simon's bedchamber, and the journals. Just to…just to look, that's all. One quick peek. Or perhaps two.

"Ah, there you are at last, slug-a-bed. Ready to go, I see, although this penchant for riding clothes day after day confounds me."

Kate froze where she was. "Adam," she said, pinning a painful smile to her face before turning around. "Ready to go where, may I— What the devil are you dressed up for? You look like one of the gardeners."

He patted at his chest with both hands. "Not the shirt, surely. Purest Irish linen. Set me back three pounds six for only a pair of them, as I recall, and I highly commend myself for sacrificing this one in such a good cause. Not that I'd come within a dozen yards of my valet's suggestion of donning his unbleached homespun. My skin chafes easily, you understand."

How had the world, for the past nearly nineteen years, refrained from squeezing the boy's neck until he turned purple? "Would you please get to the point?"

"The point? You mean I wasn't clear? We're going tunnel hunting, of course. Or cave hunting. Whatever. It's my duty to lend my assistance, you understand, brought home to me by both the marquis and your good self. And Valentine, although I admit I thought he was only attempting to frighten me. Oh, and French tailors—very important, those fellows. I'll have a go at it myself, if you don't choose to accompany me. Time I became a man, and all of that."

She looked down the hall of the west wing once more, and then resigned herself to humoring Adam, who probably wouldn't last beyond a quarter hour at most, once he either spotted a spider or remembered he wasn't at all fond of mud.

"All right, let's go," she said, sparing one last look down the hallway.

"Delicious! Your grandmother awaits us downstairs."

Now he had her full attention! "I beg your pardon?"

"You do? It's simple, really. The entire idea was hers. I awoke to a note from the dear lady, brought to me with my morning chocolate. I do adore morning chocolate, don't you, even when delivered a full two hours earlier than expected. I usually don't rise until now, which is only rational for a man of my sensibilities, but needs must when the dowager countess drives, or so Dearborn told me. Dearborn personally delivered the hot chocolate, piping hot. I think he likes me, which is more than I can say for most of the servants."

"Adam," she gritted out from between clenched teeth.

"What? Oh! I wasn't finished, was I? I'm to accompany you ladies as you tunnel hunt. In return, she's going to convince Gideon I need an increase in my quarterly allowance. Wonderful woman, the dowager countess. Smashing. And so understanding of the needs of a young gentleman of fashion on the strut."

"I'll just wager she is," Kate mumbled under her breath as she made her way downstairs, her mind whirling. Why would Trixie agree to go tunnel hunting? Worse, why would she be the one to suggest such a project? It was almost as if—

Aha! Almost as if she was being dragged from the Manor so she wouldn't see something she wasn't sup-

posed to see. Such as Simon and Richard, carrying sacks up the stairs.

Although she prided herself on never being kept in the dark for long, for her ability to ferret out almost any secret, this much was clear: Trixie was the master, Kate still the student—but she was gaining on her!

She barreled into the drawing room, deliberately going on the offensive, just as if she hadn't figured out what this *excursion* was all about. "What's going on, Trixie? Why am I being dragged Lord only knows where to look for a tunnel that might not even exist anymore? What am I not supposed to see—because *you* haven't seen this hour of the morning before unless you were just on your way home from a night of balls and routs and God knows what. Where's Simon?"

"Good morning, pet," Trixie said, unfolding herself from the fainting couch she preferred, slightly adjusting her blue-smoked spectacles. "Do you like them? I admired a pair Maxmillien was wearing, and he gifted me with my own pair. I doubt I could bear the early morning sunlight without them."

"It's closer to noon than dawn, Trixie," Kate pointed out. "Who told you about the tunnel?"

"Who? Why, Valentine, of course, in his last letter to me. Amazing boy. His letter found me still at Wickham, where I was delighting myself watching Reggie as he realized I may have bided my time, but he'd just been paid back for his insult to the Redgraves so many years ago. I suppose in time he'll find his new daughter-in-law to be a unique treasure. I did pick her specially."

"Do I need to hear this?" Kate asked. She tipped her head in Adam's direction. "Does he?"

"Probably not, although it *is* delicious. Back to Valentine and his letter. He made the whole business of the collapse inside the greenhouse sound almost jolly, but I doubt it was so at the time. I was most impressed with your heroism, Kate, leaping into the void to hold your beloved's head free of the encroaching mud until a rescue could be effected."

"He's not my— Oh, never mind. You already know, don't you? You know everything."

"Not everything, pet," Trixie said, her tone suddenly serious, "or else I could lead you to the tunnel. Shall we go? I'll be in the pony cart, observing you two adventuresome souls as you continue with whatever it is you've been doing without success. Or, if you care to hear my suggestion, to begin again, this time looking in the most unlikely places rather than the most likely. Oh, and one accessible by coach, or at least looking as if it could have been approached via coach twenty years ago."

Kate knew she shouldn't ask Trixie what she meant, not with Adam in the room. Not if she and her grandmother wcrc alone. She would never, never ask her anything about the past. Ever.

"I love you, Trixie," she said quietly, bending down to kiss the dowager countess's cheek. Ignoring the heat of the woman's powdered skin, pretending not to notice the redness and swelling around her eyes, only partially hidden by the smoked glasses. Her grandmother had been crying. Her grandmother never cried! "Thank you. Thank you, from all four of us. For everything."

"Oh, dear—sentiment," Trixie said, her voice quavering slightly. "I suppose I'll have to get used to it, won't I?"

CHAPTER EIGHTEEN

"PRETEND WE'RE NOT speaking," Kate told Simon as she looked up at him, her arms still about his neck after their kiss in a secluded area of the gardens.

"We weren't. We were kissing," he pointed out, the pads of his thumbs lightly stroking against her nipples through the thin muslin of her gown. "But, merely out of curiosity, why aren't we speaking? We spoke at dinner."

"If I told you that, we'd be speaking, and speaking at table is only polite, not to mention the fact that snubbing you across the table would only pique Trixie's interest," she pointed out, nibbling at the side of his chin. Really, men could be so thick. "Try to be logical, Simon."

"Employing my logic or yours? Because I'm afraid yours is beyond me. So here's an idea, let's just kiss again. It may be safer."

They kissed again. Kate really enjoyed kissing him, even if they both knew there was no time for anything else but kissing, as they couldn't be gone from the drawing room much longer or else be forced to return to Trixie's questions…and her subtle teasing. Kissing her and then making love to her told her he loved and wanted her. Kissing her without a chance of further… reward, meant he truly, *truly* loved her.

And she didn't care if that was her kind of logical or his kind of logical. She supposed that meant she was being romantical, which she'd always sworn she'd never be. Hadn't she been excessively silly?

But when he tried to kiss her yet again, she put her hands against his chest, signaling for him to stop. Which he did. Reluctantly, she noticed, pleased, proving he must like kissing her as much as she enjoyed kissing him.

But back to business!

"I can't believe I spent most of this afternoon chasing mare's nests with Trixie and Adam and her two yapping little monster pugs, who were constantly getting lost. Was that your idea, or hers?"

"I plead innocence about the dogs. The rest of it was more of a collaboration I'd say. You didn't enjoy yourself?"

"Not until I accidentally helped Adam trip over a tree root and he somehow ended up rump down in the stream, no. He screams worse than a pig caught in a grate, Trixie said. She was much amused, which I suppose made it all worthwhile. And at least we finally had a good excuse to call off the search—at which time I took up my own search. For the journals you and Richard carried into the west wing. They're not in your rooms. Where are they?"

"I'm sorry. I believe we're not speaking," Simon said, now fully cupping her breasts with his hands. "But damn it, woman, who told you?"

"Nobody. I saw you lugging them down the hallway toward the west wing. Stop that."

This time he didn't obey, which was nice, because she didn't really mean for him to stop. Wasn't it grand how he knew the difference?

"And you didn't come pelting after us, demanding we show you everything? My, my. Just when I thought

I was beginning to know you. No, wait. Of course you didn't come after us. You'd much rather do your own sleuthing."

"Fruitless sleuthing. Where are they? Why did you move them? Why didn't you tell me you were moving them? And, yes, we're speaking again. But we're not really on good terms, so simply ignore the fact I'm rubbing my lower body against yours if you please."

"The day I can ignore that, sweetheart, it will be time to put pennies on my eyes."

"Thank you," she said, all but preening. But then she sobered once more. "Did you read any of them?"

He shook his head. "I didn't even open any of them. My mission was clear-cut and definite. Find them, and then turn them over to the earl. Otherwise, I wouldn't have been allowed to set foot on the estate, Perceval or no Perceval. I've already written to Gideon, and I'm sure he'll be here in a few days. I'm afraid I'm fairly useless now, until we can discover more names. And so are you, by the way, which makes the two of us at loose ends, open to…other endeavors." He slid his hands lower, onto her hips. "Are you certain we'll be missed?"

Kate stepped away from him, took his hand in hers. "How long could you be alone in the drawing room with Adam before you began looking to the French doors, wondering if rescue was imminent?"

"You're right, we have to go back. But first, I have to tell you something. Do you remember Jacko?"

Kate blinked a single time at this change of subject, but recovered quickly. "The so-congenial Mr. Jacko? The giant you all but goaded into snapping your spine over his knee? How could I forget? Why are you asking?"

"Because I didn't tell you about moving the journals. Because that probably wasn't fair of me, although it was, I'll add, in part done with the intent of sparing you any more visits to the dower house. Because I truly believe you could make my life a living hell if I didn't tell you he contacted me the other day and I'm meeting with him later because the Society's smugglers will most probably be landing on Manor land sometime this moonless night."

Kate clapped her hands, actually clapped her hands. As if she was a silly little girl, and Simon had just offered her a sugary treat. Really, she needed to control herself better, now that she was a woman and all. But then she launched herself at him, hugging him fiercely about the neck.

"And you said we had nothing left to do? We're going to capture smugglers. Oh, and maybe a member or two of the Society. Or a French spy. My brothers will be shocked to their toes. *What fun!*"

Simon shook his head in obvious amazement. "Yes, that's just how we all feel. Such *fun.* Why, we're practically giddy."

She felt ridiculous. Now she couldn't even ask him what he meant by saying he'd moved the journals *in part* for her sake. What was the other part for? "You don't have to be snide. I only want to help."

"Actually, you're going to *observe,* probably from the spot we were standing as we watched Jacko drive away through the stone maze. *I'm* going to observe, as well, but from closer up, where I can be put to use if necessary. Agreed?"

"No," she said shortly. "Why can't I observe along with you? I can shoot, you know. And, unlike Adam, I don't scream."

He put his hands on her shoulders. "I love you. I adore you. I understand how badly you want to help. I'd probably do most anything, dangerous or silly, to make you happy. But not this, Kate. Not this."

She looked up at him, sighed. Love probably came with responsibilities, and this was one of them. "I'll stay on the hill. I won't like it, but I'll do it. *Now* you may kiss me again."

KATE HUNCHED DOWN beside Simon on the hill, her gaze shifting from the shore below them to the horizon. "You may think this a pointless question but what, exactly, are we supposed to see?"

Simon kept his eye to the spyglass, reluctant to admit, with no moon to assist him, he saw bloody well next to nothing. "Sails, although I doubt we'll see them until the last moment, if that. If they aren't raw amateurs, their schooner's painted black, the sails are black. They'll send out small boats with the goods if they get the all's-clear signal from somewhere here on land. Otherwise, they'll turn and sail away without us even knowing they were close."

"Won't we see the signal, as well?"

"No. The lantern will be shuttered on three sides. We could only see it if we were on the water ourselves, and even then, we'd have to know where we should be looking, as it won't flash for more than a few seconds. What we really need is a boat of our own out there on the water, and our own set of signals."

"Well, ain't you the smart one?"

Kate gasped, then quickly clapped her hand over her mouth.

Simon merely turned around. "Good evening. It's

Billy, correct? I wondered how long you'd stand back there thinking yourself brilliant."

"Here now! How did you know I was here?" the short, rail-thin man asked as he stepped closer.

"Not to put too fine a point on it, may I suggest regular bathing?" Simon said, getting to his feet. "You're telling us he's got men out there, on the water?"

"The Captain, he'll tell you what he wants you to know, not what you wants to know. Me, I ain't telling you nothin' except this. The Molly stays here. Nothin' but bad luck."

"Sorry, sweetheart, you're bad luck," Simon said tongue-in-cheek, but Kate was still peering up at Billy.

"You're a smuggler? Aiding our poorest citizens as they struggle to feed their families in these terrible times. That must take a considerable amount of courage, Mr. Billy. And God bless you, sir, for willingly endangering your life tonight for your king and country. I so admire your bravery."

Simon lowered his head, scratching at the back of his neck while whispering behind his elbow, "Won't help, sweetheart."

"I…I, um, I suppose you could come a little bit closer, miss."

Simon's smile disappeared. "She bloody well can't," he said sharply. "Billy, you're an ass, and Kate, you're a menace. Now stay here. And behave. Come on, my spindle-shanks Romeo, time to go. Let me first check on our horses."

While Billy stood with his head lowered and shoulders slumped, Simon retraced his steps to where they earlier tied Daisy and Hector, to untie Hector's reins. "And don't you take this as an invitation to start playing at Romeo, either. I need you loose if I have to have you come rescue us from the bad men." He patted the stallion's strong neck. "Let's just hope this all goes smoothly."

"Captain's waiting on you. This way," Billy said as Simon rejoined him on the hill, and with a quickly blown kiss in Kate's direction, the men made their way down the steep, rocky hillside to the stone maze below.

"Good evening, Captain," Simon said, holding out his hand to the black-clad figure half crouched behind one of the largest stones. The man was only slightly altered in his dress tonight. The cape was gone, replaced by a length of black leather draped around his neck, a pistol tied to each end. A third dull, black-handled pistol was stuffed into his waistband, and a cutlass hung from a leather strap riding low over one hip. Armed to the teeth, in the pirate way.

Kate would have been impressed all hollow and said so, although Simon doubted Ainsley Becket was as easily swayed as Billy.

"Commander," Ainsley Becket said, extending his own hand in return. "Small run tonight, which is probably better for us. The schooner's riding too high in the water, and only six men on horseback were seen riding down to the cottages. These men don't always smuggle for the profit, which first piqued our interest. On runs like these, they don't bother with tea or silk, just a few kegs of brandy for their own pleasure. No large landing parties, no pack horses or landsmen. I'm guessing human cargo tonight mostly, along with oilskin packets and opium."

Simon was surprised. "Opium?"

"Yes, I've wondered about that myself, but I trust our man who's been traveling with them. They'll be loading cargo from this end tonight before heading to Calais. Men, other oilskin packets and most of all, gold coin."

Simon had now hunkered down beside him, having given up on seeing anything in the intense dark. "To help pay and support Bonaparte's troops. One pound here's worth a pound and a half in Paris. We're definitely dealing with traitors. Desperate men who know they're destined for the hangman if captured. I'll, of course, still want them alive if that can be managed."

Even in the dark, Simon could see Becket's wide smile. "We'll do our best. They'll land on the other side of the tunnel, then come straight toward us. There has been no variation in their route, a small party or a large one, in six months. Be ready."

After that, there was nothing else to say, and there was nothing but the soft lapping of waves against the shore for the hour or more Simon spent trying to familiarize himself with his surroundings, pick out the forms of men against the darker boulders. That, and wondering if Kate was behaving herself up on the hill, if she'd had time for her agile brain to realize the journals now resided in the attics of the Manor…and if Richard was not only handy with a tinderbox, but also fleet of foot, if they'd chanced to overestimate how much lamp oil was needed to do what had to be done.

Two short, sharp whistles broke the silence, along with Becket's muttered "Sonofabitch." He was on his feet in an instant, Simon along with him, as a dozen well-armed men seemed to step out from inside rocky hidey-holes.

"What?" Simon asked as pistols were waved, knives and curved swords were unsheathed. Becket and his men pelted toward the shoreline, their boots sending up sprays of seawater as they splashed their way around the end of the rocky outcropping, to the cottage side of the beach.

"They aren't coming our way. They were spooked somehow, that's what," Jacko said from behind him. "Gone off Hythe-ways, or up the hill behind the cottages, or back out to the Channel, one of those. Leaving us who don't count running as one of their talents anymore to stand here with our thumbs up our—"

But Simon was already gone. Becket and his men could chase down the smugglers or not; Simon's concern was all for Kate, sitting at the top of the hill above him, hopefully having hidden herself, yet totally unprotected.

My fault, my fault, my fault.

He felt as if he was running through waist-deep water, struggling through clinging, clutching mud to his knees. The faster he ran and climbed, the slower he seemed to go, the longer the climb up the rocky hillside.

He couldn't call out her name, for fear he'd call attention to her presence.

He'd never reach the top, never get to her in time. Because, God help them, he knew her, and she wouldn't stay still; not if she thought she could help.

His hands and face scratched from brambles he used as handholds, not caring for or even feeling any pain, he at last made it to the spot where he'd last seen her.

The spyglass he'd left with her lay on the ground.

She wasn't there.

Simon took off toward the horses. The smugglers had broken for the hill above the cottages; men were running everywhere, so that Simon couldn't separate friend from foe. He was on his own, Kate's life was in his hands.

Let it be both of them. Please God, let it be both of them.

And it was; both horses were gone. Some one of the smugglers had probably all but run into Kate, and mounted her on Daisy, obviously, and was leading the mare by the reins. He'd use her as his hostage, his most powerful trump if they caught up with him, and let her go at some point if they didn't. Sooner probably than later, if Kate gave him trouble, which she was sure to do.

Simon drew in several deep breaths, and then, with his fingers at the corners of his mouth, whistled loud and long, praying the sound would carry through the clear, dark night, soaring over the noise of a battle taking place not one hundred yards away.

Long moments later, there was a deeper darkness in the distance. The sound of hooves churning up the loose turf. The curses of a man desperate to turn his mount about…the chilling sight of Kate atop Daisy, leading the way.

Leading the way? How was that possible?

"Here." Somehow, Courtland Becket was beside him, holding out the tied brace of pistols he'd unslung from his shoulders. "You could shoot the horse to get the man, but I have a feeling you've another plan."

Simon waved away the pistols and started to run toward Hector, pointing to his left. "Kate! Pull off! *Pull off!*"

She immediately began reining in Daisy, directing her as he'd ordered.

Hector had managed to get the bit between his teeth, and kept on coming. The smuggler was an inferior horseman, thank God.

And then, when he could nearly see the whites of the

stallion's eyes as it bore down on him, Simon yelled, *"Giddyup!"*

Hector plunged to a halt, digging in his front hooves, and the rider on the stallion's back was suddenly flying through the air toward Simon.

The unseated rider was quickly surrounded by Becket's men, even as Simon ran toward Daisy, catching Kate up neatly as she threw her leg over the pommel, clearly intending to slide to the ground on her own.

He had her in his arms in an instant, covering her face with desperate kisses. "Thank God you're safe! How did you get away from him?"

"Get away from him?" Kate went on tiptoe and planted a kiss on his nose. "I wasn't trying to get away from him. I was *chasing* him. I mean, I whistled, but Hector paid me no attention. You'll have to teach me how to— Simon? Don't look at me like that."

"How the bloody hell am I supposed to look at you? *Chasing him?* What were you planning to do when you caught up with him?"

She began stroking his chest, probably believing she was soothing him. "I couldn't catch up with him, Simon, you know that. Hector's much too fast for Daisy. But at least I could keep him in sight until you could come after us, and *you* whistled to Hector. It may be dark, but you know the West Run now, and I know it even better, so we could both make good progress on Hector, at least close enough for you to whistle. Plus, if the man were fool enough to think he could use any light from the Manor windows to cross close by and make it to the road, he'd land in the ha-ha, wouldn't he? Not that I didn't worry about Hector, in that case."

"I'm certain he appreciates that."

"Don't be facetious. The idea came clear to me in

an instant, when I saw the smuggler turning in circles at the crest of the hill, looking panicked, and then suddenly running toward the horses as if his every prayer had just been answered."

Simon made a sound low in his throat. It may have been a growl. Yes, he was fairly certain it had been a growl.

Kate frowned. "There *are* other horses here, aren't there? And you would have taken one of them and come pelting after us and— There aren't any other horses here?"

He could kill her. He could kiss her. "I'm sure there are, but all hidden out of sight. Tell me, were you prepared to follow Hector all the way to London?"

She jammed her fists against her hips. "I said it was an idea, Simon. I didn't say it was a *plan*. I hadn't gotten that far yet. Now tell me why you yelled *giddyup* and Hector *whoa-ed*."

"Because that's what I taught him. If anyone tried to steal him when I wasn't around, the thief wouldn't get very far, would he? Maybe I should try the same thing with you."

"Yes, yes, I was supposed to stay where I was. I remember, and I'm truly sorry. Shouldn't we go see who we've got? You can lecture me more later, when we've less of an audience."

Simon opened his mouth to say something, probably something very profound and astute and worthy of quoting in the future should any man find himself in the position he was in now—but he didn't say it. Nobody in this world would ever be in the same position he was in now. Because he had Kate, and they didn't.

"I love you," he said instead.

She rolled her eyes. "Really, Simon, do you actually

think this is the time for us to be— I love you, too," she ended as he slung his arm around her shoulders and, together, they approached the group of men who'd all been watching them for God knew how long.

Jacko broke away from the others and headed toward them with his seaman's rolling gait. "You can have the one, Commander, but we'll take the rest. Local men, all of them, including one of our own. Him we'll let *escape,* if you take my drift. The others need a lesson, and will get it, and time to reflect on the error of their ways once they wake up on a ship bound for Haiti. We'll also be taking the gold coin for our troubles, but you can have the brandy, as we have more than enough of our own. And here, this packet we found." He handed over the oilskin-wrapped package.

"Thank you, Jacko," Simon said, tucking the packet away as Kate surprised everyone, clearly Jacko most of all, when she ducked out from Simon's arm to give the man a hug.

Jacko smiled rather sheepishly, and then turned away, muttering, "Never live it down with my mates, that's what'll happen. Women!"

Simon threw back his head and laughed, a nearly silly joy filling him…until the sound of a pistol discharging had him running toward the circle of men. Pushing his way through, he saw the man who'd so recently met the ground thanks to Hector lying facedown there again. The first time, he was cursing. This time, he was quite dead.

"What happened?"

Billy was hanging his head, scuffing one boot against the long grass.

Ainsley Becket stepped up to Simon. "It was unexpected. He asked for some assistance in rising and Billy, always a helpful sort, bent over to give him a hand. Our dead friend pulled the pistol from Billy's belt, and turned it on himself. Loyal to their cause, these people you're after, aren't they?"

"Look away, Kate," Simon said, and then went down on one knee, to turn the body faceup. "Lantern," he ordered shortly, and one was produced, illuminating the partially shattered face of the Honorable Ambrose Webber—or at least he had been until he was drummed out of the Royal Navy after being discovered with a dead prostitute in his cabin.

Webber. Simon mentally ran down the list of code names he'd been given by Gideon. *Hammer. Weaver. Bird. Burn.* Bird had been his own brother, Holbrook, which everyone would soon learn. Webber? Yes, that could be it; a weaver could be said to make a web of sorts with thread.

So they had another name. Unfortunately, it was attached to a dead man.

"Commander."

Simon shook his mind away from his thoughts. "Yes, Captain?"

"You don't smell that?"

"Smell—?"

"I do. It smells as if something is burning, doesn't it? Oh, my God! Simon, look!" Kate took hold of his arm, shaking it. "It's the Manor. I can see the flames from here, shooting into the sky!"

Yes, maybe a barrel or three more of the lamp oil than we needed...but we couldn't trust the small army of loyal Redgrave servants not to heroically put out the fire before it did its job, could we?

"My horse, Billy," Ainsley Becket ordered swiftly. "I'll ride with you. Court, you're in charge here. Strip our dead friend, and feed him to the fish. Far enough out to be sure he doesn't return with the tide. Agreed, Commander?"

"Agreed," Simon said as two of Becket's men brought Daisy and Hector to them.

The ride back to the Manor was a race of sorts, with Kate's nervousness transferring itself to the mare, who very nearly kept up with Hector, while Becket came with them only until they were through the opened tradesman's gate before turning his horse off to the right. Simon didn't bother to ask him why; Ainsley Becket had a reason for everything he did.

It wasn't the Manor. It was the dower house. The relief Kate felt as they raced toward the closest open gate across the ha-ha and could at last see the origin of all that smoke and flame changed nearly as quickly to suspicion.

They dismounted a good distance from the scene as one of the footmen ran across the lawn to take care of their mounts. "Jacob, my grandmother. Where is she?"

"Watching from the terrace with the others, my lady, Mr. Borders and Mr. Collier and Mrs. Justis. Having tea, my lady, and even biscuits. Nothin' else for any of us to do. Mr. Dearborn says the roof's about to come slammin' down, so we needs must stay clear. All but bright as day, ain't it?"

"You did this," Kate said when Jacob took the reins and moved off. "You removed the journals, you and Richard, and then you did this." She narrowed her eyes. "How did you do it?"

"I suppose it's possible Richard and I forgot to extinguish one of the candles once we were done moving the journals," Simon said, his gaze intent on the fire.

"Possible, but not probable. Congratulations, Simon, you're learning how to answer a question without really answering. But you did it."

"Thank you, I suppose, and yes, I did it," he admitted, at last turning to look at her. "Richard lit the lamp oil at the appointed time, but the plan was my idea. Actually, I may have overdone it, and it's a good thing it's a calm night. There'll be nothing but a few stone walls and a large pit filled with rubble by the time it burns itself out. I doubt a single statue or stick of furniture or anything else will be left recognizable."

"Thank you, Simon, with all my heart," Kate said, blinking away tears as she slipped her arm through his, leaned her body against him. "My grandfather used fire to destroy. You used it to right a terrible wrong. So many terrible wrongs."

"Good evening again, Commander, my lady. Quite the spectacle you people put on," a stranger to Kate remarked from atop his horse as he joined them. He wore his wide-brimmed slouch hat low over his forehead, and a black scarf covered the top half of his face.

"Thank you, sir. We Redgraves pride ourselves on our flair for the dramatic," Kate said, peering up at him, able only to see his strangely beautiful eyes behind the half mask. She didn't remember him from seeing him earlier, although she was certain he was the one who had ridden with them through the gates to the Manor. It was obvious he didn't wish to be recognized, unlike Jacko and Billy. No, this was the man in charge of everyone else. And after what he'd done for them tonight, she knew she would have to be content with what he allowed her to see. "Yet one can look at it and only begin to imagine half of London going up in flames during the Great Fire."

"True enough. But you might find something else of interest if you were to take a moment to look in another direction. Commander, the tunnel near the stone maze is no more than thirty feet deep, and contains little but ropes used to tie casks together for hauling and some tea, unfortunately ruined by seawater. It's not what you're searching for, nor is the ancient passageway beneath the rock barrier although, architecturally, it is fascinating. Roman in origin, I believe. You will, however, locate the oilskin packet you abandoned and our late acquaintance's clothing in the cottage you visited the other day."

He half rose from his saddle, actually making quite an elegant bow. "Again, it has been my distinct pleasure. Please tender my regards to the lovely Trixie, and thank her again for her assistance that, happily, is no longer necessary. The cottage is hers once more. And give her these."

Simon's laughter was both rueful and delighted as he caught the ring of keys the man tossed him. "I'll be sure to do that, Captain."

"Thank you. Good luck to you, Commander, for you'll need all you can find—and a word of caution garnered through personal experience. A man who can convince others to execute themselves in order to protect him is a deadly dangerous man surrounded by worshipful fanatics. When you encounter them you'll have to strike first, without a thought to capturing any of them alive. Any hesitation on your part would prove fatal, for they won't hesitate to kill you, and reason is outside their realm of comprehension."

"I'll pass that along, as well," Simon said, nodding. "You're a fascinating man, Captain. I hope we might someday meet again."

The *captain* only nodded, and then turned his horse away. Looking after him, away from the brightness of the fire, Kate quickly lost him in the dark. "He is a fascinating man," she said quietly. "And he somehow knows Trixie? Let me see those keys."

"You can look at them if you wish, but I think I can already tell you the locks they fit. The tradesman's gate, the keys to the French doors for the library at the very least and one for the cottage. I'm standing here in amazement, even as I'm kicking myself for not realizing sooner—although I'll be damned if I know how the two of them met."

Kate handed back the keys. "You should be the one returning them, as I'm the one who supposedly knows nothing. You called him Captain. Don't you know his name?"

"We never exchanged names, no," Simon told her.

"As I said, you're getting better and better. I almost believed you this time. But I won't question you, as you obviously made a promise. Now tell me what he meant about something interesting to see if we were to look in another direction."

"I have no idea," he told her, squinting into the distance, slowly turning, squinting again. "Well, damn me for a tinker. That's why he went riding off, to see what we didn't see."

"What?" Kate looked at him, saw his smile and then looked in the same general direction. At first she didn't see anything, but as she looked deeper into the distance, she did. "The foaling stable. My God, Simon, it's on fire, too! Look—the grooms are leading the horses to safety."

"That's probably a good idea, although it's smoking, but not on fire. Why didn't I think of it sooner?

Kate, you said your grandfather had the foaling stable built on the foundation of the dower house. The *first* burned dower house. There had to be another tunnel leading to the new dower house, one I didn't discover, one that didn't collapse. Or a branch of the tunnel we did find—*something.* Something that's now acting as some sort of chimney for the smoke."

He picked her up and twirled her around and around. "He said we would need all the luck we could find, and even pointed some out to us. Kate, my darling, my sweet, my torment and only love—we just located the tunnel entrance!"

EPILOGUE

THE MASSIVE DOOR was no more than twenty yards from the entrance to the tunnel that disappeared into the darkness ahead of them. The tunnel itself had been cleverly located behind a false wall in the foaling stall, separated from the main stable by a stone wall with only a single door.

As the stable was only used during the spring foaling season, and occasionally to separate a sick horse from the others in the main stables, it would be easy enough to lead a group of terrified, blindfolded women into the area and through the opened panel, into the tunnel itself.

Clever man, Charles Redgrave. His grandsons had inherited his intelligence, but thankfully, not his perverted ways…although they might have had he lived, had his son, Barry, lived.

Clever woman, Trixie Redgrave. Clever woman, Maribel Redgrave. Clever, desperate and willing to risk everything, even hellfire, to protect their children.

Kate squeezed Simon's hand tightly as they approached the stout wooden door on their right, hung with thick metal bars secured by large brad spikes. There was a handle and a keyhole, but the door opened easily, as if they were expected.

"I want you to wait out here," he told her as Richard Borders stepped forward, holding up the lantern.

"But I—"

"Came with us this far because you wanted to help locate the tunnel," Simon reminded her. "At which time you promised to remain in the foaling stable, remember?"

She nodded. "Reluctantly. I agreed reluctantly."

"Happily, reluctantly or only at the point of a pistol, you promised." He shoved his lantern at her so she could light her way. "Now take yourself back to the foaling stable."

"There's such a thing as revenge, Simon Ravenbill," she called over her shoulder as she stomped off, her hips moving provocatively, although she probably didn't realize that. Then again, she probably did.

"I'm looking forward to it!" he called after her, and her laugh echoed in the tunnel.

Their initial elation on believing they'd found the tunnel entrance had been quickly tempered by what they might find inside, but Kate had determinedly chosen to be pleased, to feel victorious. Soon it would be over, their part in helping hunt down the Society a complete and utter success.

They'd discussed all of this last night, or early this morning, as no one at Redgrave Manor had climbed the stairs to their beds much before dawn. Not giving a damn to what anyone might think, Simon had entered Kate's chambers with her and then locked the doors to both the hallway and the dressing room. Not that Senorita Click-Click was inside, as she had still been in the kitchens, helping to prepare food for the house and estate workers who'd been monitoring the blaze, employing a bucket chain to keep the shrubberies nearest the terrace wet.

They'd discussed, they'd held each other, they'd discussed some more and then Kate had fallen asleep while Simon kept her cradled against his body, wondering if he could ever dare to let go of her again.

When he woke up, it was to her kisses, her provocative, roaming hands and a mutual urgency that was quickly satisfied. As she'd commented as he'd helped her slip on her riding boots, she was now probably the most compromised woman in all of England, and he the last man who'd ever be allowed to escape the parson's mousetrap.

Kate had a way about her, a way of saying she loved him without saying she loved him, and once this damn tunnel was examined, he was going to take her back to the Manor, order her a tub—the largest, deepest tub in that larger-than-life household—and show her without saying so exactly how much he loved her.

But right now, she was in the way.

"Ready?" Richard asked, holding the remaining lantern higher as he stepped in front of the door. "If what you told me yesterday is anywhere near what we're about to see, Trixie can never know. Agreed?"

"More than agreed," Simon told him, and reached past the man to push the heavy door aside.

Beyond the door was a room. Not a tunnel used as a room; a high-ceilinged room, a chamber, a gentleman's study. Marble floor, wood-paneled walls lined with bookshelves, crystal chandeliers marching in pairs across the ceiling; when lit, there wouldn't be a dark corner anywhere.

But all they had between them now was the single lantern, so they began at the beginning, advancing slowly, noting everything they could see within the small circle of light in the otherwise pitch-dark blackness.

There were large globes in stands, racks and racks of maps. Carefully drawn diagrams depicting Parliament meeting rooms, a detailing of possible routes to the prime minister's offices themselves, with all the twists and turns to exits marked with crosses. Another depicted the king's routes to Westminster, to the theatre, to Hyde Park, with notes telling of the expected number of outriders to usually accompany the coach. A rough depiction of the cortege, the coach, the outriders, had one of those soldiers marked with a drawn circle, the word "ours" scribbled beside it.

All the royal children were listed in individual journals; all their residences. Even Octavius and Alfred had journals, and they had died in the early 1780s.

A framed letter from Maximilien de Robespierre, written to Barry Redgrave, hung in place of honor below another, this one also penned to Barry, but from one Donatien Alphonse François, Marquis de Sade, then a prisoner in the Bastille.

"They were deadly serious madmen, weren't they?" Simon said, tossing down yet another diagram, this one of Traitors' Gate at the Tower of London.

"Did you notice something, Simon my boy?" Richard said, holding up the lantern over the long trestle table that was the largest piece of furniture in the room; probably where the Society met for council sessions. "There's some dust, a few dozen cobwebs, but not a patch on what we found beneath the dower house. Somebody's not only been here, they've done a little housekeeping while they were here." He took the lantern and walked down the length of the table, stopping abruptly when the light illuminated what lay beyond it. *Who* lay beyond it. "Sweet Jesus, Mary and Joseph—look at this!"

Simon made his way to Richard's side, stopped and cursed.

At the end of the table was a semicircle of marble stairs, leading up to a dais of sorts with pride of place given over to a gold gilt, high-backed throne, its massive arms made to look like lion paws, the Stuart coat of arms carved atop the high back.

On the steps were three fully-clothed skeletons, posed on their stomachs, their arms frozen in the act of reaching out; supplicants, handmaidens. One wore what had to be Saltwood livery, a periwig still on its skull. The other skeletons were encased in servant gowns and aprons, mob caps tangled in with bits of long, dark hair.

They'd found the servant Burke and his family.

Above them, seated on the throne, were the ghastly, smiling remains of their *king*.

Their well-tended monarch, Simon saw as he climbed the stairs with the lantern. The skeleton had been cleaned, and then carefully wired together, secured to the throne. The crown was still on his head. A jeweled scepter topped by a huge golden rose with a diamond as large as a pigeon egg stuck in its center still clutched in his right hand. A Stuart tartan draped one shoulder and flowed over his lower body, a golden sash over the other shoulder; small golden roses pinned to it in rows. Simon stopped counting at twenty.

They'd found Barry Redgrave.

Simon nearly jumped out of his skin when a resounding crash echoed inside the room.

"Sorry, son, I didn't see it until I was on top of it," Richard said, bending to attempt to right what seemed to be a short marble pillar with a large V top clearly meant to hold a book. A large tome, such as a bible.

"The bible?" Simon asked, careful not to step on any of the skeletons as he brought the lantern with him to the place Richard was kneeling, reaching his hands out over the floor.

"No, worse the luck. But there is this," he said, handing up what looked to be a single folded page. "Looks new compared to what we've seen. There's some writing, just above the seal."

"'Turner Collier, A Last Confession,'" Simon read. "The sonofabitch was here before he was murdered. Now what are you doing?"

"I'm not sure. Look at me, it's as if I toppled into the fireplace grate. Somebody burned something here." Richard held up two fistfuls of ashes. "You don't think it's the bible?"

Simon had already broken the seal of Collier's *Confession*. "Take the lantern, and hold it up," he ordered Richard, and then began to read.

I am a dead man, speaking to you from the grave. Behold my king, for I am his loyal subject, just as they are his servants, who were always destined to accompany him across the Rubicon. Those were the rules as set down by him, and as I followed them.

They know I continued my journal. They know about the bible, so I have destroyed it. I am the Keeper, and I know the rules. They are no more than base imposters. One of them now lies in the tunnel, having dared to follow me on my last, most holy mission, but I cannot kill them all. I should die here, but coward that I am, I take my wife and flee, while sure I cannot escape them.

Find them, destroy them. At first, I believed, but no more. They pay no honor, they disobey the rules. Their leader no king, but the devil incarnate.

Barry, dear Barry, you were always my true love.

"Well, that's that, isn't it, Richard? Let's get out of here before the sound of that crash overrides Kate's promise to remain outside. Gideon can decide what to do about everything else when he gets here, God help him. As far as Kate and Trixie are concerned, we found nothing but the ashes of the bible."

"And the tunnel?"

"It ended at the rubble from the dower house, forever blocked now," Simon improvised quickly. "Here, take the damned confession for now. Kate wouldn't dare to poke about in your pockets."

"She'd poke about in yours?" Richard asked, chuckling. "And I think you meant the *confession of the damned.* I may have nightmares for months, while the thought of taking up the religion I put down so many years ago holds some sudden appeal."

Simon nodded, his mind already concentrating on how he was going to nail the tunnel entrance panel shut with boards and nails strong enough to keep Kate out.

THE DOWER HOUSE smoldered for several days, and Trixie more than once remarked the smell just might be her new favorite scent. But that was all she'd said on the subject, probably all she would ever say. By the third day she and Richard had departed for Brighton, the pair of them looking so happy Kate would have put her mind to finding out why…except for the fact she felt fairly certain she looked more than moderately besotted herself.

Once they'd promised not to behave themselves ("Unless you've no other choice, my pets") until Gideon and Jessica arrived, and waved their goodbyes to the departing coach, she and Simon repaired to the drawing room.

Consuela had thrown up her hands the night of the fire at the idea she could continue in her role of duenna, and was once again back to harassing the upstairs servants.

Kate immediately sat herself down on one of the soft couches, slid down so that the back of her head rested on the pillowed back of the couch and plunked her riding boots on the low table in front of her, crossing her legs at the ankles.

She then turned her head and batted her eyelashes provocatively at Simon as he sat himself down beside her.

"Go on, Simon—do it," she teased.

"Do what?" he asked, but the corners of his mouth twitched slightly.

"*Relax,* silly," she told him. "If you're going to spend the rest of your life routinely in the company of us rascally Redgraves, you either learn to relax, or stick out like a vicar in a house of ill repute."

"I don't even want to know where you heard that charming saying," he told her, but then slid himself down so that he was sitting low on his spine, lifting his legs so that his boots also now rested on the table. He loosened his neck cloth slightly, unbuttoned his jacket. He then turned his head to look at Kate. "You're right. This is better." He slipped one arm around her shoulders. "And now immensely better. Shall we relax, inspect the chandelier hanging over us, or dare I steal a kiss?"

"I think you could probably dare," Kate told him, loving him so much she felt she might burst with that love. There were still questions and probably terrible answers. But those were for other people. She and Simon had done their part—brilliantly, she believed—and for the first time in her life she was not overwhelmed with curiosity about anything, determined to ferret out every secret.

He kissed the tip of her nose. "Trixie, it would seem, has friends everywhere. She's promised a special license within the week, at which point she and Richard will return. She allowed, however, that we may enjoy being *illicit* to the top of our bents, as the experience will be short-lived."

Kate giggled. "I wonder who tells Gideon."

"Dearborn, probably," Simon said, pulling her closer. *"Ahem!"*

"Speak of the devil," Kate whispered as Simon withdrew his arm. "Yes, Dearborn?"

"If you'd recall my express plea to spare the maids and the wood, my lady?"

Kate sat up, reaching behind one of the pillows, to draw out a length of padded velvet. "Lift your boots a moment, Simon, if you please," she said as she spread the length of cloth on the tabletop. Sparing a grin for him, they then both sat back and lifted their boots onto the cloth. "Happy now, Dearborn?"

"All but overcome by your kind consideration, my lady," the butler said in a resigned voice. "A special messenger delivered this only moments ago." He held out a small silver salver, a letter resting on it. "For you, my lord."

"Thank you, Dearborn. And for the record, she made me do it, so I'd still hope for a cigar after dinner."

"Simon!" Kate laughingly snatched the letter from the salver, deliberately breaking the seal and opening the single sheet. "It's from Valentine," she said, sitting up straight, holding the page away from Simon as she read it (and Dearborn lingered, attempting to read the thing over her shoulder). "Oh, my God, the *idiot!* Here, Simon, read this."

"Now there's a good idea, since it was addressed to me." And then he read aloud: "'I imagine by now congratulations are in order. You may thank me later, but for now, welcome to the menagerie. And now congratulate me, if you please. I do believe I am about to be invited to join the Society, happy degenerate that I am. For now, it's only to a party at some unnamed country house, but my hopes are high. My new bosom chum, Lord Charles Mailer, has offered to take me up with him in his traveling coach. Said party commences only a few days before the next full moon— You do remember writing to me about that, I'm sure. Coincidence? I don't think so. But it's as I told you, my new brother, some things need a lighter hand. Kisses to Kate. Tell Gideon I'll be in touch. In all modesty, et cetera, I remain your genius, Val.'"

"Genius? *Hah!* Who's this Mailer fellow? Is he one of the Society? He is, isn't he?"

"He is. One of the only two names we've discovered. In the Society's odd code, he's Post. The other, Archie Urban—known as City—is already dead."

"And if your anonymous *captain* is correct, this man Mailer would kill Valentine without a moment's hesitation, were he to realize he's been tricked. Wouldn't he?"

Simon took her hand in both of his. "He'll be careful."

Kate leaned against his shoulder, sighed. She wasn't in control, couldn't be in control. They were Redgraves, on a mission. They would all take their chances. "I know he will. Just pray there's not a woman in distress anywhere, or else our Sir Galahad will forget how careful he's supposed to be...."

* * * * *

*As the Society becomes more daring,
and more dangerous, the search for its
treasonous members grows in importance.
The only alternative left is to work
within the Society itself.
This is Valentine Redgrave's mission:
infiltrate the Society.
Alas, as his sister knows, with Val,
there's always a woman involved.
Catch all the intrigue, adventure and romance in
WHAT A GENTLEMAN DESIRES,
coming soon from Harlequin HQN.*

AUTHOR NOTE

In case you've gotten to the end of Simon and Kate's story and were left wondering: where did I see the name Ainsley Becket before, or thinking, wow, I'd like to read more about this Ainsley Becket character, here's the scoop.

Ainsley Becket is the patriarch of the Becket family, their stories told in a seven-book series with the overall title of THE BECKETS OF ROMNEY MARSH. That series begins in 1811, but when I chose the same general area for my current series, setting it in the year 1810, I thought it would be fun to give a little snippet about Ainsley—actually, I'd use any excuse to see more of Ainsley, as he and his story fascinated me so much.

The titles, in order, are *A Gentleman By Any Other Name, The Dangerous Debutante, Beware of Virtuous Women, A Most Unsuitable Groom, A Reckless Beauty, Return of the Prodigal* and *Becket's Last Stand,* all available electronically from Harlequin HQN.

You can even watch a book trailer on the Beckets of Romney Marsh series at:

http://www.youtube.com/watch?v=zXC7RoDFqyk

Enjoy!

Kasey

Join #1 *New York Times* bestselling author

STEPHANIE LAURENS

for a classic story of pursuit and surrender...

A successful horse breeder and self-proclaimed rake, Harry Lester samples women like wines. But after having his heart trampled by someone he actually loved, he has no intention of falling for a woman again, let alone be ensnared by the trap of marriage. Now, with a large inheritance to his name, Harry knows that he'd best start running from London's matchmaking mothers and widows.

Harry heads for the racing town of Newmarket, only to encounter Mrs. Lucinda Babbacombe, a beautiful, independent widow. And before he knows it, Harry vows to protect Lucinda from the town full of lonely gambling men, despite her refusal to accept his countless offers of help. Lucinda is extraordinary—an intelligent, tender woman—but will Harry let himself be taken prisoner in this most passionate of traps?

Available wherever books are sold!

Be sure to connect with us at:

Harlequin.com/Newsletters
Facebook.com/HarlequinBooks
Twitter.com/HarlequinBooks

HARLEQUIN® HQN™
www.Harlequin.com

PHSL763

New York Times bestselling author

shannon stacey

"I'm madly in love with the Kowalskis. And I love Shannon Stacey's voice!"
—*New York Times* bestselling author Nalini Singh

New York Times Bestselling Author
shannon stacey

all he ever
dreamed

Josh Kowalski is tired of holding down the fort—better known as the Northern Star Lodge—while his siblings are off living their dreams. Now that his oldest brother has returned to Whitford, Maine, for good, Josh is free to chase some dreams of his own.

As the daughter of the lodge's longtime housekeeper, Katie Davis grew up alongside the Kowalski brothers. Though she's always been "one of the guys," her feelings for Josh are anything but sisterly. And after a hot late-night encounter in the kitchen, it's clear Josh finally sees her as the woman she is.

Katie's been waiting years for Josh to notice her, but now that he has, she's afraid it's too late. Giving her heart to a man who can't wait to leave town is a sure way to have it broken. But could it be that everything Josh has ever wanted is closer than he could have imagined?

Available wherever books are sold!

Be sure to connect with us at:

Harlequin.com/Newsletters
Facebook.com/HarlequinBooks
Twitter.com/HarlequinBooks

H HARLEQUIN® HQN™
™ www.Harlequin.com

PHSS758

**#1 *New York Times* bestselling author
Linda Lael Miller returns to Stone Creek with
a sweeping tale of two strangers running from
dangerous secrets.**

LINDA LAEL MILLER

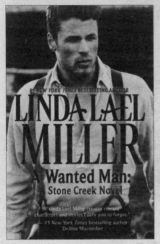

The past has a way of catching up with folks in Stone Creek, Arizona. But schoolmarm Lark Morgan and Marshal Rowdy Rhodes are determined to hide their secrets—and deny their instant attraction. That should be easy, since each suspects the other of living a lie…

Yet Rowdy and Lark share one truth: both face real dangers, such as the gang of train robbers heading their way, men Ranger Sam O'Ballivan expects Rowdy to nab. As past and current troubles collide, Rowdy and Lark must surrender their pride to the greatest power of all—undying love.

Available wherever books are sold!

Be sure to connect with us at:

Harlequin.com/Newsletters

Facebook.com/HarlequinBooks

Twitter.com/HarlequinBooks

HARLEQUIN® HQN™
www.Harlequin.com

PHLLM722

REQUEST YOUR FREE BOOKS!

2 FREE NOVELS
FROM THE ROMANCE COLLECTION
PLUS 2 FREE GIFTS!

YES! Please send me 2 FREE novels from the Romance Collection and my 2 FREE gifts (gifts are worth about $10). After receiving them, if I don't wish to receive any more books, I can return the shipping statement marked "cancel." If I don't cancel, I will receive 4 brand-new novels every month and be billed just $6.24 per book in the U.S. or $6.74 per book in Canada. That's a savings of at least 22% off the cover price. It's quite a bargain! Shipping and handling is just 50¢ per book in the U.S. and 75¢ per book in Canada.* I understand that accepting the 2 free books and gifts places me under no obligation to buy anything. I can always return a shipment and cancel at any time. Even if I never buy another book, the two free books and gifts are mine to keep forever.

194/394 MDN F4XY

Name   (PLEASE PRINT)

Address   Apt. #

City   State/Prov.   Zip/Postal Code

Signature (if under 18, a parent or guardian must sign)

Mail to the Harlequin® Reader Service:
IN U.S.A.: P.O. Box 1867, Buffalo, NY 14240-1867
IN CANADA: P.O. Box 609, Fort Erie, Ontario L2A 5X3

Want to try two free books from another line?
Call 1-800-873-8635 or visit www.ReaderService.com.

* Terms and prices subject to change without notice. Prices do not include applicable taxes. Sales tax applicable in N.Y. Canadian residents will be charged applicable taxes. Offer not valid in Quebec. This offer is limited to one order per household. Not valid for current subscribers to the Romance Collection or the Romance/Suspense Collection. All orders subject to credit approval. Credit or debit balances in a customer's account(s) may be offset by any other outstanding balance owed by or to the customer. Please allow 4 to 6 weeks for delivery. Offer available while quantities last.

Your Privacy—The Harlequin® Reader Service is committed to protecting your privacy. Our Privacy Policy is available online at www.ReaderService.com or upon request from the Harlequin Reader Service.

We make a portion of our mailing list available to reputable third parties that offer products we believe may interest you. If you prefer that we not exchange your name with third parties, or if you wish to clarify or modify your communication preferences, please visit us at www.ReaderService.com/consumerschoice or write to us at Harlequin Reader Service Preference Service, P.O. Box 9062, Buffalo, NY 14269. Include your complete name and address.

ROM13R

**If you build it, love will come...
to Hope's Crossing.**

USA TODAY **Bestselling Author**

RaeAnne Thayne

Alexandra McKnight prefers a life of long workdays and short-term relationships, and she's found it in Hope's Crossing. A sous-chef at the local ski resort, she's just been offered her dream job at an exclusive new restaurant being built in town. But when it comes to designing the kitchen, Alex finds herself getting up close and personal with construction foreman Sam Delgado....

At first glance, Sam seems perfect for Alex. He's big, tough, gorgeous—and only in town for a few weeks. But when Sam suddenly moves into a house down the road, Alex suspects that the devoted single father of a six-year-old boy wants more from her than she's willing to give. Now it's up to Sam to help Alex see that, no matter what happened in her past, together they can build something more meaningful in Hope's Crossing.

Available wherever books are sold!

Be sure to connect with us at:

Harlequin.com/Newsletters

Facebook.com/HarlequinBooks

Twitter.com/HarlequinBooks

www.Harlequin.com

PHRT747

#1 *New York Times* Bestselling Author

SUSAN WIGGS

Tess Delaney's history is filled with gaps: a father she never met and a mother who spent more time traveling than with her daughter. So Tess is shocked when she discovers the grandfather she never knew is in a coma. And that she has been named in his will to inherit half of Bella Vista, a hundred-acre apple orchard in the magical Sonoma town called Archangel.

The rest is willed to Isabel Johansen. A half sister she's never heard of.

Against the rich landscape of Bella Vista, Tess begins to discover a world filled with the simple pleasures of food and family, of the warm earth beneath her bare feet. A world where family comes first and the roots of history run deep.

Available wherever books are sold.

HARLEQUIN® MIRA®
www.Harlequin.com

KASEY MICHAELS

76764 WHAT AN EARL WANTS	___ $7.99 U.S.	___ $9.99 CAN.
77433 HOW TO BEGUILE A BEAUTY	___ $7.99 U.S.	___ $9.99 CAN.
77371 HOW TO TEMPT A DUKE	___ $7.99 U.S.	___ $8.99 CAN.

(limited quantities available)

TOTAL AMOUNT $ _____
POSTAGE & HANDLING $ _____
($1.00 FOR 1 BOOK, 50¢ for each additional) .
APPLICABLE TAXES* $ _____
TOTAL PAYABLE $ _____

(check or money order—please do not send cash)

To order, complete this form and send it, along with a check or money order for the total above, payable to Harlequin HQN, to: **In the U.S.:** 3010 Walden Avenue, P.O. Box 9077, Buffalo, NY 14269-9077; **In Canada:** P.O. Box 636, Fort Erie, Ontario, L2A 5X3.

Name: _____
Address: _____ City: _____
State/Prov.: _____ Zip/Postal Code: _____
Account Number (if applicable): _____

075 CSAS

*New York residents remit applicable sales taxes.
*Canadian residents remit applicable GST and provincial taxes.